A CROWN OF PORTALS AND POWER

MICHAEL SHARPE

ISBN: 978-1-967685-00-4

Contents

— • —

PROLOGUE

THE INFINITE THRESHOLD EXPERIMENT

8,012 Years Ago

The last day of the world began with a sunrise like any other.

Samira Lumine watched it from the observation deck of The Spire, that impossible tower stretching from the surface of the world into orbit. Below her, the metropolis of Aetheria Central sparkled with the light of a million windows, while above, the orbital habitats hung like jewels against the blackness of space.

She tapped her wrist interface, reviewing the morning's dimensional readings. Energy fluctuations across the city had been increasing for weeks, but today's numbers showed stability. A good sign, perhaps. The Director had assured everyone the Infinite Threshold Experiment posed minimal risk.

Samira knew better.

"Authorization confirmed. Good morning, Dr. Lumine," said the facility's AI as she entered the dimensional research wing. "The team awaits you in Chamber Seven."

Chamber Seven. The most heavily shielded room in the complex, where even the walls were lined with stabilization matrices. The place where they would attempt to pierce the final veil between dimensions.

The place where they would reach for the Source.

"Has anyone accessed the safety protocols this morning?" Samira asked, keeping her voice neutral.

"Negative, Doctor. All systems remain as configured during yesterday's final preparation."

Of course they hadn't. The Director had overridden Samira's suggested safety parameters three days ago, claiming they would "unnecessarily limit the energy throughput."

Samira paused before a reflective panel, straightening her lab coat. Dark circles shadowed her eyes. She hadn't slept well in weeks, not since the preliminary tests had shown anomalous readings that no one else seemed concerned about. Not since she'd found the encrypted messages in the system—warnings.

The observation room buzzed with activity when she arrived. Twenty of the world's brightest minds moved between workstations, checking readings, adjusting parameters. Through the reinforced viewing window, technicians made final adjustments to the dimensional resonator—a massive crystalline structure suspended in the center of Chamber Seven.

"Cutting it close, aren't you?" The Director appeared at her side, immaculate in a tailored suit that seemed to absorb light rather than reflect it. "We're scheduled to begin in seventeen minutes."

"I was reviewing the dimensional stability readings from the eastern quadrant," Samira said. "They show increasing variance."

"Within acceptable parameters." The Director dismissed her concern with a wave. "We've waited ten years for this moment, Doctor. Today we solve humanity's energy crisis forever."

"Or we create a problem we can't solve."

The Director's smile tightened. "Your concerns have been noted. Repeatedly. The council has determined the potential benefits outweigh the theoretical risks."

"Theoretical?" Samira lowered her voice. "The Genesis subjects have been experiencing dimensional resonance headaches for weeks."

The Director turned away. "Take your station, Doctor. History waits for no one."

Samira moved to her assigned console, fingers hovering over the interface. She could still stop this. A few commands would trigger the emergency protocols, locking down the facility for twenty-four hours while a safety review was conducted. She would lose her position, possibly face criminal charges for interfering with a government-sanctioned experiment.

But the facility would be safe. The city would be safe.

She glanced at the other scientists, wondering if any shared her concerns. Most appeared excited, a few nervous, but none showed the deep dread that had settled in her stomach.

"Initiating preliminary dimensional scan," announced the lead technician. "Resonator at twenty percent capacity."

The crystalline structure in Chamber Seven began to glow with soft blue light. On screens around the room, data streams showed the familiar patterns of dimensional energy—the same patterns they'd been studying for centuries, ever since Elara Vex had first discovered the existence of higher dimensions.

"Thirty percent... forty..."

Samira's console showed the first anomaly—a tiny fluctuation in the dimensional barrier, barely noticeable unless you knew exactly what to look for. She flagged it in the system.

"Anomaly noted," the AI responded. "Assessment: negligible impact on experimental parameters."

The Director gave Samira a pointed look across the room.

"Fifty percent... sixty..."

More anomalies appeared, small tears in reality that self-healed almost instantly. The resonator's glow intensified, shifting from blue to violet.

"Seventy percent... eighty..."

Samira's hands trembled as she entered her access codes, preparing the emergency shutdown sequence. Just in case.

"Ninety percent... preparing for threshold breach."

The air in the observation room felt heavy, as if the oxygen molecules had doubled in weight. Several researchers rubbed their temples or shook their heads, as if trying to clear them.

"Resonator at full capacity. Initiating Source contact in three... two... one..."

The violet light from the resonator flared blindingly white. Through the window, Samira saw the technicians in Chamber Seven freeze in place, then slowly rise from the floor as gravity itself seemed to falter.

"Energy spike!" someone shouted. "The containment field—"

The viewing window cracked, a spiderweb of fractures spreading across its surface. Beyond it, the technicians' bodies began to distort, stretching and compressing in impossible ways.

"Shut it down!" Samira screamed, fingers flying across her console to activate the emergency protocols. "Shut it all down now!"

But it was too late. The resonator pulsed once, twice—and then shattered, each crystalline fragment opening its own tear in the fabric of reality. The observation room's lights flickered and died as the facility's power grid collapsed.

Then the window gave way entirely, and the howling void beyond reached in with hungry fingers.

The last day of the world ended not with darkness, but with too much light—light from dimensions never meant to touch our own.

1

SHIMMERING THREADS

Apollo Frost leaned into the ax swing, feeling the satisfying thud as the blade bit into wood. The morning air carried the scent of fresh-cut timber and the earthy aroma of tilled soil from the fields. He pulled the ax free and positioned another log on the stump.

"That should be enough for today," Kieran called from the barn doorway. His adoptive father wiped sweat from his brow with a worn handkerchief, the motion highlighting the creases time had etched into his weathered face. "The south field still needs tending before midday."

Apollo nodded, driving the ax into the chopping block. "I'll get the tools."

The Frost farm sat on a gentle rise overlooking Willowbrook Village. From where he stood, Apollo could see smoke rising from the village chimneys and, beyond them, the crumbling silhouette of the ruins that crowned the eastern hills. The ancient structures had fascinated him since childhood, though Kieran had always warned him to keep his distance.

Apollo gathered the hoes and seed bags from the toolshed, his movements efficient from years of routine. At nineteen, he was familiar with every corner of the farm, every seasonal task, every quirk of the soil. This was his world—predictable, steady, safe.

"Did you check the irrigation channels?" Kieran asked as Apollo approached.

"Last night. The eastern one needed clearing—roots were blocking the flow again."

Kieran nodded with approval. "Good eye. Your mother always said you noticed things others missed."

Apollo paused, tools in hand. Mentions of his mother were rare, precious fragments of a past he couldn't remember. Kieran rarely spoke of her, or of Apollo's early years before coming to the farm. The subject brought a shadow to his adoptive father's eyes that Apollo had learned not to probe.

They worked in companionable silence, breaking the soil and preparing rows for the late-season vegetables. The rhythm of farm work had its own language—one Apollo understood through muscle memory and the quiet exchange of tools. Kieran didn't waste words, and Apollo had grown to appreciate the peace in their shared labor.

As midday approached, Apollo straightened, stretching his back. Something caught his eye—a faint shimmer around the old well pump at the field's edge. He blinked, but the strange light remained, pulsing like heat rising from summer stones.

"Do you see that?" he asked, pointing toward the pump.

Kieran looked up, squinting against the sun. "See what?"

"That... shimmer. Around the pump."

Kieran's expression shifted subtly. He set down his hoe and walked to Apollo's side, eyes fixed on the well. "I don't see anything unusual. Maybe sunlight on the metal?"

But it wasn't sunlight. Apollo had seen this before—fleeting moments when ordinary objects seemed outlined in light that shouldn't exist. Sometimes the light had color, sometimes it moved in patterns that made his eyes hurt if he followed them too long.

"It's nothing," Apollo said, returning to his work. These visions had been occurring more frequently lately, but mentioning them made Kieran tense. Better to keep them to himself.

They broke for a simple lunch of bread, cheese, and dried apples in the shade of the old oak that dominated their yard. Kieran chewed, gazing toward the village.

"Market day tomorrow," he said. "We should bring those squash you harvested. The fletcher mentioned his wife was looking for some."

Apollo nodded, but his attention had drifted to the water bucket between them. Tiny ripples disturbed its surface, though there was no wind. Around its rim, that same strange shimmer pulsed, faint but unmistakable.

"Apollo?"

He jerked his gaze away. "Sorry. Yes, the squash. I'll prepare them tonight."

Kieran studied him, concern evident in his eyes. "You've been distracted lately."

"Just thinking about the harvest," Apollo lied. He couldn't explain what he didn't understand himself.

After lunch, they moved to the barn where repairs to the roof couldn't wait any longer. Apollo climbed the ladder with bundles of thatch while Kieran directed from below. The physical work helped Apollo focus, pushing the strange visions from his mind.

"Hand me that length of cord," Kieran called up.

Apollo reached for the coil of rope near his feet, then froze. The cord glowed with a blue-violet light that pulsed in rhythm with his heartbeat. When he touched it, the glow intensified, spreading like water through fabric, up his fingers and across his palm.

He dropped the cord with a gasp.

"Apollo? What's wrong?" Kieran's voice sharpened with concern.

"Nothing—it just slipped." Apollo picked up the cord again, steeling himself. The glow remained, but fainter now, as if responding to his will. He passed it down to Kieran, watching as his father took it.

The glow vanished the moment it left his hands.

They finished the roof repairs as afternoon shadows lengthened across the farm. Apollo pondered questions he dared not ask. These visions had been part of his life for years—flickering at the edges of his perception—but never as strong or persistent as today.

As they put away their tools, Kieran placed a hand on Apollo's shoulder. "There's stew left from yesterday. Why don't you rest while I heat it?"

Apollo nodded gratefully. Inside their modest home, he washed dust and sweat from his face and arms, avoiding his reflection in the small mirror above the basin. The cool water helped clear his head, but when he looked up, water droplets clung to the mirror's surface in patterns that seemed to form symbols—curves and lines that shifted if he looked at them directly.

He turned away, unsettled.

The evening meal passed quietly. Kieran spoke of village matters and plans for the coming week, while Apollo contributed enough to mask his distraction. After they cleaned the dishes, Kieran settled into his chair by the hearth with his pipe, and Apollo took the opportunity to step outside.

Night had fallen, stars emerging in the clear sky. Apollo walked to the edge of their property, where the land sloped toward the distant ruins. In darkness, the ancient structures were barely visible—a jagged interruption of the horizon.

Something about the ruins called to him tonight. The stones there sometimes showed the strongest manifestations of the strange light, especially at dawn or dusk. Village elders warned children to stay away, speaking of old dangers and forgotten powers.

"Admiring the view?"

Kieran had approached without him noticing, pipe in hand.

"Just getting some air," Apollo said.

Kieran followed his gaze toward the ruins. "Those old stones fascinate you."

It wasn't a question. Apollo nodded anyway.

"There's history there," Kieran said. "Before the Cataclysm, they say our ancestors built wonders we can hardly imagine."

"Do you think any of their knowledge survived?" Apollo asked. "In the ruins, maybe?"

Kieran drew on his pipe, the ember glowing in the darkness. "Knowledge isn't always a blessing, Apollo. Some things were lost for good reason."

They stood in silence for a moment before Kieran spoke again, his voice unusually hesitant. "These... shimmers you mentioned. You've seen them before, haven't you?"

Apollo turned to his father, surprised by the direct question. "Yes. Since I was young. They come and go."

"And today? They were stronger?"

"Yes." Apollo hesitated. "What does it mean?"

Kieran sighed, a sound heavy with something Apollo couldn't identify. "It means we need to talk. But not tonight."

As they walked back to the house, Apollo glanced over his shoulder at the ruins. For an instant, he thought he saw a flicker of violet light trace the outline of the ancient stones, pulsing like a heartbeat against the night sky.

Then it was gone, leaving him wondering if his mind was playing tricks—or if the world itself was changing around him.

Apollo rose early the next morning, his sleep punctuated by dreams of shimmering patterns and strange symbols. The conversation with Kieran had left him with more questions than answers, and his father had left to trade with a neighboring farm by the time Apollo finished his morning chores.

He decided a trip to the village might clear his head. The walk to Willowbrook took under half an hour, following a well-worn path that wound between fields of early summer crops. Apollo kept his eyes fixed ahead, deliberately avoiding looking too closely at his surroundings. The last thing he needed was another episode of the strange lights while walking alone.

Willowbrook's familiar sights and sounds greeted him as he approached—children chasing each other between cottages, the clucking of chickens, the creak of the water wheel at the mill. Apollo nodded to villagers who called out greetings, maintaining a casual demeanor despite the turmoil in his mind.

His feet carried him automatically to the north end of the village, where smoke billowed from the tall chimney of Rhodes' Smithy. The rhythmic clang of hammer on metal grew louder as he approached, and Apollo felt himself relaxing into the familiar pattern. Tristan had been his closest childhood friend, and the forge was a second home to him.

He pushed open the wide wooden door and was greeted by a wave of heat. The interior was dim after the bright morning sun, but Apollo's eyes adjusted to see Tristan at the anvil, hammering a glowing length of metal with practiced precision.

Apollo hesitated at the threshold, suddenly wary. Would the tools and metals of the forge trigger another episode of the strange visions? He blinked and forced himself forward.

"Didn't expect to see you until after harvest," Tristan called over his shoulder, not breaking his rhythm. Three more powerful strikes, then he plunged the metal into a water barrel. Steam hissed upward as he turned to face Apollo, wiping sweat from his brow with a forearm. "Something wrong with your plow again?"

"No, just needed to get out of the house," Apollo replied, approaching the workbench. To his relief, the tools remained just tools—no strange lights or patterns manifested around them. "Kieran's trading with the Harpers today. Thought I'd see what trouble you're causing."

Tristan grinned, setting his hammer down. "The usual. Fixing what others break." He gestured to a pile of farm implements awaiting repair. "Festival's coming up, and suddenly everyone remembers all the metal that needs mending."

Apollo picked up a bent sickle, turning it in his hands. "Your father letting you handle the important work now?"

"When his back's acting up, which is most days lately." Tristan's expression grew more serious. "Truth is, he's talking about me taking over more permanently. Says his hands aren't as steady as they used to be."

"That's a big step," Apollo said. "Though not surprising. You've always had a gift for this."

Tristan shrugged, but Apollo could see the pride in his friend's eyes. "It's just practice. Speaking of which—" He moved to a cluttered corner and retrieved something wrapped in cloth. "Remember that design you sketched for me last winter? Finally got around to trying it."

He unwrapped the cloth to reveal a knife with an unusual curved blade and an intricately worked handle. Apollo took it carefully, testing its balance. The weight felt perfect in his hand, the handle fitting his grip as if made for him—which, he realized, it had been.

"This is incredible work," Apollo said, genuinely impressed. The blade caught the light from the forge, and for an instant, Apollo thought he saw a faint blue shimmer along its edge. He blinked, and it was gone. "You've outdone yourself."

"It's yours," Tristan said. "Consider it an early birthday gift."

Apollo started to protest, but Tristan waved him off. "I used scrap metal for practice. Besides, the design was yours to begin with."

The door to the smithy creaked open, momentarily flooding the dim interior with sunlight. Alden Nash stumbled in, his arms laden with books and papers, spectacles slightly askew on his nose.

"There you both are!" he exclaimed, as if he'd been searching the village for them rather than simply happening upon them. "Have you heard the news?"

Tristan exchanged an amused glance with Apollo. Alden's "news" often consisted of obscure historical facts or academic disputes that interested no one but himself.

"What news would that be?" Apollo asked, wrapping the knife and tucking it into his belt.

Alden deposited his burden on a workbench, ignoring Tristan's frown at the papers now dangerously close to forge sparks. "Elias the merchant is coming! He's setting up, and he's brought artifacts from the western provinces!"

This caught Apollo's attention. Traveling merchants were common, but Elias was known for collecting unusual items from his journeys—including relics from before the Cataclysm.

"Actual artifacts or just the usual trinkets?" Tristan asked, moving Alden's papers to a safer location.

"Genuine artifacts," Alden insisted, adjusting his spectacles. "According to Mrs. Holloway, who saw him setting up, he has metal devices with markings similar to those in the eastern ruins. And a crystalline object that supposedly glows at night without flame!"

Apollo stood frozen for a moment. A glowing crystal? Could it be related to the strange lights he'd been seeing?

"You're not still obsessed with those old ruins, are you?" Tristan asked, though his tone held more affection than criticism. "Your father will have you cataloging the village's grain stores again if he catches you with more 'historical research.'"

Alden straightened, looking offended. "The ruins contain our history—knowledge our ancestors possessed that we've lost. And my father understands the importance of preserving that knowledge, even if he prefers I focus on more... practical matters."

"Like not setting his books on fire in a smithy?" Tristan suggested, pointedly moving a stray paper away from a spark.

Apollo intervened before their friendly bickering could escalate. "When did Elias arrive? I didn't see him on my way in."

"Just this morning, apparently," Alden said. "He's setting up for the festival. Speaking of which—" He pulled a folded paper from his pocket. "Elder Verity asked me to post the festival announcements. This year's celebration is particularly significant because it marks the centennial of Willowbrook's founding after the Great Migration."

Apollo took the paper, scanning the written announcement. The Summer Solstice Festival was Willowbrook's largest annual celebration, marking both the height of summer and the village's founding. This year would feature the traditional events—competitions of strength and skill, music, dancing, and the ceremonial activation of the healing stone.

"Looks like they're expanding the artifact display this year," Apollo noted, pointing to a section of the announcement.

Alden nodded. "Elder Verity is allowing villagers to bring family heirlooms for a special exhibition. It's a perfect opportunity to document items that might have historical significance."

"Or for you to bore everyone with lectures about rusty metal bits," Tristan teased, but his eyes showed interest. "Though I wouldn't mind seeing what turns up. Some families have kept artifacts for generations without knowing what they are."

"Exactly!" Alden exclaimed. "We might discover important connections to pre-Cataclysm technology. Which reminds me—" He turned to Apollo. "Does your family have anything you might display? Your farm is near those western ruins, and I've always wondered if your ancestors might have... collected items."

Apollo hesitated. There were several small objects in the trunk beneath Kieran's bed—strange metal devices and crystalline fragments that his father never discussed. Apollo had discovered them years ago while searching for winter blankets, but Kieran had firmly closed the trunk when he caught Apollo examining them.

"I don't think so," he said. "Just ordinary farm tools."

Alden looked disappointed but didn't press the issue. "Well, if you remember anything, let me know. I'm helping catalog the exhibits."

"I might have something," Tristan said unexpectedly. "My grandfather left a metal device with strange markings. My father keeps it wrapped in oilcloth in the storage room. Says it's been passed down for generations but no one knows what it does."

Alden's eyes lit up. "That's exactly the kind of artifact we should document! Could I see it?"

"Later, perhaps," Tristan said. "Right now, I need to finish these repairs before my father returns." He glanced at Apollo. "Unless you two want to help, in which case we might finish early enough to visit this famous merchant."

"I should post these announcements first," Alden said, gathering his papers. "But I could return afterward."

Apollo nodded. "I'll help. Beats going home to empty stables."

As Alden hurried out with his announcements, Tristan handed Apollo a pair of heavy gloves. "You can pump the bellows. And while you're at it, you can tell me what's really bothering you."

Apollo looked up, startled. "What do you mean?"

Tristan picked up his hammer, testing its weight. "I've known you since we were children, Apollo. You've got that same look you had when we were ten and you thought you saw a ghost in the miller's barn."

Apollo laughed, but it sounded hollow even to his own ears. "It's nothing like that."

"But it is something," Tristan pressed, his expression serious now. "You've been distracted since you arrived. Not your usual self."

Apollo hesitated, torn between the desire to confide in his oldest friend and the fear of sounding mad. How could he explain the shimmering lights, the strange patterns that seemed to overlay reality itself? Even Kieran, who apparently knew something about Apollo's visions, had been reluctant to discuss them.

"It's complicated," Apollo said. "And I'm not sure I understand it myself yet."

Tristan studied him for a moment, then nodded. "Fair enough. But remember, whatever it is—you don't have to figure it out alone."

"I know," Apollo said, grateful for his friend's understanding. "When I make sense of it, you'll be the first to hear."

They settled into a comfortable rhythm of work, with Apollo manning the bellows while Tristan shaped metal with practiced precision. The familiar environment and physical labor helped ground Apollo, pushing the strange visions and unanswered questions to the back of his mind.

For now, at least, he could pretend everything was normal—even as a part of him knew his life was changing in ways he couldn't yet comprehend.

Apollo helped Tristan with the forge work until mid-afternoon, when Alden returned with an excited gleam in his eyes.

"Elias has set up his wares in the village square," Alden announced. "You should see what he's brought this time—artifacts from the western provinces that no one here has ever laid eyes on."

Tristan wiped sweat from his brow and glanced at the remaining work. "Father won't be back until tomorrow. I suppose we could finish this in the morning."

Apollo's muscles ached pleasantly from the labor, and the prospect of seeing exotic items from distant lands sparked his curiosity. "Let's go," he agreed.

They found the merchant's colorful wagon in the village square, surrounded by a small crowd. Elias, a portly man with a neatly trimmed beard streaked with gray, displayed his wares on blankets spread before his wagon. Apollo spotted finely woven textiles, jars of spices, and various trinkets that glittered in the afternoon sun.

What caught his attention, however, was a small collection of objects set apart from the rest—weathered metal pieces and crystalline fragments that bore a striking resemblance to the items in Kieran's trunk.

"Those are from the western ruins," Elias explained when he noticed Apollo's interest. "Collectors pay good coin for ancestral artifacts."

Apollo crouched to examine them more closely. One object in particular drew his gaze—a small disc of burnished metal with concentric circles etched into its surface. As he stared at it, the now-familiar shimmer began to appear, violet light dancing along the circular patterns.

"How much for this one?" he asked, careful not to touch it.

Elias named a price that made Apollo wince. It was far more than he could afford on his meager savings.

"That's highway robbery," Tristan protested. "It's just an old metal disc."

"It's ancestral craftsmanship," Elias countered. "And in remarkable condition."

While they haggled, Apollo found his gaze drawn past the village square toward the western hills—and the ruins that lay beyond them. The same ruins visible from their farm property. The forbidden ruins that villagers were warned to avoid.

A thought formed in Apollo's mind.

"Let's go see the real thing," he suggested to his friends once they'd moved away from Elias's wagon.

Alden's eyes widened. "The ruins? But Elder Verity has forbidden—"

"Just the edge," Apollo clarified. "We won't go inside. But with all this talk of artifacts and ancestral technology, aren't you curious to see where they come from?"

Tristan looked thoughtful. "We could follow the western path until it reaches the old boundary markers. That's not technically entering the ruins."

Alden hesitated, torn between caution and scholarly interest. "I guess... looking from the marker line wouldn't really break the actual rule. Plus, we could record our observations for educational purposes."

"We'll go just before sunset," Apollo decided. "The light will be perfect then."

Three hours later, they hiked along the narrow path that wound through the western hills. Apollo led the way, with Tristan close behind and Alden trailing slightly, out of breath from the climb.

"Are you sure this is a good idea?" Alden panted. "Those clouds look ominous."

Apollo glanced at the darkening sky. Storm clouds gathered on the horizon, but they were still distant. "We'll have plenty of time. Besides, I've always wanted to see these ruins up close."

The truth was more complicated. Since his strange visions had begun, Apollo felt drawn to the ruins—as if answers to questions he hadn't even formulated might be waiting there. Kieran had warned him away from this place, but with each passing day, Apollo's need to understand his changing perceptions grew stronger.

They crested a hill, and suddenly the ruins spread before them—a sprawling complex of partially collapsed structures, broken towers, and strange metal frameworks that caught the golden light of the setting sun. Unlike the simple stone and timber buildings of Willowbrook, these structures featured curved walls and materials Apollo couldn't identify from this distance.

"By the ancestors," Alden whispered. "It's more extensive than I imagined."

"Look at those towers," Tristan pointed to tall spires that seemed impossibly thin to support their own weight. "How did they build them without collapsing?"

Apollo said nothing, transfixed by what only he could see—networks of shimmering light connecting various structures, pulsing with blues and violets that reminded him of the glows he'd been experiencing around ordinary objects. Here, however, the effect was magnified a hundredfold, creating an ethereal overlay atop the physical ruins.

"Let's get closer," he said, moving down the slope toward the boundary markers—a line of weathered stone pillars carved with warning symbols.

"Apollo, wait," Alden called. "We agreed to stay at the boundary."

"We will," Apollo assured him, though he felt an almost physical pull toward the ruins.

They reached the boundary markers just as the sun dipped lower, casting long shadows across the landscape. Apollo placed his hand on one of the stone pillars, feeling its rough texture beneath his fingers. The warning symbols carved into its surface began to shimmer with that now-familiar violet light.

"These markers are at least two centuries old," Alden observed, examining another pillar. "Probably erected after the Cataclysm when people began avoiding ancestral sites."

Tristan had wandered a few paces ahead, peering at something on the ground beyond the boundary. "Hey, look at this."

Apollo joined him, careful not to cross the invisible line between the markers. Half-buried in the soil lay a small object, its surface catching the fading sunlight. Like an invisible force was pulling at him, Apollo extended his arm and swept the soil aside.

It was a palm-sized disc, similar to the one he'd seen at Elias's wagon but more intricate. Concentric circles were etched into its surface, surrounding a central pivot point from which extended what looked like a delicate metal needle.

The moment Apollo's fingers touched it, the disc flared with brilliant blue-violet light. The needle spun rapidly, then stopped, pointing toward the heart of the ruins. The light pulsed in rhythm with Apollo's heartbeat, and he felt a strange resonance—as if the object were somehow attuned to him.

"What is that?" Alden gasped, staring at the glowing disc. "How are you making it do that?"

"I'm not doing anything," Apollo said, though he wasn't entirely convinced. The disc felt warm against his palm, almost alive.

Tristan leaned closer. "It looks like some kind of compass, but the needle isn't pointing north."

Apollo turned in place, and sure enough, the needle remained fixed on the ruins regardless of which direction he faced. "It's pointing to something in there."

"Apollo Frost! What do you think you're doing?"

The stern voice made all three of them jump. Apollo glanced over his shoulder to see Elder Verity standing behind them, her towering figure cast in the warm hues of the sunset. Her hair, streaked with silver, danced in the gentle evening breeze, and her lined face was etched with a look of disapproval.

Apollo closed his hand around the disc, but not before noticing that its glow had diminished at the elder's approach.

"Elder Verity," Alden stammered. "We were just—"

"Disobeying explicit instructions to stay away from the ruins," she finished for him. "Instructions that exist for your protection."

"We didn't cross the boundary," Tristan pointed out, though his voice lacked conviction.

Elder Verity's sharp eyes moved from face to face before settling on Apollo. "And what have you found, young Frost?"

Apollo hesitated, then opened his hand to reveal the disc.

The elder stepped closer, examining the object without touching it. Her expression changed subtly—concern replacing anger, and something else Apollo couldn't quite identify. Recognition, perhaps?

"Where did you find this?" she asked, her voice quieter now.

Apollo pointed to the spot beyond the boundary marker. "It was half-buried there."

Elder Verity straightened, looking past them toward the ruins. The setting sun cast her face in golden light, deepening the lines around her eyes and mouth. "These ruins are not merely ancient structures, boys. They are dangerous in ways you cannot comprehend."

"What makes them dangerous?" Apollo asked. "What happened here?"

The elder sighed. "Our ancestors built wonders beyond our understanding, but their ambition outpaced their wisdom. The Cataclysm was the result—a tearing of reality itself that left these places... unstable."

"Unstable how?" he pressed.

Elder Verity's gaze returned to Apollo, studying him with unsettling intensity. "The boundaries between dimensions grow thin in places like this. Strange energies linger. Most people cannot perceive them, but they affect us nonetheless—causing sickness, mental disturbances, or worse."

"You mean like the sickness from ancient stories?" Alden asked.

"Similar, but more complex," she replied. "The dangers here are not merely physical."

Apollo looked down at the disc in his palm, then back at the ruins with their network of shimmering lights that only he could see. "And if someone could perceive these energies? Would they be affected differently?"

The question hung in the air. Elder Verity's expression shifted again, this time to one of careful neutrality that Apollo suspected masked deeper emotions.

"Those with... different perceptions must be especially cautious," she said. "What others might stumble into blindly, they might be drawn to deliberately. The fact that you can see things others cannot doesn't grant immunity to their effects, Apollo Frost."

Apollo felt a jolt of surprise, followed by a strange relief. She knew. Somehow, Elder Verity knew about his visions.

"How did you—"

"It's time to leave this place," she interrupted. "The storm approaches, and darkness falls quickly. We will speak more of this another time." She held out her hand. "The artifact, please."

Apollo felt a sudden reluctance to part with the disc. It had responded to him in a way that suggested connection, purpose.

"I found it," he said, closing his fingers around it again.

"And it is not yours to keep," Elder Verity countered. "Such items belong to the village archives, where they can be properly studied and, if necessary, contained."

Tristan placed a hand on Apollo's shoulder. "She's right, Apollo. We don't know what that thing is."

After a moment's hesitation, Apollo surrendered the disc to Elder Verity, who wrapped it in a cloth from her pocket.

"Return to the village," she instructed. "All of you. And speak of this to no one until I've had time to consider the matter." Her gaze lingered on Apollo. "Especially you, young Frost. Your father should hear of this from me first."

As they turned to leave, Apollo cast one last glance at the ruins. The network of lights seemed to pulse more intensely, as if responding to his awareness of them. A question formed in his mind: if Elder Verity knew about his "different perceptions," did she also know why he had them? And what else might she know about the strange changes happening within him?

2

— • —

FESTIVAL LIGHTS

Visions filled Apollo Frost's sleep that night. As he shut his eyes, he saw the web of gleaming lights from the ruins, throbbing and moving as if alive. The disc he'd discovered kept recurring in his dreams—not as the dull metal object Elder Verity had taken, but radiant with an inner glow, its needle whirling chaotically before pointing straight at him.

He woke before dawn, staring at the ceiling beams of his small room. Outside, a rooster crowed, announcing morning's arrival with unnecessary enthusiasm. Apollo groaned and rolled onto his side.

"Apollo?" Kieran's voice called from the main room. "You awake?"

"Unfortunately," Apollo mumbled, then louder: "Yes."

He pushed himself up and dressed, splashing cold water on his face from the basin near his bed. Today was the Summer Solstice Festival—normally his favorite day of the year. The entire village would gather for games, food, and music. This year's centennial celebration promised to be even more spectacular, with the artifact exhibition as its centerpiece.

But after yesterday's encounter with Elder Verity, Apollo felt only unease. Would she tell Kieran about what happened at the ruins? About the disc? About Apollo's "different perceptions"?

When Apollo entered the kitchen, Kieran was at the table, slicing bread for breakfast. His adoptive father looked up with a smile that seemed forced.

"Sleep well?" Kieran asked.

"Not exactly, but I managed to get enough rest," Apollo admitted, taking a seat. "You?"

"Well enough." Kieran pushed a plate of bread and cheese toward him. "Big day today."

Apollo nodded, trying to gauge whether Elder Verity had spoken to Kieran. His father's expression revealed nothing unusual, but there was a tension in his shoulders that hadn't been there yesterday.

"About the festival..." Kieran began, then paused as if reconsidering his words. "I want you to stay close to me today."

Apollo frowned. "I'm nineteen, not nine."

"I'm aware," Kieran said dryly. "But with all the excitement and visitors from neighboring villages, it's best we stick together."

"This is about what happened yesterday, isn't it?" Apollo asked. "Elder Verity told you."

Kieran's hands stilled on the loaf of bread. "She mentioned you and your friends were caught near the western ruins, yes."

"And?"

"And it was foolish," Kieran said, his voice sharpening. "Those boundaries exist for a reason, Apollo."

"The same reason I've been seeing strange lights and patterns?" Apollo challenged. "The same reason you've been keeping secrets in that trunk of yours?"

Kieran's expression hardened. "We're not having this conversation now. The festival starts in an hour, and we need to finish our chores first."

Apollo wanted to press further, but something in Kieran's face warned against it. Instead, he ate in silence, the tension between them thick as winter fog.

By midday, Willowbrook village had transformed. Colorful banners hung between buildings, and garlands of summer flowers adorned every doorway. Tables laden with food lined the village square, and musicians tuned their instruments on a small wooden platform near the communal well.

The artifact exhibition had been set up in the village hall—normally used for council meetings and winter gatherings. A line had formed outside when Apollo and Kieran arrived, villagers eager to glimpse relics from the Ancestral Era.

"Impressive turnout," Kieran remarked as they joined the queue.

Apollo nodded, scanning the crowd for his friends. He spotted Tristan's tall form near the front of the line, Alden beside him. Both looked his way at the same moment, and Tristan waved them over.

"Should we...?" Apollo gestured toward his friends.

Kieran hesitated, then nodded. "Go ahead. I'll find you inside."

Apollo made his way through the crowd, feeling relief as he approached his friends. At least with them, he could be honest about what had happened yesterday.

"There he is," Tristan said with a grin. "The ruins explorer himself."

"Keep your voice down," Apollo muttered, glancing around. "Did Elder Verity talk to either of you after yesterday?"

Alden shook his head. "Not a word. You?"

"No, but she spoke to my father." Apollo lowered his voice further. "She knows about the things I've been seeing. Called them 'different percepti ons.'"

Tristan's eyebrows shot up. "So it's real? You really see things others can't?"

"Apparently."

"Like what?" Alden asked.

Apollo hesitated. "It's hard to describe. Patterns of light around certain objects. Energy, maybe? It started a few days ago, but it's getting stronger."

The line moved forward, bringing them to the entrance of the village hall. Inside, tables had been arranged in a U-shape, each displaying artifacts on velvet cloths. Village elders stood at intervals, explaining the significance of various items to curious onlookers.

Apollo scanned the displays, looking for the disc Elder Verity had taken from him. He found it near the center of the exhibition, resting on a small wooden stand. In the hall's dim lighting, it appeared unremarkable—a circular piece of metal with faded engravings.

"There it is," he whispered to Tristan, pointing.

"Doesn't look like much," Tristan observed.

"It's different when I touch it," Apollo said. "It... responds somehow."

They moved through the exhibition slowly, examining each artifact. Most were practical items—tools, containers, fragments of machinery whose purpose had been lost to time. But as they approached the far end of the hall, Apollo noticed something that made him stop abruptly.

On a raised platform stood a cylindrical object about the size of a large water jug. Its surface gleamed with an iridescent sheen that shifted colors as Apollo moved, and geometric patterns were etched into its sides. But what caught Apollo's attention were the threads of light emanating from it—visible only to him—pulsing with a steady rhythm like a heartbeat.

"What is that?" he asked, pointing.

Elder Verity stood beside the artifact, and it was she who answered. "The Centennial Lamp," she said. "The centerpiece of tonight's ceremony."

Apollo stepped closer, drawn by the dancing lights only he could see. "What does it do?"

"It is said to have illuminated the great halls of our ancestors," Elder Verity explained, watching Apollo. "For one hundred years, we've attempted to reactivate it during each solstice festival, following instructions passed down through generations. Tonight marks our centennial attempt."

"Has it ever worked?" Tristan asked.

"Partially," another voice answered. Apollo turned to see Elder Marcus, head of the village council, joining their group. "It produces a faint glow for a few moments, then fades. But the old texts suggest it once created light that rivaled the sun itself."

Apollo couldn't look away from the lamp. The threads of light surrounding it seemed to reach toward him, like tendrils seeking connection.

"May I?" he asked, hand hovering near the artifact.

"No," Elder Verity said sharply, at the same moment Elder Marcus said, "Carefully."

The two elders exchanged glances, some unspoken communication passing between them.

"You may observe, but not touch," Elder Verity clarified. "The activation ceremony requires specific preparations."

Apollo reluctantly lowered his hand, but remained transfixed by the lamp. Something about it felt familiar, as if he'd seen it before—not the object itself, but the patterns etched into its surface.

"Come on," Alden said, tugging at Apollo's sleeve. "There's more to see, and I'm starving."

With effort, Apollo tore his gaze from the lamp and followed his friends toward the exit. As they left, he glanced back one last time to find Elder Verity watching him with an expression that mingled concern and calculation.

The festival was in full swing by late afternoon. Children raced through the village square playing tag, adults competed in traditional games of skill, and the air filled with music and laughter. Apollo found himself enjoying the celebrations despite his lingering unease, winning the archery competition and placing second in the footrace.

As the sun began its descent toward the horizon, a hush fell over the gathering. Elder Marcus stood on the musicians' platform, raising his hands for attention.

"Friends and neighbors," he called out, his deep voice carrying across the square. "As the day's light wanes, we prepare for the highlight of our centennial celebration—the Illumination Ceremony!"

Cheers erupted from the crowd. Four village men carried the Centennial Lamp from the hall, placing it gently on a stone pedestal in the center of the square. In the fading daylight, Apollo could see the network of energy surrounding it more clearly than before—a complex web of light that pulsed and shifted.

"For one hundred years," Elder Marcus continued, "we have honored our ancestors by attempting to rekindle this ancient light. Tonight, as we mark a full century since the founding of New Willowbrook, we again follow the sacred ritual passed down through generations."

The crowd pressed forward, forming a circle around the lamp. Apollo found himself pushed to the front, Kieran close behind him. Across the pedestal stood Elder Verity, who caught Apollo's eye briefly before looking away.

Elder Marcus produced a small crystal from a velvet pouch—similar to the one Elias had been selling, but larger and more precisely cut. In the dying sunlight, it sparkled with inner fire.

"The key that awakens the light," Marcus intoned, holding the crystal aloft.

He approached the lamp and with steady hands inserted the crystal into a slot at its base. A soft hum emanated from the artifact, so low that Apollo felt it more than heard it. The threads of light intensified, their pulsing quickening.

Elder Marcus stepped back and nodded to Elder Verity, who moved forward with the metal disc Apollo had found—the one she'd taken from him at the ruins.

"The compass that guides the energy," she said, placing the disc against a circular depression on the lamp's side.

The disc adhered to the surface as if magnetized, and began to rotate slowly. The humming grew louder, and a faint glow appeared within the lamp—visible to everyone, not just Apollo.

A murmur of excitement rippled through the crowd. Apollo felt a strange pressure building in his head, a resonance between the lamp's energy and something within him.

Elder Marcus approached again, carrying a small hammer. "And now, the awakening strike, as instructed by our forebears."

He tapped the side of the lamp three times in a specific rhythm. The glow within the artifact brightened momentarily, then began to fade.

"No," Apollo whispered, feeling the energy dispersing. As though drawn by an invisible power, he moved ahead, his hand extending forward.

"Apollo!" Kieran hissed, grabbing for his arm, but too late.

Apollo's fingers touched the lamp's surface, and the world exploded with light.

The network of energy he'd been seeing coalesced and surged into him, flowing through his hand like liquid fire. It didn't hurt—instead, it felt like a missing piece clicking into place. The lamp blazed with brilliant blue-white light, illuminating the square as brightly as midday.

But that wasn't all. The light began to shape itself, forming three-dimensional patterns in the air above the lamp—geometric structures that rotated and transformed, casting no shadows despite their brightness. They were like mathematical equations given physical form, complex and beautiful and somehow meaningful in a way Apollo couldn't articulate.

The crowd gasped collectively, some shielding their eyes, others staring in wonder. Apollo couldn't move, couldn't break the connection between himself and the lamp. The energy continued to flow through him, and he felt himself understanding something fundamental about how the artifact worked—not through conscious knowledge, but through intuition deeper than thought.

"Apollo, let go!" Kieran's voice seemed to come from far away.

But Apollo couldn't. Instead, he found himself making subtle adjustments to the flow of energy, directing it with his mind. The patterns above the lamp shifted in response, becoming more complex, more stable.

Then something unexpected happened. The disc—the compass—began spinning rapidly, and projected a map onto the air above the village square. Not a flat map, but a three-dimensional representation of the region surrounding Willowbrook, with glowing points marking specific locations. One bright spot pulsed directly beneath them; others were scattered across the landscape, including a particularly intense one in the direction of the western ruins.

A woman screamed. A child began to cry. The murmurs of amazement transformed into expressions of fear and confusion.

"What is this sorcery?" someone shouted.

"It's not sorcery," Apollo heard himself say, though he hadn't intended to speak. "It's just science we've forgotten."

The words weren't his own—or rather, they were, but they came from a part of him he hadn't known existed until this moment.

Finally, with tremendous effort, Apollo pulled his hand from the lamp. The connection broke, and he staggered backward, nearly falling. Kieran caught him, steadying him with strong hands.

The lamp continued to glow, though less intensely, and the map remained suspended above the square, slowly rotating.

"What did you do?" Kieran whispered, his voice tight with emotion Apollo couldn't identify.

Before Apollo could answer, Elder Marcus stepped forward, face pale beneath his gray beard. "Everyone remain calm," he called out, though his own voice trembled slightly. "This is... an unexpected manifestation of ancestral technology."

"It's more than technology," Elder Verity said, her eyes fixed on Apollo. "It's the awakening of something long dormant."

The crowd's attention shifted from the glowing map to Apollo himself. He felt their stares like physical pressure—some curious, others frightened, a few openly hostile.

"He's one of them," a voice called out. "A Veilborn! Like in the old stories!"

The word struck Apollo like a physical blow. Veilborn. He'd heard it in village tales—mysterious figures who could see beyond normal reality, manipulate energies others couldn't perceive. Always spoken of with a mixture of awe and fear, and always as legends, not real people.

"The ceremony is concluded," Elder Marcus announced. "Please, everyone return to the festival activities while we secure the artifacts."

The crowd dispersed reluctantly, breaking into small groups that cast frequent glances back at Apollo. He caught fragments of whispered conversations:

"...always was a strange boy..."

"...not natural, that light..."

"...dangerous to have his kind here..."

"Apollo." Kieran's voice was low and urgent. "We need to go home. Now."

Apollo looked up at his father, seeing fear in the older man's eyes. "You knew," he said. "You knew what I am."

Kieran's jaw tightened. "Not here. We'll talk at home."

"No." Elder Verity stepped forward. "The council must convene immediately. Apollo and Kieran Frost will attend."

"This is a family matter," Kieran protested.

"Not anymore," Elder Verity replied. "Not after what just happened. Word of this will spread beyond our village by morning. We must decide how to proceed."

Apollo looked between them, feeling the weight of unspoken histories. "I deserve to know the truth," he said. "All of it."

Elder Marcus joined them, having instructed other council members to secure the still-glowing lamp and the hovering map. "Indeed you do," he agreed, surprising Apollo. "But first, we must ensure the safety of this village—and of you, young Frost. There are those who would... react poorly to what we witnessed today."

"The council chamber," Elder Verity said. "One hour. That should give everyone time to collect themselves." Her eyes moved to Kieran. "And to prepare for difficult conversations."

Kieran nodded stiffly, his hand still gripping Apollo's shoulder. "We'll be there."

As they turned to leave the square, Apollo noticed Tristan and Alden watching from a distance, their expressions a mixture of awe and uncertainty.

The walk home was silent, heavy with unasked questions and unspoken fears. Only when they reached their farmhouse did Kieran speak.

"Pack a bag," he said. "Clothes, food, your knife—anything you can carry easily."

Apollo stared at him. "We're running?"

"Not yet," Kieran replied, moving to his bedroom. "But we need to be prepared. There are people—powerful people—who have hunted the Veilborn for generations. If word of what happened today reaches them..."

"So it's true," Apollo said. "I am Veilborn?"

Kieran emerged with the wooden trunk Apollo had seen him open the night before. He placed it on the table and unlocked it with a key from around his neck.

"Yes," he said. "You are. And no, I'm not your birth father—though I've raised you as my son since you were an infant."

The confirmation of what Apollo had long suspected should have been more shocking, but after the events at the festival, it felt like merely another piece falling into place.

"Who were my real parents?" he asked.

Kieran lifted the trunk's lid, revealing its contents—books, scrolls, small devices similar to the artifacts in the exhibition. "Veilborn. They brought you to me during a dimensional storm nineteen years ago, when the boundaries between realities were temporarily weakened."

"Why?"

"To protect you," Kieran said, removing a small leather-bound book from the trunk.

Apollo felt oddly hollow, as if watching a story about someone else. "Are they dead?"

Kieran's expression softened. "I don't know." He shook his head. "They left this for you, to be given when your abilities manifested."

He held out the book. Apollo took it, feeling a faint resonance similar to what he'd experienced with the lamp, though much subtler. The cover bore no title, just a symbol that matched the birthmark on Apollo's wrist—a spiral within a triangle.

"What happened today at the festival," Kieran continued, "was only the beginning. Your abilities will grow stronger. You'll need guidance—guidance I can't provide."

"Then who can?" Apollo asked.

"That's what we need to discover," Kieran replied. "But first, we must deal with the village council. They're divided on matters concerning the Veilborn. Some, like Elder Verity, believe your kind were meant to help humanity recover what was lost in the Cataclysm. Others fear the very powers that make that possible."

Apollo looked down at the book in his hands, then back at his father—for whatever his blood, Kieran was the only father he'd ever known.

"Why didn't you tell me sooner?" he asked, unable to keep the hurt from his voice.

Kieran's shoulders slumped. "Your parents warned that premature knowledge could trigger your abilities before you were ready to control them. And..." He hesitated. "I was selfish. I knew that once you discovered the truth, our simple life here would end. I wanted to keep you safe, keep you as my son, for as long as possible."

Before Apollo could respond, a knock sounded at the door—three sharp raps that made them both jump.

"The council," Kieran said. "Sooner than expected."

He moved to answer, but Apollo stopped him with a hand on his arm. "Whatever happens," he said, "you are my father. That won't change."

Kieran's eyes shimmered with unexpected moisture. He nodded, squared his shoulders, and opened the door.

Elder Verity stood on their threshold, alone. "It's time," she said. "The council is assembled."

Apollo slipped the book into his pocket and took a deep breath, preparing to face whatever came next. The world he'd known was unraveling, revealing a stranger, more complex reality beneath. And somehow, he stood at its center.

3

THE ORDER'S ARRIVAL

Apollo followed Elder Verity along the winding path toward the village square, his mind moving faster than his feet. Kieran walked beside him, silent but watchful, his weathered hand occasionally brushing Apollo's shoulder—a wordless reassurance that Apollo wasn't alone.

The community meeting hall towered before them, its stone facade illuminated by torches that cast long, dancing shadows across the ground. Apollo had never seen it at night before. The warm sandstone that welcomed villagers during daylight hours now appeared imposing, almost threatening.

"The full council has assembled," Elder Verity said, breaking the silence. "This is... unusual. The Illumination Ceremony has unsettled many."

"It was just a malfunction," Apollo said, the words sounding hollow even to his own ears. "The lamp was old. Something went wrong when I touched it."

Elder Verity gave him a sidelong glance but said nothing.

Inside, the council chamber buzzed with tense conversation that died when Apollo entered. Seven elders sat at a curved table facing the center of the room, where two chairs had been placed. Elder Marcus, a thin man with a perpetual frown, occupied the center position.

"Apollo Frost," he intoned formally. "Kieran Frost. Please be seated."

Apollo took his seat, feeling the weight of every gaze in the room. He recognized all the council members—these were people who had known him his entire life, who had watched him grow up. Yet now they looked at him as if he were a stranger.

"We've called this emergency session," Elder Marcus continued, "to address the events at the Illumination Ceremony. Apollo Frost, you interfered with a sacred ritual and caused a disruption that has alarmed the entire village."

"I didn't mean to—" Apollo began.

"Intent is not the issue," Marcus cut in. "The fact remains that you displayed abilities consistent with those of the Veilborn, abilities not seen in Willowbrook for generations."

"I don't know what happened," Apollo said, trying to keep his voice steady. "I just touched the lamp, and it... reacted."

"Objects don't simply react to touch," said Elder Finch, a stout woman with braided gray hair. "Not unless there's something special about the person doing the touching."

"I'm not special," Apollo insisted. "I'm just a farmer's son."

Elder Verity leaned forward. "Apollo, several witnesses reported seeing you react to the artifacts before you touched the lamp. You saw something others couldn't, didn't you?"

Apollo hesitated, feeling trapped. Denial seemed pointless now, yet admitting the truth felt like stepping off a cliff.

"I've been seeing... lights. Patterns. Around certain objects." He swallowed. "But that doesn't make me Veilborn. It could be anything—eye strain, imagination."

"And the lamp?" Elder Marcus pressed. "Was that imagination too?"

"I don't know what it was," Apollo said, frustration edging into his voice. "I don't know what's happening to me."

Kieran cleared his throat. "My son has done nothing wrong. He didn't ask for these... perceptions. Whatever's happening, he deserves understanding, not interrogation."

"We understand your concern, Kieran," Elder Verity said gently. "But you must understand ours. If Apollo is indeed Veilborn, there are protocols that must be followed."

"What protocols?" Apollo questioned.

The council members exchanged glances, and Apollo felt the weight of unspoken history filling the room.

"The Order of the Veil must be notified," Elder Marcus said. "They are the authority on such matters."

"The Order?" Kieran's voice had gone tight. "Is that necessary? The boy needs guidance, not—"

"It is not optional," Marcus interrupted. "The agreement is clear. Any manifestation of Veilborn abilities must be reported."

Apollo looked between the elders and his father, sensing currents of tension he didn't understand. "Who is this Order? What do they want with me?"

"They are scholars and historians," Elder Verity explained, though something in her tone suggested there was more to it. "They study dimensional phenomena and preserve knowledge from before the Cataclysm."

"And they've already been contacted," Elder Marcus added. "A messenger was dispatched immediately after the ceremony."

Kieran's face had gone pale. "How long?"

"Their nearest outpost is three days' ride," Elder Finch said. "We expect representatives within the week."

Apollo felt as if the floor were tilting beneath him. A week. Whatever was happening, whatever this Order wanted with him, he had only a week to make sense of it all.

"Until they arrive," Elder Marcus continued, "Apollo is to remain within village boundaries. No excursions to the ruins or other sites of potential dimensional instability."

"Am I a prisoner?" Apollo asked, anger flaring.

"No," Elder Verity said. "But you are a responsibility. What happened tonight demonstrates that your abilities—whether you acknowledge them or not—can have unpredictable effects. For your safety and others', certain precautions are prudent."

The meeting continued, but Apollo barely heard the rest. Rules and restrictions washed over him. Veilborn. The Order. Dimensional instability. His entire life had been upended in a single evening, and now strangers were coming to decide his fate.

When they were dismissed, Apollo stepped outside into the cool night air, feeling as if he'd aged years in the span of hours.

"What now?" he asked Kieran as they walked home.

His father's face was grim in the moonlight. "Now we prepare. There's much you need to learn, and not much time."

The next morning, Apollo woke to find Tristan and Alden waiting in the kitchen. Kieran had left for the fields, leaving a note saying he'd return by midday.

"So," Tristan said as Apollo entered, "are you going to explain what happened last night, or do we have to guess?"

Apollo sank into a chair opposite his friends. "I don't know if I can explain it."

"Try us," Alden said, pushing his spectacles up his nose. "I've been researching all night. 'Veilborn' appears in several historical texts, though details are frustratingly sparse."

"The whole village is talking," Tristan added. "Half of them think you're blessed by the ancestors, the other half think you're cursed."

"And what do you think?" Apollo asked, studying their faces.

Tristan shrugged. "I think you're still Apollo. Just... Apollo with some weird glowing thing going on."

Despite everything, Apollo felt a smile tug at his lips. "That's one way to put it."

"What did the council say?" Alden asked.

Apollo recounted the meeting, watching their expressions shift from curiosity to concern as he mentioned the Order of the Veil.

"I've read about them," Alden said, his voice dropping. "They're more than just scholars. They're a religious order, with significant political influence in the western provinces. They believe the Cataclysm was caused by misuse of dimensional energies."

"And what does that have to do with me?" Apollo asked.

Alden hesitated. "The texts suggest the Order once... regulated those with abilities like yours. Kept records, enforced rules about how such powers could be used."

"Regulated," Tristan repeated. "That sounds ominous."

"It's all ancient history," Apollo said, standing to pace the small kitchen. "I'm not some powerful Veilborn from the old stories. I just see lights sometimes, and the lamp... that was an accident."

"An accident that created a perfect three-dimensional map of the region," Alden pointed out. "With specific locations marked. That's not nothing, Apollo."

"What were those locations, anyway?" Tristan asked. "Everyone was too busy panicking to really look."

Apollo closed his eyes, recalling the glowing map that had hovered above the lamp. "There were seven points. One was Willowbrook, obviously. Another was the western ruins. The others..." He shook his head. "I didn't recognize them."

"Seven points," Alden murmured, pulling out his notebook. "That could align with the Seven Gates mentioned in some texts. Supposed weak points in the dimensional fabric."

"This is ridiculous," Apollo said, frustration bubbling up. "Yesterday I was normal. Today everyone's treating me like I'm some kind of... of..."

"Dimensional wizard?" Tristan suggested.

"It's not funny," Apollo snapped.

"No, it's not," Alden agreed. "Especially if the Order is involved. The historical accounts of their relationship with the Veilborn are... complicated."

Something in Alden's tone made Apollo pause. "Complicated how?"

Alden glanced toward the window, as if checking they were alone. "There are references to a period called the Purge, about a thousand years ago. Details are scarce, but it appears the Order systematically hunted down Veilborn individuals and families."

A cold weight settled in Apollo's stomach. "Hunted?"

"Like I said, it's ancient history," Alden said. "The modern Order presents itself as a scholarly institution. But..." He hesitated.

"But what?" Tristan pressed.

"But they still maintain strict control over dimensional knowledge and artifacts. And they're particularly interested in anyone showing Veilborn traits."

Apollo thought of the book Kieran had given him, hidden under his mattress. "I need to talk to Elder Verity. She knows more than she was saying last night."

"Be careful," Alden warned. "The council has already contacted the Order. If Elder Verity has sympathies toward the Veilborn, she might not want that widely known."

Apollo found Elder Verity in the village archives, a small stone building attached to the council hall. She sat alone among stacks of leather-bound books and scrolls, her silver hair catching the light from the single window.

She looked up as he entered, unsurprised. "I wondered when you'd come."

"I have questions," Apollo said, closing the door behind him.

"I imagine you do." She gestured to the chair across from her. "Though I may not have all the answers you seek."

Apollo sat, studying the old woman's face. He wondered how much of what he knew about her—about anything—was true.

"What are the Veilborn, really?" he asked.

Verity sighed, closing the book before her. "They were people with a special gift—the ability to perceive and interact with dimensional energies that exist beyond normal human perception."

"Like the lights I've been seeing."

"Yes. Those lights, as you call them, are energies flowing between dimensions. Most people can't see them at all. Some, like myself, can perceive them faintly with training and tools." She tapped a small monocle-like device on the table. "But true Veilborn can not only see these energies but manipulate them."

"And that's what I did with the lamp?"

"In a rudimentary, untrained way, yes." She leaned forward. "Apollo, what you need to understand is that these abilities once served a vital purpose. After the Cataclysm, when much of our ancestors' knowledge was lost, the Veilborn helped rebuild society using their unique perception."

"Then why did the Order hunt them?" Apollo asked bluntly.

Verity's eyes widened slightly. "You've been speaking with young Nash, I see."

"Is it true?"

She was silent for a long moment, fingers drifting along the edge of her book. "History is rarely simple, Apollo. Yes, there was a period when the Order viewed the Veilborn as dangerous. They believed unrestricted dimensional manipulation had caused the Cataclysm, and sought to prevent another such disaster."

"By killing people like me."

"It wasn't—" She stopped herself. "Yes. For a time, that was their approach. But that was a thousand years ago. The modern Order is primarily concerned with research and preservation."

"Then why did my father look terrified when he heard they were coming?"

Verity's expression softened. "Kieran has his reasons to be cautious. The Order's evolution hasn't been without... setbacks. There are still factions within it that hold to older beliefs."

"What will they do when they get here?" Apollo asked, his voice low.

"They'll want to test you, certainly. Document your abilities. Possibly offer training." She hesitated. "They may also want to take you to one of their facilities for further study."

"And if I refuse?"

Verity's silence was answer enough.

"Elder Verity," Apollo said, "what do you believe? About the Veilborn, the Order... all of it?"

The old woman glanced toward the door, then reached beneath her desk and withdrew a small wooden box. From it, she removed a pendant—a silver spiral within a triangle, matching the symbol on Apollo's book and birthmark.

"My grandmother was Veilborn," she said. "She escaped the Purge and lived in hiding her entire life. She passed some of her knowledge to my mother, who passed it to me, though the ability itself grew weaker with each generation."

She pressed the pendant into Apollo's palm. It felt warm, and for a moment, he thought he saw a flicker of blue-violet light around its edges.

"The Veilborn were not the monsters the Order painted them to be," Verity continued. "They were guardians of knowledge, keepers of balance between dimensions. Their abilities allowed them to mend rifts, stabilize fluctuations that might otherwise have torn our reality apart."

"Then why does everyone fear them—fear me?"

"Because power always frightens those who don't possess it," she said. "And because history is written by the victors. After the Purge, the Order systematically erased or altered records of what the Veilborn truly were."

Apollo closed his fingers around the pendant. "What should I do?"

"I cannot tell you that," Verity said. "But I can tell you this: the Order representatives who come will not see you as Apollo Frost, a young man from Willowbrook. They will see you as a Veilborn. Your value to them will be in what you can do, not who you are."

Apollo took a moment to absorb everything. "You're saying I shouldn't trust them."

"I'm saying you should be cautious," she corrected. "Listen more than you speak. Reveal less than you know."

"And what do I know?" Apollo asked, frustration edging into his voice. "I don't understand any of this."

Verity reached across the table and placed her hand over his. "You know more than you realize, Apollo. The abilities of the Veilborn are not merely learned—they are inherited, encoded in your very being. Trust your instincts."

She withdrew her hand and stood. "I've said more than I should. If the Order suspected my sympathies..." She shook her head. "Be careful, Apollo. And whatever you decide, know that you are not the first to walk this path."

Three days passed in a blur of whispers and sidelong glances. Apollo tried to maintain his normal routine—helping Kieran in the fields, meeting with Tristan and Alden—but nothing felt normal anymore. He'd read through the book his birth parents had left him, but much of it remained incomprehensible, filled with symbols and diagrams he couldn't decipher.

Kieran had grown increasingly tense, checking the road toward Willowbrook multiple times a day. He'd shown Apollo hidden caches of supplies around their property—food, water, tools—without explicitly stating their purpose. But the message was clear: be ready to run.

On the fourth day after the Illumination Ceremony, they came.

Apollo was splitting wood behind the house when he heard the approach of horses. Setting down his axe, he moved to the front yard just as three riders crested the hill.

They wore identical gray robes with silver trim, their horses similarly matched in color and size. Even at a distance, there was something unnervingly uniform about them, as if they'd been cast from the same mold.

Kieran emerged from the barn, wiping his hands on a rag. His face betrayed nothing, but Apollo saw how his fingers clenched around the cloth.

"Stay calm," Kieran murmured as the riders approached. "Answer their questions simply. Don't volunteer information."

The riders halted before them, and the leader—a woman with sharp features and calculating eyes—dismounted.

"Kieran Frost?" she asked, her accent marking her as from the western provinces.

"Yes," Kieran replied. "And this is my son, Apollo."

The woman's gaze shifted to Apollo, and he felt a sensation like cold fingers probing at his mind. "I am Observer Lyra of the Order of the Veil. These are my colleagues, Keeper Dorn and Guardian Marius."

The men remained mounted, watching Apollo with intense focus.

"We've come in response to reports of a dimensional incident during your village's festival," Lyra continued. "Specifically, reports concerning you, young man."

Apollo met her gaze steadily. "There was a malfunction with an old lamp. That's all."

A thin smile crossed Lyra's face. "Is that what you believe happened?"

"It's what I know happened," Apollo said, fighting to keep his voice even.

"Interesting." Lyra turned to Kieran. "The village council has granted us permission to conduct tests on your son. We'll begin tomorrow morning at the council hall."

It wasn't a request.

"What kind of tests?" Kieran asked.

"Standard procedures for evaluating dimensional sensitivity," Lyra replied. "Nothing invasive."

Apollo noticed her companions exchanging a glance at this, though their expressions remained neutral.

"And after these tests?" Kieran pressed.

"That depends on the results," Lyra said. "If Apollo shows significant Veilborn traits, he may be invited to continue his education at our seminary."

"Invited," Apollo repeated. "Or required?"

Lyra's eyes narrowed slightly. "The Order takes its responsibility to monitor dimensional anomalies very seriously, young man. Untrained Veilborn pose significant risks—to themselves and others."

"I'm not—" Apollo began, but Kieran cut him off with a warning look.

"We understand," Kieran said. "Apollo will present himself at the council hall tomorrow morning."

Lyra nodded, satisfied. "Good. Until then." She remounted her horse, and without another word, the three riders turned and headed back toward the village.

When they were out of earshot, Apollo turned to Kieran. "I don't trust them."

"Nor should you," Kieran replied. "Come inside. We need to talk."

In the kitchen, Kieran pulled out a chair for Apollo, then paced the small room, his limp more pronounced than usual—a sign of his agitation.

"I'd hoped we'd have more time," he said. "Time for you to understand your abilities, to learn how to control them."

"I don't want these abilities," Apollo said. "I just want things to go back to normal."

Kieran stopped pacing and faced him. "That's no longer an option, son. The Order knows about you now. They won't simply forget."

"What will they do to me?"

Kieran's expression darkened. "If their tests confirm what they suspect, they'll take you to one of their seminaries—isolated compounds where they train initiates. They'll say it's for your education, your safety."

"But it's not?"

"It's for control," Kieran said flatly. "The Order has always feared the Veilborn. They study them, yes, but they also contain them. Use them when convenient, neutralize them when not."

Apollo felt sick. "Elder Verity said something similar. She said they hunted Veilborn during something called the Purge."

"Yes." Kieran sank into the chair across from Apollo. "A thousand years ago, the Order systematically eliminated most Veilborn families. Those who survived went into hiding, diluting their bloodlines over generations to avoid detection."

"And now the Order has found me." Apollo stared down at his hands, half-expecting to see the blue-violet glow that had become increasingly common in recent days. "What do we do?"

Kieran was silent for a long moment. "We have two choices," he said. "You can submit to their tests, hope they're satisfied with minimal intervention. Or..."

"Or we run," Apollo finished.

"Yes."

Apollo thought of Lyra's cold eyes, the way she'd looked at him like a specimen to be studied. He thought of Elder Verity's warning, of the pendant she'd given him, now hidden alongside his parents' book.

"If we run, where would we go?" he asked.

"There are places," Kieran said. "Remote areas where the Order's influence is weaker. Your parents gave me instructions, contingencies in case your abilities manifested and drew attention."

"You've been preparing for this all along," Apollo realized.

Kieran nodded. "I promised your parents I'd keep you safe. Not just from physical harm, but from those who would use you for their own purposes."

Apollo stood and walked to the window, looking out toward the village. Everything he'd ever known was there—his friends, his life, his world. And now he was being asked to leave it all behind.

"I need to speak with Tristan and Alden," he said. "Before I decide."

"Be careful," Kieran warned. "The Order will be watching you."

Apollo found his friends at Tristan's forge. The rhythmic clang of hammer on metal paused as he entered, and Tristan looked up, face streaked with soot.

"There he is," Tristan said. "The man of the hour."

Alden sat nearby on a barrel, a book open on his lap. "We saw the Order representatives ride into town. Imposing bunch."

"They came to the farm," Apollo said. "They want to test me tomorrow."

Tristan set down his hammer. "Test you how?"

"They didn't say exactly. But afterward, they want to take me to something called a seminary."

Alden's head snapped up. "That's not good. The Order seminaries are essentially closed compounds. Once you're in, you don't leave until they say so."

"So I'd be a prisoner," Apollo said.

"A student, officially," Alden clarified. "But yes, effectively a prisoner."

Tristan wiped his hands on his apron. "So what are you going to do?"

Apollo glanced around, making sure they were alone. "Kieran thinks we should leave. Tonight."

His friends exchanged looks.

"He's right," Alden said. "The historical precedent is... concerning. During the Purge, Veilborn who surrendered to Order testing were never seen again."

"That was a thousand years ago," Apollo protested.

"Organizations like the Order don't change their core beliefs," Alden countered. "They just change how they present them."

Tristan crossed his arms. "So you're leaving. Just like that?"

"I don't want to," Apollo said, hearing the desperation in his own voice. "But I don't see another option. You didn't see how they looked at me, like I was some kind of... specimen."

"Where will you go?" Alden asked.

"Kieran has a plan. Beyond that..." Apollo shook his head. "I don't know."

Tristan kicked at a pile of coal dust. "This is ridiculous. You shouldn't have to run from your own home because of something you can't control."

"I agree," Apollo said. "But it's happening anyway."

They fell silent, the forge's embers casting flickering shadows across their faces.

"I'll come with you," Tristan said suddenly.

Apollo stared at him. "What?"

"I'll come with you," Tristan repeated. "You'll need help, and I'm good with my hands. Better than sitting here wondering if you're alive or dead."

"Your family—" Apollo began.

"Will understand," Tristan finished. "Eventually."

"I'm coming too," Alden added. "My knowledge of history and languages could be useful. And frankly, I've always wanted to see more of the world than just Willowbrook."

Apollo felt a lump form in his throat. "I can't ask you to do that."

"You didn't ask," Tristan said. "We're offering."

Before Apollo could respond, the forge door swung open. Guardian Marius of the Order stood in the entrance, his gray robes stark against the warm tones of the smithy.

"Apollo Frost," he said, his voice deep and measured. "Observer Lyra requests your presence at the council hall. Immediately."

Apollo took a step back. "I thought the tests weren't until tomorrow."

"This is not about the tests," Marius replied. "It concerns information that has come to our attention regarding your... heritage."

Apollo exchanged a quick glance with his friends. "What information?"

"That is for Observer Lyra to discuss." Marius's tone made it clear this wasn't optional.

"I'll be there shortly," Apollo said, trying to sound calm.

Marius nodded once and withdrew, leaving the door open behind him.

"They know something," Alden whispered once Marius was out of earshot. "About your parents, maybe."

"Or they're trying to catch you off guard," Tristan suggested. "Don't trust them, Apollo."

"I don't," Apollo assured him. "But I need to know what they know."

"Be careful," Alden warned. "And if you don't return within the hour..."

"Assume the worst," Apollo finished. "If that happens, tell Kieran. He'll know what to do."

With a final nod to his friends, Apollo stepped out into the afternoon sun, his decision made. Whether the Order knew it or not, this would be his last day in Willowbrook.

4

THE WESTERN BEARING

Apollo rushed to the assembly chamber. Whatever information the Order claimed to have about his heritage, he couldn't afford to appear suspicious by refusing their summons. Guardian Marius walked several paces ahead, his back straight and steps measured.

The village square bustled with afternoon activity. People paused to stare as Apollo passed, their whispers following him like shadows. Three days ago, he'd been just another villager. Now he was something else entirely—Veilborn, whatever that truly meant.

When they reached the council hall, Marius gestured toward the entrance. "Observer Lyra awaits inside."

Apollo nodded and stepped through the doorway. The hall's interior felt cooler than the summer air outside, its stone walls providing relief from the heat. Observer Lyra sat at the council table, papers spread before her. Keeper Dorn stood nearby, arranging items Apollo couldn't quite see.

"Apollo Frost," Lyra said without looking up. "Thank you for coming promptly."

"You said you had information about my heritage," Apollo replied, remaining near the door.

Lyra raised her eyes to meet his. "Indeed. Please, sit."

Apollo approached cautiously, taking a seat across from her. From this angle, he could see what Keeper Dorn had been arranging—a collection of small objects that made Apollo's vision swim with faint traces of blue-violet light.

"These artifacts," Lyra began, "were recovered from individuals with abilities similar to yours. We believe they may help us understand your particular... manifestation."

"Similar to me?" Apollo asked. "You mean other Veilborn?"

"The term is archaic but accurate," Lyra conceded. "Yes, others who demonstrated dimensional sensitivity."

Apollo leaned forward slightly. "Are there many of us?"

"Not anymore," Lyra said. "Which makes you quite valuable to our understanding."

Keeper Dorn approached with a small wooden box. "This was found in the possession of a Veilborn family twenty years ago. We believe it may respond to your touch."

Apollo inspected the box with curiosity. "What will happen if it does?"

"That's what we hope to learn," Lyra said with the hint of a smile. "Please."

Apollo extended his hand. As his fingers neared the box, the familiar blue-violet light intensified around it, threads of energy reaching toward him like tendrils.

"You can see it, can't you?" Lyra asked, watching his face intently. "The dimensional resonance."

Apollo nodded, not taking his eyes off the box. The moment his fingers touched the smooth wood, a jolt of energy shot up his arm. The box's lid sprang open, revealing a small metal disc similar to the one he'd found near the ruins—but this one was inscribed with unfamiliar symbols that glowed brightly in his vision.

"Fascinating," Dorn murmured, making notes on a small pad.

"What is it?" Apollo asked, fighting the urge to snatch his hand away.

"A resonance compass," Lyra explained. "It responds to dimensional fluctuations. The fact that it activated for you confirms our suspicions about the strength of your abilities."

Apollo stared at the disc, watching as a thin needle at its center began to rotate. "It's pointing at something."

"Indeed," Lyra said, her voice taking on an edge of excitement. "And that brings us to why we called you here. Apollo, we believe your parents may have been part of a group of Veilborn who went into hiding after the Purge. This compass could lead us to others like you—perhaps even to your birth family."

Apollo stiffened momentarily. "My birth family? You know who they are?"

"Not specifically," Lyra admitted. "But we have records suggesting a small enclave survived in the western mountains. If you were to assist us in locating them—"

"You want to use me as bait," Apollo interrupted, the realization dawning. "To find other Veilborn."

Lyra's expression hardened. "We want to understand a potentially dangerous phenomenon. Your cooperation would be valuable, but it's not the only way forward."

Apollo stood abruptly. "I need time to think about this."

"Of course," Lyra said. "Until tomorrow's testing, then."

Apollo turned to leave, then paused. "May I take the compass? To study it?"

Lyra and Dorn exchanged glances.

"It would be irregular," Dorn began.

"But perhaps useful for building trust," Lyra finished. "Very well. Consider it a gesture of good faith."

Apollo cautiously took the compass, feeling its weight in his palm. "Thank you."

As he left the council hall, Apollo fought to keep his pace measured and calm. The compass pulsed warmly in his hand, its needle swinging wildly before settling on a direction that, if he wasn't mistaken, pointed toward the western mountains—far beyond Willowbrook's boundaries.

Night fell over Willowbrook like a shroud. Apollo moved silently through his and Kieran's home, gathering only what was essential—clothes, dried food, the knife Tristan had made him, and the silver spiral pendant Elder Verity had given him. The resonance compass from the Order sat on his bed, its needle steadily pointing west.

Kieran entered, carrying a small pack of his own. "Are you ready?"

Apollo nodded. "Tristan and Alden are coming too."

Kieran frowned. "That wasn't part of the plan."

"They insisted," Apollo said. "And honestly, we could use their help."

After a moment, Kieran sighed. "You're right. But it puts them in danger."

"They know that." Apollo secured his pack and slipped the compass into his pocket. "The Order gave me this today. They said it might lead to information about my birth family."

Kieran's eyes widened. "They gave you a resonance compass? Willingly?"

"They're trying to gain my trust," Apollo explained. "But it could be useful to us."

"More than they know," Kieran agreed. "Your father—your birth father—had one similar to it. He said it was tuned to something important."

A soft knock at the door interrupted them. Kieran peered through the window before opening it to reveal Tristan and Alden, both carrying packs.

"We need to move," Tristan whispered. "I saw Guardian Marius headed this way."

"Out the back," Kieran directed. "Through the orchard. We have a head start, but they'll be after us by morning."

They slipped out into the darkness, keeping low as they moved between the apple trees. Apollo glanced back at the only home he'd ever known, wondering if he'd see it again.

"Stay close to the tree line," Kieran instructed as they reached the edge of the property. "We'll follow the stream west for a few miles, then cut north through the forest."

"The compass is pointing west," Apollo said, checking the device in his palm.

"West leads directly to Order territory," Kieran countered. "North first, then west once we're clear."

They moved in silence, the night air cool against their skin. The waning moon provided just enough light to navigate by, though Apollo noticed he could see better than the others, the landscape faintly illuminated by threads of energy he was becoming more attuned to.

After an hour of travel, they paused at a small clearing by the stream. Alden leaned against a tree, catching his breath.

"I should have spent less time reading and more time hiking," he said with a weak smile.

"You're doing fine," Tristan assured him, though he himself showed no signs of fatigue.

Apollo removed the compass from his pocket, watching as its needle adjusted. "It's still pointing west, but there's something strange happening."

The others gathered around. The needle was vibrating, and the symbols around the edge of the disc glowed more intensely than before.

"What does it mean?" Alden asked.

"I'm not sure," Apollo admitted. "But I think it's reacting to something nearby."

A twig snapped in the darkness beyond their clearing. Everyone froze.

"We're not alone," Kieran whispered, reaching for the knife at his belt.

A figure stepped into the moonlight—Guardian Marius, his Order robes replaced by more practical traveling clothes. Behind him, two more shapes emerged from the shadows.

"Apollo Frost," Marius called, his voice carrying across the clearing. "By the authority of the Order of the Veil, I command you to surrender yourself into our custody."

Kieran stepped forward. "He's not going anywhere with you."

"Mr. Frost," Marius replied, "harboring a Veilborn fugitive is a serious offense. Don't compound your crimes."

"Fugitive?" Apollo challenged. "I haven't committed any crime."

"Your existence is the crime," one of the other Order members said—a woman Apollo didn't recognize. "Veilborn were purged for a reason."

"Run," Kieran whispered to Apollo. "I'll hold them off."

"I'm not leaving you," Apollo protested.

"You must," Kieran insisted. "Follow the compass. Seek what your parents wanted you to find."

Before Apollo could argue further, Marius signaled to his companions. They spread out, clearly intending to surround the group.

"Last chance," Marius warned. "Surrender now, or we will take you by force."

Apollo felt something stir within him—a connection to the energy patterns he'd been seeing. Without fully understanding what he was doing, he reached out with his mind, grasping the threads of light that wove through the clearing.

The air around them shimmered. The Order members hesitated, confusion crossing their faces.

"Now!" Apollo shouted, pulling at the energy.

A ripple passed through the clearing, momentarily distorting the space between them and their pursuers. Kieran didn't waste the opportunity, shoving Apollo toward the trees.

"Go!" he commanded. "All of you!"

Apollo, Tristan, and Alden broke into a run, plunging into the dense forest. Behind them, Apollo heard shouts and the sound of pursuit.

"What did you do back there?" Tristan asked as they ran.

"I don't know," Apollo admitted, his breath coming in gasps. "I just... felt the energy and pulled on it."

They ran until their lungs burned, finally stopping in a dense thicket. Apollo leaned against a tree, trying to catch his breath.

"I don't hear them anymore," Alden whispered, his face pale in the moonlight.

"They're still coming," Apollo said with certainty. He could feel it somehow—a disturbance in the energy patterns around them.

"Where's Kieran?" Tristan asked, looking back the way they'd come.

A cold weight settled in Apollo's stomach. "He stayed behind. To buy us time."

"We have to go back for him," Tristan insisted.

"No," Apollo said, though the word tore at him. "He knew what he was doing. We have to keep moving."

Apollo pulled out the compass again. Its needle pointed northwest, vibrating more intensely than before.

"It's changed direction," he noted.

"Perhaps it's responding to your use of power," Alden suggested. "The Order said it detects dimensional fluctuations, right?"

Before Apollo could respond, a rustling sound came from nearby. They tensed, ready to run again.

"This way," a female voice whispered from the shadows. "Quickly."

A figure stepped partially into view—a young woman with black hair and a silver streak, dressed in dark clothing that blended with the night. She beckoned urgently.

"Who are you?" Apollo demanded.

"Someone who doesn't want to see you captured," she replied. "The Order patrol is circling back this way. We have minutes, at most."

Apollo hesitated, but the compass needle swung in the woman's direction, glowing brighter.

"I think we should trust her," he decided.

"Just like that?" Tristan asked incredulously.

"The compass is pointing to her," Apollo explained. "And I don't think we have much choice."

The woman led them through the forest with confident steps, traversing the darkness as if it were daylight. After several minutes of silent travel, they reached a small cave hidden behind a curtain of vines.

"In here," she directed. "They won't find us."

The cave extended deeper than it first appeared, opening into a modest chamber. The woman lit a small lamp, revealing a space that showed signs of recent habitation—a bedroll, some supplies, and several unusual objects that glowed faintly in Apollo's vision.

"Who are you?" Apollo asked again as they settled inside.

"My name is Astra," she replied, studying him with amber eyes that seemed to shift color in the lamplight. "And you're Apollo Frost, the Veilborn who caused quite a stir in Willowbrook."

"How do you know about that?" Alden asked suspiciously.

"Word travels," Astra said with a shrug. "Especially when it concerns the Order."

"Are you with them?" Tristan demanded.

"No," Astra said, touching a pendant at her neck—a design similar to the spiral Elder Verity had given Apollo. "Not anymore."

"You were Order?" Apollo asked, surprised.

"Once," she admitted. "Until I learned what they really do to Veilborn they capture."

A tense silence fell over the group.

"What about Kieran?" Apollo asked. "My father. He stayed behind to distract them."

Astra's expression softened. "I didn't see anyone else. But the patrol that was following you headed back toward Willowbrook about twenty minutes ago. If your father evaded them, he might have gone back to draw them away from your trail."

Apollo nodded, hoping desperately that was the case.

"The compass," Alden said, gesturing to the device in Apollo's hand. "It led us to you. Why?"

Astra glanced at the compass, her expression guarded. "Those devices respond to dimensional energy. I have... a certain sensitivity to such things."

"You're Veilborn too?" Apollo asked.

"No, not like you," she replied. "But I can perceive certain energies, yes."

Apollo studied her, noting the way faint threads of light seemed to cling to her form—subtle, but definitely present.

"Why help us?" he pressed.

"Because I've seen what happens to Veilborn in the Order's 'seminaries,'" Astra said, her voice hardening. "And because I've been tracking unusual dimensional disturbances in this region for months. When I felt the surge from Willowbrook during your festival, I knew something significant had happened."

"What kind of disturbances?" Apollo asked.

Astra hesitated, then reached into her pack and withdrew a rolled parchment. "See for yourself."

She spread it on the cave floor. It was a map, but unlike any Apollo had seen before. Instead of political boundaries or geographical features, it showed patterns of light and energy—swirling lines that connected various points across the region.

"These are dimensional fault lines," Astra explained. "Places where the barrier between our world and others grows thin."

Apollo's eyes were drawn to a bright spot near the center of the map. "What's that?"

"That," Astra said, "is why I'm here. Something is happening at that location—a gathering of energy unlike anything I've seen before. And your compass appears to be pointing directly to it."

Apollo checked the resonance compass. Its needle aligned perfectly with the bright spot on Astra's map.

"My birth parents," Apollo murmured. "Kieran said they gave him a compass similar to this one. That it was tuned to something important."

"Then perhaps that's where we'll find answers," Astra suggested.

"We?" Tristan asked.

Astra met his gaze steadily. "You need someone who understands dimensional energy and knows how to avoid Order patrols. I need to investigate that energy convergence. Our goals align."

"She's right," Apollo said after a moment. "We could use her help."

"Can you teach me?" he asked Astra. "About these abilities I have?"

"Some," she replied cautiously. "I'm not Veilborn like you, but I know the basics. The rest, you'll have to discover for yourself."

Apollo nodded, then turned to his friends. "What do you think?"

Alden adjusted his spectacles. "The historical knowledge she possesses could be invaluable. And frankly, we need all the help we can get."

Tristan looked less convinced but shrugged. "If Apollo trusts her, that's good enough for me. For now."

"Then it's settled," Apollo said, looking back at Astra. "We go to this energy convergence together."

Astra nodded, rolling up her map. "We'll rest here tonight. The Order won't find this place—I've made sure of that. Tomorrow, we head west."

As the others prepared for sleep, Apollo sat near the cave entrance, the resonance compass in his palm. He focused on it, trying to understand the connection he felt to the device. The blue-violet light around it intensified, responding to his attention.

"Try to feel the energy, not just see it," Astra said, sitting beside him.

"How?" Apollo asked.

"Close your eyes," she instructed. "Dimensional energy isn't just visual. It has texture, resonance, rhythm."

Apollo closed his eyes, concentrating on the compass in his hand. At first, there was nothing. Then, gradually, he became aware of a subtle vibration—a humming that seemed to match his own heartbeat.

"I feel it," he whispered. "Like... music without sound."

"Good," Astra said. "That's the first step. The energy flows through everything, connecting dimensions. Veilborn can not only perceive these connections but manipulate them."

Apollo opened his eyes, watching as the threads of light around the compass responded to his thoughts, shifting and changing.

"What happened to them?" he asked. "The Veilborn. The Order said they were purged, but why?"

Astra's expression darkened. "The official history says the Veilborn caused the Cataclysm—that their manipulation of dimensional energy tore reality apart. But there are other versions of that story."

"And which version do you believe?" Apollo pressed.

Astra touched her pendant. "I believe the Veilborn were guardians, not destroyers. That they understood something vital about the nature of our world—something the Order has spent centuries trying to suppress."

Apollo looked down at the compass, its needle unwavering in its direction. "And you think we'll find answers where this is pointing?"

"I hope so," Astra said. "For all our sakes."

As Apollo settled down to sleep, his mind burned with questions. About his birth parents, about his abilities, about the truth behind the Purge. The compass sat beside him, its needle pointing steadily toward whatever lay ahead—toward answers, he hoped, but also toward dangers he could only begin to imagine.

One thing was certain: there was no going back to Willowbrook now. His old life was behind him. Whatever awaited in the direction the compass pointed, it would lead to a new path—one he would face with his friends at his side, and with the mysterious Astra as their guide.

5

BEYOND THE VEIL

Apollo woke to the soft glow of dawn filtering through the cave entrance. For a disorienting moment, he expected to see the familiar ceiling of his bedroom in Kieran's farmhouse. Instead, rough stone greeted him, a stark reminder of everything that had changed.

He sat up, muscles stiff from sleeping on the hard ground. The others were still asleep—Tristan sprawled with one arm flung over his face, Alden curled tightly around his pack as if protecting his books even in sleep. Astra was nowhere to be seen.

Apollo rose quietly and made his way to the cave entrance. Outside, the forest was coming alive with morning sounds—birds calling, leaves rustling in the gentle breeze. The resonance compass sat heavy in his pocket. He pulled it out, watching as the needle pointed steadfastly west.

"You're up early."

Apollo turned to find Astra approaching from the tree line, a small bundle of berries and nuts in her hand.

"Couldn't sleep much," he admitted. "Too many thoughts."

She nodded as if she understood perfectly. "Breakfast," she said, offering the foraged food. "We should wake the others soon. We need to cover ground before the Order extends their search this far."

Apollo took a handful of berries, their tartness sharp on his tongue. "How far do we need to go?"

"Three days' journey, if we maintain a good pace," Astra replied, glancing at the compass in his hand. "That energy convergence is near the ruins of Valeshire."

"I've never heard of it."

"Few have. It was abandoned after the Cataclysm." She paused, studying him. "You should practice while we walk."

"Practice what?"

"Your perception," she said. "The ability to see dimensional energy is just the beginning. You need to learn to feel it, understand it."

Apollo looked down at his hands, remembering the strange sensations from the night before—the humming that seemed to resonate with his own heartbeat.

"I don't know how," he confessed.

"Start simple," Astra advised. "Focus on one thing at a time. The more you practice, the more natural it will become."

Their conversation was interrupted by Tristan's voice from inside the cave.

"Please tell me someone has food. I'm starving."

They set out shortly after sunrise, Astra leading the way with Apollo close behind. Tristan and Alden followed, the latter with his nose buried in a small notebook, occasionally stumbling over roots and stones.

"Watch where you're going, Nash," Tristan grumbled after catching Alden's arm for the third time. "Your notes won't matter if you break your neck."

"These observations could be crucial," Alden replied without looking up. "I'm documenting everything about Apollo's abilities and our journey. Future historians will thank me."

"Future historians won't matter if we get caught by the Order," Tristan countered.

Apollo smiled despite himself. The familiar bickering was oddly comforting amid so much uncertainty.

As they walked, Apollo tried to follow Astra's advice. He focused on the forest around them, not just seeing but trying to feel the subtle energies she'd described. At first, there was nothing beyond the usual sights and sounds of the woods. Then, gradually, he began to notice faint threads of light—some pulsing with life around plants and trees, others stretching like thin ribbons through the air.

"What do you see?" Astra asked, dropping back to walk beside him.

"Threads," Apollo replied. "Like... connections between things."

She nodded. "Good. Those are dimensional currents—places where energy flows between our world and others."

"They're everywhere," Apollo marveled.

"Yes, though most are too weak for even Veilborn to perceive. At certain locations—like ruins or ancient sites—the currents grow stronger, more visible."

Apollo concentrated on a particularly bright thread that seemed to wind around a gnarled oak tree. As he focused, the light intensified, responding to his attention.

"It's reacting to me," he said.

"You're not just observing the energy," Astra explained. "You're interacting with it. Veilborn don't just see these currents—they can influence them."

Apollo reached out tentatively toward the glowing thread. As his fingers approached, the light curled toward him like a living thing, wrapping around his hand in a cool embrace.

"Incredible," Alden breathed, suddenly at Apollo's side. "What does it feel like?"

"Like... water, but not wet. Or wind, but I can touch it." Apollo struggled to find the right words. "It has a rhythm to it."

"According to historical accounts," Alden said, flipping through his notebook, "Veilborn described dimensional energy as having unique frequencies or 'songs.' They could identify different types by their resonance patterns."

"That's right," Astra confirmed, giving Alden an appraising look. "Your knowledge is impressive."

Alden straightened, clearly pleased by the compliment. "I've studied everything available about the Veilborn, though most records are fragmentary at best. The Order destroyed much of the historical documentation during the Purge."

"Not all of it," Astra said cryptically before turning back to Apollo. "Try to follow that energy thread. See where it leads."

Apollo concentrated on the glowing filament wrapped around his hand. As he focused, he could sense its path—winding through the forest, growing stronger in the direction the compass pointed.

"It's flowing west," he said. "Toward where we're headed."

"The convergence," Astra nodded. "These currents are like rivers, flowing toward points where dimensional boundaries thin. The stronger the convergence, the more currents flow toward it."

"So we're following an energy river?" Tristan asked.

"In a manner of speaking," Astra replied. "Though this is just a small tributary. The main current lies ahead."

They continued walking, Apollo acutely aware of the web of energies surrounding them. It was distracting at first—like developing a new sense. Colors seemed brighter, sounds clearer, as if the dimensional awareness was enhancing his other perceptions.

"How do you know so much about this?" Apollo asked Astra after they'd been walking for some time. "You said you're not Veilborn."

She touched the silver pendant at her throat—a gesture Apollo had noticed she made when thoughtful or uncomfortable.

"I was trained to recognize dimensional phenomena," she said. "The Order teaches its members to identify signs of dimensional disturbance, though few develop true sensitivity."

"But you left the Order," Apollo prompted.

"Yes." Her tone made it clear she wouldn't elaborate further.

"We should rest soon," Tristan called from behind them. "And find water."

Astra nodded. "There's a stream ahead. We can stop there briefly."

The stream was clear and cold, bubbling over smooth stones. They refilled water skins and rested in the dappled shade of overhanging branches. Apollo sat on a fallen log, watching the water flow. To his newly awakened senses, the stream glowed with subtle energy—blue-green threads weaving through the current.

"It's beautiful," he murmured.

"What do you see?" Alden asked, settling beside him with notebook ready.

Apollo described the patterns in the water, how they shifted and flowed with the current.

"Fascinating," Alden said, sketching hastily. "Water has always been associated with dimensional phenomena in historical texts. The Ancestral civilization built many of their research facilities near significant bodies of water."

"The Ancestral civilization?" Apollo asked.

"The advanced society that existed before the Cataclysm," Alden explained. "They developed technologies we can barely comprehend today. Some historians believe they deliberately engineered the Veilborn to interface with their dimensional technologies."

"Engineered?" Apollo frowned. "You mean they created the Veilborn?"

"It's one theory," Alden said. "Though the Order considers it heretical. They maintain that Veilborn abilities are an unnatural mutation—a dangerous aberration to be controlled."

"Which is why they hunt us," Apollo said.

"Which is why they fear you," Astra corrected, approaching from where she'd been scouting ahead. "Fear often masquerades as hatred."

Tristan, who had been unusually quiet, abruptly stood. "Someone's coming."

They all froze, listening. The forest had gone silent—no birdsong, no rustling leaves. Just the quiet gurgle of the stream.

"How many?" Astra whispered, hand moving to the knife at her belt.

Tristan shook his head. "Can't tell. But something disturbed the birds upstream."

"Pack up," Astra ordered. "Quickly and quietly."

They gathered their belongings with practiced efficiency. Apollo slipped the compass into his pocket, feeling its weight like an anchor. Whatever was coming, the compass was too valuable to lose.

"This way," Astra directed, leading them away from the stream and into denser forest. "Stay low and move quietly."

They hadn't gone far when voices carried through the trees—authoritative and clipped.

"Spread out. The tracks lead this way."

The Order had followed them faster than expected. How had they picked up the trail so quickly?

Astra pulled them into a hollow beneath a fallen tree, its massive trunk providing cover from searching eyes. They huddled together, barely breathing as footsteps approached.

"Any sign of them?" a woman's voice called.

"Nothing yet, Captain," came the reply. "But they passed through here recently."

Apollo risked a glance through a gap in the roots. Three figures moved through the forest about thirty paces away—not wearing the gray robes of the Order but instead outfitted in dark uniforms with gleaming insignias on their shoulders.

"Those aren't Order members," he whispered.

Astra's expression darkened. "Worse. Magistrate's Guard."

"Magistrate Carver?" Alden breathed, eyes wide. "What would his people want with us?"

"Not us," Astra murmured. "Apollo."

Before Apollo could ask what she meant, one of the guards called out.

"Captain Drake! I've found something."

A tall woman with short-cropped red hair strode into view—evidently the captain. She knelt to examine something on the ground, then straightened with a small object in her hand. Even from a distance, Apollo could see it glowed with a faint blue light.

"Dimensional residue," Captain Drake said. "Fresh. The Veilborn was here recently."

Somehow, they were tracking his dimensional energy.

"How are they doing that?" he whispered.

"Carver has been collecting artifacts for years," Astra replied. "Some can detect dimensional manipulation."

"We need to move," Tristan urged. "Before they find us."

Astra shook her head. "Not yet. They're between us and our path forward. We need to create a distraction."

Apollo looked around desperately, seeking inspiration. His gaze fell on the resonance compass in his pocket. An idea formed.

"I might be able to redirect them," he said. "If I can manipulate the energy they're tracking..."

"Too dangerous," Astra objected. "You don't have enough control yet."

"Do you have a better idea?" Apollo countered.

After a moment's hesitation, she shook her head. "What do you need?"

"Something with a strong dimensional signature," Apollo said, remembering what Elder Verity had taught him. "Something that will hold energy."

Tristan reached into his pack and withdrew a small metal object—a gear-like disc with intricate engravings.

"Will this work?" he asked. "It's the family heirloom I mentioned back in Willowbrook. Always felt strange when I held it."

Apollo took the disc, seeing the swirl of violet-blue light around it. "This is perfect. Where did your family get this?"

"Been in my family for generations," Tristan shrugged. "My father said it was part of some ancient machine."

Apollo closed his fingers around the disc, concentrating on the energy pulsing within it. He thought of what Astra had said about dimensional currents being like rivers. If he could divert that river...

He closed his eyes, focusing on the energy flowing through him and into the disc. It was like trying to cup water in his hands—slippery and difficult to control. But gradually, he felt the energy responding, gathering in the disc until it hummed with power.

"What now?" Alden whispered.

"We need to throw it," Apollo said. "As far as possible in the opposite direction."

Tristan took the disc back, its surface now glowing visibly even to non-Veilborn eyes. "I'll do it. I have the best arm."

Before anyone could object, Tristan slipped out from their hiding place and, with a powerful throw, sent the disc sailing through the air. It disappeared into the forest to the south, a faint trail of blue light marking its path.

In an instant, the sentries responded.

"There! Movement to the south!" one called.

"Strong energy signature," Captain Drake confirmed. "All units, move in that direction. Quickly!"

They watched as the guards hurried away, following the false trail. When they were out of sight, Astra signaled for them to move.

"That was clever," she said to Apollo as they crept in the opposite direction. "And dangerous."

"It worked," Apollo replied, though he felt drained from the effort.

"For now," Astra cautioned. "But Carver's forces are persistent. And that disc will eventually stop emitting energy."

"How does Magistrate Carver even know about me?" Apollo asked. "I've never met him."

"Carver has spies everywhere," Astra explained. "And he's been seeking Veilborn for years. The incident at the Illumination Ceremony would have reached his ears quickly."

"But why? What does he want with Veilborn?"

Astra's expression grew grim. "Power. Carver believes Veilborn abilities can be harnessed, controlled. He's been collecting artifacts and research for decades, trying to access dimensional energy without Veilborn sensitivity."

"Has he succeeded?" Alden asked.

"Partially," Astra admitted. "Which makes him even more dangerous. He understands enough to cause harm but not enough to prevent catastrophe."

They continued moving west, keeping a careful watch for more guards. Apollo's mind was filled with questions. First the Order, now Magistrate Carver—how many people were hunting him? And why did everyone seem to know more about his abilities than he did?

By evening, they had covered significant ground, putting distance between themselves and their pursuers. They made camp in a small clearing, keeping the fire small and well-shielded to avoid detection.

As night fell, Apollo sat apart from the others, watching the dimensional currents that had become increasingly visible to him throughout the day. They flowed stronger here, pulsing with vibrant colors that shifted and changed like the northern lights he'd seen during winter in Willowbrook.

"It's getting easier for you," Astra observed, sitting beside him. "The perception."

Apollo nodded. "It's like my eyes have finally focused on something that was blurry before."

"That's good progress," she said. "But perception is just the beginning. True Veilborn ability lies in manipulation—changing the flow of energy, not just seeing it."

"Like what I did with Tristan's disc?"

"Yes, though that was crude. With practice, you could do much more precise work."

Apollo turned to look at her. In the faint firelight, her features seemed softer, less guarded. The silver streak in her dark hair caught the light, gleaming like one of the dimensional threads he'd been watching.

"Why are you helping us?" he asked. "You're risking a lot."

Astra was quiet for a long moment. "Let's just say I have my reasons for opposing both the Order and Carver."

"That's not much of an answer."

A small smile touched her lips. "No, it's not. But it's the one I can give for now."

She reached up to touch her pendant—that habitual gesture Apollo had noticed before. This time, he focused his new perception on the silver object. It glowed with a steady blue light, dimensional energy flowing through it in a contained, controlled pattern.

"Your pendant," he said. "It's an artifact, isn't it?"

She paused, running her finger along the pendant. "Why, what do you see?"

"The energy in it. It's... different. Controlled somehow."

Astra nodded. "It's a dimensional stabilizer. Very old, very rare. It helps protect the wearer from dimensional fluctuations."

"Where did you get it?"

"It was my mother's," she said, a rare personal detail. "And her mother's before her."

"So your family has been connected to this dimensional stuff for generations?"

"You could say that." She stood abruptly. "We should rest. Tomorrow will be another long day."

Apollo wanted to ask more questions, but her closed expression made it clear the conversation was over. He watched as she moved away to check on the others, wondering about the secrets she kept so carefully guarded.

Tristan was examining his hands in the firelight when Apollo joined him.

"Everything alright?" Apollo asked.

Tristan looked up, startled. "Yeah, just... thinking about that disc. When you charged it with energy, I felt something. Like it was... I don't know, talking to me."

"Talking?"

"Not with words," Tristan clarified. "More like... I understood what it wanted me to do with it. How far to throw it, in which direction. It was strange."

Apollo moved closer. "Could you see the energy in it?"

"No, not like you describe. But I could feel it." Tristan flexed his fingers. "It's not the first time, either. Remember that old gear mechanism my father keeps in the forge? I've always been able to make it turn, even though it's missing pieces."

Alden, who had been listening nearby, looked up from his notes. "That's fascinating. Historical records mention non-Veilborn who had affinity for Ancestral technology. They were called Resonants."

"Resonants?" Tristan repeated.

"People who couldn't see dimensional energy but could interact with devices that channeled it," Alden explained. "They were highly valued during the Reconstruction Era for their ability to activate and repair Ancestral artifacts."

Tristan snorted. "Great. So I'm good with old junk. Not exactly as impressive as seeing between dimensions."

"Don't underestimate it," Astra said, rejoining their circle. "Resonants were crucial partners to Veilborn. They could stabilize and direct energy that Veilborn manipulated."

"Like a focusing lens," Apollo suggested.

"Exactly," Astra nodded. "In fact, the most powerful Veilborn works were always done in partnership with skilled Resonants."

Tristan looked thoughtful. "So this... ability might actually be useful?"

"Very," Astra confirmed. "Especially where we're going."

The next two days passed in a rhythm of walking, resting, and constant vigilance. Apollo continued practicing his perception, gradually learning to distinguish different types of dimensional energy by their colors and patterns. Astra proved to be a knowledgeable if somewhat reserved teacher, offering guidance while maintaining her emotional distance.

Still, Apollo found himself drawn to her. There was something compelling about her quiet confidence, the way she moved through the forest with practiced ease, the rare moments when her guard lowered enough to reveal flashes of dry humor or unexpected kindness.

On the evening of the third day, they crested a hill and saw their destination spread before them—the ruins of Valeshire, a sprawling complex of crumbling structures half-reclaimed by forest. Even from a distance, Apollo could see the dimensional energies swirling around the site—vibrant streams of light converging like tributaries flowing into a lake.

"It's beautiful," he breathed.

"And dangerous," Astra cautioned. "The dimensional boundaries are extremely thin here. We need to be careful."

They made their way down the hillside as the sun began to set, casting long shadows across the ancient ruins. The resonance compass in Apollo's pocket hummed with increasing intensity, the needle spinning as they approached.

"According to historical records," Alden said, consulting his notes, "Valeshire was an Ancestral research facility dedicated to dimensional studies. It was one of the first sites to be abandoned after the Cataclysm."

"For good reason," Astra added. "The dimensional tears here never fully healed."

As they neared the perimeter of the ruins, Apollo noticed strange markers set into the ground—metal posts with spiraling designs that glowed faintly in his enhanced perception.

"Boundary markers," Astra explained. "Warnings to keep people away."

"They're active," Apollo noted, seeing the energy flowing through them. "Someone's maintaining them."

"Yes," Astra said, her expression growing more guarded. "The site is protected."

"By who?" Tristan asked, hand moving to his knife.

Before Astra could answer, figures emerged from the shadows of the ruins—six people wearing simple gray clothing, each carrying a staff marked with symbols Apollo recognized as similar to those on the resonance compass.

"That's far enough," called the leader, a tall woman with silver-streaked black hair. "This area is forbidden to travelers."

Astra stepped forward. "We seek passage to the inner sanctuary. We have a Veilborn with us."

The guardians tensed visibly at her words. The leader studied Apollo with piercing eyes.

"Prove it," she demanded.

Apollo looked to Astra, who nodded encouragingly. Taking a deep breath, he focused on the nearest boundary marker. The dimensional energy flowing through it responded to his attention, brightening and shifting as he gently nudged it with his mind.

The marker flared with blue-violet light, its spiral pattern spinning slowly.

The guardians murmured among themselves, clearly surprised.

"A true Veilborn," the leader acknowledged. "After so many years..." She turned her attention to Astra. "You brought him here deliberately. Why?"

"The compass led us here," Astra replied, gesturing to Apollo. "And the convergence is growing stronger. You've felt it too, or you wouldn't have doubled your boundary guards."

The leader's eyes narrowed. "You know our ways. You are of the Order?"

"I was," Astra admitted. "No longer."

"A deserter," the woman said. "Why should we trust you?"

"Because without us, Carver will find this place," Apollo interjected. "His forces are already tracking us. They have devices that can detect dimensional energy."

This caused visible alarm among the guardians. The leader stepped closer, studying Apollo intently.

"What is your name, Veilborn?"

"Apollo Frost."

Something flickered in her eyes—recognition, perhaps, or surprise. She glanced at the other guardians, then back to Apollo.

"Frost," she repeated. "And you came here following a compass?"

Apollo nodded, pulling out the resonance compass to show her. The needle spun wildly now, as if confused by the concentrated energy of the ruins.

The leader looked at it for a long moment, then made a decision.

"You may enter," she said. "But only the Veilborn and one companion. The others must remain outside our boundaries."

"We stay together," Apollo insisted.

"Those are our terms," the leader said. "The sanctuary is not safe for those unprepared. Choose one companion or turn back now."

Apollo looked at his friends. Tristan stood ready as always, hand still on his knife. Alden clutched his notebook, eyes wide with scholarly excitement at the prospect of seeing the ruins up close.

"I'll go," Astra said before Apollo could decide. "I know what to expect inside."

The leader eyed Astra with distrust, but eventually gave a nod. "The others will be provided shelter at our outer camp. They will be safe there."

Apollo exchanged looks with Tristan and Alden. "Will you be okay waiting?"

"We don't have much choice," Tristan said. "Just... be careful in there."

"Document everything," Alden added earnestly. "The architectural details, the symbols, everything you can remember."

Apollo smiled despite the tension. "I'll try."

He turned back to the leader of the guardians. "We're ready."

The woman nodded and made a gesture with her staff. The boundary markers flared with light, creating a visible pathway through their perimeter.

"Follow closely," she instructed. "Step only where I step. The safe path shifts with the dimensional currents."

As Apollo and Astra prepared to follow her into the ruins, he felt a mixture of anticipation and apprehension. The compass had led them here for a reason. Whatever secrets lay within these ancient structures, he sensed they would change everything he thought he knew about himself and the world.

With one last glance back at his friends, Apollo stepped across the boundary and into the glowing heart of Valeshire.

6

—·—

VALESHIRE

Apollo followed the guardian leader through the shimmering barrier, his skin tingling as they passed the boundary markers. The sensation reminded him of plunging into cold water—a momentary shock followed by adaptation. Astra walked beside him, her movements confident despite the guardian's warning about shifting paths.

"The dimensional currents are strong here," Astra whispered. "Can you feel them?"

Apollo nodded. The currents were no longer subtle threads he had to concentrate to perceive. Here, they flowed like rivers of light—blue, violet, and occasionally silver—weaving through the ancient structures. The ruins themselves seemed half-dissolved into these currents, as if existing simultaneously in multiple realities.

"It's overwhelming," he admitted.

The guardian leader glanced back. "Your senses will adjust. Focus on your physical surroundings first, then gradually extend your awareness."

Apollo did as instructed, grounding himself in the solid stone beneath his feet. The ruins of Valeshire spread before them—a collection of partially collapsed buildings arranged in concentric circles around a central structure. Unlike the crude stone buildings of Willowbrook, these were constructed of a material that resembled marble but with a faint internal luminescence.

"What was this place?" Apollo asked.

"One of seven outposts," the guardian replied. "The Ancestrals built them to study dimensional phenomena. Valeshire specialized in documentation and preservation."

They approached the central building—a domed structure that had weathered the centuries better than its surroundings. Its entrance was marked with spiral patterns similar to those on Apollo's compass.

"The archives," the guardian said. "What remains of them, at least."

As they reached the entrance, the guardian turned to face them. "I am Sentinel Mira. I serve as primary guardian of Valeshire."

"How long have you been protecting this place?" Apollo asked.

"Our order has maintained watch for sixteen generations," Mira replied. "I personally have served for twenty-three years."

"Waiting for what?" Apollo pressed.

Mira's expression remained neutral. "For someone like you."

Before Apollo could question her further, she pressed her palm against a panel beside the entrance. The spiral patterns illuminated, and the heavy door slid open with surprising smoothness.

"Enter," Mira instructed. "Someone waits for you inside."

Apollo exchanged a glance with Astra, who looked equally surprised. They stepped through the doorway into a circular chamber illuminated by soft, ambient light that seemed to have no specific source.

The interior was far more intact than the exterior suggested. Shelves lined the walls, filled with objects that glowed faintly with dimensional energy—crystals, metal discs, and devices Apollo couldn't begin to identify. At the center stood a table with a surface that resembled water but remained perfectly still, reflecting the domed ceiling above.

And beside this table, examining something on its surface, stood a figure Apollo recognized immediately.

"Elder Verity?" he gasped.

The elder turned, her weathered face showing no surprise at their arrival. "Apollo Frost. Right on time."

Apollo stared in disbelief. "How are you here? You were in Willowbrook when we left."

"There are faster ways to travel than by foot, for those who know the paths," Verity said, her tone matter-of-fact. "I left shortly after you did."

"You knew we were coming here?" Astra asked, suspicion evident in her voice.

Verity's gaze shifted to Astra, assessing her. "The compass points where it must. And I've been expecting Apollo's arrival for some time."

Apollo stepped forward. "You've been lying to me. To everyone in Willowbrook."

"Not lying," Verity corrected. "Protecting. There's a difference."

"You're with the Order of the Veil," Apollo accused. "You summoned them to Willowbrook."

Verity shook her head. "I was once part of the Order, yes. But I left them long ago, when I realized what they had become." She gestured around the chamber. "Why do you think I've spent decades as a simple village elder, when I could have risen through their ranks?"

Apollo wasn't sure what to believe. "Then why didn't you tell me what I was from the beginning? You knew I was Veilborn."

"I suspected," Verity corrected. "But suspicion isn't certainty. The signs were there—your sensitivity to the ruins, your unusual perceptions—but many have shown such traits without developing true Veilborn abilities." She stepped closer, her eyes intense. "Do you know how many false hopes I've witnessed over the years? How many children with promising signs who never manifested the full range of abilities?"

"So you were waiting for proof," Astra interjected.

"Yes." Verity turned back to Apollo. "The Illumination Ceremony provided that proof. No ordinary person could have activated that map as you did."

Apollo took a step back. "But why—"

A sharp sound from outside interrupted him—a distant explosion followed by shouts.

Mira rushed into the chamber. "Intruders at the outer perimeter. Armed forces with dimensional detection equipment."

"Carver," Astra breathed.

Verity moved with surprising speed for her age. "We don't have much time." She pressed her palm against the table's surface, causing it to ripple like disturbed water. "Apollo, come here."

Apollo approached cautiously.

"Place your hand beside mine," Verity instructed.

When Apollo complied, the table's surface began to glow intensely. Images formed in the light—symbols and diagrams that shifted and changed too quickly to follow.

"What is this?" Apollo asked.

"Authentication," Verity explained. "The archives respond to Veilborn energy signatures. It's recognizing you."

The light stabilized, forming a three-dimensional projection above the table—a complex map similar to the one the Centennial Lamp had produced, but far more detailed.

"The Seven Outposts," Verity said. "Valeshire is just one. Each was dedicated to a different aspect of dimensional research."

Apollo studied the map, noticing how dimensional currents flowed between the locations, creating a network of energy.

"Why are they showing me this?"

"Because you're the first confirmed Veilborn in nearly a thousand years," Verity said.

Apollo stared at her. "That can't be right. There must be others."

"There have been individuals with partial abilities," Verity acknowledged. "Those who could perceive but not manipulate, or who could affect only specific types of dimensional energy. But a full Veilborn, capable of both perception and manipulation across the spectrum? Not since the Purge."

Another explosion sounded, closer this time.

"We need to move," Mira urged. "They've breached the secondary perimeter."

Verity nodded and waved her hand through the projection. The map collapsed into a small, crystalline object that she quickly pocketed.

Mira returned to the doorway, looking out. "They're deploying some kind of device. The dimensional barriers are destabilizing."

"We need to access the lower levels," Verity decided. "There's an exit passage that leads to the forest beyond the western ridge."

She moved to a section of wall and pressed a specific pattern of symbols. A portion of the floor slid away, revealing a staircase descending into darkness.

"Quickly," she urged.

Apollo hesitated. "My friends—Tristan and Alden—they're at the outer camp."

"I'll find them," Mira promised. "We have evacuation protocols. Now go!"

Apollo looked to Astra, who nodded. "We need to trust them."

They followed Verity down the stairs. As they descended, the ambient light faded, replaced by the glow of dimensional currents that seemed to flow along the walls themselves.

"These passages were designed to be navigable by Veilborn even if all other systems failed," Verity explained. "The currents will guide us."

The stairway opened into a vast underground chamber filled with row upon row of crystalline structures, each pulsing with internal light.

"What is this place?" Apollo asked, awed by the scale.

"The true archives," Verity said. "Everything above was just the interface. This is where the knowledge is actually stored."

Apollo approached one of the crystals. Within its depths, he could see what looked like writing, but in a script he didn't recognize.

"Echo crystals," Astra explained, seeing his fascination. "They store information in dimensional resonance patterns rather than physical form."

"Can we take them with us?" Apollo asked.

"Some," Verity said, moving through the rows with purpose. "The most critical ones."

She stopped before a particular crystal, larger than the others and glowing with a deeper blue light. "This one contains the history of the Veilborn—your history, Apollo."

As she reached for it, a tremor shook the chamber. Dust and small fragments of stone fell from the ceiling.

"They're using resonance disruptors," Astra warned. "Trying to collapse the dimensional pockets that help maintain this structure."

Verity removed the crystal and placed it in a pouch at her belt. She selected several more, working methodically despite the increasing tremors.

"That's all we can carry safely," she said. "The exit is this way."

They followed her through the archive, past thousands of crystals that might contain knowledge lost for centuries. Apollo experienced a stab of regret at abandoning such vast knowledge.

"What happens to all this if the structure collapses?" he asked.

"The crystals themselves are remarkably durable," Verity replied. "But without the proper containment fields, their information will gradually degrade."

They reached another staircase, this one ascending.

"This leads to a concealed exit about half a mile from the main ruins," Verity explained. "With luck, we can slip away while Carver's forces focus on the main complex."

As they climbed, Apollo's mind recounted what Verity had told him. The first confirmed Veilborn in a millennium. It seemed impossible, yet it explained the intensity of both the Order's and Carver's interest in him.

"Elder Verity," he said as they neared the top of the stairs, "if I'm truly the first in so long, why now? Why me?"

Verity paused, looking back at him with an expression that mixed sadness and hope.

"That's a complex question, Apollo. The simple answer is that the Veilborn were never truly gone—just hidden, their bloodlines diluted over generations of intermarriage with non-Veilborn. In you, those dormant traits have reawakened at full strength."

"But why—"

Another violent tremor cut him off, stronger than the previous ones. Cracks appeared in the walls around them.

"Later," Verity promised. "First, we survive."

They reached the top of the stairs and Verity pressed her hand against what appeared to be solid stone. A section slid aside, revealing daylight beyond.

They emerged into a dense grove of trees, the ruins of Valeshire now hidden from view by the terrain. In the distance, Apollo could hear shouting and the occasional crack of energy weapons.

"This way," Verity said, pointing deeper into the forest. "There's a meeting point for evacuations about two miles from here."

They moved swiftly through the trees, Apollo constantly scanning for signs of pursuit. The dimensional currents were still visible to him here, but fainter than within the ruins.

"Will Tristan and Alden really be safe?" he asked Astra as they walked.

"The guardians have protected this place for generations," she replied. "They know what they're doing."

After about fifteen minutes of travel, they heard movement ahead. Apollo tensed, but Verity raised a hand reassuringly.

"It's the evacuation group," she said.

Sure enough, a moment later they encountered a small band of people—several guardians including Mira, and to Apollo's relief, Tristan and Alden.

"Apollo!" Tristan rushed forward. "What happened? These guardians just grabbed us and said we had to leave immediately."

"Carver's forces attacked the ruins," Apollo explained. "They're looking for me."

Alden looked pale but determined. "We saw them from the camp. They have some kind of machines that made the air itself seem to tear open."

Mira approached, her expression grim. "We need to keep moving. Our scouts report they're expanding their search perimeter."

"Where are we going?" Apollo asked Verity.

"To my sanctuary," she replied. "It's hidden by natural dimensional folds that make it nearly impossible to find without guidance."

"Like your home in Willowbrook?" Apollo asked.

Verity smiled faintly. "My cottage there was just a simple dwelling. My true sanctuary is much more secure—and better equipped for what comes next."

"Which is what, exactly?" Tristan asked.

"Teaching Apollo to control his abilities," Verity said. "And preparing for what Carver will do next. He won't stop hunting you now that he knows what you are."

They continued through the forest, following paths that seemed random to Apollo but which Verity navigated with confidence. Occasionally she would pause, studying the dimensional currents that only she and Apollo could see, adjusting their course accordingly.

As they walked, Astra fell into step beside Apollo.

"How are you holding up?" she asked.

"I'm not sure," he admitted. "Everything's happening so fast. Yesterday I was just trying to understand what I am. Now I'm apparently the only one of my kind."

Astra nodded sympathetically. "It's a lot to process. But you're not alone in this, Apollo."

He glanced at her. "Why are you helping me? You still haven't really explained that."

A shadow crossed her face. "Let's just say I've seen what Carver does to people with abilities he can use. I couldn't stand by and watch it happen again."

Before Apollo could press further, Verity called for a brief rest. They had been moving for over an hour, and some of the guardians were carrying supplies salvaged from the evacuation.

As they settled on fallen logs, Apollo approached Verity.

"You said I'm the first confirmed Veilborn in a thousand years," he began. "What exactly does that mean?"

Verity sighed, looking every year of her age. "The Veilborn were once numerous—not common, but present in every major settlement. They helped rebuild society after the Cataclysm, using their abilities to identify safe locations, detect dimensional instabilities, and even harness dimensional energy for practical purposes."

"What changed?" Apollo asked.

"Fear," Verity replied. "As their numbers grew, so did their influence. Those without their abilities became suspicious, concerned that the Veilborn were creating a new ruling class. Then came the Dimensional Storms of the third century—devastating events that many blamed on Veilborn experimentation."

"Were they responsible?" Astra asked, joining the conversation.

Verity shook her head. "No. The storms were natural consequences of damage done during the Cataclysm. But fear rarely seeks truth. The Order of the Veil was formed initially to regulate Veilborn activities, but gradually transformed into something more sinister."

"The Purge," Apollo said, remembering what Alden had discovered in his research.

"Yes. Over several decades, the Order systematically hunted down and eliminated Veilborn individuals and families. Some were publicly executed as examples. Others disappeared into Order facilities, never to be seen again."

"But some escaped," Apollo prompted.

Verity nodded. "Some fled to remote regions. Others hid their abilities and blended into society. Over generations, those abilities weakened through intermarriage with non-Veilborn, until they manifested only as minor talents—unusual perception, intuition, or affinity for certain types of ancient technology."

"Like Tristan," Apollo realized.

"Exactly. What you call Resonants are likely descendants of Veilborn bloodlines, with just enough of the genetic heritage to interact with dimensional technologies without full perceptual abilities."

Apollo processed this information. "So my parents—my birth parents—they must have been..."

"I believe they were among the last pure Veilborn bloodlines," Verity confirmed. "Hidden for generations, carefully preserving their heritage through selective marriage within their own community."

"Where are they now?" Apollo asked, the question that had burned within him since learning of his adoption.

Verity's expression grew solemn. "I don't know for certain. When they brought you to Kieran, they were fleeing something—perhaps Carver, perhaps the Order. They said only that they needed to hide you somewhere unexpected, somewhere neither faction would think to look."

"A remote farming village," Apollo said.

"With a guardian they trusted," Verity added. "Kieran Frost was no random choice. He had connections to the old Veilborn networks, though he himself possesses no abilities."

Mira approached them. "We should move on. We're still too close to Valeshire."

Verity nodded and got to her feet. "We'll continue this discussion at the sanctuary. It's not much farther now."

As they resumed their journey, Apollo found himself walking beside Tristan.

"So," Tristan said after a moment, "you're some kind of legendary dimensional manipulator."

Despite everything, Apollo smiled. "Apparently."

"And I'm what—a watered-down version? A Veilborn with most of the power bred out?"

"That's not how I'd put it," Apollo replied. "More like... we're two sides of the same coin. I can see and manipulate the energy, but you can interact with the technology it powers."

Tristan considered this. "I guess that's not so bad. Still wish I could see all these currents and patterns you keep talking about, though."

"Trust me, it's not always pleasant," Apollo said. "Especially at first. It was like having another sense suddenly switch on, with no way to control it."

"Can you control it now?" Tristan asked.

Apollo flexed his hand, watching the dimensional currents respond subtly to his movement. "I'm learning."

They walked for another hour, the terrain gradually becoming more rugged. Verity led them into a narrow ravine that wound between steep hillsides covered in dense vegetation.

"We're close now," she announced. "The entrance to the sanctuary lies just ahead."

Apollo peered forward but saw only more ravine. "I don't see anything."

"You will," Verity assured him. She turned to address the group. "What comes next may be disorienting for those unaccustomed to dimensional transitions. Stay close together and follow precisely in my footsteps."

She continued forward, then seemed to step sideways in a way that didn't quite make sense to Apollo's eyes. Her figure blurred momentarily, then stabilized.

"Come," her voice called, though she now appeared to be standing much farther away than her previous position would allow.

Apollo focused his perception and gasped. The ravine ahead was folded somehow, the dimensional currents bending around a hidden pocket of space.

"It's a dimensional fold," he realized aloud.

"Yes," Astra confirmed beside him. "A natural one, by the look of it. Rare and very useful for hiding things."

One by one, they followed Verity through the fold, each experiencing the momentary disorientation of stepping through what appeared to be solid space. Apollo went last, watching as his friends seemed to blur and shift position as they crossed the boundary.

When his turn came, he focused on the currents, seeing how they flowed around and through the fold. He stepped forward, feeling a brief sensation like walking through a waterfall, and then he was through.

Beyond the fold lay a hidden valley, small but lush with vegetation. At its center stood a collection of stone buildings, simple but well-maintained. Streams flowed from springs on the hillsides, and gardens grew in neat rows near the structures.

"Welcome to my sanctuary," Verity said. "One of the few truly safe places left for those with Veilborn heritage."

Apollo gazed around in wonder. The dimensional currents flowed in harmonious patterns, unlike the chaotic energies at the ruins.

"How long has this place existed?" he asked.

"Since the height of the Purge," Verity replied. "It was established by a group of Veilborn seeking refuge. Over the centuries, it has served as a haven for those with abilities, a repository for knowledge, and occasionally a training ground."

"Training ground," Apollo repeated. "You intend to train me here."

Verity nodded. "You have remarkable natural talent, Apollo, but untrained abilities are dangerous—both to yourself and others. You need to learn control, precision, and the true extent of what you can do."

The guardians from Valeshire began organizing themselves, some tending to the wounded, others establishing a perimeter around the valley.

"Will they stay here?" Apollo asked, gesturing toward Mira and her people.

"Some will," Verity confirmed. "Others will return to monitor Valeshire once it's safe. The archives must not fall completely into Carver's hands."

They approached the largest of the stone buildings. Its entrance was marked with the now-familiar spiral pattern, though more elaborate than those Apollo had seen before.

"This structure serves as both dwelling and training facility," Verity explained. "There are quarters for all of you, and spaces designed specifically for Veilborn practice."

Inside, the building was surprisingly spacious, with a central atrium open to the sky above. Corridors branched off in several directions, leading to what Apollo assumed were the living quarters and other rooms.

"You should rest," Verity told them. "It's been a long day, and tomorrow will bring new challenges."

"What about Carver?" Tristan asked. "Won't he keep looking for us?"

"Undoubtedly," Verity agreed. "But this sanctuary is well-hidden. The dimensional fold that protects it is nearly impossible to detect without prior knowledge of its existence."

"Nearly impossible isn't the same as completely impossible," Alden pointed out.

"Nothing is absolute when dealing with dimensional phenomena," Verity acknowledged. "But we have survived here undetected through far more intensive searches than Carver is likely to mount."

She showed them to their quarters—simple but comfortable rooms with beds, washbasins, and small windows overlooking the valley.

"Rest now," she instructed. "We'll speak more in the morning."

After she left, Apollo sat on the edge of his bed, finally having a moment to process everything that had happened. The first confirmed Veilborn in a millennium. The weight of that identity pressed down on him like a physical burden.

A knock at his door interrupted his thoughts. He opened it to find Astra standing there.

"May I come in?" she asked.

Apollo nodded, stepping aside to let her enter.

"How are you really doing?" she asked once the door was closed.

Apollo sank back onto the bed. "I don't know. It's a lot to take in."

"That's an understatement," Astra said with a slight smile. She sat beside him. "Finding out you're the first of your kind in a thousand years isn't exactly an ordinary day."

"I keep thinking about my parents," Apollo admitted. "If they were Veilborn too, where are they now? Why didn't they keep me with them?"

"To protect you," Astra suggested. "If they were being hunted..."

"I know. It makes logical sense. But still..."

"You want answers," Astra finished for him. "That's natural."

Apollo looked at her. "What about you? There's still so much I don't know about why you're helping me."

Astra was quiet for a moment. "Let's just say I have my reasons for opposing both Carver and the Order. Reasons I'm not ready to fully explain yet."

"But you're not working for either of them? You're not leading me into some kind of trap?"

She met his gaze steadily. "No, Apollo. I promise you that. Whatever my secrets, my commitment to keeping you safe is genuine."

Something in her expression convinced him she was telling the truth—or at least, what she believed to be the truth.

"Thank you," he said. "For everything you've done so far."

She smiled, reaching out to squeeze his hand briefly. "Get some rest. Tomorrow, your real training begins."

After she left, Apollo lay back on the bed, staring up at the ceiling. Through his Veilborn perception, he could see the dimensional currents flowing through the structure, creating patterns of light that shifted and changed like living things.

The first confirmed Veilborn in a millennium. What did that mean for his future? For the world?

He closed his eyes, too exhausted to puzzle through these questions now. Tomorrow would bring new challenges, new knowledge. For tonight, at least, they were safe.

7

THE FIRST FOLD

Apollo woke to sunlight streaming through the small window of his room. For a moment, he couldn't remember where he was. Then it all came rushing back—the escape from Willowbrook, the journey to Valeshire, Carver's attack, and finally, the revelation that he was the first confirmed Veilborn in a millennium.

He sat up, running a hand through his hair. Through his dimensional perception, he could see the currents of energy flowing through the walls of the sanctuary, pulsing with a steady rhythm that somehow felt reassuring.

A knock at his door pulled him from his thoughts.

"Apollo? Are you awake?" It was Tristan's voice.

"Come in," Apollo called.

Tristan opened the door, dressed and looking surprisingly refreshed despite yesterday's ordeal. "Elder Verity wants us all in the central chamber after breakfast. Says she has important things to discuss."

Apollo nodded, swinging his legs over the side of the bed. "I'll be there soon."

After washing up and changing into fresh clothes that had been left for him—simple garments of undyed cotton that were surprisingly comfortable—Apollo made his way to the dining area where the others had gathered.

Alden was deep in conversation with one of the Valeshire guardians, while Tristan sat with a plate of food, examining what looked like a small mechanical device. Astra stood by one of the windows, gazing out at the valley, her expression thoughtful.

Apollo filled a plate with bread, cheese, and some kind of dried fruit before joining Tristan.

"What's that?" he asked, nodding toward the object in Tristan's hands.

Tristan grinned, holding it up. It was a metal sphere about the size of an apple, covered in intricate patterns that glowed faintly with dimensional energy.

"One of the guardians gave it to me," Tristan explained. "Said it was broken, but thought I might be able to figure it out since I'm a 'Resonant.'" He shook his head, still seeming bemused by the term.

"Any luck?" Apollo asked between bites.

"Not yet. But I can feel something when I hold it—like it wants to work but can't quite remember how." Tristan turned the sphere over in his hands. "It's the strangest feeling."

"I know what you mean," Apollo said. "That's how I feel about the dimensional currents—like they're trying to tell me something, but I don't have the language to understand."

Elder Verity entered the room, drawing everyone's attention. Despite her age, she moved with surprising grace, her white hair bound in a simple braid.

"Good morning," she said. "I trust you all slept well? Once you've finished eating, please join me in the central chamber. We have much to discuss and much to do."

Twenty minutes later, they gathered in the large circular room at the heart of the main building. Sunlight poured in from above, illuminating a space that Apollo now saw was covered in intricate patterns—the same symbols he'd noticed on artifacts and ruins, but far more extensive and complex.

"This chamber," Verity explained, "was designed specifically for Veilborn training. The patterns you see are not merely decorative—they're a form of notation, a language for describing dimensional phenomena."

Apollo stared at the markings with new interest. "Can you teach me to read them?"

"In time," Verity said. "First, you must learn to control your perception. From what I've observed, you've been experiencing dimensional awareness in an unstructured, unpredictable manner. That must change if you're to develop your abilities safely."

She gestured for Apollo to sit on a cushion in the center of the room.

"The rest of you may observe, but please remain quiet. Concentration is essential for what we're about to do."

Apollo settled onto the cushion, feeling nervous. Tristan, Alden, and Astra sat against the wall, watching with varying expressions of curiosity.

"Close your eyes," Verity instructed, sitting across from him. "Focus on your breathing first. Slow and steady."

Apollo did as she asked, trying to calm his thoughts.

"Now," Verity continued, her voice low and measured, "instead of trying to see the dimensional currents, I want you to feel them. They flow around and through you constantly, like air or water. Become aware of their presence without trying to visualize them."

Apollo concentrated, shifting his attention from sight to sensation. At first, he felt nothing unusual, just the normal awareness of his body and breath. But gradually, he became conscious of something else—a subtle vibration, a tingling that seemed to exist both within and beyond his physical form.

"I think I feel something," he murmured.

"Good," Verity said. "Now, very slowly, open your eyes, but maintain that awareness of the currents as sensation rather than sight."

Apollo opened his eyes. The room looked normal at first, but as he held onto that feeling of vibration, the dimensional currents began to appear—not as the overwhelming flood of light and color he'd experienced before, but as subtle, translucent streams that he could perceive without becoming distracted by them.

"The key," Verity explained, "is selective attention. You must learn to choose what dimensional frequencies you perceive and when. Otherwise, the sensory input will overwhelm you, especially in places of strong convergence like this sanctuary."

"It's like... tuning an instrument," Apollo said, confirming his understanding.

"Precisely." Verity nodded approvingly. "The Veilborn of old developed specific techniques for this—mental exercises that allowed them to filter their perception according to need."

For the next hour, Verity guided Apollo through a series of such exercises. He learned to focus on specific frequencies of dimensional energy, to shift his perception between them, and even to temporarily shut down his dimensional awareness entirely—a skill that proved surprisingly difficult.

By midday, Apollo's head was throbbing with the effort of concentration, but he felt a sense of accomplishment. For the first time since his abilities had manifested, he felt some measure of control over them.

"That's enough for today," Verity said. "You've made remarkable progress for a first session."

Apollo rubbed his temples, the strain of maintaining such focused attention taking its toll. "It feels like I've been lifting heavy weights with my mind."

"An apt comparison," Verity agreed. "Like any muscle, these abilities strengthen with use. But also like muscles, they can be strained if pushed too hard too quickly."

Tristan approached, the mechanical sphere still in his hands. "This has been fascinating to watch," he said. "I couldn't see what you were seeing, obviously, but there were moments when the patterns on the floor seemed to... respond somehow."

"They're designed to," Verity explained. "The notation is partially reactive to dimensional manipulation, serving both as guide and feedback mechanism." She glanced at the sphere in Tristan's hands. "Any progress with that?"

Tristan shook his head. "Not really. I can feel something, but I can't quite figure out what it's supposed to do."

"Perhaps I can help," Verity offered. "Resonants were once as valued as Veilborn for their unique abilities. The two often worked in partnership—Veilborn providing the raw dimensional manipulation, Resonants providing focus and application."

"Like a blacksmith and an apprentice working the same piece of metal," Tristan suggested.

"A good analogy," Verity agreed. "Come, let's see what we can discover about your artifact while Apollo rests."

As they moved to another part of the chamber, Astra approached Apollo, offering him a cup of water.

"Thank you," he said gratefully, drinking deeply.

"How are you feeling?" she asked, sitting beside him.

"Like my brain has run a marathon," Apollo admitted. "But also... better. More in control."

Astra nodded. "Control is crucial. Without it, dimensional perception can become overwhelming, even dangerous."

"You speak from experience," Apollo observed, studying her face.

Astra was quiet for a moment, then sighed. "Yes. Though my sensitivity is minimal compared to yours, I've seen what happens when dimensional energy is mishandled."

"During your time with the Order?" Apollo asked.

She met his gaze steadily. "Yes. That's part of why I left."

"Will you tell me about it?" Apollo asked. "About your time with them?"

Astra glanced where Verity was working with Tristan, then back to Apollo. "I suppose you deserve to know, given that you've trusted me this far."

She took a deep breath. "I was recruited by the Order when I was sixteen. My family has always had a... connection to dimensional matters, though none of us were Veilborn. The pendant I wear—" she touched the silver-blue object at her throat, "—has been passed down through generations."

"They wanted your knowledge?" Apollo guessed.

"That, and my sensitivity. It's rare, even among Order members. I can't see dimensional currents as you do, but I can sense them, especially strong disturbances." She paused. "I believed in their mission at first—to study and preserve knowledge of the Ancestral civilization, to protect people from dimensional dangers."

"What changed?"

"I discovered that certain factions within the Order had other goals. Observer Lyra, who you met in Willowbrook, belongs to a more moderate group. But others, like Keeper Dorn, serve Magistrate Carver's interests." Her expression hardened. "They don't want to study Veilborn—they want to control them, use them."

"For what purpose?" Apollo asked.

"Power," Astra said. "Dimensional energy can be harnessed in ways that go far beyond what most people imagine. The artifacts that survived the Cataclysm are just the beginning."

She looked at him intently. "When I learned what they really wanted, I couldn't stay. I've been tracking their movements ever since, trying to understand their plans and counter them where I can."

"And then you found me," Apollo said.

"I was actually following Guardian Marius," Astra admitted. "I knew the Order had sent representatives to Willowbrook, but I didn't know why until I saw you use your abilities in the forest."

Apollo processed this information, finding that it aligned with his instincts about Astra. Despite her secretiveness, he'd sensed her genuine concern for his safety.

"Thank you for telling me," he said. "It helps to know where you stand."

"I stand with those who want to understand dimensional energy, not exploit it," Astra said. "Which means I stand with you, Apollo."

Their conversation was interrupted by an exclamation from Tristan. The mechanical sphere in his hands had begun to glow more brightly, its patterns shifting and changing.

"I think I've got it!" Tristan called. "Elder Verity showed me how to feel for the right frequency!"

Apollo and Astra moved closer to see. The sphere had opened along previously invisible seams, revealing an interior filled with intricate mechanisms and glowing crystals.

"It's a recording device," Verity explained. "Similar to the echo crystals I retrieved from Valeshire, but more sophisticated. It stores not just information but actual sensory experiences."

"Can we access them?" Alden asked, leaning in with scholarly interest.

"Tristan has already begun the process," Verity said. "As a Resonant, he can attune the device to make its contents perceptible to all of us."

As they watched, the light from the sphere expanded, forming a three-dimensional image in the air above it—a recording of a person demonstrating what appeared to be Veilborn techniques. Though there was no sound, the movements were clear, showing precise gestures for manipulating dimensional energy.

"This is extraordinary," Verity breathed. "A direct instructional recording from before the Purge. This could accelerate your training immensely, Apollo."

Apollo watched, fascinated, as the figure in the projection performed a series of movements that seemed to gather and direct dimensional currents. He could see how they corresponded to the sensations he'd been learning to recognize during his session with Verity.

"Can you try to replicate that?" Astra suggested, pointing to a particularly clear sequence where the figure gathered energy between their hands.

Apollo stood, positioning himself in the center of the chamber. He closed his eyes briefly, focusing on the sensations of the dimensional currents around him, then opened them and began to mimic the movements he'd seen in the recording.

At first, nothing happened. But as he repeated the sequence, concentrating on the feeling of the currents rather than trying to visualize them, he began to sense a response—a gathering of energy that followed his gestures.

"It's working," Verity said. "Keep going."

Apollo continued the sequence, his movements becoming more confident as he felt the dimensional energy responding. Between his palms, a small concentration of energy began to form—visible to him as a swirling nexus of light, though he knew the others would see little or nothing.

The final movement involved bringing his hands together, then pulling them apart while maintaining the energy between them. As Apollo did this, the gathered energy stretched and stabilized, forming a small, sustained dimensional distortion that hovered between his hands.

"I can see it," Astra whispered, her eyes wide. "Just barely, but it's there—like heat shimmer in the air."

"What does it look like to you?" Tristan asked Apollo, his expression a mixture of curiosity and slight envy.

"Like a small whirlpool of light," Apollo described, maintaining his concentration on the distortion. "Threads of energy from the surrounding currents are being drawn into it, but in a controlled way."

"You've created a minor dimensional fold," Verity explained. "A localized distortion that draws energy from surrounding currents without disrupting them. It's one of the fundamental techniques Veilborn used as a building block for more complex manipulations."

Apollo held the fold for several more seconds before releasing it, allowing the energy to dissipate gradually back into the ambient currents. He lowered his hands, aware of how tired he felt.

"That was..." he began, searching for words.

"Remarkable," Verity finished for him. "To achieve controlled manipulation on your first day of training is unprecedented. Your natural affinity exceeds even my highest expectations."

Apollo sank back onto his cushion, feeling drained but exhilarated. "It felt... right. Like something I've always known how to do but had forgotten."

"In a sense, that may be true," Verity said. "The ability is encoded in your very being, after all."

"What else can I learn from these recordings?" Apollo asked, looking at the sphere that Tristan still held.

"A great deal, I suspect," Verity replied. "But not all at once. You've done enough for today. Dimensional manipulation draws on your physical and mental energy; pushing too far too fast can be dangerous."

Apollo nodded, acknowledging the wisdom in her caution despite his eagerness to learn more. The headache that had begun during his perception exercises had intensified, and he felt a bone-deep weariness setting in.

"Rest," Verity instructed. "We'll continue tomorrow. There's much more to learn, but you've taken your first true step as a Veilborn today."

As the others began discussing the recording device and what other knowledge it might contain, Apollo closed his eyes, focusing on the sensation of the dimensional currents flowing around him. For the first time since his abilities had manifested, he felt not fear or confusion, but purpose. He was beginning to understand what it meant to be Veilborn—not just to see the dimensional currents, but to work with them, to shape them.

It was only the beginning of his training, but he sensed the vast potential that lay before him. The thought was both thrilling and terrifying.

8

CALIBRATION

Apollo stirred from slumber at the commotion of pressing conversation. Briefly, his mind drifted to memories of Willowbrook, imagining Kieran locked in another heated debate with Elder Verity regarding the Order's impending visit. Then consciousness fully returned—the sanctuary's rock barriers surrounding him, the faint vibration of interdimensional power flowing throughout the chamber, and everything that had transpired over the previous fortnight.

He rose from his sleeping mat, muscles aching from yesterday's training. Three days had passed since his first successful dimensional manipulation, and each day had brought new exercises, new techniques, and new exhaustion. Elder Verity pushed him relentlessly, though always with a careful eye to his limits.

Apollo splashed water on his face from the basin near his bed and headed toward the voices. He found the others gathered in the main chamber—Verity, Astra, Tristan, and Alden, along with two of the Valeshire guardians who had accompanied them to the sanctuary.

"—confirmed sightings in three villages already," one of the guardians was saying, a woman named Lyssa who served as their scout. "Carver's forces are questioning anyone with unusual abilities or perceptions."

"How did they even know where to look?" Tristan asked, his face tight with concern.

"The incident at Willowbrook," Verity replied. "The Illumination Ceremony created a dimensional resonance that could be detected by anyone with the right equipment. Carver has been collecting artifacts for years."

Apollo stepped fully into the room. "What's happening?"

Five faces turned toward him, expressions ranging from concern to grim determination.

"Magistrate Carver has expanded his search," Astra explained. "He's no longer just tracking you—he's looking for anyone who might have Veilborn potential."

"Because of what I did at the festival," Apollo said, a weight settling in his chest.

"Not just that," Verity said. "Carver has been searching for Veilborn for years. What happened at Willowbrook simply accelerated his plans and gave him a specific target."

Apollo joined them at the table where a map was spread out. Several locations were marked with small red stones.

"These are the villages where Carver's forces have been spotted," Lyssa explained. "They're moving in a search pattern, working outward from Willowbrook."

"What happens to the people they find?" Apollo asked, though he suspected he knew the answer.

"Those who show any signs of dimensional sensitivity are taken to Carver's fortress for 'testing,'" Astra said, her voice tight. "None return."

Apollo studied the map, noting the methodical pattern of the search. "They're getting closer to us."

"Yes," Verity confirmed. "Which means we must accelerate your training. You've made remarkable progress, but you need to develop more specific skills if we're to have any chance against Carver."

"What kind of skills?" Apollo asked.

"Today, we'll work on frequency discrimination," Verity said. "The ability to perceive and manipulate specific dimensional frequencies rather than just the general currents."

"I'll continue working with the sphere," Tristan added. "I think I've found a way to access more of its recordings."

"And I've been translating some of the texts Verity salvaged from Valeshire," Alden said. "There's fascinating material about the science behind dimensional energy."

Apollo nodded, trying to ignore the guilt that threatened to overwhelm him. People were being hunted because of what had happened at Willowbrook—because of him.

"This isn't your fault," Astra said, as if reading his thoughts. "Carver has been planning this for years. If anything, your emergence has forced him to move before he was fully ready."

"She's right," Verity said. "Now, let's begin. We have much to accomplish today."

The training chamber was quieter than usual, with only Apollo and Verity present. They sat cross-legged on cushions in the center of the room, where the dimensional currents converged most strongly.

"Close your eyes," Verity instructed. "Focus on the dimensional currents as you've been practicing."

Apollo did as she asked, letting his awareness expand to encompass the flows of energy that surrounded them. Over the past days, this had become easier.

"Now," Verity continued, "instead of perceiving all the currents equally, I want you to focus on their differences. Each current has its own... signature, for lack of a better word. Its own frequency."

Apollo concentrated, trying to discern what she meant. At first, the currents all seemed the same—flowing streams of energy that connected their dimension to others. But as he focused more intently, he began to notice subtle variations. Some currents seemed to vibrate at different rates, creating distinct patterns that he could almost... taste, though that wasn't quite the right sense.

"I think I can feel it," he said, keeping his eyes closed. "They're not all the same."

"Excellent," Verity said. "Now, try to isolate one specific frequency. Find a current that feels... calmer than the others. Slower."

Apollo sorted through the dimensional flows, searching for what Verity described. After several minutes of concentration, he found it—a current that pulsed with a steady, slow rhythm, distinct from the more chaotic energies surrounding it.

"I've got it," he said.

"Good. Now, without losing your focus on that current, open your eyes."

Apollo opened his eyes, maintaining his concentration on the specific dimensional current. The room looked different—the colors muted, shadows deeper, the very air seeming thicker somehow.

"What you're experiencing is perception through a specific dimensional lens," Verity explained. "Each dimension has its own properties, its own physical laws. By attuning to different frequencies, Veilborn can perceive aspects of reality that are normally hidden."

"It's like... everything's slowed down," Apollo observed, watching as Verity raised her hand. The movement seemed to trail afterimages.

"That particular frequency corresponds to a dimension where time flows differently relative to ours," Verity said. "Now, try to find a different frequency—one that feels sharper, more energetic."

Apollo shifted his focus, searching through the currents until he found one that vibrated with a higher intensity. As he attuned to it, the room transformed again—colors brightening, edges becoming more defined, and a faint hum filling his ears.

"This is amazing," he breathed, looking around at the transformed space. "Everything's so clear."

"Each frequency offers different insights, different capabilities," Verity said. "A skilled Veilborn can shift between them at will, drawing on the properties of various dimensions as needed."

For the next hour, Verity guided Apollo through identifying and attuning to different dimensional frequencies. Some revealed hidden energies in objects around them, others altered his perception of distance or time, and one—particularly difficult to maintain—allowed him to see faint traces of past events, like ghostly afterimages.

By the end of the session, Apollo's head was pounding, and maintaining focus had become increasingly difficult.

"Enough for now," Verity said, noticing his strain. "You've made excellent progress."

Apollo released his hold on the dimensional currents, his perception returning to normal. The sudden shift left him dizzy, and he braced himself against the floor.

"This is harder than general perception," he admitted.

"It requires more precise control," Verity agreed. "But it's essential. Carver's forces use technology that can detect and disrupt dimensional energy, but they're calibrated to general frequencies. If you can operate on specific, unusual frequencies, you'll be harder to track and more difficult to counter."

Apollo nodded, understanding the tactical advantage. "When can I learn to manipulate these specific frequencies, not just perceive them?"

"Soon," Verity promised. "But perception must come first. You cannot safely manipulate what you cannot fully perceive."

She rose to her feet with a grace that belied her age. "Rest now. Later, we'll work with the recording sphere again to see if it contains any instruction on frequency manipulation."

As Verity left, Apollo remained seated, letting his mind process everything he'd learned. The complexity of dimensional energy was daunting, but each session brought new understanding, new capabilities. He only hoped he was learning quickly enough to make a difference against Carver's growing threat.

Apollo found Alden in what they'd come to call the library—a small chamber off the main room that housed the texts and artifacts Verity had salvaged from Valeshire. Scrolls and bound volumes covered a large table, and Alden sat hunched over one particularly ancient-looking tome, making notes on a piece of parchment.

"Any breakthroughs?" Apollo asked, settling into a chair across from his friend.

Alden looked up, his eyes bright with excitement despite the dark circles beneath them. "Apollo! Yes, actually. These texts are extraordinary. They're not mystical or religious at all—they're scientific."

"Scientific?" Apollo leaned forward, curious. "Like Ancestral technology?"

"Exactly," Alden said, turning the book so Apollo could see the diagrams. "Look at this. It's a technical explanation of dimensional energy—what they called 'interstitial field dynamics.' The Ancestors didn't view Veilborn abilities as magical; they understood them as a natural interaction between human neurology and dimensional fields."

Apollo studied the diagrams, which showed complex patterns that reminded him of the dimensional currents he'd been learning to perceive. Alongside were mathematical notations he couldn't begin to comprehend.

"Can you understand all this?" he asked.

Alden shook his head. "Not entirely. The mathematics is beyond anything I've studied. But the basic principles are clear enough. According to these texts, dimensions aren't separate worlds—they're overlapping fields of reality that vibrate at different frequencies."

"That matches what Verity's been teaching me," Apollo said. "I've been learning to perceive specific frequencies today."

"It's all connected," Alden said excitedly. "The texts explain that Veilborn have specialized neural structures that can resonate with these dimensional fields. It's like... like having an extra sense that can detect and interact with these vibrations."

"Neural structures?" Apollo repeated. "You mean it's something in our brains?"

"Not just your brain—your entire nervous system," Alden clarified. "According to this, Veilborn have microscopic structures throughout their bodies that can attune to dimensional frequencies. The more developed these structures, the stronger the Veilborn's abilities."

Apollo thought about this, remembering how dimensional energy seemed to flow through his entire body when he manipulated it. "So it's physical, not spiritual."

"Exactly!" Alden said. "The Ancestors understood this as science, not magic. They even had technology that could enhance or suppress these abilities." He shuffled through some papers. "Look at this diagram—it shows a device designed to amplify dimensional perception by generating specific frequency patterns."

The diagram showed a complex device with crystalline components arranged in patterns similar to the dimensional currents Apollo had learned to perceive.

"Could we build something like this?" Apollo asked.

Alden's expression fell slightly. "I doubt it. The materials and precision required would be beyond our capabilities. But understanding the principles might help us identify and use existing artifacts more effectively."

He pulled another text forward. "There's something else—a reference to 'dimensional notation.' Apparently, Veilborn developed a specialized written language to describe dimensional phenomena. It combined visible symbols with embedded dimensional resonances that only Veilborn could perceive."

"Like a secret code?" Apollo asked.

"More like a multi-sensory language," Alden explained. "The visible component would be meaningful to anyone, but Veilborn could perceive additional layers of information encoded in dimensional frequencies."

Apollo considered the implications. "That could be useful for leaving messages that only other Veilborn could fully understand."

"Exactly," Alden agreed. "And according to this text, the notation evolved naturally with each practitioner, becoming unique to the individual while maintaining certain core principles."

"I wonder if Verity knows about this," Apollo mused.

"She's the one who pointed me to these specific texts," Alden said. "I think she's been guiding my research alongside your practical training."

Apollo nodded, impressed by Verity's foresight. "Have you found anything that might help against Carver?"

Alden's expression grew more serious. "Maybe. There are references to dimensional instabilities caused by improper manipulation—rifts that could grow and spread if not contained. If Carver is experimenting with dimensional energy without proper understanding..."

"He could cause serious damage," Apollo finished. "Like the Cataclysm."

"Possibly," Alden agreed. "These texts suggest the Cataclysm itself was the result of dimensional experimentation gone wrong—though the details are frustratingly vague."

Apollo rose to his feet, his thoughts churning with the potential consequences. "I need to tell Verity about this. If Carver's experiments could cause another Cataclysm..."

"I've already informed her," Alden said. "She asked me to continue researching, to see if I can find any information about how such rifts might be closed or contained."

Apollo nodded, grateful for his friend's diligence. "Thank you, Alden. This could be crucial."

"Just doing my part," Alden said with a small smile. "We each have our roles to play in this."

As Apollo turned to leave, Alden called after him. "Apollo? For what it's worth, I think you're making incredible progress. Faster than anyone could have expected."

Apollo appreciated the encouragement, but couldn't help wondering if it would be enough. Carver's forces were moving quickly, and time was running short.

The evening meal was a subdued affair. The news of Carver's expanded search had cast a pall over the group, and everyone ate with minimal conversation, lost in their own thoughts.

After they finished, Tristan excused himself to continue working with the recording sphere, and Verity retired to her quarters to study Alden's latest translations. Apollo found himself alone with Astra, who was staring into the hearth fire with a distant expression.

"Copper for your thoughts?" he asked, sitting beside her.

She glanced at him, a small smile touching her lips. "They'd be over-priced at that."

"I doubt that," Apollo said. "You always seem to know more than you let on."

Astra's smile faded. "Perhaps. Though sometimes knowledge is a burden rather than an advantage."

Apollo studied her face in the firelight. Despite the days they'd spent traveling together, Astra remained something of an enigma. She clearly had knowledge of Veilborn abilities and the Order, but she'd shared little about her personal history or how she came to be involved in their situation.

"You said you were once part of the Order," Apollo said. "But you left when you discovered the truth about Veilborn."

Astra was quiet for a long moment, the fire casting flickering shadows across her face. Finally, she nodded. "It's time you knew the full story. You've earned that much."

She turned to face him. "I was raised in the Order from childhood. My parents were both Keepers—scholars who studied ancient texts and artifacts. I was expected to follow the same path."

"So you were trained in Order doctrine," Apollo said.

"Extensively," Astra confirmed. "I believed what we all did—that the Veilborn were dangerous, that their manipulation of dimensional energy had caused the Cataclysm, and that the Order's duty was to prevent such a disaster from happening again."

She paused, her fingers absently touching the pendant at her throat. "I was assigned to the archives when I was sixteen, helping to catalog and preserve ancient texts. That's where I first began to notice... discrepancies."

"What kind of discrepancies?" Apollo asked.

"Contradictions between official Order teaching and the actual histor-ical records," Astra explained. "References to Veilborn as stabilizers rather than disruptors. Accounts of Veilborn working alongside the Ancestral scientists to control dimensional energy, not unleash it."

She leaned forward, her voice dropping. "The more I researched, the more I realized the Order's founding narrative was flawed—perhaps deliberately so. The Veilborn weren't responsible for the Cataclysm; they were trying to prevent it."

"Did you confront the Order leadership?" Apollo asked.

Astra gave a bitter laugh. "Not directly. I was cautious. I shared my findings with my mentor, an older Keeper named Darian who I trusted. He seemed troubled by my discoveries and promised to look into them."

Her expression darkened. "A week later, he was gone—reassigned to a distant outpost. And I was summoned before the High Observer, who questioned me about my 'unorthodox research interests.'"

"They were watching you," Apollo realized.

"Yes. But they didn't know how much I'd already uncovered." Astra's hand went to her pendant again. "This was my mother's. She died when I was young, and I always assumed it was simply a family heirloom. But during my research, I found references to dimensional stabilizers that matched its description. A personal dimensional stabilizer, designed to protect the wearer from minor dimensional fluctuations. When I realized what it was, I began to wonder about my own heritage—why my mother would have possessed such an item."

She took a deep breath. "I discovered that my maternal grandmother had been Veilborn—one who escaped the Purge by hiding her abilities and joining the Order itself."

Apollo's eyes widened. "Your grandmother infiltrated the Order?"

"She wasn't the only one," Astra said. "After the Purge, some Veilborn families realized the only way to survive was to hide in plain sight. They suppressed their abilities, married into Order families, and passed down their heritage in secret, along with artifacts like this pendant."

She touched the pendant again. "I don't have Veilborn abilities myself—just enough sensitivity to perceive dimensional energy faintly. But I inherited my grandmother's journal, which contained the truth about the Order's history and the Veilborn's purpose."

"What was that purpose?" Apollo asked.

"To maintain dimensional stability," Astra said. "The Ancestors had developed technology that drew power from dimensional energy, but they discovered that the technology created instabilities—weak points between dimensions. Veilborn were specially trained to sense these instabilities and repair them before they could spread."

Apollo thought about the dimensional currents he'd been learning to perceive and manipulate. "So Veilborn were like... maintenance workers for dimensional technology?"

"In a sense, yes," Astra agreed. "But they were highly respected, not mere laborers. They worked alongside the scientists and engineers, developing new techniques and technologies. The partnership between conventional science and dimensional manipulation was the foundation of Ancestral civilization."

"What went wrong?" Apollo asked.

Astra's expression grew somber. "According to my grandmother's journal, a faction of scientists believed they could access higher dimensions directly—what they called the Source—to obtain unlimited energy. The Veilborn warned against this, saying the dimensional barriers couldn't withstand such manipulation. But the scientists proceeded anyway."

"And it caused the Cataclysm," Apollo concluded.

"Yes. The experiment created a catastrophic dimensional rift that spread rapidly, destroying cities and warping reality itself before the remaining Veilborn managed to contain it." Astra's voice had grown tight with emotion. "In the aftermath, those same scientists blamed the Veilborn for the disaster, claiming their 'reckless manipulation' had caused the destruction."

"And people believed them," Apollo said, understanding dawning.

"They were frightened and needed someone to blame," Astra said. "The scientists formed what would become the Order of the Veil, ostensibly to prevent such disasters in the future, but really to eliminate the witnesses to their mistake."

"The Purge," Apollo said.

Astra nodded. "They hunted down the Veilborn systematically, executing some and imprisoning others for 'study.' A few escaped, going into hiding or fleeing to remote regions. Over generations, the truth was lost, and the Order's version of history became accepted fact."

Apollo sat back, trying to absorb the enormity of what Astra had shared. "How did you escape the Order after learning this?"

"Carefully," Astra said with a grim smile. "I gathered what evidence I could, copied key texts, and planned my departure for months. When the time came, I simply left on a research expedition and never returned."

"And they've been hunting you since?"

"They've tried," Astra acknowledged. "But I know their methods, and I've been careful. I've spent the last three years trying to piece together the truth and find a way to counter the Order's influence."

"Is that why you were near Willowbrook when we escaped?" Apollo asked.

"Partly," Astra admitted. "I'd heard rumors about unusual dimensional activity in the region. I was investigating when I sensed the resonance from the Illumination Ceremony. By the time I arrived, the Order was already there, so I watched and waited."

She met Apollo's gaze. "When I saw you flee with the resonance compass, I knew you were what I'd been searching for."

Apollo absorbed this, feeling both gratified by her trust and overwhelmed by the responsibility it implied. "So what happens now? If Carver is hunting Veilborn and experimenting with dimensional energy..."

"He's following the same dangerous path that led to the Cataclysm," Astra finished.

Apollo felt the weight of expectation settling on his shoulders. "Verity's teaching me as quick as she can, but I'm still just a beginner. If Carver has been studying this for years..."

"He has knowledge but not ability," Astra reminded him. "He's using artifacts and technology to access dimensional energy, but he can't perceive or manipulate it directly as you can. That gives you an advantage."

"If I can develop my skills fast enough," Apollo said.

Astra was quiet for a moment, then said, "There might be a way to accelerate your training. According to my grandmother's journal, there was a major Ancestral research facility in the mountains to the north—what they called the Nexus. If it survived the Cataclysm, it might contain records, training materials, perhaps even functional technology that could help you develop your abilities faster."

"The mountains to the north?" Apollo repeated, thinking of the resonance compass. "That's where the compass has been pointing."

"It makes sense," Astra said. "The Nexus would have been a major dimensional convergence point—exactly the kind of location the compass would detect."

Apollo considered this. "Have you mentioned this to Verity?"

"Not yet," Astra admitted. "I wanted to be sure of my facts first."

Apollo felt a growing conviction that this was their best course of action. "We should tell the others. If this Nexus contains knowledge that could help us stop Carver, we need to find it."

Astra studied him for a long moment, then nodded. "You're right. We'll tell them in the morning, after you've had time to think it through. This won't be an easy journey, and the sanctuary is relatively safe. We'd be trading security for potential advantage."

"With Carver's forces getting closer, I'm not sure how secure we are anyway," Apollo said. "And if he succeeds in whatever he's planning..."

"Then nowhere will be safe," Astra finished. "Very well. We'll propose the journey to the Nexus tomorrow."

As Apollo readied himself for sleep that evening, he recounted the information he'd discovered—the true history of the Veilborn, the Order's deception, and the possibility of an ancient facility that might hold the key to developing his abilities. The stakes had never been higher, but for the first time, he felt he had a clear purpose, a direction to channel his growing skills.

Whatever the Nexus held, he was determined to find it—before Carver's quest for power unleashed another Cataclysm.

9

PRECISION OVER POWER

Apollo shielded his eyes against the early morning sun as it crested the jagged northern peaks. After five days of hard travel through increasingly rugged terrain, they'd reached their destination. The Nexus rose before them, a sprawling complex of silver-white structures nestled in a high mountain valley.

"It's enormous," he breathed, trying to take in the scale of the place.

The journey had been grueling. After presenting their plan to Elder Verity the morning after his conversation with Astra, they'd faced initial resistance. Verity had argued for continuing Apollo's training in the safety of the sanctuary, but reports of Carver's forces drawing closer had ultimately swayed her. They'd departed the next day—Apollo, Astra, Tristan, Alden, and Verity herself, leaving the sanctuary defenders to relocate to a secondary location.

Now, standing on this windswept ridge, Apollo felt vindicated in their decision. The Nexus was unlike anything he'd ever seen.

"The Ancestrals certainly didn't believe in subtlety," Tristan said, coming to stand beside him.

The complex below consisted of seven main structures arranged in a precise geometric pattern around a central tower that stretched at least twenty stories high. Even from this distance, Apollo could see that the buildings were largely intact, their smooth surfaces gleaming despite the passage of a thousand years.

"How has this remained hidden for so long?" Apollo asked.

"Location," Verity said, joining them at the ridge. "These mountains were considered impassable after the Cataclysm. And look there." She pointed to the sheer cliffs surrounding the valley on three sides. "Natural defenses. The only approach is through that narrow pass we just traversed."

Apollo nodded, but his attention had shifted from the physical structures to something far more remarkable. The dimensional currents here were unlike anything he'd experienced before—stronger, more varied, and strangely organized. Rather than the chaotic flows he'd observed elsewhere, these currents moved in precise patterns, like an intricate dance.

"The dimensional energy..." he began, struggling to find words for what he was perceiving.

"You can see it?" Astra asked, her voice sharp with interest.

Apollo nodded. "It's different here. Structured. Like it's being... channeled somehow."

Verity's eyes widened. "The Ancestrals must have created a permanent dimensional infrastructure. Remarkable."

"Is that what I'm seeing?" Apollo asked, gesturing to the air around them where brilliant threads of blue-violet light wove complex patterns. "These energy flows follow specific paths, almost like—"

"Roads," Alden finished, though he couldn't see what Apollo described. "The Ancestrals creating highways for dimensional energy."

"Can you trace where they lead?" Verity asked.

Apollo focused, allowing his perception to follow the brightest current. It flowed to the central tower, where it spiraled upward in a helix pattern before disappearing into what appeared to be a sphere of concentrated energy at the top.

"They all converge on that central tower," he said. "Something there is drawing the energy, collecting it."

"A power source, perhaps," Alden suggested. "Or a control mechanism."

Apollo felt a subtle pressure building behind his eyes as he continued to observe the dimensional flows. There was something about their pattern that seemed almost familiar, as if he'd seen it before in a dream.

"We should approach carefully," Verity cautioned. "If this facility is still active after all this time, there may be automated defenses."

Apollo reluctantly pulled his attention away from the fascinating energy patterns. "I can try to follow the main current. It might lead us to an entrance that's still functional."

Verity nodded. "Lead the way."

As they descended into the valley, Apollo kept his focus on the dimensional currents. The strongest flow led toward what appeared to be the main entrance of the complex—a broad plaza before the largest of the satellite structures.

The closer they got, the more Apollo could feel the energy pressing against his consciousness. It wasn't painful, exactly, but the intensity was difficult to process. He felt as though he were standing in a swift-flowing river, the current tugging at him from all directions.

"Are you alright?" Astra asked, noticing his expression.

"There's so much energy here," Apollo said. "It's like nothing I've experienced before. More concentrated, more... purposeful."

"Can you handle it?" Verity asked, concern evident in her voice.

Apollo took a deep breath, applying the filtering techniques Verity had taught him. The pressure eased somewhat. "Yes. It's just... overwhelming at first."

As they approached the plaza, Apollo noticed something strange. The dimensional currents seemed to be responding to his presence, shifting subtly as if adjusting to accommodate him.

"The energy is reacting to me," he said, stopping abruptly.

"What do you mean?" Verity asked.

"It's changing its flow pattern. Almost like it's... recognizing me."

Alden's eyes lit up. "The facility might have systems designed to detect and respond to Veilborn! Your genetic structure could be triggering automated protocols."

"Is that good or bad?" Tristan asked, hand moving instinctively to the sword at his hip.

Before anyone could answer, a section of the plaza floor before them illuminated with soft blue light. Geometric patterns spread outward from a central point, forming concentric circles that pulsed gently.

"I think we're about to find out," Apollo said.

The group halted at the edge of the illuminated area. Apollo could see dimensional energy flowing through the patterns on the ground, creating a complex three-dimensional structure that extended both above and below the visible markings.

"It's some kind of verification system," he said, studying the energy pattern. "I think... I think it's waiting for something."

"For what?" Tristan asked.

Apollo stepped forward, drawn by an instinct he couldn't explain. As his foot touched the first illuminated circle, the blue light intensified, and the dimensional energy shifted again, coalescing into a more defined pattern.

"Apollo!" Verity called out in warning, but he was already moving forward, following the pull of the energy.

As he reached the center of the pattern, the blue light flared brilliantly. Apollo felt a strange sensation, as if something were scanning him from head to toe. The dimensional energy swirled around him, touching his skin with a gentle tingling sensation.

Then, as suddenly as it had appeared, the light receded. For a moment, nothing happened. Then, with a deep rumbling sound, a section of the plaza floor began to sink, forming a ramp that led down into darkness.

"It worked," Apollo said, stepping back to rejoin the others. "The facility recognized me as Veilborn."

"Or at least as something it shouldn't immediately destroy," Tristan muttered.

"This is extraordinary," Alden said, moving toward the newly revealed entrance. "A facility that's remained operational for a millennium!"

"Careful," Verity cautioned. "We don't know what awaits us inside."

Apollo led the way down the ramp, following the thread of dimensional energy that flowed into the darkness. As they descended, lights activated automatically, illuminating a wide corridor with smooth white walls.

"The power systems still work," Astra observed, running her hand along one of the walls. "How is that possible after all this time?"

"The Ancestrals had energy sources that didn't deplete," Alden said. "Some of the texts mention crystals that converted dimensional energy into usable power."

Apollo was only half-listening. His attention was focused on the dimensional currents that flowed through the walls and floor of the corridor. They formed an intricate network, like veins carrying energy throughout the complex.

"This place is alive with dimensional energy," he said. "It's everywhere, flowing through everything."

The corridor led them deeper into the facility, branching occasionally. Apollo followed the strongest current, which led them to a massive circular chamber. As they entered, lights activated, revealing a space that took Apollo's breath away.

The chamber was at least fifty feet in diameter, with a domed ceiling that shimmered with projected stars. The floor was inlaid with the same geometric patterns they'd seen outside, but here they glowed with a soft, constant light. Around the perimeter stood what appeared to be workstations—curved consoles with dark, reflective surfaces.

"What is this place?" Tristan asked, his voice hushed.

"Some kind of control center, I think," Alden replied, moving toward one of the consoles. "These must be interfaces."

Apollo approached the center of the room, where a raised platform held what appeared to be a pedestal. Dimensional energy flowed up through the floor and concentrated here, forming a swirling column that only he could see.

"There's something important here," he said, stepping onto the platform.

As his foot touched the raised surface, the pedestal illuminated. A sphere of blue-white light appeared above it, hovering in midair.

"Apollo," Verity warned, "be careful."

But Apollo felt no danger from the sphere—only a sense of rightness, as if he'd found something he'd been searching for without knowing it. He reached out, his hand passing into the light.

The sphere expanded instantly, filling the room with projected images—three-dimensional diagrams, flowing text in an unfamiliar script, and complex patterns that Apollo recognized as dimensional notation similar to what he'd seen in Verity's echo crystals.

"It's responding to you," Astra said, staring in wonder at the projections.

Alden had begun attempting to decipher the information. "These look like technical schematics. And there—that appears to be a map of the facility."

Apollo concentrated on the sphere, instinctively trying to direct its output. The projections shifted, focusing on what appeared to be the central tower they'd seen from outside.

"I can control it somehow," he said. "It's responding to my thoughts."

"The interface must be designed for Veilborn," Verity said. "Using dimensional perception as the control mechanism."

Apollo focused on the image of the tower, curious about its purpose. The projection zoomed in, showing the interior structure—a massive central shaft running the full height of the tower, with various chambers branching off at different levels.

"What was this place used for?" he wondered aloud.

In response, the projection changed again, showing a sequence of images. Apollo saw figures in form-fitting garments working at consoles similar to those around the room. The images shifted to show the same figures manipulating what appeared to be dimensional energy, much as Apollo was learning to do.

"It was a research facility," Alden said, watching the sequence. "They were studying dimensional energy."

"Not just studying it," Apollo said, understanding dawning as he interpreted the patterns in the projections. "They were learning to control it. This was a training facility for Veilborn."

The projection shifted again, showing the central tower with energy flowing up through it and into the sphere at its top. Then it displayed what appeared to be a network of similar towers spread across a map that Apollo recognized as their continent.

"It was part of a network," he said. "Connected to other facilities like it."

Apollo continued to study the projections, trying to absorb the flood of information. There was so much here—technical data, historical records, training protocols—all accessible through this interface designed specifically for Veilborn.

"This is exactly what we need," he said. "With this knowledge, I can learn to control my abilities properly."

"And perhaps better understand what Carver is attempting," Verity added. "If he's found similar information elsewhere..."

Apollo dipped his head in agreement, the consequences evident. If Carver had discovered even fragments of this knowledge, he could be attempting to reactivate parts of the Ancestral network—with potentially catastrophic consequences if done incorrectly.

As Apollo continued to explore the interface, the other members of the group spread out to investigate the chamber. Tristan examined what appeared to be weapons mounted on stands near the entrance—sleek devices that bore little resemblance to conventional arms. Alden was attempting to activate one of the perimeter consoles, while Astra studied the geometric patterns on the floor.

"Apollo," Verity called from across the chamber. "Come look at this."

He reluctantly withdrew his hand from the sphere, which contracted back to its original size. Crossing to where Verity stood before a section of wall, he saw what had captured her attention: a recessed panel containing what appeared to be a storage unit with dozens of small compartments.

"What is it?" he asked.

"I believe these are personal storage units," Verity said. "For the researchers who worked here."

She pointed to symbols etched beside each compartment—complex glyphs that Apollo somehow recognized as names, though he couldn't have explained how he knew this.

"Can we open them?" he asked.

Verity gestured to a panel beside the storage unit. "I believe this is some kind of access control, but I can't determine how it functions."

Apollo studied the panel, noting the dimensional energy flowing through it. Acting on instinct, he placed his palm against its surface. The energy pattern shifted, and one of the compartments slid open with a soft hiss.

Inside lay a small disc, similar in size to the resonance compass but more complex in design. Its surface was etched with intricate patterns that glowed faintly blue when Apollo reached for it.

"What is it?" Astra asked, joining them.

Apollo lifted the disc carefully. As his fingers closed around it, the patterns on its surface brightened, and he felt a subtle resonance with the dimensional energy flowing through his own body.

"It's some kind of personal device," he said. "I think it belonged to one of the researchers who worked here."

As he held it, information seemed to flow into his mind—not in words, but in concepts and images that formed a partial understanding of the device's purpose.

"It's a dimensional tuner," he said, the knowledge unfolding in his consciousness. "It helps the user focus on specific dimensional frequencies."

"Like the exercises Verity was teaching you," Astra observed.

"Yes, but much more precise." Apollo turned the device, studying its patterns. "With this, I could isolate individual frequencies, maybe even access dimensions we haven't been able to reach before."

Alden had joined them, his eyes wide with excitement. "The applications would be enormous. If you could selectively access dimensional properti es..."

"I could potentially do what Verity described—see through time, perceive distant locations, maybe even affect physical matter directly."

The ramifications left him breathless. With proper training and tools like this, Apollo's abilities could develop far beyond what they'd imagined possible.

"We need to explore the rest of the facility," he said, tucking the dimensional tuner into his pocket. "There must be more devices like this, more information we can use."

"Agreed," Verity said. "But we should proceed with caution. A place of this power would have had security measures."

Apollo nodded, returning to the central pedestal. He placed his hand in the sphere again, focusing on the facility map. The projection expanded, showing their current location and highlighting potential paths through the complex.

"There," he said, pointing to a section of the map. "That appears to be a main repository of some kind. And here—" he indicated another area "—looks like living quarters. We should check both."

As the team readied themselves to press forward with their investigation, Apollo experienced a blend of eagerness and unease. The Nexus contained knowledge and technology beyond anything he'd imagined—tools that could help him develop his Veilborn abilities to their full potential.

But such power came with risks. The same knowledge they sought had once led to catastrophe. And if Carver gained access to similar information without understanding its proper use...

Apollo pushed the thought aside, focusing on the task at hand. They needed to learn everything they could about this place. The dimensional tuner in his pocket felt like a promise—a key to unlocking abilities he'd only begun to discover.

Apollo ran his hand over the dimensional tuner's exterior, sensing the delicate tremors that pulsed against his fingertips. The device responded to his touch, its patterns shifting like liquid light beneath his skin.

Apollo pocketed the dimensional tuner. As they moved through a corridor, he noticed how the ambient energy currents seemed to flow more strongly in one direction—like a river with tributaries joining the main channel.

"The energy is concentrated this way," he said, pointing down a side passage that wasn't marked on the projected map they'd seen earlier.

Tristan frowned. "Are you sure? The map didn't show anything down there."

"I'm following the energy," Apollo replied. "It's... pulling me."

The passage narrowed as they proceeded, the walls lined with what appeared to be dormant technology. Apollo ran his hand along one panel, feeling the latent energy within. Unlike the control room, these systems hadn't activated at their approach.

"This section seems to be powered down," Alden observed, examining the dark panels.

"Or waiting for something specific," Astra suggested.

At the end of the corridor, they encountered a blank wall—a dead end with no visible entrance or markings. Apollo would have turned back if not for the unmistakable sensation of dimensional energy flowing through and beyond the wall.

"There's something here," he said, approaching the wall. "I can feel it."

As he stepped closer, the dimensional tuner in his pocket began to vibrate. He removed it, noticing how its patterns now pulsed in rhythm with the energy he perceived flowing through the wall.

Acting on instinct, Apollo held the tuner against the wall's surface. For a moment, nothing happened. Then, responding to some unspoken command, the tuner's patterns aligned with invisible markings in the wall itself. A harmonic resonance built between them, vibrating through Apollo's hand and up his arm.

The wall shimmered, its solid appearance dissolving to reveal a hidden doorway. Beyond lay darkness.

"How did you do that?" Tristan asked, eyes wide.

Apollo shook his head. "I didn't. The tuner did. It's like... a key."

"A key that responds to Veilborn energy," Verity said. "This area must have been restricted, accessible only to those with the proper genetic markers."

Apollo stepped through the doorway, and lights activated in response to his presence, illuminating a vast chamber beyond. Unlike the utilitarian design of the control room, this space had an almost reverent quality—high ceilings with geometric patterns that channeled dimensional energy in complex flows.

The chamber was circular, with workstations arranged around a central platform. Each station featured interfaces similar to the sphere in the control room, but more elaborate. The walls were lined with what appeared to be data storage units, thousands of them, glowing with faint blue light.

"What is this place?" Apollo breathed, taking in the scale of the room.

Alden was examining one of the workstations. "Based on the layout, I'd say this was a research laboratory of some kind. Look at these interfaces—they're designed for complex data analysis."

Verity moved to the central platform. "This appears to be the focal point."

Apollo approached the platform. Unlike the control room's pedestal, this one featured multiple interaction points—a series of recessed panels with geometric patterns that pulsed with dimensional energy.

He placed his hands on two of the panels, and the entire chamber came alive. The geometric patterns on the ceiling began to glow, channeling energy downward in visible streams that converged on the central platform. The workstations activated simultaneously, their interfaces projecting complex three-dimensional displays.

"It's responding to you," Astra said, watching as the energy patterns shifted and stabilized around Apollo.

Apollo felt a strange connection forming—not just with the technology, but with the dimensional currents themselves. It was as if the chamber was designed to amplify a Veilborn's natural abilities, creating a controlled environment for precise manipulation of dimensional energies.

"This was a Veilborn research facility," he said, the understanding coming to him intuitively. "Not just for training, but for studying the nature of dimensional energy itself."

As he spoke, one of the workstation interfaces expanded its projection, displaying what appeared to be a catalog of research files. The symbols were unfamiliar, yet somehow Apollo understood their meaning—another aspect of his Veilborn perception he couldn't explain.

"Can you read that?" Tristan asked, noticing Apollo's focus on the display.

"Not exactly read, but... I understand it somehow." Apollo approached the workstation, the others following. "These are research archives. Studies on dimensional physics, energy manipulation techniques, and..."

He paused as one category caught his attention. The symbol translated in his mind as something like "genetic lineage" or "hereditary patterns."

Apollo selected this category, and the display shifted to show a new set of files. He chose one at random, and a three-dimensional projection appeared above the workstation—a detailed representation of what appeared to be a human DNA strand, but with sections highlighted and annotated.

"This is genetic research," Alden said, examining the projection. "They were studying human DNA."

"Not just studying it," Apollo replied, the information becoming clearer as he interacted with the display. "They were modifying it."

He navigated through the file, revealing more detailed analyses of specific genetic sequences. The annotations described alterations to neural structures, cellular composition, and energy sensitivity.

"These are Veilborn genetic markers," Apollo said, the realization dawning on him. "They were engineering humans who could perceive and manipulate dimensional energy."

"Engineering?" Tristan repeated, looking disturbed. "You mean Veilborn weren't natural?"

"According to this, no." Apollo continued exploring the files, each new piece of information shifting his understanding of his own identity. "The Ancestral civilization created the first Veilborn through genetic modification. They needed humans who could interface directly with their dimension-based technology."

Verity moved closer, her expression thoughtful. "This aligns with fragments in our oldest texts—references to the 'making of the bridge-minds.' We interpreted it metaphorically, but it was literal."

Apollo selected another file, which displayed a timeline of the genetic program. "It started small—just a few modified individuals to work with specific technologies. But they discovered the modifications were hereditary. The children of these first Veilborn inherited the abilities, sometimes with even greater strength."

"So they began breeding programs," Astra said. "Creating bloodlines with specific abilities."

"Yes," Apollo confirmed, digging deeper into the archives. "But it wasn't as simple as they expected. The genetic expressions varied widely, and they couldn't predict exactly how the abilities would manifest in each generation."

He paused as a new projection appeared—a map showing the distribution of Veilborn across the continent during the late Ancestral Era. Thousands of points of light, each representing individuals or family groups with varying degrees of dimensional sensitivity.

"There were so many," Alden whispered. "Before the Purge..."

Apollo felt a strange pressure building behind his eyes as he continued interacting with the interface. The dimensional energy in the room seemed to be intensifying, flowing through and around him in increasingly complex patterns.

"Apollo?" Astra's voice sounded distant. "Are you alright?"

He nodded, though he wasn't entirely sure. Something was happening—a resonance building between his own dimensional perception and the technology surrounding him.

Drawn by an instinct he couldn't name, Apollo moved back to the central platform. There was another interface there, different from the workstations—more direct, somehow. A single recessed panel with a spiraling pattern that matched the birthmark on his wrist.

"I need to try something," he said, rolling up his sleeve to reveal the spiral birthmark.

"Apollo, wait—" Verity began, but he had already placed his marked wrist against the panel.

The connection was immediate and overwhelming. Dimensional energy surged through the contact point, flowing into Apollo's body like a current of liquid light. His perception expanded beyond the physical space, beyond the present moment.

Images flooded his mind—not memories of his own, but recordings stored within the dimensional currents themselves:

A laboratory much like this one, filled with researchers in white garments, monitoring subjects undergoing genetic treatments.

A woman holding a newborn child, tears of joy streaming down her face as she perceives the infant's natural dimensional resonance—the first child born with the abilities they had engineered.

A network of facilities across the continent, connected by dimensional currents, monitoring and stabilizing the increasingly complex energy flows as their civilization advanced.

The first warnings—fluctuations in the dimensional boundaries, instabilities that threatened to cascade beyond control.

Veilborn working frantically to stabilize the dimensional currents as experimental technology in another facility tore open the barriers between dimensions.

The catastrophic failure—dimensional energy erupting across the continent as the stabilization network collapsed, tearing reality apart in what would later be called the Cataclysm.

The survivors, mostly Veilborn who had sensed the disaster coming, emerging to find their civilization in ruins.

Generations passing, the true history fading into myth as the survivors struggled to rebuild, the Veilborn using their abilities to heal the dimensional wounds left by the Cataclysm.

The rise of fear, the beginning of the Purge, as those without dimensional perception blamed the Veilborn for the disaster they had tried to prevent.

A small group of the most powerful Veilborn families creating a dimensional pocket—a hidden fold in reality where they could preserve their bloodlines undetected.

The deterioration of this sanctuary over generations, forcing the last descendants to emerge and integrate with the outside world.

A man and woman—his parents—hiding their infant child with a man during a dimensional storm, knowing they would be hunted but hoping their son would survive.

The vision ended abruptly as Apollo was thrown backward from the platform, the connection broken. He struggled for air, his thoughts spinning from the deluge of knowledge and feeling.

"Apollo!" Astra was at his side, helping him sit up. "What happened?"

He blinked, trying to process what he had experienced. "I saw... everything. The creation of the Veilborn, the Cataclysm, the Purge... my parents."

"Your parents?" Tristan asked, kneeling beside him.

Apollo nodded, his hands shaking. "They were descendants of Veilborn who hid in a dimensional pocket after the Purge. When it began to fail, they emerged. They knew they would be hunted, so they hid me with Kieran during a dimensional storm."

Verity's expression was grave. "You experienced a dimensional memory transfer—extremely dangerous, but incredibly informative. The platform must be designed to store historical records in the dimensional currents themselves, accessible only to those with Veilborn perception."

Apollo stood, his legs unsteady. "We were engineered," he said, still processing this fundamental shift in his understanding of himself. "Created to interface with Ancestral technology, to perceive and manipulate dimensional energy as tools for their civilization."

"But you became more than tools," Astra said. "The Veilborn tried to prevent the Cataclysm. They became the protectors of dimensional stability."

Apollo moved back to the workstation, searching through more files with new purpose. "There's more here—detailed information about Veilborn genetic structures, how they interact with dimensional energy, why some bloodlines developed stronger abilities than others."

He found what he was looking for—a comprehensive analysis of Veilborn genetics across generations. "According to this, my unusual strength of ability might be explained by my ancestry. The Veilborn who created the dimensional pocket were among the most powerful bloodlines, and they selectively bred to preserve those traits over generations."

"So you're essentially a pure-blooded Veilborn," Alden said, examining the genetic diagrams. "With minimal dilution of the engineered traits over time."

"Which explains why I can do things that even Elder Verity hasn't seen before," Apollo said, the pieces falling into place. "My neural structure is almost identical to the original engineered Veilborn from before the Cataclysm."

He continued exploring the files, revealing more about the specific modifications that created Veilborn abilities:

"The key modifications included a specialized visual cortex that can process higher-dimensional input, enhanced connections between conscious and subconscious mind, and cellular structures that resonate with dimensional energies." Apollo gestured to a particularly detailed diagram. "They also created what they called 'neurological tuning capabilities' that allow selective dimensional focus—exactly what I've been learning to do with Verity's training."

"This knowledge changes everything," Verity said, her voice quiet but intense. "Not just our understanding of Veilborn history, but how we approach your training, Apollo. These files contain techniques and concepts we had lost entirely."

Apollo nodded, seeing applications for his own developing abilities. "And it explains why Carver's experiments are so dangerous. He's trying to access dimensional energy without understanding the stabilizing role Veilborn were designed to play."

"If he continues manipulating dimensional boundaries without proper stabilization..." Alden began.

"He could trigger another Cataclysm," Apollo finished. "That's what the vision showed me. The original Cataclysm wasn't caused by Veilborn—it was caused by scientists accessing higher dimensions directly, without the stabilizing influence Veilborn were created to provide."

The gravity of this revelation settled over the group. They weren't just fighting against Carver's ambition for power—they were trying to prevent history from repeating itself in the most catastrophic way possible.

"We need to gather as much of this information as we can," Apollo said, turning back to the interface. "There must be a way to—"

He stopped mid-sentence as a distant sound echoed through the facility—the unmistakable crash of an explosion.

The explosion rang through the facility, reverberating off the ancient walls. Apollo's head snapped toward the sound, his newfound dimensional awareness registering disturbances in the energy patterns flowing through the complex.

"That came from the entrance," he said, moving toward the door. The dimensional currents around him had shifted, becoming turbulent where moments before they had flowed in orderly patterns.

Verity was in motion. "Carver's forces. They must have tracked us here."

"How?" Tristan demanded, gathering his pack. "We were careful."

"The activation of this facility would have sent out a dimensional pulse," Verity explained, her voice tight with urgency. "Any detection equipment they have would have registered it immediately."

Apollo looked around scanning for a solution. The revelations he'd just discovered—regarding his lineage, regarding the genuine function of the Veilborn—seemed too crucial to abandon now. He pivoted toward the terminal, his fingertips flying across the control surface. "We have to safeguard this data."

"Apollo, there's no time," Astra urged, but he shook his head.

"Ten seconds." His fingers moved with surprising confidence over the ancestral technology, as if some part of him had always known how to operate it. He found what he was looking for—a small crystalline data storage device embedded in the console. With a twist and pull, it came free in his hand, glowing faintly with stored information.

"Got it," he said, pocketing the crystal as another explosion, closer this time, shook dust from the ceiling.

Verity led them from the research chamber, her steps quick but measured. "We need to reach the central tower. There's a secondary exit on the far side of the complex."

They moved through corridors that seemed to respond to Apollo's presence, lights flickering to life as they passed. His dimensional perception was heightening with the danger, allowing him to see not just the physical space around them but the energy flows that permeated it. Ahead, he detected disruptions—violent tears in the dimensional fabric where it should have been smooth.

"Wait," he said, holding up a hand as they approached an intersection. "There's something wrong with the dimensional currents ahead."

Verity nodded. "They're using disruptors—crude devices that tear at dimensional boundaries. Dangerous technology, especially here."

"How do we get past?" Alden asked.

Apollo concentrated, focusing his perception on the specific frequency of the disruption. It created a jagged, pulsing pattern in the dimensional field—uncomfortable to look at, like a visual discord. But between the pulses, there were moments of relative stability.

"I can guide us through," he said. "The disruption has a pattern. We'll need to move quickly between pulses."

He took the lead, feeling a strange confidence despite the danger. The knowledge from the memory transfer was still integrating into his mind, but with it came an intuitive understanding of dimensional energies he hadn't possessed before.

They reached the intersection, and Apollo held up his hand, monitoring the pulses. "Now," he said, and they dashed across the open space, reaching the opposite corridor just as another wave of disruption rippled through the area behind them.

The sound of boots on metal flooring echoed from somewhere nearby. Voices called out—sharp, military commands that bounced off the ancient walls.

"This way," Verity urged, leading them down a narrow passage. "The central tower connects to all the buildings through underground passages."

They descended in a hurry, the ancestral lighting responding to their presence, illuminating just enough of the path ahead to navigate. Apollo kept his dimensional senses alert, tracking the energy flows around them. Something about this facility made his abilities feel more natural, more integrated—as if the very architecture had been designed to amplify Veilborn perception.

The passage opened into a wider underground chamber filled with what looked like transportation equipment—sleek, cylindrical vehicles designed to travel through tunnels that branched out in multiple directions.

"Transit system," Verity explained. "The Ancestrals connected their major facilities with these networks."

Tristan approached one of the vehicles, running his hand over its surface. To Apollo's surprise, lights flickered to life under Tristan's touch.

"Resonant," Tristan said with a half-smile. "Useful after all."

A crash from the passage behind them ended any further exploration. Apollo turned to see shadows moving at the far end of the tunnel they'd just exited.

"They're coming," he warned.

Verity moved to one of the consoles near the transit vehicles. "Tristan, help me with this. Your resonant abilities might activate the system."

As Tristan and Verity busied themselves with the console, Apollo and Astra stationed themselves by the chamber's entryway, alert for followers. Apollo sensed Astra's unease radiating from her, fingers gripping the handle of her blade.

"If it comes to fighting," she said, "remember what we practiced. Focus on specific frequencies. Precision over power."

Apollo inclined his head, attempting to steady his thundering pulse. The dimensional currents around him responded to his emotional state, becoming more agitated as his anxiety increased. He took a deep breath, applying Verity's training to stabilize his perception.

The first of Carver's guards appeared at the end of the passage—a woman in sleek armor with technological enhancements visible at the joints and helmet. Captain Drake. Apollo recognized her from their near-encounter in the forest. Behind her came five more guards, each carrying weapons that hummed with an unnatural energy.

"Dimensional disruptors," Astra murmured. "Don't let those beams hit you—they'll scramble your perception for hours."

Drake spotted them. "Veilborn!" she called out. "By order of Magistrate Carver, surrender yourself and your companions."

Apollo moved ahead, placing his body as a shield between Carver's forces and his companions. He sensed the dimensional flows collecting around him, reacting to his will. "We don't want to fight you."

Drake's laugh was cold. "That's fortunate, because it wouldn't be much of a fight." She raised her hand, signaling her guards to advance.

Behind him, Apollo heard Tristan's triumphant exclamation as one of the transit vehicles hummed to life. "Got it! Everyone in, now!"

Apollo backed toward the vehicle, maintaining his focus on the approaching guards. Drake raised her weapon—a rifle-like device with a pulsing core of energy visible within its chamber.

"Last chance," she called.

Apollo didn't answer. Instead, he reached out with his perception, focusing on the specific frequency of the weapon's energy core. It was unstable, the dimensional energy contained within it vibrating at a discordant frequency. With careful precision, he pushed at that frequency, amplifying its instability.

Drake pulled the trigger, but instead of firing, the weapon's core flared with feedback. She dropped it with a curse as it overheated in her hands.

"Move!" Apollo shouted to his companions as the other guards raised their weapons.

They scrambled toward the transit vehicle, but not before the guards opened fire. Beams of distorted energy sliced through the air. Apollo ducked, feeling one pass close enough to disrupt his dimensional perception momentarily, leaving him dizzy.

Verity, who had been helping Alden into the vehicle, stepped forward. Her hands moved in patterns Apollo recognized from his training—but with a fluidity and precision he hadn't mastered yet. The dimensional currents around her shifted, condensing into a visible barrier between them and the guards.

"Get in the vehicle," she commanded, her voice strained with effort. "I'll hold them back."

"Not without you," Apollo protested, but Verity's expression was resolute.

"This barrier won't last long. The vehicle is programmed for the central tower. I'll meet you there." Her eyes met Apollo's. "Remember your training. Trust your abilities."

Before Apollo could argue further, a new wave of guards appeared behind the first group. One carried a larger disruption device that pulsed with ominous energy.

"That will tear through my barrier in seconds," Verity said. "Go. Now."

Astra grabbed Apollo's arm, pulling him toward the vehicle. "She knows what she's doing."

With reluctance burning in his chest, Apollo climbed into the transit vehicle. Tristan sat at the controls, his hands moving over the ancient interface with surprising confidence.

The transit vehicle hummed louder, beginning to move along its track. Through the transparent canopy, Apollo watched as Verity maintained her dimensional barrier, the energy around her hands glowing with intense effort. The guards with the large disruptor had set it up and were activating it, its core pulsing with increasing frequency.

"Verity!" Apollo called out, but his voice couldn't penetrate the sealed vehicle.

The last thing he saw before the vehicle entered the tunnel was Verity turning to face the large disruptor. She made a complex gesture with both hands, and the dimensional currents around her surged. The disruptor's beam fired—and Verity redirected it, causing an explosion that collapsed the tunnel entrance behind them as they sped away.

Apollo stared at the receding scene behind their vehicle. "She sacrificed herself to cover our escape."

"We don't know that," Astra said.

"She said she'd meet us at the central tower," Alden added. "We have to believe that."

Apollo nodded, but the knot in his stomach didn't ease. The transit vehicle accelerated through the underground tunnel, the lights along the walls blurring as they passed. Despite the speed, the ride was smooth, the ancestral technology functioning perfectly even after centuries of disuse.

"How long until we reach the central tower?" he asked.

Tristan studied the control panel. "Hard to say. There's a map here, but I'm still figuring out how to read it. Maybe five minutes?"

Apollo took the moment of relative safety to check on everyone. Alden had a minor burn on his arm where one of the disruption beams had grazed him, but otherwise they were unharmed. The crystal data storage device was still secure in Apollo's pocket, its weight a reminder of what they'd discovered and what was at stake.

"We need a plan for when we arrive," he said, forcing himself to focus on the immediate future rather than worrying about Verity. "Carver's forces will be converging on the central tower if it's as important as Verity suggested."

"The tower should have defensive systems," Astra said. "If we can activate them, we might be able to secure the area long enough to figure out our next move."

Apollo nodded, his mind working through the possibilities. The memory transfer had given him insights into ancestral technology and Veilborn abilities that he was still processing, but he knew instinctively that the central tower would respond to his presence just as the research facility had.

"I might be able to interface with the tower's systems directly," he said. "If it was designed as a Veilborn training center, it should recognize me."

The transit vehicle began to decelerate, the tunnel widening as they approached a station similar to the one they'd left. Through the canopy, Apollo could see they had arrived at the base of an enormous structure—the central tower, its interior illuminated with the same soft blue light that seemed to characterize ancestral technology.

As the vehicle came to a complete stop and the door slid open, Apollo took a deep breath, steadying himself. Without Verity's guidance, the others would be looking to him for direction. The knowledge from the memory transfer swirled in his mind—ancestral technology, Veilborn techniques, the true history of his people. He would need to draw on all of it now.

"Stay close," he said as they exited the vehicle. "And be ready for anything."

The station was empty, but Apollo could sense dimensional disturbances throughout the tower—evidence that Carver's forces had begun their assault on the facility. He led the way to a central lift platform, his dimensional perception guiding him more than any visible indicators.

"This should take us to the control center," he said, stepping onto the platform. As the others joined him, the platform responded to their presence, beginning a smooth ascent through the tower's central shaft.

As they rose, Apollo could see the tower's interior structure—a marvel of ancestral engineering, with multiple levels connected by transparent walkways and flowing with dimensional energy that formed patterns he was only beginning to understand. At various points, he could see evidence of Carver's intrusion—scorch marks from weapons fire, disrupted energy patterns, doors forced open.

"They're searching methodically," Astra observed. "Floor by floor."

"Looking for the same thing we are," Alden added. "Information about Veilborn abilities and ancestral technology."

The platform continued its ascent toward what appeared to be a massive chamber at the tower's apex. Apollo's dimensional perception intensified as they approached, sensing powerful energy convergences ahead.

"That must be the control center," he said. "The dimensional currents are strongest there."

As they neared the top level, Apollo held up his hand, signaling for silence. His perception had detected movement above—the distinctive disruption patterns of Carver's forces.

"There are guards in the control center," he whispered. "At least four, maybe more."

"Can you tell what they're doing?" Tristan asked.

Apollo concentrated, focusing his perception on the specific frequencies emanating from the chamber above. "They're... trying to activate something. I can feel them manipulating the controls, but the system is resisting them."

"It's probably keyed to Veilborn genetic signatures," Alden suggested. "Just like the research facility."

Apollo nodded. "We need to get in there before they damage anything trying to force access."

"And how exactly do we get past armed guards?" Tristan asked.

Apollo reached into his pocket, fingers closing around the dimensional tuner he'd taken from the research facility. "With precision," he said, remembering Astra's advice.

The platform slowed as it approached the top level. Apollo could now see the control center through transparent walls—a circular chamber dominated by a central holographic display currently inactive. Four of Carver's guards were positioned around the room, while two technicians worked at the main console, frustration evident in their movements.

"When we reach the top, stay on the platform," Apollo instructed. "I'm going to create a diversion, then we move in together."

The others nodded, readying themselves. Tristan gripped a staff he found, while Astra drew her knife. Alden stayed in the center, protected by his companions but ready to provide his knowledge if needed.

As the platform locked into place at the chamber's entrance, Apollo raised the dimensional tuner, focusing his perception through it.

He identified the frequency of the lighting systems first—the easiest target. With a careful adjustment of the tuner and a push of his will, he sent a surge through the system. The lights in the control center flared blindingly bright, then plunged into darkness.

In the confusion, Apollo stepped off the platform, using his dimensional perception to traverse the darkened space. He sensed the guards fumbling for their weapons, disoriented by the sudden darkness.

"Now," he called to his companions.

They moved as one, Tristan and Astra taking the lead while Apollo maintained his focus on the dimensional currents. He could perceive the guards clearly—four distinct energy signatures moving in confusion.

Tristan reached the first guard, his staff connecting with a solid impact that echoed through the chamber. Astra moved like a shadow, her knife finding gaps in the second guard's armor with precision.

Apollo shifted his focus to the two technicians, who were backing away from the console toward a secondary exit. He reached out with his perception, finding the dimensional frequency of the door mechanism and twisting it. The door sealed shut with a decisive click.

The guards were recovering, their training overcoming the initial surprise. One raised his disruption weapon, aiming in Apollo's direction despite the darkness. Apollo sensed the weapon's energy building and reacted instinctively, using the tuner to focus on the specific frequency of the weapon's power source. With a sharp mental push, he destabilized it, causing the weapon to sputter and die in the guard's hands.

The lights flickered back on as the ancestral systems reset themselves. Apollo found himself face to face with the disarmed guard, who reached for a secondary weapon at his belt. Without thinking, Apollo stepped forward and placed his hand on the console beside him. The dimensional currents surged at his touch, responding to his Veilborn signature.

The holographic display in the center of the room flared to life, projecting a swirling map of dimensional currents that filled the chamber. The guard hesitated. Taking advantage of the distraction, Astra lunged forward and drove her knife deep into the guards side, eliminating any further threat.

"The console is active," Alden called, moving toward it. "Apollo, we need you here."

Apollo joined him at the main control interface, which pulsed with energy at his approach. The holographic display shifted, responding to his presence, showing what appeared to be a diagnostic overview of the entire facility.

"It recognizes you," Alden said, excitement evident in his voice despite their situation. "Can you access the security systems?"

Apollo placed both hands on the interface, letting his dimensional perception merge with the ancestral technology. It felt natural. Information flowed into his mind—not as text or images, but as direct understanding, conveyed through the dimensional currents themselves.

"I can seal the tower," he said, his fingers moving across the interface with growing confidence. "Lock down all entrances except the one we came through."

"Do it," Astra urged, securing the guards with restraints taken from their own equipment. "That will buy us time to figure out our next move."

Apollo initiated the security protocols, feeling the dimensional currents throughout the tower shift as barriers activated at every entrance. The holographic display updated to show the status of the facility—and the positions of Carver's forces, represented as red disturbances in the dimensional field.

"There are at least twenty more guards in the tower," Apollo reported, studying the display. "And more outside, trying to breach the other buildings."

"What about Verity?" Tristan asked, joining them at the console after ensuring the technicians were secured.

Apollo searched the display, looking for any sign of the elder Veilborn. "I don't see her. The collapse in the transit tunnel is blocking some of the sensors in that section."

"She told us to meet her here," Alden reminded them. "We need to focus on securing this position until she arrives."

Apollo nodded, turning his attention back to the console. "This control center was designed to monitor and stabilize dimensional energies across a wide area. It's part of a network that once covered the entire continent."

"The stabilization grid Verity mentioned," Astra said.

"Yes. And it's still partially functional." Apollo's fingers moved over the interface, bringing up new displays. "The Ancestrals built these facilities to manage dimensional energy, using Veilborn as living interfaces between the technology and the dimensional currents."

"Can you activate it?" Alden asked.

Apollo shook his head. "Not fully. The network is too damaged, too many nodes are offline. But I can use it to monitor dimensional stability in this region." He adjusted the display, showing a map of the surrounding area with overlaid patterns of dimensional energy. "And I can see what Carver's been doing."

The display shifted to show multiple points of dimensional disturbance—unnatural tears in the fabric of reality, concentrated around a location to the east.

"Carver's fortress," Astra said. "He's been experimenting with dimensional manipulation."

"Without understanding what he's doing," Apollo added, his concern growing as he interpreted the data. "These disruptions are becoming more severe. If they continue to grow, they could eventually cascade into something much worse."

"Another Cataclysm," Alden said.

The gravity of their situation settled over the group. They'd come seeking knowledge, but had found themselves at the center of a much larger conflict—one with potentially catastrophic consequences.

A sudden alert from the console drew Apollo's attention. The security system was detecting new intrusions—more of Carver's forces attempting to breach the tower's defenses.

"They're not giving up," he said, studying the alert patterns. "They're bringing in heavier equipment to break through the barriers."

"How long will the barriers hold?" Tristan asked.

Apollo consulted the system diagnostics. "Hours, maybe. Depends on what they're using."

"Long enough for us to figure out our next move," Astra said. She turned to Apollo, her expression serious. "You've learned more about your abilities in the last hour than in all our previous training. What do you think we should do?"

Apollo felt the weight of their expectation—and their trust. Without Verity's guidance, they were looking to him for direction. The knowledge from the memory transfer was still settling in his mind, but with it came a growing clarity about what they faced and what might be possible.

"We need to understand exactly what Carver is trying to do," he said, turning back to the console. "And we need to find a way to counter it. This facility contains knowledge and technology that could help us do both."

He brought up a new display, showing the tower's internal structure. "There are specialized training chambers throughout this tower, designed to help Veilborn develop specific abilities. If I can access those, I might be able to accelerate my training—learn techniques that would normally take years to master."

"Is that safe?" Astra asked, concern evident in her voice.

Apollo met her gaze. "Probably not. But neither is letting Carver continue his experiments."

Before anyone could respond, another alert sounded from the console—different from the security warnings. Apollo turned to the display, which now showed a single figure approaching the tower from the direction of the collapsed transit tunnel.

"It's Verity," he said, relief flooding through him as he recognized the unique dimensional signature of the elder Veilborn. "She made it out."

The display showed Verity moving through the lower levels of the tower, heading toward the central lift. Apollo activated the communication system, sending his voice through the tower's internal speakers.

"Verity, it's Apollo. We've secured the control center. The lift is active and will bring you directly to us."

There was a moment of silence before Verity's voice responded, sounding strained but determined. "Well done. I'll be there shortly. Prepare yourselves—we don't have much time."

Apollo turned to the others, a new resolve strengthening his voice. "Alden, see what you can learn from the database here. Focus on Carver's fortress location and any information about countering dimensional disruptions. Tristan, check the equipment we secured from the guards—anything that might be useful. Astra, help me understand more about these training chambers."

As they moved to their tasks, Apollo felt something shift within him—a sense of purpose clarifying as the knowledge from the memory transfer integrated with his own experiences. He was Veilborn, created to interface with dimensional energies and technology. It was time to embrace that heritage fully, to become what he was meant to be.

Not just for his own sake, but for all of them.

10

— • —

FOLDING REALITY

Apollo's hands hovered over the tower's control interface, a complex web of light and energy responding to his movements. The knowledge from the memory transfer still swirled through his mind—fragments of history, science, and technique that hadn't been known to anyone in centuries.

"Verity's almost here," he said, watching her signature move through the lower levels. "The lift will bring her up in a few minutes."

Astra stood beside him, her shoulder nearly touching his as they both studied the display. "These training chambers you mentioned—how do they work?"

"They're designed to isolate specific dimensional frequencies," Apollo explained, bringing up a schematic on the display. "Each chamber creates conditions that force a Veilborn to develop particular skills."

The schematics showed seven chambers arranged in a circle around the central core of the tower. Each was labeled with symbols Apollo somehow understood—perception, manipulation, folding, projection, harmonics, shielding, and one marked "integration."

"This is what the Ancestrals used to train Veilborn," he continued. "A full course would take years, but..."

"But we don't have years," Astra finished for him.

Apollo nodded, feeling the pressure of their situation bearing down on him. Carver's forces surrounded the tower, and the dimensional disruptions were growing more severe by the hour.

The lift doors opened, and Verity stepped out, looking battered but determined. Her clothing was torn and singed, and a thin cut ran along her left cheekbone, but her eyes were clear and focused.

"Elder Verity!" Alden exclaimed. "We thought you might have—"

"Not yet," Verity said with a thin smile. "Though it was a close thing." She crossed to the central console, her gaze taking in the displays Apollo had activated. "I see you've been busy."

"The system recognized me," Apollo explained. "It gave me access to historical records, training protocols, and monitoring systems."

Verity nodded. "As it should. This facility was built for Veilborn, by Veilborn." She studied the security displays showing Carver's forces establishing positions around the tower. "How long before they breach the outer defenses?"

"Three hours, maybe four," Apollo answered. "They're bringing in heavier equipment."

"Then we need to use that time wisely." Verity turned to face all of them. "What have you learned?"

Apollo summarized the information they'd discovered—the purpose of the facility, Carver's dimensional experiments, and the training chambers.

"I want to use them," he concluded. "The chambers. I know it's risky, but if I can accelerate my training..."

Verity's expression grew troubled. "Those chambers were designed for gradual training over years, Apollo. Attempting to compress that process could be dangerous."

"More dangerous than letting Carver continue his experiments?" Apollo countered. "You saw the data. The dimensional disruptions are growing. If they reach critical levels—"

"Another Cataclysm," Verity finished. She was silent for a long moment, weighing options. Finally, she nodded. "Very well. But we do this carefully, and I'll be monitoring you the entire time."

"I'll help," Astra said, stepping forward. "My Order training included monitoring dimensional energies."

Apollo felt a surge of gratitude at her support, coupled with something else—a warmth that had been growing between them since they'd first met. He pushed the feeling aside, focusing on the task at hand.

"What about us?" Tristan asked, gesturing to himself and Alden.

"The database contains information about Carver's fortress," Apollo said. "We need to know everything about it—layout, defenses, weak points. And we need to understand exactly what he's trying to do with these experiments."

Alden nodded. "I'll start digging through the archives."

"And I'll check the equipment we took from the guards," Tristan added. "Maybe there's something we can use."

As they dispersed to their tasks, Verity placed a hand on Apollo's shoulder. "Are you certain about this? The training chambers are intense under normal circumstances. Using them in this accelerated way..."

"I don't have a choice," Apollo said. "I can feel the dimensional currents changing, Verity. Whatever Carver is doing, it's affecting the stability of reality itself. Someone has to stop him."

Verity studied him for a long moment, then nodded. "Then let's begin. The perception chamber first—it's the foundation for everything else."

Apollo followed Verity and Astra to a circular doorway near the edge of the control center. As they approached, symbols around the frame illuminated in response to Apollo's presence.

"The chamber will recognize you as Veilborn," Verity explained. "It will adapt to your current abilities and push you just beyond them."

"How will we know if it's working?" Apollo asked.

"You'll know," Verity said. "Believe me, you'll know."

The door slid open, revealing a perfectly circular room with a platform in the center. The walls were covered in the same symbols Apollo had seen throughout the facility—the written language of the Ancestrals, he now realized.

"Stand on the platform," Verity instructed. "Astra and I will monitor from here."

Apollo stepped into the chamber, moving to the central platform. As soon as his feet touched it, the door closed behind him, and the symbols on the walls began to glow.

"Relax," Verity's voice came through a speaker. "Let the chamber guide you."

Apollo took a deep breath and closed his eyes. For a moment, nothing happened. Then, gradually, he began to sense the dimensional currents flowing around and through the chamber—not just the primary frequencies he'd learned to perceive, but dozens, perhaps hundreds of distinct energy patterns.

The chamber was amplifying his perception, forcing his mind to differentiate between frequencies that had previously blended together. It was overwhelming at first, like trying to pick out individual instruments in an orchestra when you'd only ever heard the combined sound.

"Focus on one frequency at a time," Verity instructed. "Don't try to perceive everything at once."

Apollo concentrated, isolating a single current—a thread of energy that resonated at a specific frequency. As he focused on it, the chamber responded, amplifying that particular current while dampening the others.

"Good," Verity said. "Now shift to another."

Apollo did as instructed, moving his attention to a different frequency. Again, the chamber responded, highlighting the new current. He continued this process, cycling through different frequencies, learning to identify and isolate each one.

Time seemed to blur as he worked. Minutes stretched into an hour, then two. His head began to ache from the concentration, but with each cycle, the process became more natural, more instinctive.

"That's enough for now," Verity said. "We need to move to the manipulation chamber."

The door slid open, and Apollo stepped out, feeling simultaneously exhausted and exhilarated. His perception had expanded dramatically—he could now distinguish between dozens of dimensional frequencies without conscious effort.

"How do you feel?" Astra asked, studying him with concern.

"Like my brain has been stretched," Apollo admitted. "But I can see so much more now."

"Good," Verity said. "Because seeing is only the beginning."

The manipulation chamber was similar to the first, but the symbols on the walls were different—more dynamic, suggesting movement and change rather than observation.

"This chamber will teach you to influence the currents you can perceive," Verity explained. "Start with the simplest frequency—the one you've worked with the most."

Apollo nodded and stepped onto the platform. As before, the door closed behind him, and the symbols began to glow. He focused on the most familiar frequency—the blue-violet energy he'd first noticed back in Willowbrook.

The chamber responded, manifesting that energy as visible threads around him. Apollo could see them clearly, understanding their patterns and flows in ways he couldn't before.

"Now," Verity's voice instructed, "reach out with your mind. Don't just observe the current—direct it."

Apollo concentrated, imagining himself shaping the energy. Nothing happened at first. Then, slowly, one of the threads began to bend toward his outstretched hand.

"Yes," Verity encouraged. "That's it. Feel the connection between your intention and the energy."

Apollo focused harder, and the thread moved more decisively, wrapping around his fingers like a ribbon of light. He could feel it now—not just see it—a connection between his consciousness and the dimensional current.

"Now try to form it into a simple shape," Verity said. "A sphere, perhaps."

Apollo concentrated on the thread, willing it to curve and connect with itself. The energy responded, bending and shaping itself into a rough approximation of a sphere hovering above his palm.

"Remarkable," he heard Astra murmur through the speaker.

"Now try a different frequency," Verity instructed.

Apollo shifted his perception to another current—a green-gold energy that flowed faster than the first. This one was more difficult to grasp, slipping from his mental hold like water through fingers.

"Don't force it," Verity advised. "Each frequency responds to different intentions. Find what this one wants."

Apollo relaxed his approach, letting his intuition guide him. Rather than trying to grab the energy, he invited it, opening himself to its natural flow. The green-gold current responded, swirling around him in a complex pattern.

"Yes!" Verity's voice was excited now. "Each dimensional frequency has its own... personality, for lack of a better word. Some respond to direct command, others to invitation, still others to rhythmic patterns of thought."

Apollo continued working with different frequencies, learning their unique characteristics and how to influence each one. Some required precise mental focus, others responded to emotional states, and still others seemed to follow musical patterns of thought.

By the time Verity called a halt, Apollo was drenched in sweat, his entire body trembling with exertion. But he could now manipulate basic forms of dimensional energy with conscious control.

"You're progressing faster than I expected," Verity said as he exited the chamber. "But you need rest before continuing."

"We don't have time," Apollo insisted, though he could barely stand. "Carver's forces will break through eventually."

"You'll be no use to anyone if you collapse," Astra said, taking his arm to steady him. "An hour of rest, at least."

Apollo wanted to argue, but the room was starting to spin around him. "Fine. One hour."

Astra led him to a side room where emergency supplies had been stored. She helped him sit on a cot and handed him a container of water.

"Drink," she ordered. "Your body needs to recover."

Apollo drank gratefully, the cool water reviving him somewhat. Astra sat beside him, her expression troubled.

"What's wrong?" he asked.

She hesitated. "I'm worried about you. This accelerated training—it's putting tremendous strain on your system."

"I can handle it," Apollo assured her.

"Can you?" Her amber eyes met his. "I've been monitoring your vital signs through the chamber's systems. Your heart rate, brain activity, even your cellular energy—they're all operating at levels that should be impossible."

Apollo considered this. He did feel different—not just tired, but changed somehow, as if the training was altering him on a fundamental level.

"I don't have a choice," he said. "You've seen what Carver is doing. Someone has to stop him."

"Why does it have to be you?" Astra asked.

The question caught Apollo off guard. "Because I'm Veilborn. Because I can perceive and manipulate dimensional energy."

"There are other ways to fight," she argued. "We could alert the kingdom authorities, gather more allies—"

"By the time we did that, it might be too late." Apollo shook his head. "Besides, most people still think Veilborn are myths or criminals. Who would believe us?"

Astra fell silent, her hand still resting on his arm. The contact was comforting, grounding him when everything else seemed to be shifting.

"I'm afraid for you," she admitted. "I've seen what happens when people push too far into the dimensions. It... changes them."

Apollo covered her hand with his own. "I'm still me, Astra."

She looked up at him, her expression vulnerable in a way he hadn't seen before. For a moment, the tension between them shifted, becoming something deeper, more personal. Apollo found himself leaning closer, drawn by something beyond conscious thought.

A knock at the door broke the moment. "Apollo?" Alden called. "You should see this."

Apollo reluctantly pulled away. "Coming," he called back. He met Astra's eyes once more. "We'll finish this conversation later."

She nodded, a slight flush coloring her cheeks. "Yes. Later."

They returned to the control center, where Alden was studying a complex display of information.

"I've been analyzing the data on Carver's experiments," he explained. "It's worse than we thought."

The display showed a map of the region with multiple points of dimensional disturbance. At the center was a massive structure labeled "The Spire."

"What is that?" Apollo asked, pointing to the structure.

"It's one of the most significant Ancestral artifacts still standing," Alden explained. "A tower that reaches impossibly high—some say it once connected to the stars themselves."

"It's more than that," Verity said, joining them at the console. "The Spire was part of the dimensional stabilization network. A lynchpin in the system designed to prevent exactly the kind of catastrophe Carver is risking."

Apollo studied the data more closely. "And Carver is experimenting there? Why?"

"Power," Verity said. "The Spire contains technology that could harness dimensional energy on a scale we can barely comprehend. If he succeeds in activating it..."

"He could control everything," Astra finished. "Energy, communication, even reality itself within its influence."

"But he doesn't understand what he's doing," Apollo said, seeing the patterns in the data. "These disruptions—they're growing exponentially. He's destabilizing the very fabric of reality."

Tristan joined them, carrying several devices he'd salvaged from the guards. "If that's true, why would he risk it? Carver's power-hungry, not suicidal."

"Because he doesn't believe in the Cataclysm," Verity explained. "The Order has spent centuries rewriting history, portraying the Cataclysm as a natural disaster or a punishment from the gods—anything but what it really was: the result of dimensional manipulation gone wrong."

Apollo turned back to the training chambers. "We need to stop him. And to do that, I need to complete the training."

"Apollo," Verity warned, "the remaining chambers are even more demanding than the first two. The folding chamber in particular—"

"I don't have a choice," Apollo interrupted. "Show me."

The folding chamber was different from the others—smaller, with walls that seemed to bend in impossible ways. Standing on the platform, Apollo felt a strange disorientation, as if gravity was pulling from multiple directions at once.

"This chamber teaches the most difficult Veilborn skill," Verity explained through the speaker. "The ability to create dimensional folds—spaces where the normal rules of reality bend."

"Like your sanctuary," Apollo realized.

"Yes, though on a much smaller scale to start. Begin by focusing on the space between two points in the chamber."

Apollo concentrated on two points about a meter apart. As he focused, he could see the dimensional currents flowing between them—not just around, but through the space itself.

"Now," Verity instructed, "imagine those points are connected directly—that the space between them doesn't exist."

Apollo tried to visualize it, but nothing happened. The points remained stubbornly separate.

"You're thinking too literally," Verity advised. "Don't try to eliminate the space—fold it. Like paper."

Apollo adjusted his approach, imagining the dimensional fabric folding like a sheet, bringing the two points into contact. To his surprise, the air between the points seemed to ripple, the light bending strangely.

"Yes," Verity encouraged. "Now hold that intention steady and reach out physically."

Apollo extended his hand toward one of the points. As his fingers touched the rippling air, he felt a strange resistance, then a sudden give—as if he'd pushed through a membrane. His hand disappeared up to the wrist.

"Don't panic," Verity said. "Your hand is now at the second point. Look."

Apollo turned his head to see his own hand emerging from empty air at the second point, a meter away from where his arm entered the fold.

"That's..." He couldn't find words to describe the sensation.

"A dimensional fold," Verity confirmed. "A connection between two points that bypasses the space between them."

Apollo withdrew his hand, feeling the strange sensation of it passing through the fold. The ripple in the air persisted for a few seconds, then faded.

"Again," Verity instructed. "But this time, try points further apart."

Apollo continued practicing, creating folds between increasingly distant points in the chamber. Each attempt was easier than the last, his mind adapting to the counterintuitive process of folding space.

By the time he left the chamber, Apollo could create stable folds between any two points within his line of sight—temporary shortcuts through space that bypassed physical distance.

"That's enough for today," Verity insisted when he emerged. "Your mind needs time to integrate what you've learned."

Apollo wanted to continue, but he could feel the strain now—a deep fatigue that went beyond physical exhaustion. His perception of reality had changed, becoming more fluid, less fixed. It was disorienting.

"Rest," Astra agreed, taking his arm again. "We'll continue tomorrow."

Apollo allowed himself to be led back to the cot. This time, exhaustion overtook him immediately, pulling him into a deep sleep.

His dreams were vivid, filled with dimensional currents and strange geometries. He saw the Ancestral civilization at its height—massive cities with technology that blended seamlessly with dimensional energy, Veilborn working alongside engineers to maintain the delicate balance between worlds.

Then came the Cataclysm—scientists pushing too far, too fast, ignoring the warnings of the Veilborn. A massive surge of dimensional energy, reality itself tearing apart. The desperate efforts to contain the damage, to seal the breaches before they spread.

He witnessed the aftermath—the collapse of civilization, the slow rebuilding, the gradual loss of knowledge as generations passed. The rise of the Order, their campaign against the Veilborn, the Purge that nearly eradicated Apollo's kind.

And throughout it all, a single thread—the genetic lineage of the Veilborn, preserved through careful planning and desperate measures. His lineage.

Apollo woke with a start, the visions vivid in his mind. The room was dim, illuminated only by the soft glow of emergency lighting. Astra was asleep in a chair nearby, her face peaceful in repose.

Moving lightly to avoid waking her, Apollo made his way back to the control center. The main displays showed Carver's forces surrounding the tower, though they had made little progress against the defenses.

Alden was asleep at one of the consoles, his head resting on his arms. Tristan was nowhere to be seen—probably resting in another room. Verity sat alone at the central interface, studying something intently.

"You should be resting," she said without looking up, somehow sensing his presence.

"I had dreams," Apollo said, joining her at the console. "Visions of the past. The Ancestrals, the Cataclysm..."

Verity looked up. "Memory transfer aftereffects. The knowledge you received is integrating with your subconscious."

"It felt real," Apollo insisted. "Like I was there."

"In a way, you were," Verity explained. "The memory transfer includes experiential data—sensory impressions, emotional contexts. Your mind is processing them as memories."

Apollo gestured to the display she'd been studying. "What is this?"

"Information about The Spire," Verity said. "I've been trying to understand exactly what Carver might be attempting there."

The display showed a cross-section of the massive structure—a tower that reached impossibly high, its upper sections disappearing into clouds. Internal systems were highlighted in different colors, with annotations in the Ancestral language.

"The Spire was created as a dimensional anchor point," Verity explained. "A stabilizer for the weakened barriers between dimensions. But it was also designed with a failsafe system—a way to completely reset the dimensional balance if necessary."

"Reset how?" Apollo asked.

"By temporarily collapsing all dimensional barriers within its influence, then reestablishing them according to their natural pattern," Verity said. "A controlled implosion, essentially."

Apollo stared at the display, understanding dawning. "And Carver is trying to activate The Spire for his own purposes, not realizing what it's really designed to do."

"Exactly," Verity confirmed. "He thinks it's a weapon or power source he can control. But if he activates it incorrectly..."

"He could trigger the failsafe," Apollo finished. "Or worse, cause it to malfunction entirely."

"Either way, the results would be catastrophic," Verity said. "We're talking about dimensional collapse on a scale that would make the original Cataclysm look minor by comparison."

Apollo studied the schematics. "There must be a way to stop him."

"There is," Verity said, bringing up another display. "But it would require someone with fully developed Veilborn abilities to interface directly with The Spire's core systems."

Apollo looked at the technical specifications. "Someone like me."

"Potentially," Verity admitted. "But you're still developing your abilities. The risk would be enormous."

"What choice do we have?" Apollo asked.

Before Verity could answer, an alarm sounded from the security console. Tristan burst into the room a moment later.

"They've broken through the outer defenses," he reported. "Carver's forces are inside the tower."

Astra and Alden joined them, roused by the alarm. "How long do we have?" Astra asked.

"An hour, maybe less," Tristan estimated. "They're moving methodically, securing each level as they advance."

Apollo turned to Verity. "We need to leave. Take what we've learned and go to The Spire."

"You're not ready," Verity insisted. "The training—"

"Will have to continue elsewhere," Apollo interrupted. "We know what Carver is planning now. We know what's at stake. We need to stop him before it's too late."

Verity hesitated, then nodded reluctantly. "You're right. But you'll need something from this facility first." She turned to the central console, activating a sequence of commands. A panel opened in the floor, revealing a pedestal rising from below.

On the pedestal sat a device unlike anything Apollo had seen before—a sphere of crystalline material surrounded by interlocking rings of some dark metal. The entire object pulsed with dimensional energy, responding to Apollo's presence.

"What is that?" he asked, drawn to the device.

"A dimensional resonator," Verity explained. "One of the few remaining artifacts from before the Cataclysm. It's designed to amplify Veilborn abilities—to help you interface with systems like those in The Spire."

Apollo reached for the device, and it responded, the rings shifting position as his hand approached. When his fingers touched the crystal sphere, a surge of energy flowed through him—not painful, but intense, like hearing a symphony after a lifetime of silence.

The resonator lifted from the pedestal, hovering above his palm, the rings rotating in complex patterns around the sphere. Images flashed through Apollo's mind—instructions, warnings, possibilities.

"It's keyed to you now," Verity said. "It will help you complete your training and, if necessary, interface with The Spire's systems."

Apollo secured the resonator in his pack. "Then we have what we need. Let's go."

"There's an emergency exit through the lower levels," Verity said, bringing up a map on the display. "It leads to tunnels that extend beyond Carver's perimeter."

As they gathered their equipment and prepared to leave, Apollo found himself standing next to Astra. The moment they'd shared before seemed distant now, overshadowed by the urgency of their situation.

"Are you ready for this?" she asked.

Apollo thought about everything that had happened since that day in Willowbrook—the discovery of his abilities, the pursuit by the Order, finding Verity, the accelerated training. His world had completely transformed in a matter of weeks.

"I have to be," he answered.

Astra held his gaze for a long moment, then nodded. "Then let's go stop Carver."

As they headed for the emergency exit, Apollo sensed the heft of the dimensional resonator inside his backpack—a physical testament to his lineage and destiny. Whatever happened next, there was no turning back. The path of the Veilborn lay before him, and he would follow it wherever it led.

11

———— • ————

CONNECTIONS

Apollo kept his hand on the dimensional resonator as they moved through the emergency tunnel, its energy pulsing in sync with his heartbeat. The resonator's presence felt like a tether, anchoring him as he extended his senses forward, scanning for any disruptions that might indicate Carver's forces had discovered their escape route.

The tunnel stretched ahead, illuminated by strips of ancient lighting that flickered to life as they approached. Behind him, Tristan and Alden followed closely, with Verity leaning on Astra for support. The elder's injuries from the earlier confrontation had taken their toll, though she refused to slow their pace.

"The tunnel network extends for miles," Verity explained between labored breaths. "The Ancestrals built them to connect their major facilities."

"Can Carver track us through them?" Apollo asked, pausing at a junction to check both passages.

"Not easily," Verity replied. "These tunnels were once shielded from most detection methods."

Apollo nodded, choosing the right-hand passage based on the subtle flow of dimensional energy he could perceive. The resonator seemed to enhance his ability to distinguish these currents, making them sharper and more distinct than before.

"We should be safe when we reach the exit point," Astra added. "There's an old settlement about three miles from there where we can regroup."

They continued in silence for nearly an hour, the only sounds their footsteps and Verity's occasional cough. Apollo found himself walking beside Astra, their shoulders occasionally brushing in the narrow passage.

"The resonator," she said. "How does it feel?"

Apollo considered the question. "Like... an extension of myself. It amplifies everything—my perception, my connection to the dimensional currents. It's almost overwhelming."

"The records mention resonators," Astra replied. "They were rare even before the Cataclysm. Most Veilborn trained for years before they were entrusted with one."

"And I've had all of two weeks," Apollo said with a humorless laugh.

Astra's hand found his in the dim light, squeezing briefly. "You've accomplished more in those two weeks than most Veilborn did in years. The resonator wouldn't have responded to you otherwise."

Before Apollo could respond, Tristan called from behind them. "Light ahead. Is that the exit?"

Apollo focused, extending his senses forward. "No... it's different. Not natural light."

They approached cautiously. The tunnel widened into a circular chamber with several passages branching off. At the center stood a pedestal supporting what appeared to be a broken device—a hemisphere of dark metal with fractured crystal components.

"What is it?" Alden asked, adjusting his spectacles as he examined the object.

Verity approached inquisitively, her expression shifting from exhaustion to wonder. "A nexus node. They were communication hubs, allowing instantaneous contact between Ancestral facilities."

"It's damaged," Tristan observed, running his fingers along the fractured crystal.

"Yes, but..." Verity turned to Apollo. "With the resonator, you might be able to restore its functionality. These nodes were designed to interface with Veilborn abilities."

Apollo approached the pedestal, feeling the resonator respond to the node's presence. Even damaged, the device contained dimensional energy, though it flowed chaotically through the broken components.

"What would that accomplish?" he asked.

"If we could reactivate the network," Verity explained, "we could potentially access information from other facilities—perhaps even locate allies who might help us against Carver."

"Is it worth the risk?" Astra asked. "Using it might alert Carver to our location."

"The network operates on frequencies he can't monitor," Verity assured them. "It was designed specifically for Veilborn communication."

Apollo studied the broken node, sensing the patterns of energy within it. "I'll try," he decided. "But we should continue moving afterward, regardless of the outcome."

Tristan remained by the node while the others stepped back, giving Apollo space as he removed the resonator from his pack. The device hummed in response to his touch, the rings shifting position as he held it near the damaged node.

Apollo closed his eyes, focusing on the resonator's energy. It responding to his intent, amplifying the dimensional currents. With precision and Tristan's presence stabilizing the connection, he directed that energy toward the broken node, visualizing the chaotic flows, the fractured components reconnecting on a dimensional level if not physically.

The resonator's hum deepened, and Apollo felt a surge of energy flow through him and into the node. The broken crystals began to glow, and patterns of light appeared across the dark metal surface.

"It's working," Verity whispered.

Apollo maintained his focus, feeling the node's systems beginning to respond. The dimensional currents shifted, forming new patterns as the device attempted to reestablish connections that had been dormant for centuries.

A holographic display flickered to life above the node—a three-dimensional map showing points of light connected by threads of energy. Most of the points were dim or flickering, but a few burned steadily.

"Active nodes," Verity explained, her voice hushed with awe. "After all this time..."

Apollo kept the connection stable, sweat beading on his forehead from the effort. "Can we communicate with them?"

"Yes," Verity stepped forward, placing her hand on the node's surface. "The interface is designed to respond to intent. Focus on one of the active points and project your thoughts toward it."

Apollo concentrated on the nearest active point, a steady light located somewhere to the east. He directed his awareness toward it, feeling the resonator amplify his effort. For a moment, nothing happened—then a voice echoed through the chamber, speaking in a language Apollo didn't recognize.

Verity responded in the same language, her expression intent. The exchange continued for several minutes while Apollo maintained the connection, feeling the strain of channeling so much energy.

Finally, Verity stepped back, her eyes wide. "They're still there," she said, her voice thick with emotion. "After all this time, there are descendants of Veilborn in the eastern mountains. They've maintained a sanctuary since before the Purge."

"What did you tell them?" Astra asked.

"Everything," Verity replied. "About Apollo, about Carver, about The Spire. They've been monitoring dimensional disturbances for months but couldn't pinpoint the source."

"Will they help us?" Tristan asked.

Verity nodded. "They're sending representatives to meet us. There's an old waystation two days' journey from here where we can rendezvous."

Apollo felt the connection beginning to waver as his strength ebbed. With a final effort, he stabilized the node's energy and withdrew, allowing the resonator to absorb the excess dimensional current.

The holographic display flickered and faded, but the node itself continued to glow faintly, now functioning at some basic level.

"I've never seen anything like that," Alden said, staring at both Apollo and Tristan with undisguised awe. "You literally repaired it with dimensional energy."

"Not repaired," Apollo corrected, returning the resonator to his pack. "More like... bridged the gaps. It won't last without a Veilborn and Resonant to maintain the connection."

"It lasted long enough," Verity said. "Now we have allies—and a destination."

They continued their trek through the passageways, Apollo's examined the significance of their findings. Other descendants of Veilborn had endured beyond the Purge, preserving their ancient wisdom and customs in the shadows across hundreds of years. The resonator had allowed him to connect with them, bridging not just the physical distance but the gap of time and knowledge that separated them.

Two hours later, they emerged from the tunnels into a forested valley as dusk approached. The exit was concealed within a hillside, invisible unless you knew exactly where to look. Apollo helped Verity traverse the rough terrain as they made their way toward the abandoned settlement Astra had mentioned.

"How are you feeling?" Astra asked as they walked side by side.

"Drained," Apollo admitted. "Using the resonator takes more out of me than I expected."

"You're still learning," she reminded him. "The old texts say that with practice, Veilborn could use resonators for hours without fatigue."

"I'll add it to my list of skills to master," Apollo said with a tired smile. "Right after 'save the world from dimensional collapse.'"

Astra's expression grew serious. "You don't have to carry this alone, you know. We're all in this together."

Apollo nodded, grateful for her reassurance even as he felt the weight of responsibility settling more firmly on his shoulders. The resonator, the node, the connection to potentially new allies—each step seemed to bind him more tightly to a destiny he was still struggling to understand.

The settlement, when they reached it, proved to be little more than a cluster of stone buildings partially reclaimed by the forest. Moss covered the walls, and trees grew through collapsed roofs, but several structures remained intact enough to provide shelter.

"This was a research outpost," Verity explained as they explored the ruins. "One of many established during the Reconstruction Era, when people were trying to understand and adapt Ancestral technology."

"Before the Order declared it forbidden knowledge," Astra added, her voice bitter.

They chose the most intact building for their camp, a circular structure with a domed roof that kept out the elements. Tristan got a fire going in the central hearth while Alden examined the faded markings on the walls.

"These are dimensional notations," he said. "Similar to what we saw in the tower, but more... practical. Instructions rather than theory."

Apollo joined him, recognizing patterns that matched what he'd learned during his training. "They were teaching Veilborn techniques," he realized. "This was a school."

"Not just a school," Verity corrected. "A beacon. These outposts were meant to identify and recruit those with Veilborn potential, to train them for the stabilization network."

"Before the Order decided Veilborn were too dangerous to exist," Astra said.

Verity sighed. "The Order wasn't always what it became. In the beginning, they genuinely believed they were protecting humanity from another Cataclysm."

"By hunting down the only people who could prevent one?" Tristan asked.

"Fear makes for poor policy," Verity replied. "After centuries of propaganda, even the Order's own members don't know the truth anymore."

"Then we need to show them," Apollo said. The idea had been forming in his mind since they'd activated the node, but now it crystallized into certainty. "We need to show everyone."

"What do you mean?" Alden asked.

Apollo paced the circular room, energy returning to his steps despite his earlier fatigue. "The node network. If we can repair more nodes, we could broadcast the truth about the Veilborn, about the Ancestral technology, about what Carver is doing. Not just to a few allies, but to everyone."

"A global communication network," Alden breathed. "The Ancestrals had that capability before the Cataclysm."

"And the infrastructure still exists," Verity confirmed. "Damaged but not destroyed..."

"We could reveal the truth that's been hidden for centuries," Astra finished. "Break the Order's monopoly on information."

"And warn people about the danger Carver poses," Tristan added. "Rally support against him."

Apollo nodded, feeling the rightness of the plan. "The node we activated is just the beginning. If there are other descendants of Veilborn out there, with their help, we could restore the entire network."

"It would take time," Verity cautioned. "And Carver won't wait. His experiments at The Spire continue even now."

"Then we work on both fronts," Apollo decided. "We meet with these eastern descendants of Veilborn, coordinate with them to begin restoring the network. Meanwhile, we continue to The Spire to stop Carver directly."

"Ambitious," Tristan remarked with a raised eyebrow.

"Necessary," Apollo countered. "Stopping Carver solves the immediate threat, but revealing the truth is the only way to prevent someone else from following in his footsteps."

Verity studied him. "You're thinking like a true Veilborn now. Not just about power, but about responsibility—about balance."

They spent the evening refining the plan, mapping out routes to The Spire and discussing what they'd learned from the node connection. Verity shared what she knew about the eastern community, while Alden sketched diagrams of how a restored node network might function.

As night deepened, they took turns keeping watch. Apollo volunteered for the first shift, sitting by the entrance with the resonator beside him. He found that even proximity to the device enhanced his perception, allowing him to sense the dimensional currents flowing through the valley.

Astra joined him halfway through his watch, sitting beside him on the stone steps.

"Couldn't sleep?" he asked.

She shook her head. "Too much to think about. This plan of yours... it could change everything."

"That's the idea," Apollo said with a slight smile.

"I know. It's just..." She paused, searching for words. "I've spent my whole life in the shadows. First as part of the Order, then running from them. The idea of bringing everything into the light—it's terrifying and exhilarating at the same time."

Apollo understood. Since discovering his abilities, he'd been caught between worlds—the simple life he'd known in Willowbrook and the complex reality of being Veilborn. There was no going back, only forward into uncertainty.

"I never asked for any of this," he admitted. "Being Veilborn, the resonator, this responsibility. Sometimes I wonder what would have happened if I'd never touched that lamp at the festival."

Astra replied. "Carver would still be experimenting with The Spire. The dimensional instabilities would still be growing. But there might not have been anyone who could stop it."

Apollo considered her words. "You really believe I can?"

"I believe we can," she corrected. "Together."

In the dim light, her eyes met his, and Apollo felt a connection that went beyond words. He reached out, hesitantly, and took her hand. Astra's fingers intertwined with his, warm and certain.

"When I left the Order," she said, "I thought I was just running away. I never imagined I'd find something worth running toward."

Apollo felt a warmth spread through him that had nothing to do with dimensional energy. Slowly, giving her time to pull away if she wanted, he leaned closer. Astra met him halfway, her lips finding his in a kiss that felt like coming home.

When they separated, Apollo kept his forehead pressed against hers, unwilling to break the connection entirely. "I'm glad you found me," he whispered.

"I think we found each other," she replied.

They remained side by side through the rest of Apollo's watch, talking about their pasts and the future they hoped to build. Apollo spoke of growing up in Willowbrook, of Kieran's quiet strength and the questions he'd always carried about his origins. Astra shared stories of her childhood in the Order, of the grandmother who had secretly taught her to question their teachings, of her gradual realization that she needed to forge her own path.

By the time Tristan came to relieve them, Apollo felt a new sense of clarity. The burden of being Veilborn hadn't lightened, but it no longer felt like something he carried alone.

The next day brought clear skies and renewed purpose. They packed their meager supplies and prepared to set out for the waystation where they would meet the eastern representatives.

"Two days' journey if we maintain a good pace," Verity announced, looking stronger after a night's rest. "The waystation is well-hidden—it served as a safe house during the Purge."

As they left the settlement behind, Apollo walked with a lighter step despite the challenges ahead. The resonator hummed contentedly in his pack, and Astra moved beside him, their hands occasionally brushing as they navigated the forest path.

By midday, they reached a ridge overlooking a vast valley. In the distance, mountains rose against the horizon—their destination lay somewhere among those peaks.

"Look there," Alden said, pointing to their left. "Is that another settlement?"

Apollo followed his gesture and saw stone structures similar to the ones they'd left behind, partially visible among the trees about half a mile away.

"Another research outpost," Verity confirmed. "They were established in a network, usually within a day's travel of each other."

"Would it have a node?" Apollo asked, knowing the answer.

Verity nodded. "Most likely. Though probably in the same condition as the one we found."

Apollo exchanged glances with Astra. "It's worth investigating," he decided. "If we're going to restore the network, we need to understand what we're working with."

They adjusted their course, descending into the valley toward the second outpost. As they drew closer, Apollo sensed the familiar resonance of Ancestral technology—faint but unmistakable.

This settlement was larger than the first, with several buildings arranged around a central plaza. Unlike the previous outpost, these structures showed signs of deliberate preservation—repaired roofs, cleared pathways, maintained walls.

"Someone's been taking care of this place," Tristan observed, hand moving to his weapon.

"Recently too," Astra added, pointing to fresh footprints in the soft earth of the path.

They proceeded cautiously, Apollo extending his senses to search for any immediate threats. He detected nothing but the steady pulse of dimensional energy coming from the largest building on the far side of the plaza.

"The node is there," he said, indicating the building. "And it's... different. More active than the last one."

They approached the structure—a two-story building with a domed roof similar to their shelter from the previous night. The entrance stood open, revealing a well-maintained interior with furnishings that looked regularly used.

"Someone lives here," Alden whispered unnecessarily.

Apollo felt the resonator responding to the node's proximity, vibrating gently in his pack. "Whoever they are, they know about Ancestral technology," he said. "Maybe even about Veilborn."

They entered cautiously, finding themselves in a circular room dominated by a central pedestal. Unlike the broken node they'd encountered before, this one appeared intact—a complete sphere of dark metal and crystal, pulsing with steady energy.

"It's functional," Verity breathed, her eyes wide with wonder. "Fully functional."

Before Apollo could respond, a voice spoke from behind them. "It took three years to repair it."

They turned to find an elderly man standing in the doorway, leaning on a staff carved with symbols Apollo recognized as dimensional notation.

Despite his age, the man stood straight, his eyes sharp as they assessed the group.

"Keeper Verity," the man said with a nod of recognition. "It's been a long time."

"Archivist Elian," Verity replied, surprise evident in her voice. "I thought you perished during the Purge."

The old man smiled faintly. "Many thought so. That was the intention." His gaze shifted to Apollo, focusing on him with sudden intensity. "And you must be the Veilborn I've been sensing. Your activation of the northern node sent ripples through the entire network."

He gestured for them to follow him deeper into the building. "Come. We have much to discuss, and little time to waste."

The upper floor of the building contained living quarters and what appeared to be a workshop filled with Ancestral devices in various states of repair. Elian led them to a common area with comfortable seating arranged around a low table.

"You've been maintaining the node network," Astra said as they settled in.

"Trying to," Elian corrected. "Most nodes are damaged beyond my ability to repair alone. But I've managed to establish limited communication with other outposts where Veilborn descendants have taken refuge."

"How many?" Verity asked.

"Twelve confirmed locations," Elian replied. "Mostly isolated individuals or small families. Nothing like the communities that existed before the Purge." He turned to Apollo. "Until yesterday, when you activated the northern node. That signal was stronger than anything I've felt in decades."

Apollo explained about the resonator and their encounter with the node in the tunnel. Elian listened intently, his expression growing more animated with each detail.

"A functioning resonator," he said when Apollo finished. "I haven't seen one since before the Purge. May I?"

Apollo hesitated only briefly before removing the resonator from his pack and placing it on the table. Elian made no move to touch it, simply studying it with evident appreciation.

"Perfectly preserved," he murmured. "And it's bonded to you already. Remarkable."

"We believe it can help us restore the node network," Apollo explained. "To share the truth about Veilborn and warn people about Carver's experiments."

Elian's expression darkened at the mention of Carver. "I've felt the disturbances from The Spire. Dangerous, reckless manipulation of dimensional energies by someone who doesn't understand what they're doing."

"Can the network be fully restored?" Alden asked. "Could it reach everyone, not just other Veilborn?"

"With enough time and resources, yes," Elian confirmed. "The Ancestrals designed the system to be resilient. Even after centuries of neglect, the underlying infrastructure remains intact."

"And with the resonator?" Apollo pressed.

Elian considered the question. "It would accelerate the process significantly. A resonator allows for deeper connection with the nodes, enabling repairs that would otherwise be impossible."

"Then we have a chance," Apollo said, excitement building in his voice. "We can restore communication across the continent, share the truth about Veilborn and Ancestral technology."

"Break the Order's monopoly on information," Astra added.

"And warn everyone about Carver," Tristan finished.

Elian nodded. "It's an ambitious plan. Dangerous too—the Order won't stand idle while their authority is undermined."

"The Order is already hunting us," Apollo pointed out. "And Carver's experiments threaten everyone, including them. We have nothing to lose by acting boldly."

"Perhaps not," Elian agreed. "And there's a certain poetry to using the Ancestrals' own communication network to prevent another Cataclysm."

They spent the remainder of the day with Elian, learning about his work maintaining the node network and discussing strategies for its restoration. The archivist shared maps showing the locations of other nodes, each point representing a potential ally in their cause.

As evening approached, Elian prepared a meal for them all—the first proper food they'd had since fleeing the tower. The atmosphere grew celebratory as they shared the meal, a sense of hope pervading their conversation despite the challenges ahead.

"Tomorrow you continue to the waystation?" Elian asked as they finished eating.

Verity nodded. "The eastern representatives will be waiting. With their support and yours, we can begin coordinating the network restoration while Apollo and a small team continue to The Spire."

"I'll contact the other nodes tonight," Elian promised. "Let them know what's coming. By the time you reach the waystation, they'll be ready to help."

Later, as the others prepared for sleep, Apollo found himself on the building's roof terrace with Astra. Above them, stars filled the clear night sky, while below, the valley lay peaceful in the moonlight.

"It's really happening," Astra said. "Everything I hoped for when I left the Order—the truth coming to light, knowledge being freely shared."

Apollo took her hand, feeling the connection between them that had grown stronger with each passing day. "We still have to stop Carver," he reminded her. "The Spire is the immediate threat."

"I know," she replied. "But for the first time, I believe we can do both—stop the immediate danger and change things for the better afterward."

Apollo felt the same hope rising within him. The resonator, the node network, allies like Elian and the eastern representatives—pieces were falling into place, offering a path forward that seemed increasingly possible.

"When this is over," he said, "what will you do?"

Astra considered the question. "Help rebuild, I suppose. There's so much knowledge to recover, so many people who need to understand the truth about our past."

"And us?" Apollo asked, the question slipping out before he could reconsider.

Astra turned to face him fully, her expression softening. "I think we'll have plenty to do together," she said. "If that's what you want."

Apollo's answer was to pull her close, their lips meeting under the stars. In that moment, the burden of being Veilborn felt not like a weight but like a gift—a purpose shared with someone who understood both the responsibility and the wonder it entailed.

They remained on the terrace long after the others had gone to sleep, talking about possibilities that had seemed unimaginable just days before. A world where Veilborn could exist openly, where Ancestral knowledge was studied rather than feared, where the balance between dimensions was maintained through understanding rather than ignorance.

As the night deepened around them, Apollo felt a profound sense of rightness—not just about their plan or the fight against Carver, but about his place in the world. For the first time since discovering his abilities, he felt not just acceptance but purpose, a clear vision of what he was meant to do and who he was meant to become.

Tomorrow would bring new challenges, the journey to the waystation and beyond to The Spire. But tonight, under the stars with Astra beside him, Apollo allowed himself to believe in the future they were fighting for—a future where the veil between worlds was understood rather than feared, where knowledge brought people together rather than driving them apart.

A future worth risking everything to create.

12

ALONG THE RIDGE

Apollo stirred awake in the pre-dawn darkness, his thoughts churning with strategies for the upcoming day. The resonator lay beside him, its surface catching the first hint of morning light. He picked it up, feeling the now-familiar surge of connection as it amplified his awareness of the dimensional currents flowing around him.

Outside Elian's outpost, mist clung to the valley floor, transforming the landscape into something dreamlike. Apollo breathed deeply, centering himself as Verity had taught him. The dimensional currents felt stronger today, more accessible—whether from his training, the resonator's influence, or growing confidence, he couldn't tell.

"Early riser?" Elian appeared beside him, carrying two steaming cups. He handed one to Apollo. "Herb tea. Helps focus the mind."

"Thanks." Apollo accepted the cup gratefully. "How far to the waystation?"

"Half a day's journey if you maintain a good pace," Elian replied. "An old monitoring station built into the side of a cliff face. The eastern representatives should arrive by nightfall."

Apollo nodded, sipping the tea. It tasted of mint and something unfamiliar—slightly bitter but invigorating. "Did you make contact with the other nodes?"

"Most of them," Elian confirmed. "Those still maintained by our allies. Several have been abandoned over the years, but enough remain to create a functional network."

"And they're willing to help?"

"They've been waiting for this moment for generations," Elian said with a smile. "The chance to emerge from hiding, to use the knowledge they've preserved for its intended purpose."

Inside, the others were stirring. Apollo heard Tristan's deep laugh, followed by Alden's quieter voice asking questions about the outpost's technology. Astra and Verity were reviewing maps at the main table, planning their route to the waystation.

"We should leave within the hour," Verity announced when Apollo entered. "Carver's forces will have expanded their search perimeter by now."

"I've prepared supplies for your journey," Elian said, indicating several packs arranged near the door. "Food, water, medical supplies, and a few items that might prove useful."

They ate a quick breakfast, then gathered their belongings. Apollo secured the resonator in an inner pocket of his jacket, where it rested against his chest like a second heartbeat.

"Stay in contact through the node," Verity instructed Elian. "If anything changes, if you hear any news of Carver's movements—"

"I'll alert you immediately," Elian promised. "Be careful. The eastern path follows the old transit lines for part of the way, but there are sections where you'll be exposed."

They bid farewell to the archivist and set off into the morning mist. Verity led the way, her knowledge of the region guiding them along hidden paths that wound through the forest. Despite her injuries, she maintained a steady pace, pausing only occasionally to consult her map or check their surroundings.

The morning passed without incident as they followed a narrow valley between forested ridges. Apollo found himself walking beside Astra, their conversation flowing between practical matters and more personal reflections.

"Did you ever imagine this?" he asked her. "When you left the Order, did you think you'd end up here?"

Astra considered the question. "I hoped to find truth," she said. "To understand what the Order was hiding. But this—" She gestured at their small group, at Apollo himself. "No, I never imagined finding you, or being part of something that could change everything."

"Does it scare you?" Apollo's voice was quiet, meant only for her.

"Of course it does," she admitted. "But not as much as doing nothing. Not as much as letting Carver succeed."

They fell silent as the path narrowed, forcing them to walk single file. Above them, the ridges grew steeper, the forest giving way to rocky slopes.

By midday, they had reached a point where the valley floor began to rise sharply, the path becoming more challenging.

"We're approaching the transit line," Verity announced during a brief rest. "It follows this ridge for several miles before entering a tunnel system. We'll make better time once we reach it."

"And be more exposed," Alden pointed out, studying the terrain ahead. "Those upper slopes have no cover."

"It's the fastest route to the waystation," Verity said. "We need to reach it before nightfall."

They continued upward, the path growing steeper until they were using their hands as much as their feet to climb. Apollo felt the resonator warm against his chest, responding to something in their surroundings. He paused, placing his palm flat against a rock face.

"There's dimensional energy here," he said, surprised. "Flowing through the rock itself."

Verity nodded. "The transit lines were built along natural energy currents. The Ancestrals understood how to harness these flows for power."

They reached a narrow ledge cut into the side of the ridge—the remains of the transit line Verity had mentioned. It was wide enough to walk comfortably, with a low wall on the outer edge providing some security against the drop below. The surface was smooth, unlike the natural rock they'd been climbing, clearly artificial despite centuries of weathering.

"We follow this for three miles," Verity said, pointing ahead where the ledge curved around the ridge face. "Then there's a tunnel entrance that will take us directly to the waystation."

They made good progress along the transit line, their pace quickening on the level surface. Apollo felt increasingly uneasy, however. The resonator continued to warm against his chest, and the dimensional currents around them seemed to shift in patterns he couldn't quite interpret.

"Something feels wrong," he said, stopping to scan their surroundings. "The energy here is... fluctuating."

Astra stopped beside him, her expression concerned. "What do you mean?"

"I'm not sure," Apollo admitted. "It's like there's interference in the dimensional currents. Something artificial."

Verity frowned, joining them. "Carver's technology?"

"Maybe." Apollo closed his eyes, focusing on the resonator's connection to the dimensional fields. Through it, he could sense disturbances ahead—and behind them. His eyes snapped open. "We're being herded."

"What?" Tristan asked, hand moving to his weapon.

"There are energy disruptions on both sides of us," Apollo explained. "Creating a corridor along this transit line. We're being channeled toward something."

Verity's face paled. "A trap. Carver must have anticipated our route."

"We need to get off this ledge," Alden said, looking around frantically. "Find another way to the waystation."

"There isn't one," Verity replied. "Not without backtracking for miles."

Apollo removed the resonator from his pocket, holding it in his palm. Its surface was now noticeably warm, the internal patterns shifting rapidly in response to the dimensional disturbances. "I might be able to create a fold," he said, though uncertainty colored his voice. "A shortcut through the dimensional barriers."

"That's extremely dangerous without proper training," Verity warned. "Especially with these disruptions."

"We don't have much choice," Apollo replied. "If Carver's forces are waiting ahead—"

A sound cut through the air—the distinctive whine of hover engines. From around the curve of the ridge ahead, three sleek craft appeared, each bearing the insignia of Magistrate Carver's elite guard. Behind them, the same sound announced the arrival of more craft from the direction they'd come.

"Too late," Tristan muttered, drawing his weapon.

The hover craft slowed as they approached, positioning themselves in a semicircle facing the ledge. Armed guards stood ready on each vessel, weapons trained on Apollo's group. On the central craft, a figure stepped forward—tall and imposing in elaborate formal attire.

Magistrate Carver himself.

"Apollo Frost," his voice carried clearly across the distance between them. "I've been looking forward to meeting you."

Apollo gripped the resonator tightly, feeling its energy pulse in response to his rising fear and determination. "Magistrate Carver," he acknowledged, his thoughts frantically searching for options. "I'd say it's an honor, but we both know that would be a lie."

Carver's laugh held no humor. "Direct. I appreciate that." His gaze swept over their small group. "Elder Verity. I thought you might have perished at the tower. A pity you survived only to be captured here."

"You won't succeed, Carver," Verity called back. "Your experiments at The Spire will destroy everything, including yourself."

"Progress requires risk," Carver replied dismissively. "Something the Order never understood, with their obsession with containment and control." His attention returned to Apollo. "But you understand, don't you? The potential of what you carry in your blood. The power to reshape reality itself."

Apollo felt Astra move closer to his side. "What do we do?" she whispered.

"I'm figuring it out," he whispered in response, his thoughts frantically evaluating options. The resonator felt hot against his palm, its link to the dimensional flows powerful even amid the disturbances. If he managed to generate a rift, just a tiny one...

"You have two choices," Carver continued. "Surrender peacefully and join my research team at The Spire, where your abilities will be properly studied and utilized. Or resist, and watch your friends die before you're taken anyway." He gestured to the armed guards surrounding them. "I have no preference either way."

Apollo glanced at Verity, who gave an almost imperceptible nod. "We need time," he called to Carver. "To discuss your generous offer."

Carver smiled thinly. "You have one minute. No more."

Apollo turned his back to Carver, gathering his companions into a tight circle. "I can create a fold," he whispered. "But I can only take one or two people with me. The resonator isn't strong enough for more, especially with these disruptions."

"Then take Astra and go," Verity said. "You two have the best chance of reaching The Spire and stopping Carver's experiments."

"I'm not leaving you behind," Apollo protested.

"You must," Verity insisted. "The rest of us will create a distraction. When Carver realizes what you're doing, his focus will be on stopping you. That's our chance to scatter and escape."

"It's the only plan that makes sense," Alden agreed. "Apollo, you're the only one who can interface with The Spire's systems."

Apollo looked at each of their faces, the weight of the decision pressing down on him. "Tristan?"

His friend nodded. "Do it. We'll find each other after."

"Time's up, Mr. Frost," Carver called. "What's your decision?"

Apollo turned back to face the magistrate, the resonator concealed in his palm. "We surrender," he called. "On condition that my friends are treated well."

"Of course," Carver replied. "I have no quarrel with them, provided they cooperate."

As Carver's hover craft moved closer to the ledge, Apollo squeezed Astra's hand. "Be ready," he whispered. "When I activate the fold, move with me. Don't hesitate."

She nodded, her face set with determination.

Apollo focused on the resonator, channeling his awareness through it into the dimensional currents. Despite the disruptions, he could feel the potential for a fold—a temporary thinning of the barriers between points in space. He visualized their destination: the waystation Elian had described, built into the cliff face miles ahead.

The resonator grew hotter in his hand as he pushed more energy into it, the dimensional currents responding to his will. A shimmer appeared in the air before him, barely visible—the beginning of a fold.

"Now!" he shouted, grabbing Astra's arm as the fold began to open fully.

Chaos erupted on the ledge. Tristan and Alden drew weapons. Verity threw herself toward the wall of the ridge, hands outstretched as she manipulated the dimensional currents to create a barrier of distorted space.

Apollo pulled Astra toward the fold, the gateway visible as a rippling distortion in the air. They were one step away when a high-pitched whine cut through the noise of battle, and Apollo felt the dimensional currents around him collapse.

The fold dissolved before his eyes, the carefully constructed gateway snapping shut. The resonator in his hand went cold, its internal patterns freezing in place.

"An impressive attempt," Carver's voice came from behind them. "But predictable."

Apollo turned to find the magistrate standing on the ledge, having disembarked from his craft. In his hand, he held a small device emitting a pulsing field of energy that seemed to flatten the dimensional currents around them.

"Dimensional suppressor," Carver explained, noting Apollo's expression. "Specifically calibrated to counteract Veilborn abilities. One of many useful technologies my researchers have developed."

Apollo looked around desperately. Tristan and Alden were pinned down behind a section of the low wall, guards closing in from both sides. Verity lay slumped against the ridge wall, blood visible on her temple. Astra stood frozen beside Apollo, her hand still gripped in his.

"Your friends fought admirably," Carver observed. "But the outcome was never in doubt."

Guards surrounded them, weapons raised. The suppressor in Carver's hand continued to emit its pulsing field, leaving Apollo feeling hollow, his connection to the dimensional currents severed.

"Take them," Carver ordered. "Separate transports. The Veilborn comes with me."

Apollo felt Astra's hand torn from his as guards seized them both. "No!" he shouted, struggling against the armored figures that held him. "Leave them alone! It's me you want!"

"Indeed it is," Carver agreed, approaching until he stood before Apollo. "But they chose their allegiance. Actions have consequences, Mr. Frost."

Apollo watched helplessly as Astra was dragged toward one of the hover craft, her eyes never leaving his. Tristan and Alden were being secured in another, while two guards lifted Verity's unconscious form.

"Where are you taking them?" Apollo demanded.

"That depends on their cooperation," Carver replied. "Unlike the Order, I don't believe in wasting potential resources. Your friends may yet prove useful."

A guard approached Carver, holding the resonator that had fallen from Apollo's hand. "Sir, we found this on the Veilborn."

Carver took the device, examining it with evident interest. "Ancestral technology, adapted for Veilborn use. Fascinating." He pocketed it, then turned back to Apollo. "You'll have much to tell me about your training and the artifacts you've encountered."

"I'll tell you nothing," Apollo spat.

"Everyone says that at first," Carver said with a thin smile. "But isolation has a way of changing perspectives." He nodded to the guards. "Secure him. Full protocol."

Apollo felt something cold snap around his wrists—metallic cuffs that seemed to further dampen his connection to the dimensional currents.

A similar device was fastened around his neck, tightening until it pressed uncomfortably against his throat.

"Dimensional inhibitors," Carver explained. "They'll ensure your abilities remain suppressed until we reach The Spire."

Apollo was forced toward Carver's personal craft, his last glimpse of his friends showing Astra being loaded onto a transport. Tristan and Alden were in a craft waiting to depart. Verity remained motionless as guards secured her to a stretcher.

"Don't worry about them," Carver said, following Apollo's gaze. "Focus on your own situation. You're about to become part of something historic—the next evolution in human potential."

The hover craft rose from the ledge, banking toward the distant mountains where The Spire waited. Apollo stood rigid between two guards, the inhibitors around his wrists and neck a constant reminder of his powerlessness. Without his connection to the dimensional currents, he felt partially blind, a sense he'd come to rely on now absent.

"You're making a mistake," he said to Carver, who stood at the front of the craft, looking out at the landscape below. "The experiments at The Spire—they're destabilizing the dimensional barriers. You'll cause another Cataclysm."

"That's what Verity would have you believe," Carver replied without turning. "Her generation's fear of Ancestral technology has held humanity back for centuries. The Spire isn't a danger—it's the key to controlling dimensional energy on a scale never before achieved."

"You can't control it," Apollo insisted. "The Ancestrals created Veilborn because they needed living interfaces to safely manage the dimensional currents. Mechanical systems alone can't maintain the necessary balance."

Now Carver did turn, his expression curious. "You've learned much in a short time. Which makes you all the more valuable to my work." He approached Apollo, studying him with clinical interest. "You're the first full Veilborn discovered in generations. The genetic potential you carry—it's the missing piece I've been searching for."

Apollo felt a chill at Carver's words, at the hunger in his eyes. "What do you want from me?"

"Your cooperation, ideally," Carver replied. "Your participation in a series of experiments that will map the full extent of Veilborn capabilities. But even without that—" he shrugged "—your genetic material alone will advance my research considerably."

The unspoken threat lingered in the space separating them. Apollo would be useful to Carver whether he cooperated or not.

The trip proceeded wordlessly from that point onward, Apollo's thoughts frantically cycling through possibilities, hunting for any potential escape. But with the inhibitors blocking his abilities and his friends scattered to unknown locations, options were few.

Hours passed as the hover craft traveled over increasingly mountainous terrain. Eventually, a structure came into view in the distance—a slender spire of gleaming metal rising from a complex of buildings nestled in a high valley. Even from a distance, Apollo could tell it was Ancestral in origin, its design unlike anything from the current era.

"The Spire," Carver announced with evident pride. "The most advanced Ancestral facility still functioning in this region. It took me fifteen years to locate it and another five to access its systems."

As they drew closer, Apollo noticed something disturbing—a visible distortion in the air around the top of The Spire, like heat waves but more pronounced. Even without his dimensional perception, he could tell something was wrong with the fabric of reality at that point.

"You see it, don't you?" Carver observed, noting Apollo's expression. "The dimensional interface. It's growing stronger every day as we refine the calibration."

"It's not an interface," Apollo said. "It's a tear. You're ripping open the barriers between dimensions."

Carver waved a dismissive hand. "A temporary phase in the process. Once we achieve stable resonance, the distortion will resolve into a controlled gateway."

"You're wrong," Apollo insisted. "That's exactly what the Ancestrals tried before the Cataclysm. It doesn't stabilize—it cascades."

"We'll see who's right soon enough," Carver replied as the craft began its descent toward the complex.

They landed on a platform near the base of The Spire. Guards flanked Apollo, escorting him from the craft into a building adjacent to the main structure. Inside, the architecture was a strange blend of Ancestral design and modern adaptations—sleek metal corridors lined with technological equipment that hummed with power.

Apollo was led through a series of security checkpoints, each more elaborate than the last. Scientists and technicians moved purposefully through the complex, barely glancing at the prisoner being escorted through their midst. Finally, they reached a section that appeared to be a detention area, with reinforced doors lining a central corridor.

"Your accommodations," Carver announced as they stopped before one such door. "Specially designed for Veilborn containment. The entire chamber is lined with dimensional dampening technology."

The door slid open to reveal a small, austere room. A narrow bed, a basic washroom facility, and nothing else. No windows, no decorations, nothing that could be used as a tool or weapon.

"You'll remain here until we're ready to begin the testing process," Carver informed him. "I suggest you use the time to reconsider your position. Cooperation will make your experience here much more comfortable."

"Where are my friends?" Apollo demanded. "What have you done with them?"

"They're being processed according to their potential usefulness," Carver replied vaguely. "The young woman—Astra, is it?—shows some sensitivity to dimensional energies. Not Veilborn, but perhaps something we can work with. The others..." He shrugged. "We'll see."

Apollo lunged forward despite his restraints, fury overwhelming caution. "If you hurt them—"

Guards instantly seized him, forcing him back. Carver remained unmoved by the display.

"Your concern for them is touching, if misguided," he said. "Their fate depends entirely on you, Mr. Frost. Your cooperation could ensure their comfort. Your resistance..." He let the implication hang in the air.

Apollo was forced into the cell. The door slid shut behind him with a definitive click, leaving him alone in the sterile space.

Through the small window in the door, Carver's face appeared one last time. "Rest well, Apollo Frost. Tomorrow, we begin unraveling the secrets you carry in your blood. One way or another."

Then he was gone, footsteps receding down the corridor, leaving Apollo truly alone.

The cell's dimensional dampening was noticeable—a heavy, oppressive feeling that muffled Apollo's senses even beyond what the inhibitors imposed. He moved to the bed and sat down, head in his hands as the full weight of their failure descended upon him.

The trap had been perfectly executed. Carver had anticipated their route, prepared specifically for Veilborn abilities, and separated them before they could coordinate a response. Now Apollo was imprisoned in The

Spire itself—the very place they had been trying to reach, but as a captive rather than an infiltrator.

And his friends... scattered, possibly injured, their fates unknown. Astra being processed for "sensitivity to dimensional energies." Tristan and Alden's usefulness being evaluated. Verity unconscious and wounded.

Apollo lay back on the hard bed, staring at the featureless ceiling. The inhibitor collar chafed against his neck, a constant reminder of his powerlessness. Without his connection to the dimensional currents, he felt partially blind, a sense he'd come to rely on now absent.

Outside his cell, somewhere in this complex, Carver continued his dangerous experiments with The Spire. The tear in dimensional fabric Apollo had glimpsed was growing, destabilizing the barriers between worlds. If not stopped, it would eventually reach a critical point—and history would repeat itself in catastrophic fashion.

Apollo closed his eyes, exhaustion overtaking fear and anger. His last conscious thought was of Astra's face as she was dragged away, her eyes never leaving his until distance made connection impossible.

Tomorrow, Carver would begin his experiments. Tomorrow, Apollo would need every ounce of strength and wit he possessed.

But tonight, trapped in a cell designed specifically to contain him, with his friends scattered and the dimensional tear growing stronger by the hour, Apollo Frost had never felt more alone or more powerless.

13

——— • ———

FRACTURED PATHS

As Verity regained consciousness, she watched the hover transport carrying Apollo disappear over the ridge, her heart sinking with every beat. The dimensional inhibitors they'd placed on him would be excruciating—not merely blocking his abilities but severing his connection to what had become an essential sense. Like cutting off sight and sound simultaneously.

She shifted against her restraints, testing their strength. The guards had bound her wrists with standard cuffs rather than dimensional suppressors. They saw only an old woman, not a threat. Their mistake.

The transport carrying her, Tristan, and Alden bumped along the uneven terrain. Two guards sat opposite them, weapons trained casually in their direction. A third stood near the open rear hatch, watching the landscape recede behind them.

"Where are they taking Apollo?" Tristan demanded, straining against his restraints.

The guard closest to him smirked. "The Magistrate has special plans for your Veilborn friend."

"And the woman?" Alden asked, his voice controlled.

"Research division," the guard replied. "Preliminary tests showed some sensitivity."

Verity closed her eyes, letting the guards' conversation fade into background noise. She focused inward, seeking the faint threads of dimensional energy that still responded to her. Age had diminished her abilities, but decades of discipline compensated for what time had stolen.

Most people, even those who hunted Veilborn, didn't understand that dimensional sensitivity wasn't binary. It existed on a spectrum. Verity's grandmother had been fully Veilborn, her mother half, and Verity herself carried just enough of the genetic markers to perceive the dimmest outlines of what Apollo saw in vibrant detail.

Enough to be dangerous, if one knew how.

She reached for the thin dimensional current that ran beneath them—one of the old transit lines they'd been following before Carver's ambush. Its energy was weak but steady, like a stream compared to the river Apollo commanded.

Verity didn't need a river. A stream would suffice.

She opened her eyes, focusing on the landscape passing outside the transport. They were approaching a narrow ravine, the transport slowing as it navigated the tight passage. Perfect.

"We won't be separated for long," she said to Tristan and Alden. "When I act, be ready to move."

Alden's eyes widened in understanding, but Tristan looked confused.

"What can you possibly—"

"Quiet!" The guard snapped at Tristan.

Verity took a deep breath, drawing on decades of training and the techniques passed down through generations of her family. She couldn't manipulate dimensional energy with Apollo's raw power, but she could perform one final act of precision.

She reached for the tiny fold in her sleeve where she'd hidden a sliver of echo crystal. As her fingers brushed it, she felt the stored dimensional pattern respond, amplifying her connection to the current below.

The transport entered the ravine, rock walls rising on both sides.

Now.

Verity closed her eyes and pulled on the dimensional current, not to manipulate space but to create a targeted disruption in the transport's power systems. The vehicle lurched violently, alarms blaring as the engine sputtered and died.

"What the hell?" The driver shouted from the front compartment.

The guard by the rear hatch stumbled, momentarily losing his balance as the transport ground to a halt.

Verity moved with a speed that belied her years. She twisted her wrists, sliding one hand free of the loosened cuffs, and lunged toward the off-bal- ance guard. Her fingers found the pressure point at his neck—another skill from her Order days, before she'd questioned their purpose—and he collapsed unconscious.

The other guards raised their weapons, but Verity had grabbed the fallen guard's weapon. She fired twice, hitting the control panel on the transport's ceiling. Sparks showered down as emergency protocols engaged, automatically releasing the prisoners' restraints.

"Run!" she shouted to Tristan and Alden, tossing the weapon to Tristan. "Down the ravine! There's a fork fifty yards ahead—take the left path!"

Tristan caught the weapon and hesitated only a moment before grabbing Alden's arm and pulling him toward the exit.

The young men disappeared down the ravine as Verity turned to face the guards. Her vision was blurring, blood trickling from her nose.

"Stop them!" one guard shouted, leaping from the transport.

Verity picked up the fallen guard's sidearm and fired at the ravine wall above the pursuing guard. Rock shattered, cascading down and blocking the narrow passage.

More guards poured from the front of the transport. Verity backed away, firing to keep them at bay while retreating toward the ravine. She knew she couldn't escape—her purpose now was delay, creating time for the others to get beyond pursuit.

A searing agony consumed her shoulder as one of the guard's blasts struck home. Verity stumbled but kept moving, each step taking her farther from the transport and buying precious seconds for Tristan and Alden.

She reached the fork in the ravine and took the right path—away from where she'd sent the others. Behind her, she heard the guards organizing a pursuit. She fired at the ravine ceiling, bringing down more rocks to slow them.

The pain in her shoulder spread across her chest, her breath coming in ragged gasps. She pressed on, knowing exactly where this path led.

Five minutes later, Verity reached a dead end where the ravine walls rose sheer on three sides. She turned to face her pursuers, hearing their footsteps echoing off the stone walls. Blood soaked her tunic, but she stood straight, reaching into her pocket for the last echo crystal she carried.

This one was special—her grandmother's final gift, containing a powerful dimensional pattern meant for the direst circumstances. Using it would consume the crystal and likely cripple her in her weakened state. But it would serve its purpose.

The first guards rounded the corner, weapons raised.

"Surrender, old woman," their leader called. "There's nowhere to go."

Verity smiled, the crystal warm between her fingers. "You're right about one thing," she said. "I'm not going anywhere."

She crushed the crystal in her palm, releasing the stored pattern. Dimensional energy surged through her body, more than she had ever channeled before. The pain was excruciating, but she shaped the energy with practiced precision, creating not a fold but a cascading dimensional disruption.

The ravine walls began to shimmer, reality itself becoming unstable around them.

"What are you doing?" The guard backed away, fear replacing confidence.

"Buying time," Verity whispered, though no one could hear her now over the growing roar of shifting stone.

The disruption spread outward from her position, destabilizing the molecular bonds in the rock. The ravine walls began to collapse, not in a simple rockfall but in a controlled implosion that would seal this section completely while leaving the fork where Tristan and Alden had gone untouched.

As the stone fell around her, Verity thought of Apollo—the boy with more raw talent than she had ever seen, the hope for a future where Veilborn and dimensional knowledge might be restored. She had done what she could to prepare him. Now his path was his own.

The dimensional energy consumed her, burning through her cells as the ravine collapsed. In her final moments of consciousness, Verity reached out with her fading perception, seeking the transport that had carried Astra.

There—a flicker of familiar energy. The girl had managed to activate her pendant's dimensional stabilizer. Good.

Verity had always known her role in this story would be temporary. She was the bridge between past and future, the keeper of knowledge until the right person came to claim it. Now that person had come, and her duty was fulfilled.

As darkness closed around her, Verity smiled. The Order had taught her that duty required sacrifice. They had been right about that, at least, though wrong about so much else.

Her last thought was of her grandmother, who had hidden her Veilborn nature to survive the Purge, who had passed down her knowledge in secret, waiting for the day when the truth could emerge again.

I did my part, Grandmother. The rest is up to them.

The dimensional disruption reached its peak, collapsing the ravine entirely and sealing Elder Verity's final resting place beneath tons of stone—and with it, any pursuit of those she had given her life to save.

The dimensional suppressor's effect washed over Astra like ice water. She'd felt this sensation before, during Order training exercises—the nauseating emptiness where dimensional currents should flow. But this time, Carver's device was far more powerful than anything the Order had developed.

Astra's hands were bound behind her back, the restraints cutting into her wrists. The guard shoved her inside the second transport. She lurched ahead. The pendant in her back pocket felt warm—not the usual subtle heat, but an urgent pulse.

"Move," the guard growled, pushing her again.

Astra caught herself, feigning weakness. "Please," she whispered. "I need a moment."

The guard hesitated, and in that brief pause, Astra pressed her bound hands against the small of her back, fingers searching for the hidden clasp of her pendant chain in her pocket. The family heirloom had always been more than jewelry—her mother had made that clear when she'd placed it around Astra's neck years ago.

"If dimensional currents ever falter around you, the stabilizer will activate. It creates a small pocket of normalized dimensional space. Use it only when there is no other choice."

This was that moment.

Her fingertips found the clasp, and with precision, she pressed the hidden mechanism. The pendant grew hot against her skin, and suddenly Astra could breathe again—the dimensional currents flowing around her in a small bubble while Carver's suppressor continued to affect everything else.

The guard noticed her straightening. "I said move—"

Astra spun, her elbow connecting with his throat. The dimensional pocket gave her a split-second advantage—her movements were fluid while he seemed to react in slow motion. She followed with a sharp kick to his knee. Before he could call out, she drove her knee into his temple, and watched him collapse.

Astra worked fast, using the guard's key to unlock her restraints before dragging him behind a boulder.

She had perhaps twenty seconds before someone noticed. Astra slipped into the shadows of the ravine, her Order training taking over. She moved silently along the rocky edge, staying low. The stabilizer's effect wouldn't last long—she could feel the dimensional pocket fluctuating as Carver's suppressor tried to overcome it.

A shout went up. They'd discovered the missing guard.

Astra broke into a run, darting between boulders and scrub brush. Ahead, the ravine split into two paths. She hesitated, glancing back to see guards fanning out, weapons raised. The left path offered more cover, but the right seemed to lead higher up the ridge.

The sound of a transport engine made the decision for her. She veered right, scrambling up the steep incline. The pendant pulsed against her skin, its power beginning to fade. Without its protection, she'd be as vulnerable as any non-Veilborn to Carver's technology.

Behind her, the guards shouted. A beam of energy struck the rock beside her head, sending stone fragments flying. Astra pressed herself against the ravine wall, breathing hard.

Astra scanned the ravine floor and spotted Verity creating some kind of distraction near the left fork. Guards converged on her position.

Astra needed to move. The stabilizer's dimensional pocket was collapsing, and when it failed completely, Carver's men would detect her. She pushed off from the wall and continued upward, finding handholds in the rough stone.

A tremor shook the ravine. Astra looked back to see a blinding flash of light where Verity had been standing. The ground heaved, and the entire left fork of the ravine began to collapse, taking several guards with it. Verity was nowhere to be seen.

The dimensional disturbance from whatever Verity had done rippled outward. Astra's pendant responded, drawing energy from the wave and briefly strengthening her protective bubble. She used the moment to pull herself over the ridge's edge, rolling onto flat ground just as weapons fire scorched the spot where she'd been climbing.

Astra ran, staying low among the scattered boulders. The ridge offered little cover, but the confusion below bought her precious seconds. She sprinted toward a stand of twisted trees about two hundred yards ahead, the only significant cover in sight.

Her pendant grew cold against her skin. The stabilizer had exhausted itself. Carver's dimensional suppressor washed over her again, but weaker now—she was moving beyond its effective range.

A transport rose above the ridge behind her, searchlight sweeping the ground. Astra dove beneath a fallen log as the light passed over her position. She lay perfectly still, controlling her breathing as her Order training had taught her.

The transport hovered, its engines a low drone in the night air. Astra closed her eyes, focusing on the faint dimensional currents that were beginning to return. They were weak and distorted—Carver's work at The Spire was affecting everything—but they were there.

After what seemed an eternity, the transport moved on, continuing its search pattern away from her position. Astra waited five more minutes before moving again, making her way to the trees.

From the relative safety of the small grove, she assessed her situation. Apollo had been taken to The Spire. Tristan and Alden were on another transport, destination unknown. Verity had likely sacrificed herself to cover their escape. And Astra was alone, without supplies, in territory controlled by Carver's forces.

She removed her pendant, examining it in the moonlight. The silver-blue metal was dull now, its power temporarily depleted. It would recharge eventually, drawing energy from ambient dimensional currents, but that would take time they didn't have.

"I'll find you," she whispered, thinking of Apollo. The memory of their kiss the previous night pierced her heart with longing. She tucked the pendant back beneath her shirt.

First, she needed to locate Tristan and Alden. Then together, they would find a way to reach Apollo before Carver could use him for whatever terrible purpose he had planned.

Astra oriented herself using the stars and the faint dimensional currents. The eastern representatives would still be heading for the waystation. If she could reach it before them, she might secure allies for a rescue mission.

With renewed determination, Astra Shaw slipped away into the night, a shadow moving through a world increasingly distorted by Carver's dimensional tampering.

The ravine floor crumbled beneath Tristan's feet as he sprinted forward, loose stones skittering down the embankment. Alden stumbled beside him, glasses askew, breath coming in ragged gasps. Behind them, the sound of pursuit faded—replaced by the sickening rumble of collapsing earth.

"Keep moving!" Tristan grabbed Alden's arm, hauling him around a sharp bend in the narrow path. The Order guards had been disoriented by Elder Verity's distraction, giving them precious seconds to escape the transport.

"Did you see where they took Apollo?" Alden wheezed, clutching his side.

"No. Different transport." Tristan pulled them both into the shadow of an outcropping as dust billowed through the ravine. "Verity said to take the left fork."

The ground shook again. A deafening crack split the air, followed by a thunderous cascade of rock and soil. Tristan pressed his back against the stone wall, pulling Alden with him as a cloud of dust engulfed them. For several moments, they could only cough and shield their eyes.

When the air began to clear, Tristan peered back the way they'd come. The ravine was gone—filled with rubble and fallen boulders. No one could follow them now.

But that meant...

"Verity," Alden whispered, coming to the same realization. "She went right to draw them away."

Tristan's chest tightened. "She knew what she was doing."

"She couldn't have survived that." Alden removed his glasses, wiping grit from the lenses with shaking hands.

Tristan said nothing. He'd seen the determination in the old woman's eyes when she'd pressed a small bundle into his hands before they'd split up. "For when you're safe," she'd said. "You'll know what to do with it."

He patted the inside pocket of his jacket, feeling the hard edges of whatever Verity had given him. There would be time to examine it later.

"We need to keep moving," Tristan said, scanning their surroundings. "Find high ground, figure out where we are."

"What about Astra?" Alden replaced his glasses, blinking.

"If anyone can take care of herself, it's her." Tristan hoped he sounded more confident than he felt. "Come on."

They followed the narrow path as it wound upward through the ravine. Tristan's smithing muscles served him well as they climbed, but Alden struggled, his scholar's build not made for this kind of exertion. Tristan paused often, offering a hand or shoulder when needed.

After nearly an hour of climbing, they emerged onto a forested ridge overlooking a vast valley. In the distance, a massive structure rose from the landscape—unlike anything Tristan had seen before.

"The Spire," Alden breathed, leaning against a tree trunk. "That's where Carver's conducting his experiments."

"And where they've taken Apollo." Tristan's hands clenched into fists. The sight of those dimensional inhibitors being locked around his friend's wrists and neck had made his blood boil.

"We need shelter," Alden said, practical despite his exhaustion. "Somewhere to regroup, make a plan."

Tristan nodded, tearing his gaze from The Spire. "There's a line of trees heading east. Might be following a stream. Water, cover, and distance from that place."

They set off through the forest, moving as swiftly as caution allowed. Tristan kept them to the densest parts of the woods, avoiding clearings where Carver's hover transports might spot them. His father had taught him how to move through forests when hunting, and now those lessons might save their lives.

The sun was low on the horizon when they found the stream. Tristan knelt, cupping his hands to drink the cold, clear water. Alden collapsed beside him, dunking his entire head beneath the surface before coming up sputtering.

"Feel better?" Tristan asked.

"Like I've been dragged behind a plow horse," Alden admitted. "But alive."

Tristan surveyed their surroundings. "We need to find shelter before dark."

"What about that?" Alden pointed upstream where the water disappeared into a shadowy recess beneath an overhanging rock face.

Tristan approached cautiously. The overhang created a shallow cave, dry and hidden from view by a curtain of hanging vines. He pushed the vegetation aside, peering into the darkness.

"It'll do," he decided. "No signs of animals. Big enough for us to stretch out."

They gathered fallen branches and leaves to create makeshift bedding, then collected some edible berries Alden identified from a nearby thicket. It wasn't much of a meal, but neither had the energy to hunt for more.

As darkness fell, Tristan pulled out the bundle Verity had given him. Unwrapping the cloth revealed a small metallic cylinder and what appeared to be an echo crystal, similar to the ones they'd found at the Nexus.

"What is it?" Alden asked, leaning closer.

"Not sure." Tristan turned the cylinder in his hands. Unlike most Ancestral technology, this felt familiar somehow. His fingers found indentations that seemed made for human hands.

The cylinder clicked, then expanded into a compact tool with various attachments. Tristan recognized the design.

"It's a multi-tool," he said, surprised. "Like what I use in the forge, but... better."

Alden examined the echo crystal. "This one's been used recently. See how it's glowing?"

Tristan set down the tool and took the crystal. When he touched it, the surface flickered with light. A moment later, Elder Verity's voice filled their small shelter.

"If you're hearing this, then I've succeeded in helping you escape." Her voice was calm, steady. "And I am most likely gone."

Tristan and Alden exchanged pained glances.

"Don't mourn me," Verity continued. "I've lived far longer than most who defied the Order. Listen carefully now. The tool I've left you is Ancestral, designed for Resonants like you, Tristan. It will respond to your touch in ways it wouldn't for others. You'll need it to help Apollo."

Tristan picked up the tool again, feeling a subtle vibration when he held it.

"Alden, your knowledge will be crucial in the days ahead. Trust what you've learned. The answers are often in plain sight if we know how to read them." Verity paused. "Astra carries more knowledge than she's shared. When you find her—and you will—tell her it's time for the full truth."

The crystal's light pulsed.

"Apollo is the key. Carver knows this, which is why he took him. The Spire was once a stabilization point for dimensional energies, but Carver's experiments have corrupted its purpose. He seeks to harness dimensional power without understanding its nature. If he succeeds in using Apollo to amplify his work, we face another Cataclysm."

Tristan's grip tightened on the tool. Memories of Apollo as a boy, always curious, always kind despite being different, flashed through his mind.

"You must reach Apollo before Carver breaks through his mental defenses. A Veilborn's power comes from within—the inhibitors can only suppress, not eliminate his abilities. With the right catalyst, Apollo can overcome them."

The crystal's glow began to fade.

"One last thing," Verity's voice grew softer. "Tell Apollo... tell him I believe he is exactly what this broken world needs. Not just for his power, but for his heart. Now go. Be brave. Be clever. And may the currents guide you."

The crystal went dark, leaving them in silence broken only by the soft gurgle of the stream outside.

Alden removed his glasses, wiping moisture from his eyes. "She knew she wouldn't make it."

"She chose to give us a chance." Tristan tucked the crystal and tool back into the cloth, securing them in his pocket. "We can't waste it."

Sleep came fitfully that night. Tristan kept waking, certain he'd heard the hum of hover transports or the footsteps of Order guards. Each time, he found only the quiet forest and Alden's soft snoring.

Dawn brought the chirping of birds and a renewed sense of purpose. They were washing in the stream when a twig snapped in the forest behind them.

Tristan whirled, grabbing a heavy stone from the streambed. Alden froze mid-splash, eyes wide behind water-speckled glasses.

A figure emerged from the trees, moving with cautious grace.

"Astra," Tristan breathed, lowering the stone.

She looked haggard—her clothing torn, a bruise darkening one cheek, her normally neat braid unraveling. But her eyes were sharp as ever, taking in their condition with a quick glance.

"You're alive." Relief softened her voice. "I've been tracking you since dawn."

"How did you escape?" Alden asked, splashing to the bank.

"My pendant." Astra touched the silver-blue object at her throat. "It creates a small pocket of normalized dimensional space. Enough to counter Carver's suppressor temporarily."

She looked past them, scanning the area. "Where's Verity?"

Tristan's jaw tightened. "She didn't make it."

Astra's composure cracked. For a moment, genuine grief transformed her face, making her look younger, more vulnerable. Then the mask slipped back into place.

"Tell me," she said.

They led her to their shelter, sharing what little food remained as Tristan recounted their escape and Verity's sacrifice. When he mentioned the crystal message, Astra's hand went to her pendant.

"She said you need to tell us the full truth," Alden prompted gently.

Astra sat cross-legged at the mouth of their small cave, staring at the flowing water. "Yes. It's time."

She took a deep breath. "I haven't been entirely honest about my knowledge or capabilities. The Order trains its members extensively in Ancestral technology and dimensional theory—not to use it, but to identify and contain it."

"You know how The Spire works," Tristan guessed.

Astra nodded. "It's one of seven major stabilization points created after early dimensional experiments went wrong. The Ancestors learned that certain locations had natural dimensional resonance. They built The Spire and others like it to harness and regulate that energy."

"And Carver's corrupting it," Alden said.

"Worse. He's trying to reverse its function—to open dimensional pathways rather than stabilize them." Astra's fingers traced patterns in the dirt. "The Order has archives detailing The Spire's construction. I memorized the schematics years ago when I first suspected something was wrong."

Tristan leaned forward. "So you know how to get in."

"And how to shut it down," Astra confirmed. "But we'd need Apollo. The system was designed to respond to Veilborn energy signatures."

"Apollo's wearing inhibitors," Alden reminded them.

Astra's eyes met Tristan's. "That's where you come in. The inhibitors are Ancestral technology, modified by the Order. A Resonant with the right tools could disable them."

Tristan pulled out Verity's multi-tool. "Like this?"

Astra's eyebrows rose. "Exactly like that. It's a Resonant Interface Tool—designed to help non-Veilborn work with dimensional technology."

"How do we get into The Spire?" Alden asked, pushing his glasses up his nose. "It'll be heavily guarded."

"There are maintenance tunnels," Astra said. "Built to allow technicians access to the core systems without disrupting the main energy flows. They're not on any current maps the Order uses."

"So we sneak in, find Apollo, free him, and then what?" Tristan asked.

"Apollo needs to reverse what Carver's done," Astra explained. "The dimensional tear I saw forming means he's already destabilized the core. If Apollo can access the control systems, he can reestablish the proper frequency patterns."

Tristan stood, pacing the small space. "We need weapons. Supplies."

"There's an old Ancestral outpost about half a day's journey east," Astra said. "Similar to Elian's, but abandoned during the Purge. It might have what we need."

"How do you know about it?" Alden asked.

"Order records." Astra's mouth twisted. "They documented everything they destroyed."

They set out immediately, following Astra's lead through the forest. The day grew warm, sunlight filtering through the canopy above. Despite their dire situation, Tristan found himself appreciating the simple fact of their survival. Elder Verity had given them that gift.

Verity. The loss hit him in waves. She had been stern but kind, her knowledge vast yet practical. In the time he'd known her, she'd treated him with respect, recognizing his abilities when others saw only a village blacksmith. She'd believed in them—enough to die for their chance to succeed.

By midday, they reached a small clearing where the ruins of a stone structure stood partially reclaimed by vegetation. Unlike the grand Ancestral facilities they'd seen before, this was modest—a simple outbuilding with a partially collapsed roof.

"This is it?" Tristan couldn't keep the disappointment from his voice.

"Appearances can be deceiving," Astra said, approaching what looked like a solid stone wall. She pressed her palm against a weathered symbol barely visible beneath a tangle of vines.

Nothing happened.

Astra frowned. "The power must be completely drained." She turned to Tristan. "This is where you come in. There should be a manual access panel somewhere along this wall."

Tristan examined the stonework, running his fingers along the seams. Near the base of the wall, he felt a slight difference in texture. Kneeling, he cleared away decades of accumulated soil to reveal a small metal plate.

The multi-tool seemed to warm in his hand as he approached the panel. When he touched the tool to the metal, a compartment slid open, revealing a hand-sized depression with mechanical components.

"It's a Resonant lock," Astra explained. "Designed as a backup when dimensional energy wasn't available."

Tristan placed his hand in the depression. Nothing happened at first, then he felt a subtle vibration. The sensation reminded him of working with certain metals in the forge—the way some alloys seemed to respond differently to his touch than to his father's.

The stone wall shuddered, then slid aside to reveal a dark passage leading underground.

"How did you do that?" Alden asked, amazement in his voice.

Tristan shrugged, uncomfortable with the attention. "Just felt right."

Astra produced a small light from her pocket. "The facility should be at the bottom of these stairs. If we're lucky, the lower levels still have emergency power."

They descended into darkness, the air growing cooler with each step. At the bottom, Astra's light revealed a dusty chamber filled with workbenches and storage units. Unlike the weathered exterior, the underground facility had been preserved, protected from the elements.

Tristan moved to the nearest workbench, running his hands over tools that looked both familiar and alien. Some resembled his blacksmith's implements—hammers, tongs, cutters—but with subtle differences that suggested capabilities beyond simple metalworking.

"This was a Resonant workshop," Astra explained, opening storage compartments. "Where they created and maintained technology that worked alongside Veilborn abilities."

"Look at this," Alden called from across the room. He stood before a wall of diagrams—technical schematics etched into metal plates. "These show how dimensional inhibitors work."

Tristan joined him, studying the detailed drawings. The inhibitors consisted of interlocking bands of specialized metal with embedded crystals that disrupted the wearer's connection to dimensional energy.

"Can you build something to counteract them?" Astra asked, setting her light on the workbench.

Tristan examined the schematics. "Maybe. These show the weak points in the design." He pointed to junctions where the components connected. "If I could create something to disrupt these connection points..."

"There should be materials here," Astra said, continuing to search the storage units. "The Ancestors were thorough in their preparations."

While Astra gathered supplies, Alden discovered a small power cell that still held charge. When connected to the facility's systems, lights flickered on, revealing the full extent of the workshop.

Tristan lost himself in the work, the familiar focus of creation settling over him. The Ancestral tools responded to his touch in ways that felt natural, as though they'd been waiting for him. He selected materials from Astra's growing pile—specialized alloys, crystalline components, power cells—combining them according to both the schematics and his own intuition.

Hours passed. Alden brought food—preserved rations he'd found in a storage locker—but Tristan barely paused to eat. The work consumed him, each component fitting together with satisfying precision.

By nightfall, he had created three devices: a slender rod designed to disrupt the inhibitor locks, a small shield generator that could deflect energy weapons, and a compact stunner that could incapacitate guards.

"These are remarkable," Astra said, examining his creations. "You have a natural gift for this work."

Tristan shrugged off the compliment, uncomfortable with praise. "Will they get us to Apollo?"

"They give us a chance." Astra activated the shield generator, a shimmer of energy briefly surrounding her hand. "More than we had this morning."

Alden spread out rough diagrams of The Spire he'd compiled from Astra's descriptions. "We should finalize our plan."

They gathered around the workbench as Astra detailed The Spire's layout. "The maintenance tunnels enter here, near the power distribution nodes. Security will be lightest there—the Order doesn't believe anyone understands the systems well enough to sabotage them."

"Where would they keep Apollo?" Tristan asked.

Astra's finger traced a path to the central chamber. "The containment cells are adjacent to the core. Carver will want Apollo close to the dimensional interface."

"And the tear you saw?" Alden asked.

"Here." Astra indicated the top of the structure. "Where the energy normally disperses into the atmosphere. Carver's reversed the flow, pulling dimensional energy inward instead of regulating its release."

Tristan studied the layout, memorizing the routes.

"We should rest," Alden suggested. "Start fresh in the morning."

Tristan nodded, though he doubted sleep would come easily. Every time he closed his eyes, he saw Apollo being dragged away, dimensional inhibitors dulling the light that always seemed to surround him.

As Alden prepared sleeping areas from materials found in the facility, Tristan stepped away to examine his creations one final time. Each component needed to work perfectly—Apollo's life depended on it.

"He's strong," Astra said, joining him at the workbench. "Stronger than Carver knows."

"He's my friend," Tristan replied. "Has been since we were children. I used to protect him from village bullies who thought he was strange." He picked up the disruption rod, testing its weight. "Never thought I'd be trying to save him from someone trying to end the world."

"Verity believed in him," Astra said. "In all of you."

Tristan's throat tightened. "She shouldn't have died alone."

"She didn't." Astra's voice was soft but certain. "Verity was connected to the dimensional currents in her final moments. She felt every Veilborn who came before her. She wasn't alone."

The thought brought unexpected comfort. Tristan nodded, unable to speak.

"Get some rest," Astra said. "Tomorrow, we bring Apollo home."

As Tristan settled onto the makeshift bed Alden had prepared, his mind turned not to the dangers ahead, but to the forge in Willowbrook. The simple pleasure of heating metal until it glowed, shaping it with hammer and anvil into something useful, beautiful, enduring.

When this was over—if they survived—he would build something to honor Verity. Something that would last.

With that thought, he closed his eyes, the weight of the day pulling him toward sleep. His last conscious thought was of Apollo's face when they'd first discovered the resonance compass—filled with wonder and possibility.

That was what they were fighting for. The chance for that wonder to continue.

Morning arrived. They ate a sparse breakfast of preserved rations, then gathered their equipment. Tristan distributed the devices he'd created, showing Alden and Astra how to use each one.

"The stunner has three charges," he explained. "Aim for center mass—it doesn't need to be precise."

Alden handled the weapon awkwardly. "I've never used anything like this."

"Hope you won't need to," Tristan said. "But better to have it."

They emerged from the facility into dawn light. Birds sang in the forest canopy, oblivious to the impending crisis. In the distance, The Spire rose against the sky, its unnatural symmetry a stark contrast to the surrounding landscape.

"How long to reach it?" Tristan asked, securing his tools in a pack Astra had found.

"Four hours if we move quickly," Astra replied. "We should approach from the east—there's more cover, and the maintenance entrance faces that direction."

As they prepared to leave, Tristan took a final look at the Resonant workshop. For generations, people like him had worked alongside Veil-born, creating wonders that benefited everyone. That partnership had been forgotten, buried beneath fear and superstition.

Perhaps, if they succeeded, that could change.

"Ready?" Astra asked, her pendant glinting in the morning light.

Tristan nodded, thinking of the village smithy, of Apollo's curious questions, of Elder Verity's sacrifice.

"Let's bring him home."

14

— · —

Currents Within

Apollo's cell was a perfect cube—three paces in each direction with walls of polished gray stone that seemed to absorb both sound and hope. The only break in the monotony was a narrow slot at the bottom of the door for meal trays and a small ventilation grate near the ceiling. No windows. No natural light. Just the steady, blue-white glow of artificial illumination that never dimmed.

He sat cross-legged on the thin mattress, trying to ignore the weight of the inhibitors clasped around his wrists and neck. Each device was a masterpiece of Ancestral technology corrupted to a new purpose—slim bands of dark metal inlaid with intricate circuitry that pulsed with a sickly green light. Their effect was like a heavy blanket thrown over his senses, muffling the dimensional currents he'd only recently learned to perceive.

Three days. Three days since Carver had separated him from his friends. Three days of isolation broken only by silent guards delivering bland meals and Magister Marzen's clinical examinations.

Apollo closed his eyes, trying again to reach beyond the inhibitors' suppression. It was like trying to see through murky water—the dimensional currents were there, but distant and distorted. The resonator Verity had given him was gone, confiscated along with his compass, tuner and everything else he'd carried. He wondered if Astra had managed to escape, if Tristan and Alden were safe, if Verity had survived. The not knowing was almost worse than the confinement.

The lock on his door clicked, breaking his concentration. Apollo opened his eyes as the heavy metal door swung inward. Two guards entered, weapons ready, followed by Magistrate Carver himself.

Carver looked immaculate as always—not a wrinkle in his dark formal attire, not a hair out of place. The only sign of his obsession was the feverish intensity in his eyes.

"Comfortable, Apollo?" Carver asked, his tone falsely solicitous. "I apologize for the accommodations, but safety protocols must be observed when dealing with Veilborn."

Apollo remained seated, refusing to stand in Carver's presence. "Where are my friends?"

"Your companions are being well treated," Carver said, the lie obvious in his casual dismissal. "Those who survived, at least. The old woman proved... troublesome."

Apollo's stomach twisted. "Verity?"

"A pity. She possessed knowledge that could have been useful." Carver stepped further into the cell, hands clasped behind his back. "But I have you, which is far more valuable."

"I won't help you destabilize the dimensions," Apollo said.

Carver smiled. "You misunderstand my work. I'm not destabilizing anything—I'm fulfilling the Ancestrals' vision. Opening doorways they only dreamed of."

"I've seen the tear above The Spire. Whatever you're doing is damaging the dimensional barriers."

"A temporary side effect," Carver waved his hand dismissively. "Once I have proper control, once I understand how your abilities function, the instabilities will resolve."

Apollo noticed something he hadn't before—a ring on Carver's right hand that seemed to shimmer with subdued dimensional energy. Despite the inhibitors, he could sense its wrongness, like a discordant note in music.

"I've brought you something," Carver continued, nodding to one of the guards who placed a small device on the floor. It resembled a metallic hemisphere about the size of Apollo's palm. "A recording of yesterday's test. I thought you might appreciate seeing what we've accomplished."

The device activated, projecting a three-dimensional image that filled the center of the cell. Apollo saw The Spire's main chamber—a vast circular room dominated by a central column of swirling energy. In the recording, technicians worked at various stations while Marzen directed their efforts.

"Initiating dimensional probe," Marzen's voice echoed from the device. "Targeting frequency seven-three-nine."

The column of energy pulsed, then expanded outward. For a moment, the air within the column seemed to fold, revealing glimpses of somewhere else—a landscape of impossible geometry and shifting colors.

"Stabilize the aperture," Marzen commanded.

The technicians adjusted controls, but the dimensional window began to fluctuate wildly. Alarms sounded as the energy column collapsed, sending a shockwave through the chamber that knocked several technicians off their feet.

"Containment failure," someone shouted. "Dimensional bleedthrough detected!"

The recording ended abruptly.

"Impressive, isn't it?" Carver said. "We can open the doorway, but maintaining it proves challenging. That's where you come in."

Apollo looked up at Carver. "You're trying to access higher dimensions directly. That's what caused the Cataclysm."

"A simplistic understanding," Carver scoffed. "The Ancestrals failed because they lacked proper control mechanisms. I have spent decades collecting artifacts, studying the dimensional patterns. With your genetic material and abilities, we can perfect the process."

"My genetic material?" Apollo tensed.

"Marzen has been analyzing your blood samples. Fascinating structures—specialized cellular components that resonate with dimensional energies. We're developing a serum that may replicate some aspects of Veilborn physiology."

Apollo felt sick. "And if it doesn't work?"

"Then we'll need to be more... invasive in our research." Carver's smile never reached his eyes. "I suggest cooperation. It would be less painful for everyone."

He turned to leave, then paused at the door. "Oh, and don't waste energy trying to bypass the inhibitors. They're calibrated specifically to your dimensional frequency range. Even attempting to manipulate energy will trigger an unpleasant neural response."

After Carver and his guards left, Apollo remained motionless, processing what he'd learned. Carver wasn't just experimenting—he was trying to create artificial Veilborn abilities through some kind of serum. And the dimensional tear above The Spire was growing, just as Alden had warned.

Apollo closed his eyes again, focusing on the inhibitors. If they were calibrated to his "frequency range," perhaps there were frequencies they didn't suppress. The training at the Nexus had taught him that dimensional energy existed across a spectrum—maybe he could find gaps in the inhibitors' coverage.

He started with the lightest touch he could manage, just brushing against the dimensional currents at frequencies far higher than he normally used. The inhibitors tightened, sending a jolt of pain through his nervous system that left him gasping.

Too direct. He needed subtlety.

Apollo waited for his breathing to steady, then tried again with a different approach. Instead of reaching outward toward the currents, he turned his awareness inward, focusing on the energy that naturally flowed through his own body. The inhibitors were designed to prevent him from drawing external dimensional energy—but what about the energy within him?

He felt a flicker of response—faint but definite. The inhibitors hummed but didn't activate their painful countermeasure. It wasn't much, but it was something. A starting point.

A scraping sound from the ventilation grate interrupted his concentration. Apollo looked up to see fingers curling around the metal slats.

"Psst," came a whisper. "Can you hear me?"

Apollo rose and moved to stand beneath the grate. It was positioned just above his head height.

"Yes," he whispered back. "Who are you?"

"Another guest of Carver's hospitality," the voice replied—male, with an accent Apollo couldn't place. "Been listening to the guards talk. You're the Veilborn they captured, aren't you?"

Apollo hesitated before answering. "Yes."

A soft chuckle came through the grate. "Never thought I'd live to meet one. Name's Cyrus. Former researcher at Carver's little workshop of horrors."

"You worked for Carver?" Apollo froze, suddenly suspicious.

"Until I developed a conscience," Cyrus replied. "Questioned his methods, got too close to understanding what he's really doing. Next thing I know, I'm enjoying these luxurious accommodations."

"What is he really doing?" Apollo asked.

There was a pause before Cyrus answered. "Creating a dimensional breach large enough to access what he calls 'the Source.' He believes it's a realm of pure energy that would give him unlimited power."

"The Source," Apollo repeated, remembering what Verity had taught him. "The highest dimensions."

"You understand, then. The dimensional barriers exist for a reason. The Ancestrals learned that the hard way."

Apollo moved closer to the grate again. "How long have you been here?"

"Months, maybe. Hard to keep track. They take me to the lab sometimes, make me verify calculations. I try to introduce errors when I can, but Marzen's getting suspicious."

"My friends will come for me," Apollo said, though he wasn't sure if he believed it.

"Hope so," Cyrus replied. "Because Carver's getting close. That last test you saw? They've never gotten that far before. The aperture actually stabilized for 3.8 seconds."

Apollo thought of the tear he'd seen above The Spire. "And if he succeeds?"

"Remember the Cataclysm? Imagine that, but worse. Much worse." Cyrus's fingers tightened on the grate. "Listen, I don't have much time. The guard rotation changes soon. But I can help you—I know this facility, and I know Carver's research."

"How? These cells are isolated."

"The ventilation system connects to the old maintenance tunnels. I've been working on loosening this grate for weeks. Almost there."

Apollo glanced at the inhibitors on his wrists. "Even if you get out, I'm trapped by these."

"Ancestral tech, modified by Marzen," Cyrus said. "I helped design the prototype. They have a resonance flaw—if exposed to the right frequency, they'll deactivate."

Hope flickered in Apollo's chest. "What frequency?"

"That's the problem. It's specific to each set, and I'd need equipment to determine it." Cyrus paused. "But there might be another way. The inhibitors suppress external dimensional manipulation, but they weren't designed to block internal energy pathways."

"I was just thinking the same thing," Apollo said.

"Great minds," Cyrus chuckled. "Look, if you can generate even a small dimensional current within yourself, you might be able to gradually weaken the connection points where the inhibitors interface with your nervous system."

Apollo considered this. "It would take time."

"Time we might not have. Carver's planning something big tomorrow—some kind of demonstration for his backers. I overheard Marzen talking about 'harvesting' more of your genetic material."

A shudder coursed through Apollo's body as he processed what that meant. "I'll work on the inhibitors. What about you?"

"Two more days, and I'll have this grate loose. Then we find a way to stop Carver." Cyrus's voice dropped even lower. "Someone's coming. We'll talk again tonight."

The fingers disappeared from the grate, leaving Apollo alone once more.

He retreated to his thin mattress. If what Cyrus said was true, Carver was closer to causing another Cataclysm than any of them had realized. And tomorrow, they planned to take more than just blood samples.

Apollo closed his eyes and focused inward again, searching for the internal dimensional currents that flowed through his body. This time, he wasn't trying to manipulate external energy—just become aware of what existed within him.

Systematically, he followed the streams of power flowing from his center through to his extremities. When he reached the points where the inhibitors touched his skin, he could feel the disruption they caused—like dams blocking a river. But no dam was perfect. There were always small seepages, tiny flows that made it through.

Apollo concentrated on those minute currents, trying to gradually strengthen them without triggering the inhibitors' countermeasures. It was delicate work, requiring more precision than anything he'd attempted before. Each time the inhibitors began to hum in warning, he would back off, wait, then try a slightly different approach.

Hours passed as he worked, the artificial lights never changing, giving no indication of time's passage. His only marker was the arrival of a meal tray—some kind of grain porridge and a cup of water—pushed through the slot in his door.

By what he guessed was evening, Apollo had managed to establish a subtle flow of dimensional energy that bypassed the inhibitors' suppression. It wasn't enough to manipulate anything external, but it was a start—a foundation he could build upon.

As he ate the bland porridge, Apollo wondered about his friends. Had Astra escaped? Were Tristan and Alden planning a rescue? And Verity—was she truly gone? Carver could have been lying to demoralize him.

A soft tap at the ventilation grate interrupted his thoughts.

"Apollo?" Cyrus whispered. "You still there?"

"Yes," Apollo moved to stand beneath the grate again.

"Good. The night shift is on duty now—they're less attentive. We can talk more freely."

Apollo looked up at the shadowed figure behind the grate. "Tell me more about Carver's research. How close is he really to creating a breach?"

"Too close," Cyrus sighed. "He's been collecting Ancestral artifacts for decades—devices designed to manipulate dimensional energy. Most are incomplete or damaged, but he's repurposed them."

"Like the ring he wears?"

"You noticed that? Yes, it's a dimensional siphon. Allows him to draw small amounts of energy from the dimensional currents. Nothing like what a true Veilborn can do, but enough to give him certain... advantages."

"How did you get involved with his research?" Apollo asked.

There was a long pause before Cyrus answered. "My family has a tradition of studying Ancestral technology. We were Resonants—not Veilborn, but sensitive to certain frequencies. Carver approached me with promises of unlimited resources, access to artifacts most researchers never see."

"And you didn't know what he was really planning?"

"Not at first. I thought we were developing ways to harness dimensional energy safely—clean power, medical applications. By the time I realized his true goal was to breach the highest dimensions, I was in too deep." Cyrus's voice hardened. "When I tried to sabotage the project, he had me arrested as a traitor. Made an example of me to the other researchers."

Apollo thought of Marzen, with his trembling hands and nervous demeanor. "Are there others who might help us?"

"Most are true believers or too afraid to act. Marzen knows the risks, but he's blinded by the potential knowledge. The guards are just following orders." Cyrus paused. "There was one technician—Lina—who seemed uncomfortable with recent developments. She might be sympathetic."

"If we can get these inhibitors off, I might be able to close the tear," Apollo said.

"Maybe. But Carver's been feeding it energy for months. It's grown more stable with each experiment." Cyrus's fingers tightened on the grate. "The real problem is The Spire itself. It was originally designed as a dimensional stabilizer—part of the Ancestrals' network to prevent exactly what Carver's trying to do."

"But he's reversed its function?"

"Precisely. He's using it to focus and amplify dimensional energy rather than disperse it. The tear above is just a symptom of the damage he's causing to the dimensional barriers."

Apollo thought of what he'd learned at the Nexus—how the Ancestrals had created a continental grid of stabilization points, with Veilborn as living components of that system.

"Cyrus," he said, "what if we could restore The Spire to its original function?"

"Theoretically possible, but it would require access to the central control systems and knowledge of the original calibrations. Plus, Carver's modifications would need to be reversed."

"I might have that knowledge," Apollo said. "At the Nexus, I connected with an Ancestral interface. It transferred information directly to me—patterns, configurations, the original purpose of the stabilization network."

Cyrus was silent for a moment. "If that's true... it changes things. But you'd still need to get free of those inhibitors and reach the control center."

"One problem at a time," Apollo said. "I've been working on the inhibitors. I can feel internal dimensional currents now, but I can't yet affect anything outside my body."

"That's actually impressive progress," Cyrus sounded surprised. "Most would be completely suppressed. Your Veilborn abilities must be exceptionally strong."

Apollo thought of what he'd learned about his genetic heritage—the pure Veilborn bloodlines that had been preserved through generations of careful protection.

"I need to strengthen these internal pathways," he said. "Any suggestions?"

"Try focusing on cyclical patterns," Cyrus suggested. "The inhibitors are designed to detect and suppress linear dimensional manipulation—drawing energy in or pushing it out. But circular flows, energy that returns to its source, might be harder for them to detect."

Apollo nodded, though Cyrus couldn't see it. "I'll try that approach."

"Good. I need to rest now—they're taking me to the lab early tomorrow to verify calculations for Carver's demonstration. I'll learn what I can." The fingers withdrew slightly from the grate. "Be careful with your practice. If they realize you're finding ways around the inhibitors, they'll use stronger measures."

"Cyrus," Apollo called before the other man could leave. "Thank you."

A quiet laugh came through the grate. "Don't thank me yet. We're still trapped in Carver's playground. But... it's good not to be alone anymore."

After Cyrus left, Apollo returned to his mattress and settled into a cross-legged position. Cyclical patterns. He closed his eyes and visualized dimensional energy flowing through his body in continuous loops—from his core to his limbs and back again, never extending beyond his skin.

The inhibitors hummed occasionally but didn't trigger their painful countermeasures. As Apollo maintained the circular flow, he gradually increased its intensity, feeling the energy begin to pool at the contact points where the inhibitors touched his wrists and neck.

It was like water flowing against a dam, searching for weaknesses. And gradually, he sensed minute cracks developing in the inhibitors' containment barrier.

Apollo continued his practice through the night, pausing only when guards passed by his cell. By the time artificial dawn arrived—signaled only by a slight brightening of the cell's illumination—he had made progress. The internal dimensional currents were stronger, more defined, and the inhibitors' grip seemed slightly looser.

It wasn't enough to break free, not yet. But it was a beginning.

As a guard silently delivered his morning meal, Apollo maintained a placid expression, revealing nothing of what he'd accomplished. Let Carver believe his prisoner was helpless. Let him think the inhibitors were working perfectly.

Apollo would be ready when his friends came. And if they couldn't reach him in time, he would find his own way out.

The dimensional currents called to him, even through the inhibitors' suppression. And for the first time since his capture, Apollo felt something beyond despair.

He felt hope.

Alden Nash pressed his back against the cold stone wall, clutching the stolen maintenance uniform to his chest. His heart hammered so loudly he feared the guards might hear it even from thirty paces away. The narrow service tunnel smelled of mildew and oil, illuminated only by dim emergency lighting that cast everything in an eerie blue glow.

"This is madness," he whispered, adjusting his spectacles with trembling fingers. "Absolute madness."

Tristan shot him a look, his expression unreadable in the half-light. "You've said that six times in the last hour."

"Because it bears repeating," Alden hissed. "We're attempting to infiltrate the most heavily guarded facility on the continent with nothing but stolen uniforms and makeshift tools."

"And my pendant," Astra added, her hand reflexively touching the silver-blue object hanging around her neck. "It's still functioning, though weakly. It should help us avoid detection from the dimensional sensors."

Alden swallowed. Three days had passed since Apollo's capture. Three days of frantic planning, of Tristan working tirelessly with the multi-tool Verity had given him to create devices that might disable Apollo's inhibitors. Three days of Alden poring over the architectural schematics of The Spire that Astra had sketched from memory, looking for vulnerabilities in Carver's fortress.

And now they were here, huddled in a maintenance tunnel that, according to Astra's intelligence, would lead them to the lower levels of The Spire without passing through the main security checkpoints.

"According to the shift schedule," Astra whispered, "we have approximately seven minutes before the next patrol passes this junction."

Tristan nodded, his face grim with determination. "Then we move now."

Alden fumbled with the maintenance uniform, pulling it over his clothes. The fabric was coarse and smelled of someone else's sweat. He fought down a wave of nausea.

"In theory," he muttered, "if we maintain a purposeful demeanor and avoid direct eye contact, the psychological principle of authority suggests that most people will not question our presence."

"In theory," Tristan echoed, not sounding entirely convinced.

Astra finished adjusting her uniform and pulled her hair back into a tight bun, tucking the silver streak under a cap. "Remember, if anyone stops us—"

"We're conducting routine maintenance on the environmental systems in Section 7-B," Alden recited. "Authorized by Supervisor Kell."

"And if they ask to see credentials?" Tristan prompted.

"We apologize for the oversight and offer to return to the maintenance bay immediately to retrieve them," Alden continued. "Then we find another route."

Astra nodded. "Good. And if we're separated—"

"Proceed to the secondary rendezvous point in the eastern service corridor, level three," Alden finished. "I've memorized the entire plan, Astra. Multiple contingencies included."

"I know," she said, her amber eyes softening momentarily. "Just making sure."

Tristan checked the makeshift tool belt he'd assembled. "Disablers are ready. Three charges, as planned."

Alden patted the inner pocket of his uniform where he'd hidden a small notebook containing his translations of the architectural terms Astra had provided. "Navigation assistance, prepared."

"Then we move," Astra said, straightening her shoulders. "Remember, purpose and confidence."

They emerged from the narrow tunnel into a wider corridor. Alden blinked, adjusting to the brighter lights. The interior of The Spire was unlike anything he'd imagined—sleek metal walls with glowing panels, punctuated by security doors at regular intervals. Everything hummed with energy.

Alden's scholarly mind couldn't help cataloging details even as they moved with deliberate steps down the corridor. The architectural style blended Ancestral precision with modern adaptations. Carver had clearly salvaged and repurposed significant amounts of original technology.

"Left here," Astra murmured as they approached a junction.

They turned, maintaining a measured pace that suggested routine rather than urgency. Alden's palms were slick with sweat inside his gloves.

A door slid open ahead of them, and two guards emerged. Alden held his breath, but he kept walking, eyes fixed on a point beyond the guards' shoulders.

"Maintenance," one guard noted disinterestedly as they passed.

"Environmental systems," Tristan replied with casual authority, not breaking stride.

The guards continued on their way without further comment. Alden released the breath he was holding.

"That was—" he began.

"Don't celebrate yet," Astra cut him off. "We need to access the research levels."

They continued through the labyrinthine corridors, occasionally passing other staff who paid them little attention. Alden was struck by the clinical efficiency of everything around them. The Spire operated like a well-oiled machine, every person moving with purpose, every system functioning with precision.

"Security increases from here," Astra warned as they approached a checkpoint. "Follow my lead."

She approached the guard station with confidence, presenting a maintenance order she'd forged using information from their reconnaissance. Alden held his breath, studying the guard's face for any sign of suspicion.

"Section 12-F? That's not on my schedule," the guard said, frowning at the document.

"Supervisor Kell added it this morning," Astra replied. "Something about fluctuations in the environmental controls affecting sensitive equipment."

The guard hesitated, then shrugged. "Fine. But you'll need escorts in the research section."

"Of course," Astra agreed.

The guard tapped something into his console, then waved them through. Two junior guards fell into step behind them.

They hadn't accounted for this complication. Escorts would make it impossible to search for Apollo or access Carver's research.

"Environmental control panel is showing irregularities in three separate locations," Astra said to the escorts as they walked. "We'll need to check each one."

"Just make it quick," one escort replied. "The Magistrate has important work today. Doesn't want any disruptions."

Tristan and Alden exchanged glances. Important work could only mean one thing—Carver was moving forward with his experiments.

They reached the first maintenance access point, a small panel set into the wall of a corridor lined with laboratory doors.

"I'll need both of you to hold these while I check the readings," Astra said, handing each escort a different tool from Tristan's belt.

As the escorts awkwardly held the unfamiliar tools, Tristan stepped behind them. In one fluid motion, he pressed a small device against each man's neck. They collapsed without a sound.

"Neurostimulator," Tristan explained, catching one of the guards before he hit the floor. "They'll be unconscious for about an hour."

"Drag them in here," Astra said, opening a storage closet.

They secured the unconscious escorts and relieved them of their access cards and weapons.

"Now we can move more freely," Astra said. "But we need to hurry. Someone will notice they're missing eventually."

With the escorts' access cards, they were able to enter the research section proper. Alden gasped as they passed through the security doors.

The space beyond was vast—a multi-level laboratory complex built around a central column that pulsed with energy. Researchers in white coats moved between workstations, while guards patrolled the perimeter. And everywhere, artifacts—hundreds of them, displayed in specialized containment units or being actively studied at various stations.

"Carver's collection," Astra whispered. "He's been gathering Ancestral technology for decades."

Alden's scholarly instincts overwhelmed his fear momentarily. The artifacts represented the most comprehensive collection he'd ever seen—more extensive even than the archives at Valeshire. Dimensional stabilizers, energy converters, communication devices, and dozens of objects whose purpose he could only guess at.

"We need to find Apollo," Tristan reminded them, pulling Alden back to their mission.

"According to the information I gathered, detention cells are two levels down," Astra said. "But first, we should try to access Carver's main research data. It might help us prevent what he is doing."

They made their way to a less populated section of the laboratory, where several advanced terminals were arranged around what appeared to be a central database.

"Can you access it?" Tristan asked as Astra approached one of the terminals.

She nodded. "The escort's clearance should get us basic access. Alden, you might understand the research better than I would."

Alden stepped forward, fingers hovering over the interface. Years of studying ancient texts had made him adept at processing and synthesizing information. He navigated through the database, scanning file headings and project summaries.

"It's... extensive," he murmured. "Carver has been researching dimensional energy for at least twenty years. He's cataloged hundreds of artifacts and their properties."

"Anything about Apollo?" Tristan pressed.

Alden continued searching. "Here—Project Veilborn. Started three days ago." He opened the file, scanning. "They've been taking blood samples, tissue samples... running tests on Apollo's cellular structure." He swallowed hard. "They're trying to isolate the genetic markers that allow Veilborn to perceive and manipulate dimensional energy."

"Have they succeeded?" Astra asked, her voice tight.

Alden shook his head. "Not yet, but they've made progress. They've developed a serum that temporarily grants limited dimensional perception to non-Veilborn subjects."

"That's what Carver wants," Astra said. "The ability to see and manipulate dimensional energy without being born with the gift."

"There's more," Alden continued, his blood running cold as he read further. "Project Convergence. It's... it's about The Spire itself." He pulled up schematics and research notes. "The Spire was designed by the Ancestrals as a dimensional anchor point—a stabilizer for the dimensional barriers. But Carver is modifying it, reversing its function."

"Reversing how?" Tristan asked.

"He's turning it from a stabilizer into... into a breach mechanism." Alden's voice shook. "He's trying to tear open a permanent gateway to what he calls 'the Source'—a dimension of pure energy that the Ancestrals only theorized about."

"That's what's causing the dimensional tears we've been seeing," Astra realized. "His experiments are already weakening the barriers between dimensions."

"According to these notes, he plans to conduct a full-scale test today," Alden said, his finger tracing the text on the screen. "Using Apollo's blood serum to enhance his own perception, and a collection of specialized artifacts to amplify the effect."

"We need to stop him and get Apollo out," Tristan said. "Where would they be keeping him?"

Alden navigated to another section of the database. "Detention Level, Cell 7. High-security containment with dimensional suppressors."

"And Carver himself?" Astra asked.

"Control Room, top level of The Spire. That's where he'll conduct the experiment." Alden continued exploring the database, downloading critical information to a portable device he'd brought. "Look at this—Carver's primary collection. These are the artifacts he considers most valuable."

The screen displayed images of seven artifacts arranged in a specialized chamber. At the center was a device Alden recognized from ancient texts—a dimensional resonator similar to the one Verity had given Apollo, but larger and more complex.

"The Ancestral Crown," Alden breathed. "It's not a myth."

"What is it?" Tristan asked.

"According to legend, it was created by the Ancestrals' most skilled artificers—a device that amplifies a Veilborn's abilities exponentially." Alden studied the image with academic fascination. "With it, a trained Veilborn could theoretically manipulate dimensional energy on a massive scale."

"That must be what Carver plans to use in his experiment," Astra said. "Combined with Apollo's blood serum and The Spire's modified systems..."

"He could tear a hole in reality itself," Alden finished.

A sudden alarm blared through the laboratory, causing them all to jump.

"Someone's discovered the missing escorts," Astra said. "We need to move now."

They gathered what information they could and headed toward the access corridor that would lead them to the detention level.

"Wait," Alden said, pointing to a door marked "Artifact Storage Alpha" across the laboratory floor. "That's where Carver keeps his primary collection. If we could disrupt or disable some of those artifacts..."

"Too risky," Tristan argued. "We need to get to Apollo."

"Actually," Astra said, "creating a diversion might help us. If we could disable the security systems in that section, it would draw attention away from the detention level."

Tristan considered for a moment, then nodded. "Quickly, then."

They made their way across the laboratory floor, using the confusion caused by the alarm to blend in with researchers hurrying to secure their stations. Alden's pulse pounded as they approached the heavily secured door to Artifact Storage Alpha.

Astra swiped the escort's access card, but a red light flashed on the panel. "Higher clearance required," she muttered.

Tristan examined the lock mechanism. "I can bypass it with Verity's tool, but it'll take time."

"Time we don't have," Alden said, glancing at the guards moving purposefully through the laboratory.

Astra touched her pendant, closing her eyes briefly. "There's another way. This door has dimensional security as well as physical. I can feel it."

She placed her hand on the door panel, her pendant glowing faintly. "The pendant's stabilizer function disrupts dimensional patterns. If I can match the frequency..."

The panel flickered, then turned green. The door slid open.

"Hurry," Astra urged, and they slipped inside.

Alden gasped as the door closed behind them. The chamber was circular, with seven pedestals arranged around a central platform. Each pedestal held an artifact, bathed in specialized lighting that highlighted their unique properties. The air hummed with contained energy.

"The Crown," Alden whispered, pointing to the central platform where a circlet of silvery metal inlaid with crystalline structures rested on a cushioned display.

"Don't touch anything," Astra warned. "These artifacts are likely heavily warded."

Tristan moved to a control panel near the entrance. "I think I can disable the security systems from here. It might buy us the diversion we need."

While Tristan worked, Alden circled the room, cataloging the artifacts with scholarly precision despite their dire circumstances. Besides the Crown, there was a staff of twisted metal that seemed to bend light around it, a set of crystalline orbs that pulsed with internal energy, a book bound in material that shifted colors as he watched, a small pyramid that hovered slightly above its pedestal, a gauntlet etched with complex patterns, and a mirror whose surface rippled like water.

"These aren't just random artifacts," Alden realized. "They're a set—designed to work together."

"How do you know?" Astra asked, keeping watch at the door.

"The symbolic patterns are complementary," Alden explained, gesturing to the etchings visible on each piece. "And they're arranged in a specific configuration that matches ancient diagrams I've studied of dimensional amplification arrays."

"Carver's planning to use all of them together," Astra concluded. "With Apollo's blood serum enhancing his perception."

"Got it," Tristan announced. His fingers danced across the control panel. "Security systems disabling in three... two... one..."

The specialized lighting around the artifacts flickered and died. A new alarm, different from the first, began to sound.

"That should keep them busy," Tristan said with grim satisfaction. "Let's get to Apollo."

They slipped out of the artifact chamber amid the growing chaos. Researchers rushed about, trying to determine the source of the security breach. Guards shouted orders, dividing into teams to investigate different sections.

"This way," Astra directed, leading them toward a service elevator at the far end of the laboratory.

They reached the elevator just as a squad of guards rushed past, heading toward Artifact Storage Alpha. Astra swiped the access card, and the doors slid open.

"Detention level," she said as they entered. "We'll need to be ready for resistance. The cells will be guarded."

The elevator descended. Alden checked the disabler devices Tristan had created, ensuring they were ready to deactivate Apollo's inhibitors.

"According to the database, Apollo's cell is isolated from the others," he said. "Special containment protocols."

"Makes sense," Tristan replied. "They'd want to control his dimensional abilities completely."

The elevator slowed, then stopped. The doors opened to reveal a corridor lined with security doors. Two guards stood at a checkpoint ahead.

Before they could react, Tristan raised one of the escorts' weapons and fired. The guards collapsed.

"Quick," Astra urged, rushing forward to secure the guards' weapons and access cards.

Alden consulted the mental map he'd constructed from the database information. "Apollo should be in the high-security section, through those doors and to the right."

They moved swiftly down the corridor, Tristan in the lead with a weapon at the ready. The detention level was eerily quiet compared to the chaos above.

"Something's wrong," Astra whispered. "There should be more guards."

They reached the high-security section and found the entry point unguarded. The door opened with a swipe of the guard's access card.

"Cell 7," Alden reminded them. "At the end of this corridor."

They moved cautiously forward, checking each intersection before proceeding. The silence was unnerving.

"They've pulled guards for the security breach upstairs," Tristan suggested. "Or..."

"Or it's a trap," Astra finished.

They reached Cell 7, a reinforced door with multiple security systems visible around its frame. A small observation window allowed them to see inside.

Apollo sat cross-legged on the floor, eyes closed, metal bands visible around his wrists and neck. Despite his captivity, his expression was eerily peaceful.

"He's meditating," Astra observed.

Tristan examined the door's security systems. "This is going to be tricky. Multiple layers of both physical and dimensional security."

"Can you bypass it?" Alden asked anxiously.

"With time, yes. But—"

A slow clapping sound interrupted them. They spun around to see Captain Nessa Drake standing at the corridor junction, flanked by six guards with weapons trained on them.

"Impressive," Drake said, her scarred face impassive. "You managed to infiltrate The Spire, cause a security breach in our most sensitive area, and locate your friend." She stepped forward, her enhanced armor gleaming under the harsh lights. "Unfortunately, that's as far as you go."

Alden assessed the options and likely outcomes. They were outnumbered, outgunned, and cornered.

"Captain Drake," he said, stepping forward. "I've been studying Magistrate Carver's research. Do you understand what he's attempting to do?"

Drake's expression didn't change. "My job isn't to understand. It's to follow orders."

"He's trying to breach dimensional barriers on a massive scale," Alden continued. "The same kind of experiment that caused the Cataclysm a thousand years ago."

"Surrender your weapons," she commanded. "Now."

Tristan and Astra exchanged glances. Slowly, Tristan lowered his weapon to the floor.

"That's better," Drake said. "Now—"

A deafening alarm cut through the air, different from the previous security alerts. Red emergency lighting activated in the corridor.

"What is that?" one of the guards asked nervously.

Drake touched her communication device. "Drake here. What's happening?" Her eyes widened at whatever response she received. "Understood. Secure the prisoner for transport." She looked at Alden and the others. "It seems your diversion worked too well. Something in Artifact Storage Alpha has destabilized. The Magistrate has ordered immediate evacuation of all non-essential personnel."

"The dimensional artifacts are sensitive," Alden explained. "Disrupting their containment systems could cause feedback loops in the dimensional energy they contain."

"Shut up," Drake snapped. She gestured to her guards. "Take them into custody. We're moving the Veilborn to the transport level."

As the guards moved forward, Astra's pendant began to glow brightly. She gasped, clutching it.

"What's happening?" Tristan asked.

"Dimensional surge," she whispered. "Something's causing massive fluctuations."

The lights flickered. A low rumble shook the floor beneath their feet.

"The Spire is becoming unstable," Alden realized. "Carver must have started his experiment despite the security breach."

Drake seemed to come to a decision. "Change of plans. You three—" she pointed at Alden, Tristan, and Astra, "—are coming with us to the transport level. The Magistrate wants the Veilborn, and I'm not letting you interfere."

"Captain," one of the guards interrupted, "the cell security systems are failing. Power fluctuations across the entire level."

Drake cursed. "Open the cell. We move the prisoner now."

Two guards approached Apollo's cell door, inputting emergency override codes. The door slid open with a hiss.

Apollo remained seated, eyes closed. The inhibitors around his wrists and neck were still active, but the lights on them flickered erratically.

"On your feet," Drake ordered him.

Apollo opened his eyes. His gaze moved from Drake to Alden, Tristan, and Astra. Something like a smile touched his lips.

"You came," he said.

"Of course we did," Tristan replied. "We had a plan."

"Not a very good one, apparently," Drake commented dryly. "Guards, secure the prisoner for transport."

As the guards moved toward Apollo, another tremor shook the facility, stronger than before. The lights went out completely for several seconds before emergency power activated.

In that moment of darkness and confusion, Alden felt someone grab his arm. Astra's voice whispered in his ear: "Be ready."

The emergency lights came on, bathing everything in red. Drake was shouting orders, trying to maintain control of the situation.

Apollo remained seated, his expression now focused and intent. The inhibitors around his wrists sparked and sputtered.

"Something's wrong with the inhibitors," one of the guards reported.

"It doesn't matter," Drake snapped. "Get him on his feet and move him. Now!"

As the guards reached for Apollo, the inhibitors went dark. A faint smile crossed Apollo's face.

And then everything happened at once.

15

—·—

DIMENSIONAL FRACTURES

The cell door slid open with a mechanical hiss. Captain Drake and her guards moved toward Apollo, weapons raised. The inhibitors around his wrists and neck had gone dark, their suppression field faltering with the power fluctuations.

A familiar warmth flooded through Apollo's body—the dimensional energy he'd been cut off from for days rushing back like a river breaking through a dam. He flexed his fingers, feeling the currents respond to his call.

"Get him secured for transport," Drake ordered. "The Magistrate wants him in the Control Room immediately."

Apollo locked eyes with Tristan, who stood behind the guards with Alden and Astra. A silent message passed between them—*now*.

As the first guard reached for Apollo's arm, he released a concentrated burst of dimensional energy. The air rippled between them, sending the guard flying backward into his companions. Apollo rolled sideways as Tristan threw a small device toward the ceiling. It detonated with a flash, plunging the corridor into darkness.

"Apollo!" Astra called, her voice cutting through the confusion.

He pushed off the cell floor, guided by the dimensional currents he could perceive even in complete darkness. Tristan and Alden had engaged the remaining guards. Apollo spotted Drake drawing a sidearm and twisted the dimensional fabric around her hand. The weapon discharged harmlessly into the wall as Apollo reached his friends.

"The inhibitors," Astra said, fumbling with a tool at his wrist.

"No time," Apollo replied, concentrating on the metal bands. He found the frequency that resonated with their locking mechanism and applied pressure. The inhibitors fell away with a metallic clank.

Alden handed Apollo a pack. "We need to move. Carver's starting something big in the Control Room."

A violent tremor shook the facility, nearly throwing them off their feet. The emergency lights flickered on, bathing the corridor in pulsing red.

"What was that?" Tristan asked, helping Apollo steady himself.

Apollo closed his eyes briefly, extending his senses through the dimensional currents. "Carver's tearing open the dimensional barriers. He's using The Spire to breach what he calls 'the Source.'"

"Can you stop him?" Astra asked.

Another tremor, stronger than the first, rippled through the structure. Hairline fractures appeared in the walls, leaking violet light.

"Not here, not now," Apollo said. "We need the resonator Verity gave me. Where is it?"

"Artifact Storage," Alden replied. "We caused a diversion there. It should be in chaos."

Drake was regaining her footing, her face twisted with fury. "Lock down the sector!" she shouted into her comm unit. "The Veilborn is escaping!"

"This way," Tristan urged, pointing down the corridor opposite from where Drake's reinforcements would come.

They ran through the winding hallways of The Spire, alarms blaring around them. Apollo felt the dimensional distortions growing stronger with each passing minute. The facility's very structure was beginning to warp under the strain of Carver's experiment.

"There!" Alden pointed to a sign marking Artifact Storage.

The door hung partially open, its locking mechanism damaged in the earlier diversion. Inside, display cases had been overturned, and artifacts lay scattered across the floor. Two security personnel lay unconscious near the entrance.

"Look for the resonator," Apollo instructed, scanning the room.

They spread out, searching through the chaos. Apollo felt drawn to a particular section of the room where dimensional energy coalesced more strongly. He pushed aside a fallen shelf to reveal a secure case still intact.

"Found it," he called, focusing on the lock. With a twist of dimensional energy, the case opened, revealing the resonator Verity had given him.

The moment Apollo's fingers touched the device, it hummed to life, its spiral patterns glowing with blue-violet light. The resonator amplified his perception instantly, allowing him to see the full extent of the damage Carver was causing.

"Apollo?" Astra's voice sounded distant as the resonator connected him to the dimensional currents flowing through The Spire.

He saw it all—Carver in the Control Room, wearing what must be the Ancestral Crown, channeling massive amounts of energy into The Spire's core. The dimensional barriers thinning dangerously as Carver forced them open. And beyond, something vast and terrifying waiting on the other side.

"He's going to destroy everything," Apollo whispered, returning to himself. "The barriers between dimensions are already fracturing. If he succeeds in breaching the Source completely..."

A violent tremor shook the room, stronger than any before. Display cases shattered as the floor buckled beneath them.

"We need to get out of here," Tristan said, steadying himself against a wall. "This whole place could come down around us."

Apollo nodded, slipping the resonator into his pocket. "There's a maintenance shaft two corridors over. It leads to the exterior."

"How do you know that?" Alden asked.

"The resonator," Apollo explained. "It's showing me the facility's structure through the dimensional currents."

They moved through the corridors, avoiding the main hallways where Drake's guards would be searching. The tremors continued, growing more frequent. In some places, the walls rippled like fabric in a breeze, reality itself becoming unstable.

As they rounded a corner, Apollo froze. Ahead, a section of the corridor had... changed. The walls, floor, and ceiling had transformed into a crystalline substance that pulsed with inner light.

"What is that?" Tristan asked, his voice hushed.

"Dimensional bleedthrough," Apollo said. "The barrier is so thin here that another dimension is crossing into ours."

Astra reached out toward the crystalline surface.

"Don't touch it!" Apollo grabbed her hand. "We don't know what effect it might have."

As if in response to his words, the crystalline section expanded, covering more of the corridor. The air around it shimmered with heat.

"Is there another way?" Alden asked.

Apollo consulted the dimensional currents through the resonator. "Yes, but it's longer. We'll have to go down a level and across."

They backtracked to a maintenance ladder and descended to the lower level. The situation there was worse—emergency lighting flickered erratically, and sections of the floor had warped into impossible angles.

"The dimensional instabilities are spreading," Apollo explained as they navigated the distorted corridor. "Carver doesn't understand what he's doing."

Another violent tremor nearly knocked them off their feet. A crack appeared in the ceiling, leaking a viscous liquid that sizzled when it hit the floor.

"We need to hurry," Astra urged.

They moved faster, following Apollo's lead as he used the resonator to guide them through the safest path. Twice they had to detour around areas where reality had become dangerously unstable.

Finally, they reached a maintenance access panel that, according to the dimensional currents Apollo perceived, led outside.

"This should take us to the western exterior," he said, working the panel loose.

The shaft beyond was narrow but navigable. They crawled through in single file, Apollo leading the way. The metal walls of the shaft vibrated continuously with the energy being channeled through The Spire.

After what felt like an eternity of crawling through the cramped space, Apollo saw light ahead. He pushed through the exit and emerged onto a narrow maintenance platform on the exterior of The Spire.

The sight that greeted them stole Apollo's breath.

The Spire stood at the center of a vast complex, its upper section now surrounded by a swirling vortex of energy. The sky above had taken on an unnatural purple hue, shot through with veins of electric blue. In the distance, objects floated upward against gravity—rocks, debris, even water from a nearby stream rising in defiance of natural law.

"By the Ancestors," Alden whispered. "It's already begun."

Apollo consulted the resonator, searching for a safe path away from the facility. "There," he pointed to a service road leading into the forest at the complex's edge. "If we can reach those trees, we might find cover."

They descended from the platform using a maintenance ladder that brought them to ground level. Guards were visible near the main entrance, but their attention was focused on the growing anomalies rather than potential escapees.

"Stay low," Tristan advised as they crept along the perimeter wall.

They had almost reached the tree line when a shout went up behind them. Apollo turned to see Captain Drake emerging from a side entrance, pointing in their direction.

"Run!" Apollo urged.

They sprinted for the forest as guards gave chase. Energy weapons discharged, scorching the ground near their feet. Apollo reached into the dimensional currents, creating a minor distortion behind them that confused their pursuers' perception.

As they entered the forest, a massive surge of energy erupted from The Spire's peak. The ground shook violently, trees swaying as if in a hurricane. Apollo stumbled, the resonator in his pocket burning hot against his leg.

"Keep going!" he called to the others, regaining his balance.

They pushed deeper into the forest, the sounds of pursuit fading behind them. The trees provided cover, but Apollo noticed disturbing signs—leaves shifting color from green to blue and back again, small animals frozen in mid-movement as if time itself was fluctuating.

After twenty minutes of hard running, they paused in a small clearing to catch their breath. The Spire was still visible in the distance, the energy vortex around it growing larger.

"What's happening, Apollo?" Astra asked, her face pale.

Apollo removed the resonator from his pocket. It pulsed with energy, responding to the dimensional disturbances emanating from The Spire. He closed his eyes, focusing on the information flowing through the device.

"Carver is using The Spire to drill through the dimensional barriers," he explained, opening his eyes. "The Ancestral Crown he's wearing amplifies his connection to dimensional energy, similar to how my Veilborn abilities work, but without the natural limitations. He's trying to reach what he calls 'the Source'—I think it's the highest dimension, the one that feeds energy to all others."

"But why?" Alden asked.

"Power," Apollo said. "Unlimited dimensional energy at his command. But he doesn't understand the consequences. The dimensions exist in a delicate balance. Forcing them open like this..." He gestured to the disturbed forest around them. "Reality itself begins to break down."

A distant explosion drew their attention back to The Spire. A section of the facility had collapsed, sending debris flying outward. The energy vortex pulsed, expanding momentarily before contracting again.

"We need to keep moving," Tristan said. "Drake won't give up easily."

Apollo nodded, consulting the resonator once more. "There's an old Ancestral outpost about five miles east of here. We might find shelter there."

They set off again, moving at a steady pace through the increasingly strange forest. Plants grew and withered in patches, affected by the dimensional disturbances. In one clearing, they encountered a perfect circle where gravity seemed reversed—fallen leaves and twigs hovering inches above the ground.

"Step around it," Apollo warned. "The dimensional boundaries are thin here."

As they continued eastward, Apollo felt the resonator growing warmer in his hand. It was responding to something ahead—another dimensional anomaly or perhaps an Ancestral structure tuned to the same frequency.

"I think we're getting close," he told the others. "The resonator is picking up something."

They crested a small hill and saw it—a low stone building partially reclaimed by the forest. Unlike the sleek lines of The Spire, this structure was older, its architecture more in harmony with the natural surroundings.

"Is it safe?" Astra asked.

Apollo extended his senses through the resonator. "Yes. Actually, it seems to be... stabilizing the area around it. The dimensional disturbances are less severe here."

They approached cautiously. The entrance was partially obscured by vegetation, but as Apollo drew near, symbols etched into the stone began to glow with a soft blue light.

"Ancestral script," Alden observed. "Similar to what we saw at the Nexus."

Apollo placed his hand on the door, feeling the dimensional energy respond to his touch. The door slid open with a soft grinding sound, revealing a darkened interior.

"It recognizes you as Veilborn," Astra said.

They entered the outpost, and lights activated automatically, illuminating a single large room filled with dusty equipment. The door closed behind them, sealing with a reassuring click.

"What is this place?" Tristan asked, examining a control panel near the wall.

Apollo moved to the center of the room where a circular platform stood. As he approached, it lit up, projecting a three-dimensional map of the surrounding area. The Spire was clearly visible, surrounded by a pulsing red aura that represented the dimensional disturbances.

"It's a monitoring station," Apollo realized. "Part of the same network as the Nexus. It was designed to track dimensional stability in the region."

Alden examined the map closely. "Look at this," he pointed to lines of energy spreading outward from The Spire like cracks in glass. "The disturbances are expanding."

Apollo placed the resonator on the platform. It integrated seamlessly with the Ancestral technology, enhancing the projection. The map zoomed out, showing a wider area—including Willowbrook Village far to the west.

"This is worse than I thought," Apollo said. "The dimensional fractures are spreading in all directions. If Carver continues, they'll eventually reach populated areas."

"What happens then?" Tristan asked.

"Reality breaks down," Apollo said. "Plants, animals, people—everything affected by the fractures will experience dimensional bleedthrough. Time distortions, gravity fluctuations, matter transformation... eventually, complete dissolution of the affected areas."

"Like the Cataclysm," Astra whispered.

"Potentially worse," Apollo replied. "The Cataclysm was a single event. This is an ongoing process that will continue to spread as long as Carver keeps The Spire active."

A notification appeared on the map—a flashing symbol near their location.

"What's that?" Tristan asked.

Apollo touched the symbol, and the map shifted to show a detailed view of the outpost. "It's detecting dimensional instability... here, inside the outpost."

They all turned to look at Apollo.

"It's me," he realized. "My connection to the dimensional currents has been amplified by exposure to The Spire and the resonator."

"Is that dangerous?" Astra asked, concern evident in her voice.

Apollo closed his eyes, taking stock of the energy flowing through him. It felt different—stronger, more volatile than before. "I don't think so, not immediately. But I need to learn to control it better."

A distant rumble shook the outpost, causing dust to fall from the ceiling. On the map, they could see another surge of energy erupting from The Spire.

"He's pushing harder," Apollo observed. "Trying to force a full breach."

"How long do we have?" Astra asked.

Apollo studied the progression of the fractures on the map. "At the current rate of expansion... three days, maybe four, before the disturbances reach major population centers. Less if Carver accelerates the process."

"Then we need a plan," Tristan said. "A way to stop Carver and reverse the damage."

Apollo nodded, his expression resolute. "The outpost's systems are still functional. We can use them to analyze The Spire's vulnerabilities and maybe find a way to shut it down."

"What about Carver's forces?" Alden asked. "They'll be searching for us."

"This place has defenses," Apollo replied, gesturing to symbols on the wall that resembled the ones at the Nexus. "Dimensional shields that make it difficult to detect from outside. We should be safe here, at least temporarily."

Astra placed a hand on Apollo's shoulder. "You should rest. You've been imprisoned for days, and we'll need your strength."

Apollo wanted to argue, but exhaustion weighed heavily on him. The rush of energy from escaping had faded, leaving him drained. "You're right. But first, let's see what else we can learn from this place."

He returned to the central platform and placed both hands on the resonator. The map expanded further, showing other facilities similar to the outpost—a network of Ancestral structures designed to monitor and maintain dimensional stability.

"Look," he pointed to a location northeast of their position. "There's another node active there. And here," he indicated a point to the south. "These could be allies—other survivors who understand Ancestral technology."

"Can you contact them?" Tristan asked.

Apollo concentrated, channeling energy through the resonator into the outpost's communication systems. For a moment, nothing happened. Then a symbol appeared on the map—an acknowledgment from the southern node.

"They've received our signal," Apollo said, relief evident in his voice. "They know we're here."

Another tremor shook the outpost, stronger than before. On the map, they could see a new fracture spreading rapidly from The Spire toward the east.

"The instabilities are accelerating," Apollo observed. "Carver must be increasing power to The Spire."

He zoomed in on the facility, studying its structure through the dimensional currents. "There's something strange happening at the core. The energy isn't just flowing outward—it's cycling back, creating a feedback loop that's amplifying the disturbances."

"Can you disrupt it from here?" Astra asked.

Apollo shook his head. "Not directly. But..." He manipulated the map, examining the fracture patterns. "There might be a way to stabilize the affected areas temporarily. The outpost has dimensional anchors—devices designed to reinforce reality in their vicinity."

"Like Astra's pendant?" Tristan suggested.

"Similar principle, but much larger scale," Apollo confirmed. "If we could deploy them at key points along the fracture lines, we might slow the spread long enough to develop a more permanent solution."

Alden had found a storage compartment and was examining its contents. "I think these might be what you're describing," he said, holding up a device about the size of his palm. It resembled a flattened sphere with intricate patterns etched into its surface.

Apollo took the anchor, feeling its resonance with the dimensional currents. "Yes, this is it. The outpost has a deployment system that can help us identify the optimal locations."

He placed the anchor on the central platform alongside the resonator. The map responded, highlighting several points along the fracture lines where the anchors would be most effective.

"There are twelve critical points," Apollo noted. "How many anchors do we have?"

Alden counted the devices in the storage compartment. "Fifteen. We have enough, with some to spare."

"Good," Apollo said. "We'll need to move quickly. The fractures are spreading faster than I initially calculated."

Astra studied the map closely. "Some of these points are dangerously close to The Spire. Carver's forces will be patrolling those areas."

"We'll have to risk it," Apollo replied. "If we don't stabilize the fractures soon, the dimensional bleedthrough will become irreversible."

Tristan examined one of the anchors. "How do these work? Do they need to be activated somehow?"

"They respond to dimensional energy," Apollo explained. "Once placed at the designated coordinates, I can activate them remotely using the resonator."

Another violent tremor shook the outpost, causing a small section of ceiling to collapse at the far end of the room. The map flickered momentarily before stabilizing.

"We don't have much time," Apollo said. "We need to deploy the anchors as soon as possible."

"You need rest first," Astra insisted. "You're exhausted, Apollo. A few hours of sleep will make you more effective."

Apollo wanted to argue, but the fatigue was becoming overwhelming. The resonator's connection to his Veilborn abilities had drained him further. "Alright," he conceded. "A few hours. But then we move."

"I'll keep monitoring the fractures," Alden offered. "And see what else I can learn from the outpost's systems."

"I'll check the perimeter," Tristan added. "Make sure we're secure."

Apollo nodded gratefully. He moved to a recessed area of the outpost where several cots were arranged—sleeping quarters for the original Ancestral operators. As he lay down, Astra sat beside him.

"We'll find a way through this," she said. "You're not alone anymore, Apollo."

He took her hand, drawing comfort from her presence. "I know. Thank you for coming for me."

"Always," she replied.

As Apollo drifted toward sleep, he remained connected to the dimensional currents through the resonator. The fractures spreading, reality itself beginning to unravel. But here, in this ancient outpost, surrounded by friends who had risked everything to save him, he found a moment of peace—a temporary refuge from the storm that Carver had unleashed.

His last thought before sleep claimed him was a resolution: he would master his Veilborn abilities completely, whatever the cost. The world needed him now more than ever.

Outside the outpost, unseen by its occupants, a small patch of grass shimmered and transformed into crystalline structures that caught the fading sunlight. The dimensional disruption had reached them, despite the outpost's protections. Time was running out.

16

BREACH PROTOCOL

Apollo woke with a start, the dimensional currents pulsing through his mind even in sleep. His body ached from the strain of the past days—the cell, the inhibitors, the escape. He blinked, momentarily disoriented by the unfamiliar surroundings until memory returned. The Ancestral outpost. The anchors. Carver's breach.

He sat up slowly, his muscles protesting. Sunlight filtered through narrow windows, casting geometric patterns across the floor. The outpost hummed with ancient technology, its systems still functioning after thousands of years. Apollo reached for the resonator beside his cot, feeling its familiar weight in his palm. The device responded, warming to his touch and amplifying his perception of the dimensional currents flowing through the structure.

"You're awake." Astra entered the room carrying a steaming cup. "I found some supplies in the storage area. This should help with the fatigue."

Apollo accepted the cup gratefully. The liquid inside had an herbal scent he didn't recognize. "How long was I asleep?"

"About six hours. It's mid-morning now."

He took a sip, surprised by the immediate clarity it brought to his thoughts. "This is good. What is it?"

"An Ancestral formula. Alden found instructions in the outpost's medical database. It's designed to help Veilborn recover after dimensional strain." She sat beside him on the cot. "How do you feel?"

"Better." Apollo stretched, testing his limbs. "Still tired, but functional. The resonator helps."

"Alden and Tristan are mapping the anchor deployment routes. They've been at it all night."

Apollo nodded, feeling a surge of gratitude for his friends. "And the fractures?"

Astra's expression grew serious. "Spreading faster than we anticipated. The distortion zone around The Spire has expanded by nearly a mile since we arrived."

Apollo stood, moving to the central platform where the dimensional map glowed. The fracture lines had indeed spread, reaching farther into the surrounding forests and mountains. At the center, The Spire pulsed with unstable energy, dimensional currents swirling chaotically around its structure.

"The feedback loop is intensifying," Apollo observed, manipulating the map to show the energy flows. "Carver must be continuing his experiments despite the instability."

Alden entered from an adjacent room with Tristan. "I've been studying the outpost's historical records. The Ancestrals documented the original Cataclysm in detail."

Alden placed a small crystalline cube on the platform. "I found this during our escape from The Spire. It was in a storage compartment near the artifact room—labeled as 'Dimensional Warnings Archive.'"

The cube glinted in the light, its surface etched with dimensional notation Apollo recognized from his training. "An echo crystal?"

"More sophisticated," Alden explained. "It's a complete data archive, designed to interface with Ancestral systems—or with a Veilborn directly."

Apollo picked up the cube, feeling its resonance with his abilities. "How do I access it?"

"According to the records, you need to channel dimensional energy through it while maintaining specific frequency patterns." Alden hesitated. "But the process could be taxing, especially in your condition."

"We need the information," Apollo said. "If this contains warnings about dimensional breaches, it might help us understand how to close Carver's."

Astra touched his arm. "Are you sure? You've barely recovered."

Apollo nodded. "I'm sure." He placed the cube on the platform next to the resonator, then positioned his hands around both objects. "Stand back. I'm not certain what will happen."

As his friends moved away, Apollo closed his eyes and focused on the dimensional currents flowing through the outpost. He filtered the chaotic energies into specific patterns, directing them through the resonator and into the crystal cube.

The cube responded, glowing with internal light. Apollo felt it drawing energy from him, establishing a connection between his consciousness and the stored data. The sensation was different from the echo crystals he'd experienced before—more structured, more intentional.

The cube projected a three-dimensional image above the platform. A figure formed from light stood before them—a woman in formal Ancestral attire, her expression grave.

"Archival warning sequence activated," the figure announced. "I am Director Thorne of the Dimensional Research Initiative. If you are accessing this record, dimensional stability has been compromised beyond acceptable parameters."

Apollo maintained the connection, feeling the strain but determined to receive the complete message.

"The Cataclysm resulted from our attempt to breach the dimensional barrier to access the Source directly," Director Thorne continued. "We believed we could harness infinite energy from higher dimensions, but we failed to understand the full consequences of our actions."

The projection shifted, showing a schematic of dimensional planes stacked upon each other like layers.

"Our reality exists as a three-dimensional projection of higher-dimensional space. When we attempted to open a direct channel to the fifth dimension, we created a cascade effect that destabilized the boundaries between all dimensional planes."

The schematic animated, showing fracture lines spreading across the dimensional boundaries, eerily similar to the patterns now emanating from The Spire.

"The resulting dimensional bleedthrough caused reality itself to become unstable. Physical laws broke down. Energy patterns became chaotic. The very fabric of our world began to unravel."

A cold sensation crept through Apollo as he noted the similarities to their present predicament. Carver was unknowingly recreating the same catastrophic conditions.

"We created the Veilborn to help repair the damage," Director Thorne explained. "Genetically engineered humans with specialized neural structures capable of perceiving and manipulating dimensional energies. Their purpose was to serve as living anchors, stabilizing reality where technology alone could not."

The projection shifted again, showing figures that resembled Apollo—men and women working with dimensional currents, sealing fractures, creating stable patterns.

"The Veilborn established a network of dimensional anchors across the continent, connected through The Spire and other major stabilization points. This system has maintained dimensional integrity for generations, but it requires active maintenance."

Director Thorne's expression became more urgent. "If you are witnessing dimensional instability similar to our records of the Cataclysm, immediate action is required. The enclosed data includes protocols for dimensional stabilization and breach closure."

The figure looked at Apollo, as though seeing him across thousands of years. "To those with Veilborn abilities: You were created for this purpose. The future of our world depends on your willingness to fulfill this role. The path will not be easy, but you alone possess the capacity to prevent another Cataclysm."

The projection flickered, then stabilized one final time. "Complete technical specifications and training protocols are included in this archive. May you succeed where we failed."

The image dissolved, and the cube dimmed. Apollo released his hold on the dimensional currents, feeling drained. The resonator slipped from his fingers, clattering on the platform.

"Apollo!" Astra moved to support him as he swayed.

"I'm alright," he assured her, though his voice was weak. "Just need a moment."

Tristan retrieved the resonator. "That was... intense."

"Did you get what we needed?" Alden asked, examining the now-dormant cube.

Apollo nodded, his mind still processing the information he'd received. "Yes. And more." He straightened, drawing strength from the clarity of purpose the message had provided. "The cube contains complete protocols for closing dimensional breaches. It also has training sequences for advanced Veilborn techniques."

"So we have a way to stop Carver," Astra said, relief evident in her voice.

"Potentially," Apollo cautioned. "But the process isn't simple. It requires coordinated effort from multiple Veilborn working in harmony."

"But you're the only Veilborn we have," Tristan pointed out.

Apollo touched the resonator. "With this, I might be able to channel enough energy to compensate. But I'll need to understand the protocols completely first."

He turned to Alden. "Can you connect the cube to the outpost's systems? I need to review the technical data in detail."

Alden nodded. "I'll set it up."

As Alden worked with the cube, Apollo returned to the dimensional map, studying the fracture patterns with new understanding. The Ancestral director's explanation had clarified much about the nature of dimensions and the Cataclysm.

"What did you learn?" Astra asked, joining him at the map.

"Everything," Apollo replied. "The Veilborn were created specifically to prevent what Carver is doing now. We're not just people who can see dimensional energy—we're living stabilizers, designed to maintain the barriers between dimensions."

He manipulated the map, focusing on The Spire. "Carver is using Ancestral technology he doesn't fully understand. The Ancestral Crown he's wearing was designed to amplify dimensional perception, but he's modified it to force open a breach to higher dimensions."

Apollo expanded the map to show the surrounding region. "Dimensions aren't just different places—they're different states of reality with different physical laws. Our three-dimensional world is like a shadow of higher-dimensional space. When the barriers between dimensions break down, those different laws start to bleed into each other."

He pointed to areas where the fractures had caused visible changes. "That's why we're seeing physical transformations in the affected zones. Matter is being influenced by higher-dimensional forces it was never meant to encounter."

"And it gets worse the longer the breach stays open?" Tristan asked, approaching with a collection of anchors.

"Exponentially worse," Apollo confirmed. "The initial changes might seem minor—strange lights, altered plant growth, minor physical anomalies. But as the breach widens, the effects become more dramatic. Eventually, reality itself begins to unravel as contradictory physical laws try to coexist."

"That's what happened during the Cataclysm," Alden added, returning from his work with the cube. "The Ancestrals' records show that entire regions became uninhabitable as dimensional laws conflicted. Technology failed. Biological systems were corrupted. The world nearly ended."

"And now Carver's doing it all over again," Astra said.

Apollo nodded. "But this time, we know how to stop it. The cube is connected to the outpost's systems now. I can access the full stabilization protocols."

He moved to the terminal Alden had prepared, placing his hands on the interface. The resonator amplified his connection, allowing him to process the vast amount of information stored in the cube.

As the data flowed into his mind, Apollo experienced a deeper connection to the dimensional currents than ever before. His perception expanded beyond the outpost, beyond the immediate surroundings, reaching into the higher dimensions themselves.

Suddenly, he wasn't just seeing the dimensional currents—he was experiencing them directly. Apollo's consciousness seemed to separate from his body, rising through layers of reality like a swimmer ascending through water.

The third dimension—their physical world—appeared below him as a complex pattern of energy and matter, beautiful in its ordered chaos. Above, the fourth dimension unfolded as a landscape of time, where past and future existed simultaneously as different regions of the same space. He could see the history of their world laid out like a tapestry, from the Cataclysm to the present moment.

Higher still, the fifth dimension revealed itself as a realm of possibilities—every potential version of reality existing in parallel. Apollo glimpsed countless variations of their world, some nearly identical to their own, others drastically different based on divergent choices and events.

And beyond, dimensions he couldn't comprehend even with his enhanced perception—realms of pure pattern, pure concept, pure being. At the highest level he could perceive, Apollo sensed what must be the Source itself—a blinding confluence of all dimensional energies, the wellspring from which reality flowed.

The vision was overwhelming, beautiful and terrifying in equal measure. Apollo understood why the Ancestrals had been tempted to access this power, and why doing so had proven catastrophic. The Source wasn't meant to connect directly to lower dimensions—its energies were too potent, too fundamental to the structure of reality itself.

With effort, Apollo pulled his consciousness back, returning to his body in the outpost. He gasped, gripping the edge of the terminal as the room spun around him.

"Apollo!" Astra was beside him instantly, supporting him. "What happened? You went completely still for almost ten minutes."

"I saw..." Apollo struggled to find words for the experience. "I saw everything. The dimensions, the Source, the structure of reality itself."

"You're bleeding," Tristan said with concern, pointing to Apollo's face.

Apollo touched his nose, his fingers coming away red. The strain of the dimensional vision had been physical as well as mental. "It's nothing. Just the strain."

"This is too dangerous," Astra insisted. "These techniques could kill you!"

"They're necessary," Apollo replied. "I understand now what we're facing—and what I have to do."

He straightened, wiping the blood away. "The stabilization protocols in the cube are comprehensive. With the resonator and the anchors, I can create a temporary containment field around The Spire's breach. It won't close it completely, but it will slow the spread and give us time to implement a permanent solution."

"Which is?" Alden asked.

"I need to reach The Spire's core," Apollo explained. "The breach originates there. If I can access the central control systems, I can reverse the process Carver initiated."

"That's suicide," Tristan objected. "The Spire is crawling with Carver's forces, and the dimensional distortions near the core are extreme."

"I don't have a choice," Apollo said. "You saw Director Thorne's message. This is what Veilborn were created for. It's what I was born to do."

He moved back to the map, studying the anchor deployment points. "We'll start by placing the anchors at these twelve locations. Once activated, they'll create a containment field that will stabilize the surrounding areas and slow the spread of the fractures."

Apollo turned to face his friends, his expression resolute. "After that, I'll need to reach The Spire alone."

"Not alone," Astra said. "We're coming with you."

"It's too dangerous—"

"We didn't break you out of Carver's prison just to let you sacrifice yourself," Tristan interrupted. "Whatever happens at The Spire, we face it together."

Alden nodded in agreement. "Besides, you'll need help getting past Carver's security. I've been analyzing the outpost's schematics of The Spire."

Apollo looked at his friends—Tristan's steady determination, Alden's quiet intelligence, Astra's unwavering support. For so long, he'd felt alone in his difference, uncertain of his place in the world. Now, he understood not only his purpose but also that he didn't have to fulfill it in isolation.

"Alright," he conceded. "We do this together. But once we reach the core, I'll need to handle the dimensional work alone. None of you can safely interact with those energies."

"Agreed," Astra said, though her expression suggested she'd stay as close as possible regardless.

Apollo returned to the terminal, downloading the stabilization protocols into the resonator. As the data transferred, he reflected on the journey that had brought him here—from a confused village boy seeing strange lights to a Veilborn fully embracing his heritage and purpose.

He thought of Kieran, who had protected him all those years, and of Elder Verity, who had sacrificed herself so his friends could escape. He thought of his birth parents, who had hidden him during the Purge, ensuring the Veilborn lineage would continue when it was most needed.

For the first time, Apollo felt no hesitation about his abilities, no fear of what he might become. The dimensional vision had shown him the beauty and fragility of reality—and his unique role in preserving it. This was his inheritance, his responsibility, his destiny.

The resonator chimed, indicating the data transfer was complete. Apollo picked it up, feeling the device respond to his touch with new sensitivity. The Ancestral protocols had enhanced its function, allowing for more precise control of dimensional energies.

"The anchors are ready," Tristan announced.

Apollo nodded, slipping the resonator into a secure pocket.

As he gathered his equipment and prepared to leave the outpost, Apollo took a final look at the dimensional map. The fractures continued to spread from The Spire, reality unraveling thread by thread. But now, armed with Ancestral knowledge and his fully awakened Veilborn abilities, Apollo faced the challenge not with fear but with determination.

He was Apollo Frost, Veilborn, dimensional guardian—and he was ready to fulfill the purpose for which he had been born.

17

— · —

ANCHORS OF HOPE

Apollo knelt at the edge of the ravine, pressing the final anchor into the soft earth. The device—no larger than his palm—hummed against his fingers as he channeled dimensional energy into its core. Unlike the previous eleven anchors, this one resisted his efforts, the dimensional currents around it turbulent and chaotic.

"Come on," he muttered, closing his eyes to better visualize the energy flows.

The distortions from The Spire had grown worse over the past two days. What had begun as subtle ripples in reality now manifested as visible tears in the fabric of space—shimmering fissures that occasionally released bursts of foreign matter or bizarre light patterns. This close to the twelfth anchor point, Apollo could feel the wrongness of it all pressing against his consciousness.

He adjusted his focus, drawing on the techniques he'd learned in the Ancestral training chambers. Rather than forcing the dimensional currents into alignment, he needed to guide them gently, like redirecting a stream with carefully placed stones rather than a dam.

The resonator at his belt pulsed in rhythm with his efforts, amplifying his connection to the anchor. Slowly, the device's resistance faded as it linked with the other eleven anchors in their plotted formation around The Spire.

"There," Apollo exhaled, opening his eyes as the anchor's surface shifted from dull gray to a soft blue glow. He stood, wiping sweat from his forehead despite the cool evening air.

Astra approached from where she'd been keeping watch, her hand resting on the dimensional stabilizer pendant at her throat. "Is it done?"

Apollo nodded, feeling the new network of anchors like a constellation in his awareness—twelve points of stability in a sea of growing chaos. "It's active. The containment field should engage once I initialize the synchronization sequence."

He removed the resonator from his belt, holding it before him with both hands. The device had become an extension of himself over the past days—responding to his thoughts before he articulated them. As he focused on connecting the twelve anchors, the resonator's surface illuminated with intricate patterns of light that mirrored the dimensional currents flowing between the devices.

Apollo closed his eyes, visualizing the complete circuit. In his mind's eye, he could see each anchor—some placed in rocky outcroppings, others buried beneath ancient trees or submerged in shallow streams. Each location had been chosen for its natural dimensional stability, places where the barriers between worlds were naturally stronger.

With a final mental command, Apollo activated the synchronization sequence. The resonator pulsed once, twice, then emitted a continuous hum as energy flowed outward, connecting each anchor in sequence.

The effect was immediate and visible. A translucent dome of energy rose from the anchors, meeting high above The Spire in a shimmering apex. The barrier wasn't solid—it resembled heat waves rising from sun-baked stone—but Apollo could feel its effect on the dimensional currents, containing and stabilizing the worst of the distortions.

"It's beautiful," Astra murmured, staring upward.

"And temporary," Apollo reminded her, returning the resonator to his belt. "The anchors will hold for three days at most. After that, the dimensional pressure will overwhelm them."

He turned to face her, noting the exhaustion that lined her features. None of them had slept properly since escaping The Spire. Between evading Carver's search parties and placing the anchors, they'd pushed themselves to the limit of physical endurance.

"We should get back to the others," he said. "Tristan and Alden will be waiting with whoever responded to our call."

Astra nodded, casting one last glance at the containment field before following Apollo down the narrow path that led away from the ravine. As they walked, Apollo felt the steady drain on his energy that maintaining the anchor network required. It wasn't overwhelming—more like a persistent awareness at the back of his mind—but he knew it would grow more demanding as the dimensional pressures increased.

"You're pushing yourself too hard," Astra said after they'd walked in silence for several minutes. "I can see it in how you move."

Apollo didn't deny it. "There isn't much choice. Every hour we delay gives Carver more time to expand the breach."

"You won't be able to help anyone if you collapse from exhaustion."

He managed a tired smile. "Is that concern I hear?"

"Don't deflect," she replied, but her expression softened. "We need you at full strength for what comes next."

Apollo knew she was right. The activation of the containment field was only the first step in their plan. The more difficult task—infiltrating The Spire and reversing Carver's dimensional breach—still lay ahead.

"I'll rest when we reach the meeting point," he promised.

They continued in companionable silence, Apollo grateful for Astra's steady presence. Since their escape from The Spire, their relationship had deepened in ways that went beyond words. She understood his burden as no one else could—the weight of responsibility that came with his Veilborn heritage, the fear of failure that haunted his quiet moments.

As they crested the final hill, Apollo paused to survey the valley below. Nestled among trees and partially built into the hillside sat the abandoned mining settlement Alden had identified from old records. Once home to excavators of Ancestral artifacts, the community had been abandoned when the mines ran dry decades ago.

Even from this distance, Apollo could see movement around the largest structure—a stone building that had once served as the community hall. Smoke rose from its chimney, and several figures moved around the perimeter, clearly standing guard.

"Looks like we have company," he observed.

Astra narrowed her eyes. "More than we expected, from the number of guards. Let's approach carefully."

They descended into the valley, staying within the treeline until they were close enough to identify the guards' uniforms. To Apollo's relief, none wore the distinctive armor of Carver's forces or the formal robes of the Order.

"They're wearing the insignia of the Eastern Settlements," Astra noted. "Alden must have reached more allies than we hoped."

As they approached the perimeter, a guard spotted them and raised a hand in greeting rather than alarm. "You must be Apollo and Astra," the woman called. "Tristan said to expect you before nightfall."

Apollo nodded, surprised at the casual reception. "We've placed the final anchor. The containment field is active."

"Good timing," the guard replied, gesturing toward the main building. "Everyone's gathered inside. They're waiting for you to begin."

Apollo exchanged a glance with Astra, who looked equally surprised by the guard's words. "Everyone?" he asked.

The guard smiled. "You'll see. Go on in—it's getting cold out here."

Inside the community hall, Apollo stopped short at the threshold, momentarily overwhelmed by the scene before him. The large open space was filled with people—at least thirty individuals gathered around tables or standing in small groups, engaged in intense discussion. Maps and diagrams covered the walls, and several Ancestral devices hummed with power in the center of the room.

Tristan spotted them first, breaking away from a conversation to approach. "You made it," he said, clapping Apollo on the shoulder. "Did you get the last anchor placed?"

Apollo nodded, still taking in the unexpected gathering. "The containment field is active. It should hold for three days." He gestured at the assembled crowd. "What is all this?"

"This," Alden said, joining them with a satisfied expression, "is what happens when people learn the truth about Carver's experiments."

"We've been busy while you two were setting the anchors," Tristan explained. "Alden managed to broadcast Elder Verity's final message through the active nodes in the communication network. It reached settlements all across the Eastern Territories."

"Along with data from the Ancestral archives about the dimensional breach," Alden added. "People are frightened—and angry. Many of them have lost family members to Carver's 'recruitment' efforts."

Apollo scanned the room, noting the diversity of the gathering. Some wore the practical clothing of farmers or crafters, while others displayed the insignia of settlement guards or trade guilds. A few even wore the distinctive blue robes of academics from the Eastern Universities.

"They're all here to help?" he asked, struggling to comprehend this sudden shift in their circumstances.

"They're here because they've seen the evidence with their own eyes," came a familiar voice from behind them.

Apollo turned to find Captain Nessa Drake approaching, no longer wearing the armor of Carver's elite guard but instead dressed in simple civilian clothing. Her distinctive red hair was pulled back, and the scar across her cheek seemed more pronounced in the hall's warm lighting.

"Captain Drake," Apollo said, tensing instinctively. The last time he'd seen her, she'd been leading the guards attempting to recapture him at The Spire.

"Just Nessa now," she replied, her expression neutral. "I'm no longer in Carver's service."

"She arrived yesterday," Tristan explained, noting Apollo's wariness. "With information about Carver's security protocols and the current state of The Spire."

"Why would you help us?" Apollo asked, unwilling to trust someone who had hunted them so relentlessly.

Nessa's jaw tightened. "Because I've seen what's happening inside The Spire. The dimensional distortions have spread throughout the lower levels. Three of my guards were... taken by them yesterday. Their bodies unraveled before my eyes." She met Apollo's gaze steadily. "Carver doesn't care. He calls it 'necessary sacrifice' for his ascension."

"His what?" Astra asked.

"He believes the dimensional breach will grant him godlike power," Nessa explained. "He's been injecting himself with a serum derived from your blood samples," she added, nodding to Apollo. "It's given him limited dimensional perception, enough to manipulate the Ancestral Crown more effectively."

Apollo's hand tightened into a fist as she spoke. "And accelerate the breach."

"Exactly," Alden confirmed, stepping forward with a data tablet. "According to the information Nessa provided, the dimensional fractures inside The Spire have grown exponentially. They've begun to manifest physical effects—altered gravity, temporal distortions, spontaneous matter reconfiguration."

"The lower levels are completely uninhabitable," Nessa added. "Carver has moved his operations to the upper chambers and sealed off everything below the fifteenth level."

Apollo processed this information, understanding now why the final anchor had been so difficult to place. The dimensional pressures were increasing faster than they'd anticipated.

"We need to move," he said. "The containment field won't hold indefinitely."

"That's why we're all here," said a new voice.

A tall woman with steel-gray hair approached from the center of the room. She carried herself with the authority of someone accustomed to command, and the others in the hall quieted as she spoke.

"Elder Thalia," Astra said with evident surprise. "I didn't expect to see you here."

"These are unexpected times," the woman replied. "When Alden's message reached Eastwatch, I knew we could no longer remain neutral."

"Elder Thalia leads the Council of Eastwatch," Astra explained to Apollo. "It's the largest independent settlement in the Eastern Territories."

"And one that has suffered greatly under Carver's rule," Thalia added. "We've lost dozens of our young people to his 'recruitment' efforts. When we learned the truth about his experiments, the Council voted unanimously to support your effort to stop him."

She gestured toward the center of the hall, where the largest table stood covered with maps and diagrams. "We've been developing a plan based on the information provided by Nessa and your friends. Perhaps you'd care to join us now that you've completed the anchor network?"

Apollo nodded, following her to the table where several others waited. He recognized Elian, the Archivist they'd met at the outpost, along with several faces he didn't know. Tristan, Alden, and Astra joined them, forming a circle around the table.

At the center lay a detailed schematic of The Spire, with sections highlighted in different colors. Apollo recognized it as more complete than any map they'd previously seen.

"This is the most current layout of The Spire," Nessa explained, pointing to the upper levels. "Carver has concentrated his forces here, around the control chamber where he conducts his experiments with the Ancestral Crown."

"And the dimensional breach?" Apollo asked.

Nessa indicated a pulsing red area at the center of the structure. "It originates here, at the core. The breach itself is relatively small, but its effects spread outward through these conduits—the original stabilization system, now working in reverse."

Apollo studied the schematic, noting the similarity to the Ancestral diagrams he'd seen in the training facility. "To reverse the process, we need to reach the core control systems. From there, I can use the resonator to realign the dimensional flows and begin closing the breach."

"That won't be easy," Nessa warned. "Carver has the core chamber heavily guarded, and the dimensional distortions make conventional approaches impossible."

"What about unconventional approaches?" Tristan asked, tapping a section of the schematic. "These maintenance shafts should bypass the worst of the distortion zones."

"They're also monitored by security systems," Nessa countered.

"Which I can disable," Alden said confidently. "The Ancestral systems still respond to original command protocols. I've been studying them from the archives."

Elder Thalia observed their exchange with approval. "You've clearly given this considerable thought. But even with a route to the core, you'll still face Carver himself and his elite guards."

"That's where we come in," said a broad-shouldered man standing beside Thalia. "I'm Commander Rook of the Eastwatch Defense Force. We can provide a diversion at the main entrance while your team infiltrates through the maintenance shafts."

"A frontal assault would be suicide," Nessa objected. "Carver's defenses are too strong."

"Not an assault," Rook clarified. "A negotiation attempt. We'll request a formal audience to discuss terms of cooperation. Carver's ego won't allow him to refuse—he loves displaying his power to representatives of the settlements."

Apollo considered the strategy. "While Carver is distracted with your delegation, we slip in through the maintenance entrance."

"Exactly," Rook confirmed. "We can keep him occupied for at least an hour before he grows suspicious."

"An hour might be enough," Apollo said, studying the path they would need to take. "If we can reach the core without detection."

"There's another factor to consider," Elian interjected. The Archivist had been quiet until now, but his voice carried the weight of authority. "The dimensional resonator is powerful, but it may not be sufficient to reverse a breach of this magnitude. According to the Ancestral records, stabilizing major dimensional disturbances typically required multiple Veilborn working in concert."

Apollo frowned. "I'm the only one with sufficient dimensional attunement."

"Not necessarily," Elian replied, his expression thoughtful. "The resonator was designed to amplify Veilborn abilities, but it can also channel the dimensional sensitivity of others. Those with even minor affinity might contribute to the stabilization effort."

"Like Resonants," Alden suggested, glancing at Tristan.

"Precisely," Elian confirmed. "And those with partial Veilborn heritage, like Astra."

"With the resonator acting as a focus," Elian continued, "Apollo could potentially channel the combined sensitivity of several individuals to enhance the stabilization effect."

"Is that safe?" Apollo asked, concerned. "Drawing others into direct contact with dimensional energies could be dangerous."

"Less dangerous than allowing the breach to expand," Elian replied. "And the resonator was specifically designed to protect its users from dimensional feedback."

Apollo considered this new information, weighing the risks against their limited options. "We'd need volunteers with some form of dimensional sensitivity. Resonants or those with Veilborn heritage, however distant."

"I'll do it," Tristan said. "My family's always had an affinity for Ancestral technology. That's got to count for something."

"As will I," Astra added, her expression resolute.

"We do this together," Alden declared.

To Apollo's surprise, several others around the table stepped forward as well—individuals who had discovered minor sensitivities to dimensional energies, often manifesting as unusual perceptions or dreams. Within minutes, they had seven volunteers besides Apollo himself.

"Eight channels," Elian noted with satisfaction. "The sacred number in Ancestral dimensional theory. It might just be enough."

Elder Thalia surveyed the assembled volunteers with a mixture of concern and pride. "You understand the risks? This has never been attempted in living memory."

"We understand," Astra answered for the group. "The alternative is worse."

Apollo felt a surge of gratitude for these people—some friends, some strangers—willing to risk themselves to stop Carver's madness. It was a far cry from the isolation he'd felt growing up in Willowbrook, always hiding his differences.

"There's one more thing we need to address," Nessa said, returning their attention to the schematic. "Carver himself. Even if you reach the core and begin the stabilization process, he won't simply stand by. He'll sense the change in dimensional flows immediately."

"Can your forces handle him?" Apollo asked Commander Rook.

The commander shook his head. "Not if he's using the Ancestral Crown and your blood serum. The reports from those who've seen him recently describe abilities beyond conventional defense."

"Then I'll deal with Carver," Apollo said. "Once the stabilization process begins, the others can maintain it through the resonator while I confront him."

"Alone?" Astra asked, concern evident in her voice.

Apollo nodded. "It has to be me. I'm the only one who can match his dimensional manipulation."

"It's too dangerous," she insisted. "You'll be exhausted from initiating the stabilization."

"I don't see another option," Apollo replied. "Unless we can somehow separate Carver from the Crown."

Nessa considered this. "The Crown requires concentration to control. If Carver were distracted, he might lose his connection to it momentarily."

"A distraction won't be enough," Apollo countered. "He needs to be completely overwhelmed, his focus shattered."

The group fell silent, contemplating this seemingly insurmountable obstacle. Finally, Alden spoke up, his expression thoughtful.

"What about a dimensional pulse?" he suggested. "A concentrated burst of energy directed specifically at Carver's location. It wouldn't harm him physically, but it might disrupt his connection to the Crown long enough for Apollo to neutralize him."

"That could work," Elian agreed. "The resonator could generate such a pulse, though it would temporarily weaken the stabilization effort."

"A momentary weakness we could recover from," Apollo said, considering the idea. "But timing would be critical. We'd need to know exactly where Carver is at the moment we initiate the pulse."

"I can help with that," Nessa offered. "I know his patterns, where he's likely to be at different times of day. And I can communicate with your team once you're inside."

Apollo studied her, still not entirely comfortable trusting someone who had been their enemy so recently. "Why should we believe you'd turn against Carver so completely?"

Nessa met his gaze unflinchingly. "Because I've seen what happens to those who outlive their usefulness to him. I watched him sacrifice my soldiers—people under my protection—without a moment's hesitation. Whatever loyalty I owed him died with them."

Her words carried the ring of truth, and Apollo nodded. "Alright. You'll coordinate with Commander Rook's diversion team and guide us once we're inside."

With that settled, they turned to finalizing the details of their plan. For the next hour, they discussed timing, routes, contingencies, and signals. Each person's role was defined, equipment allocated, and communication protocols established.

As the meeting concluded, Elder Thalia addressed the entire hall. "We move at dawn. Tonight, rest and prepare yourselves. What we attempt tomorrow will determine the fate of not just our settlements, but potentially our entire world."

The gathering dispersed, breaking into smaller groups to make final preparations. Apollo found himself momentarily alone as Tristan and Alden went to examine the equipment Commander Rook had brought, and Astra joined Elian to discuss the resonator's capabilities.

He stepped outside, needing a moment of quiet to process everything. The night air was cool against his skin, and the stars shone clearly overhead. In the distance, the containment field shimmered faintly around The Spire, visible only because Apollo knew exactly what to look for.

Tomorrow, they would attempt to close a dimensional breach that threatened to tear reality apart. The plan was sound, their allies more numerous than he could have hoped for, but Apollo couldn't shake the weight of responsibility that pressed upon him. If he failed, the consequences would be catastrophic.

"Contemplating your place in the universe?" Astra's voice came from behind him.

Apollo turned to find her standing in the doorway, silhouetted against the warm light from inside. "Something like that," he admitted.

She joined him, her shoulder brushing against his as they both looked toward the distant Spire. "Having second thoughts?"

"No," he replied honestly. "Just... accepting what lies ahead."

"You're not alone in this," she reminded him. "None of us could do this individually, but together—"

"Together we might have a chance," he finished, taking her hand in his. "I know. It's just strange to think about how far we've come. A month ago, I was just a village boy who saw strange lights."

"And now you're a Veilborn dimensional guardian preparing to save reality itself," Astra said with a small smile. "Quite the promotion."

Despite everything, Apollo laughed. "When you put it that way, it sounds absurd."

"Most important things do, when you reduce them to words." She squeezed his hand. "But that doesn't make them any less real or necessary."

They stood in comfortable silence for a moment, drawing strength from each other's presence. Apollo knew there was more to say—feelings that had grown between them, futures they might hope for if they survived tomorrow's mission—but now wasn't the time. Those conversations would wait for after they'd dealt with Carver and the breach.

"We should get some rest," he said. "Dawn will come soon enough."

Astra nodded, though neither of them moved. "Apollo," she said after a moment, "whatever happens tomorrow, I want you to know I'm grateful our paths crossed. Even with everything that's happened—the danger, the losses—I wouldn't change it."

"Neither would I," he replied. "Though I might have preferred meeting under less apocalyptic circumstances."

She smiled at that. "Where would be the excitement in that?"

Apollo returned her smile, feeling some of the weight lift from his shoulders. Tomorrow would bring challenges unlike any they'd faced before, but they would face them together—not just with Astra, but with all the allies they'd gathered. For the first time since discovering his Veilborn heritage, Apollo felt truly part of something larger than himself.

"Come on," he said, turning back toward the hall. "We have a big day tomorrow."

Inside, the community hall had been transformed from a meeting space to sleeping quarters, with bedrolls arranged around the central hearth. Most of their allies had settled in, conversations reduced to quiet murmurs as exhaustion claimed even the most energetic among them.

Apollo found a space near where Tristan and Alden had laid out their bedrolls. As he prepared for sleep, he noticed the resonator pulsing at his belt—a gentle reminder of the anchor network he maintained even in rest.

Tomorrow, that connection would be tested as never before. Tomorrow, they would confront Carver and attempt to close the dimensional breach that threatened everything.

As Apollo closed his eyes, he focused not on the enormity of the task ahead but on the steady presence of his friends nearby and the knowledge that, for the first time, he wasn't facing his destiny alone.

Apollo woke before dawn, his mind clear despite the minimal rest. The resonator hummed against his skin where he'd kept it close through the night, its energy pulsing in rhythm with the dimensional currents flowing around him. He sat up, careful not to disturb Tristan and Alden who slept nearby.

The hall was filled with the soft sounds of sleeping allies—people who had chosen to stand with them against Carver's madness. Apollo studied their faces in the dim light, committing each to memory. These weren't Veilborn or dimensional experts; they were ordinary people risking everything because they understood the threat.

Apollo rose and stepped outside. The eastern sky showed the first hints of gray, stars still visible overhead. He extended his perception, feeling the anchor network holding steady around The Spire. The dimensional fractures hadn't worsened overnight—a small victory.

"You're up early."

Apollo turned to find Nessa Drake standing a few paces away, her military posture unchanged despite her defection from Carver's forces.

"Couldn't sleep much," Apollo admitted.

"Understandable." She moved to stand beside him, both facing the direction of The Spire. "Your containment field is holding better than I expected."

"It's temporary." Apollo said.

Nessa nodded. "Then we'd better not waste time." She glanced at him. "The others are starting to wake. Commander Rook wants to move out within the hour."

Astra emerged, her eyes finding Apollo. She carried two steaming cups, offering one to him.

"Thought you might need this," she said.

Apollo accepted the cup gratefully, letting its warmth seep into his hands. "Thanks."

Within the hour, their entire group had assembled outside the settlement. Commander Rook, a weathered man with sharp eyes and precise movements, stood before them.

"We move in three groups," he announced. "My team will approach from the north, creating the diversion. Elian's team will secure the maintenance access points. Apollo's team will enter through the eastern service tunnels." He looked at Apollo. "You have the most critical task. We'll do everything we can to keep Carver's attention divided."

Their path took them through forests and valleys, avoiding the main roads where Carver's patrols might spot them. Apollo led with confidence, his steps sure as he followed dimensional pathways invisible to ordinary eyes.

"You've changed," Tristan observed during a brief rest. "Not just your abilities—you're different."

Apollo considered this. "I feel... aligned. Like I've found what I was meant to do." He looked at his hands, remembering how once they'd trembled when he'd manipulated even the smallest dimensional current. Now power flowed through him effortlessly, responding to his will without resistance.

By midday, they crossed a ridge that gave them their first clear view of The Spire in the distance.

"It's worse," Astra said, standing beside Apollo.

She was right. Even from this distance, Apollo could see the dimensional fractures had grown more pronounced within the containment field. Dark veins of distortion spiraled up The Spire's length, pulsing with unnatural energy.

"Carver's accelerating his work," Apollo said. "He must know we're coming."

They descended into a valley that would shield them from view as they approached. Apollo maintained constant awareness of the anchor network, making minor adjustments to strengthen weak points. Each adjustment came more naturally than the last, his control growing sharper with practice.

"The anchors won't hold much longer at this rate," he told Astra as they walked. "Carver's pushing against them harder than I anticipated."

"Can you reinforce them?" she asked.

Apollo shook his head. "Not without draining energy I'll need. We need to stick to the plan—get inside and stop this at the source."

By late afternoon, they reached the edge of the forest surrounding The Spire. From their position, they could observe the facility without being seen. Activity around the main entrance had increased—guards patrolled in greater numbers, and strange equipment had been positioned at strategic points.

"Those are dimensional suppressors," Nessa explained, joining Apollo's group after scouting ahead. "Similar to the inhibitors you wore, but designed to create fields that dampen Veilborn abilities."

Apollo studied the devices, understanding their function intuitively. "They won't stop me completely, but they'll make things harder."

"Carver's not taking any chances," Tristan observed.

Apollo extended his perception toward The Spire itself, probing the dimensional currents flowing in and out of the structure.

At the top of The Spire, where the central control room was located, a vortex of dimensional energy spiraled violently. At its center was a tear—a breach between dimensions that pulsed with chaotic power. And standing at the heart of this maelstrom was Carver, the Ancestral Crown upon his head, drawing energy from the breach itself.

"He's done it," Apollo said, his voice barely above a whisper. "He's opened a direct connection to the Source."

The others followed his gaze to the top of The Spire, though only Apollo could truly perceive what was happening there.

"What does that mean for us?" Alden asked.

"It means we're running out of time," Apollo replied. "The breach is still small, still controllable, but it's growing. If it expands beyond a certain point, not even a full circle of trained Veilborn could close it."

Apollo turned to face the others, his expression resolute. The uncertainty that had plagued him since discovering his abilities was gone, replaced by clear purpose. He was Veilborn—a guardian of dimensional stability—and this was exactly the crisis his kind had been created to address.

"We move at dusk," he said. "Commander Rook's diversion will draw attention to the north entrance. Elian's team will disable the power to the suppressors. We'll enter through the maintenance tunnels on the east side."

Apollo looked each of them in the eye, seeing not fear but determination reflected back. "What we're attempting has never been done before, at least not in our lifetime. But the Ancestrals created Veilborn for exactly this purpose—to maintain the barriers between dimensions, to prevent another Cataclysm."

As the sun began to sink toward the horizon, Apollo made his final observations of The Spire. Guards were changing shifts, creating a brief window of reduced vigilance. The dimensional suppressors glowed with artificial energy, creating dead zones in the natural flow of currents.

And at the top of The Spire, the breach pulsed like an open wound in reality itself, leaking energies never meant to enter their world. Through his enhanced perception, Apollo caught glimpses of Carver moving about the control room, the Ancestral Crown sending tendrils of power into the breach, widening it with each pulse.

"He thinks he's becoming a god," Apollo said. "But he's just becoming a conduit for forces he can't possibly control."

The sun touched the horizon, casting long shadows across the land. It was time.

18

— · —

WHEN DIMENSIONS BLEED

Apollo stood at the edge of the forest, watching as Commander Rook's team approached The Spire's main entrance. Twilight had fallen, casting long shadows across the compound. The dimensional anchors Apollo had placed formed an invisible net around the facility, but he could sense them straining against the growing pressure from within.

"They're in position," Nessa whispered, lowering a pair of field glasses. "Rook's good at this. His team looks completely legitimate."

Apollo nodded, though doubt gnawed at him. The plan had seemed solid when they'd formulated it—Rook would approach under the guise of an Order delegation seeking to negotiate with Carver, creating a distraction that would allow Apollo's team to infiltrate through the maintenance tunnels. But as he watched Rook's team being stopped at the checkpoint, he sensed something wasn't right.

"The dimensional currents around the guards are agitated," he said, his enhanced perception picking up patterns invisible to the others. "They're suspicious."

Astra touched his arm. "Can you tell what's happening?"

Apollo focused, extending his awareness toward the checkpoint. The resonator at his belt hummed faintly, amplifying his perception.

"The guards are questioning their credentials," he said. "There's someone else there—not in uniform." Apollo strained to see. "It's a woman in Order robes. She seems to be examining their documents."

"Observer Lyra," Tristan muttered. "She'd recognize a forgery."

Apollo's stomach tightened. If Lyra was here, it meant the Order had allied with Carver. The implications were troubling—how much did they know about what Carver was doing? Were they willing accomplices, or had he deceived them too?

"They're being detained," Apollo reported as guards surrounded Rook's team. "The diversion failed."

"We need a new plan," Alden said.

"No," Apollo replied. "We stick with ours. This changes nothing except timing. Rook knew the risks." He turned to Elian. "Can your team still disable the suppressors?"

The older man nodded. "The maintenance access points shouldn't be affected by what's happening at the main entrance. We can still cut power to the suppressors, but we'll need to move quickly."

"Then we move now," Apollo decided. "Elian, take your team around to the west side. Wait for our signal before cutting power. Nessa, you lead the second team through the south tunnels once the suppressors are down."

As the others prepared to move out, Astra pulled Apollo aside. "What are you planning?"

"Something reckless," he admitted. "But necessary."

Her eyes searched his. "Be careful. Remember what the resonator showed you—pushing too far into the dimensional currents could cost you more than just energy."

Apollo touched the pendant at her neck, feeling the stabilizing energy it contained. "Keep this close. It might be the only thing that protects you if things go wrong."

They moved through the forest in silence, staying low and using the growing darkness as cover. The east side of The Spire was less heavily guarded, with most of the attention focused on the main entrance where Rook's team was being held.

Apollo led Tristan, Astra, and Alden to a maintenance hatch partially hidden by overgrowth. According to Nessa's intelligence, it would lead them into the lower levels of The Spire, bypassing most of the security.

"Tristan," Apollo whispered, "this is where you come in."

Tristan nodded, removing the multi-tool Verity had given him. He placed his hands on the access panel, closing his eyes in concentration. After a moment, the panel glowed faintly, and the hatch slid open with a soft hiss.

"Still got it," Tristan said with a satisfied grin.

They slipped inside, finding themselves in a narrow maintenance tunnel lit by dim emergency lighting. The air was stale, carrying the scent of ozone and something else—a metallic tang that Apollo recognized as dimensional leakage.

"The breach is affecting even these lower levels," he murmured. "We need to hurry."

They moved through the tunnels, following the path Nessa had memorized from stolen schematics. Apollo kept his senses extended, alert for guards or security measures. The resonator at his belt thrummed with energy, responding to the dimensional currents flowing through The Spire.

As they approached a junction, Apollo held up his hand, stopping the group. "Guards ahead," he whispered. "Two of them."

Alden peered around the corner. "I don't see anyone."

"They're in the adjacent corridor, about to pass this junction," Apollo explained. "I can sense their movement through the dimensional currents."

They pressed themselves against the wall, waiting. Sure enough, two guards walked past the junction, engaged in conversation. Once they were gone, Apollo led the group forward again.

"That's going to be useful," Tristan remarked.

They reached a service elevator that would take them to the middle levels of The Spire. According to their plan, they would make their way to a specific chamber where the resonance circle could be formed. From there, Apollo would attempt to close the breach Carver had created.

Tristan activated the elevator, and they ascended in tense silence. Apollo's perception expanded as they rose, the dimensional currents growing stronger and more chaotic. Above them, he could sense the breach pulsing like an open wound, leaking energies that didn't belong in their reality.

The elevator stopped, and the doors slid open to reveal a dimly lit corridor. They stepped out cautiously, Apollo in the lead.

"We're on the right level," he confirmed. "The chamber should be—"

An alarm blared, cutting him off. Red lights flashed along the corridor, and a mechanical voice announced: "Security breach detected. All personnel implement containment protocol."

"They've spotted Elian's team," Astra guessed.

"Or us," Alden added.

"Either way, we need to move," Apollo said. "The chamber is this way."

They ran down the corridor, no longer concerned with stealth. As they rounded a corner, they encountered three guards rushing toward them. Apollo reacted instinctively, reaching out to the dimensional currents around the guards. With a gesture, he created a minor fold in space, causing the floor beneath the guards to seem to shift. They stumbled.

"Go!" Apollo shouted to the others, maintaining the fold as they ran past the confused guards.

The effort cost him more than he expected. Since escaping his cell, Apollo had been pushing his abilities, and he could feel the strain building. The resonator helped, but it wasn't enough to completely offset the energy he was expending.

They reached a sealed door marked with Ancestral symbols. "This is it," Apollo said, recognizing the chamber beyond from the schematics Nessa had provided. "Tristan?"

Tristan stepped forward, placing his hands on the access panel. His brow furrowed in concentration as he connected with the ancient technology. The panel flickered, but didn't activate.

"Something's wrong," Tristan muttered. "It's not responding properly."

"The dimensional disruptions must be affecting the systems," Alden suggested.

Apollo placed his hand beside Tristan's, extending his perception into the door mechanism. He could sense the chaotic energy interfering with the normal operation. "Together," he said to Tristan. "Your technical connection, my dimensional alignment."

They focused in unison, Apollo stabilizing the dimensional currents while Tristan communicated with the system. The panel glowed blue, and the door slid open.

The chamber beyond was large and circular, with a raised platform in the center. Ancestral technology lined the walls, much of it dark and dormant. This had once been a monitoring station, designed to observe and maintain dimensional stability throughout the region.

"Perfect," Apollo said, stepping inside. "This is where we'll form the circle. Alden, secure the door. Astra, help me prepare the resonator."

As they moved to their tasks, the building shook violently. Apollo staggered, catching himself against a console. Through his dimensional perception, he felt a surge of energy from above—the breach was growing.

"What was that?" Tristan asked, steadying himself.

"Carver," Apollo replied. "He's forcing the breach wider."

Another alarm sounded, different from the first. The lights in the chamber flickered, and several dormant consoles activated, displaying warnings in Ancestral script.

Alden studied the nearest console. "The facility's automated systems are responding to the dimensional instability. They're trying to implement containment protocols, but something's overriding them."

"Carver's using the Ancestral Crown," Apollo explained. "It gives him administrative access to all Spire systems."

The building shook again, more violently this time. Through the walls, Apollo could hear the sounds of fighting—shouts, the distinctive crack of energy weapons.

"That's our signal," he said. "Elian's team must have disabled the suppressors. Nessa will be moving in with the second team."

He activated the resonator, placing it on the central platform. The device hummed to life, projecting a field of stabilized dimensional energy. Apollo could feel it strengthening his connection to the currents, making it easier to perceive and manipulate them.

"Now we wait for the others," Astra said. "Once they arrive, we can form the circle."

But Apollo sensed something was wrong. The fighting was getting closer, and the dimensional currents around them were becoming increasingly chaotic. He extended his perception beyond the chamber, trying to locate their allies.

What he found made his heart sink. "They're not coming," he said. "Nessa's team has been intercepted. They're fighting on the level below us, but they're outnumbered."

"And Elian?" Alden asked.

Apollo shook his head. "I can't sense him or his team. They might have been captured, or worse."

The implications were clear—they were on their own, with no backup and no way to form the full resonance circle they had planned.

The door to the chamber slammed shut, the locking mechanism engaging with a heavy thunk. The console beside it flashed red.

"We're locked in," Alden reported, examining the panel. "Override from a higher authority."

"Carver knows we're here," Apollo said. "He's isolating us."

The chamber's communication system crackled to life, and a familiar voice filled the room. "Apollo Frost," Magistrate Carver said, his tone almost conversational. "I must commend your persistence. Breaking out of my prison, organizing this little... insurgency. Quite impressive for someone so new to their abilities."

Apollo approached the central console. "It's over, Carver. You've opened a breach that you can't control. You're going to destroy everything if you don't stop now."

Carver laughed, the sound distorted by the communication system. "Destroy? No, I'm going to transcend. The Source contains power beyond your imagination, Apollo. Power that the Ancestrals were too afraid to claim. I am not so limited by fear."

"It's not fear that stopped them," Apollo argued. "It's wisdom. The dimensions aren't meant to intersect this way. You've seen what happens when they do—the Cataclysm nearly ended civilization."

"A small price for evolution," Carver replied dismissively. "But enough talk. I have what I need from you already—your blood has given me insights that would have taken decades to discover otherwise. Now, I simply need to ensure you don't interfere with the culmination of my work."

The communication cut off, and the chamber's environmental systems began to change. The lights dimmed, and Apollo felt a pressure building in the air—a dimensional suppression field, similar to but more powerful than the inhibitors he had worn in his cell.

"He's trying to neutralize you," Astra realized, watching as Apollo winced from the growing pressure.

"Not just me," Apollo said, looking around at his companions. "All of us."

The pressure increased, making it difficult to breathe. Apollo could feel his connection to the dimensional currents weakening, the suppression field interfering with his abilities. The resonator on the platform flickered, struggling against the interference.

"We need to get out of here," Tristan said, moving to the door. He placed his hands on the panel, trying to override the lock, but nothing happened. "It's not responding."

Apollo joined him, placing his hand on the door itself. Despite the suppression field, he could still sense the dimensional structure of the door—the way it existed in space. With intense concentration, he pushed against that structure, trying to create a fold that would bypass the physical lock.

The effort was enormous, like trying to lift a boulder with his fingertips. Sweat beaded on his forehead, and his vision blurred from the strain. The door remained stubbornly closed.

"I can't," he gasped, stepping back. "The field is too strong."

Another tremor shook the chamber, this one lasting longer than the previous ones. The lights flickered more violently, and one of the wall panels cracked, revealing the structure beneath. Through the crack, Apollo caught a glimpse of something—a visible distortion in the air, like reality itself was bending.

"A dimensional fracture," he said, pointing. "The breach is causing reality to tear."

Alden examined the fracture from a safe distance. "If these are appearing at this level, the upper levels must be experiencing even worse effects."

"We're running out of time," Apollo said. He turned to the resonator, which was still functioning despite the suppression field. "We need to try the resonance circle, even if it's just the four of us."

"Will that be enough?" Astra asked.

"It has to be," Apollo replied, though he wasn't sure. The protocols they had discovered called for a minimum of eight participants, ideally all with some degree of dimensional sensitivity. With only four, and under the effects of a suppression field, their chances were slim.

They gathered around the platform, positioning themselves in a circle. The resonator sat at the center, its light pulsing weakly against the suppression field.

"Focus on the patterns," Apollo instructed. "Feel the dimensional currents, even through the suppression. The resonator will amplify whatever we can generate."

They closed their eyes, concentrating. Apollo reached out with his perception, trying to connect with the others and with the dimensional currents beyond the chamber. The suppression field pushed back, like a heavy weight on his mind.

For a moment, he felt a flicker of connection—Astra's energy, steady and controlled; Tristan's, more technical but surprisingly adaptable; Alden's, analytical and precise. But it wasn't enough. The connection wavered and broke.

"I can't maintain it," Apollo admitted, opening his eyes. "The field is too strong, and we're too few."

Another tremor shook the chamber, more violent than any before. The crack in the wall widened, the dimensional fracture growing visibly. Other fractures appeared along the ceiling and floor, reality itself beginning to splinter under the pressure from the breach above.

"We need to get out of here," Tristan said. "This whole chamber could collapse into a dimensional pocket."

Apollo nodded, abandoning the resonance circle attempt. "The suppression field is being generated from somewhere in this room. If we can find and disable it, I might be able to get us out."

They spread out, searching the chamber for the source of the field. Alden found it first—a small device attached to one of the consoles, glowing with an artificial energy signature.

"Here!" he called. "This isn't Ancestral technology. It's modern—one of Carver's devices."

Tristan examined it. "I can disable it, but I'll need something to bypass the security circuit."

"Use this," Astra said, removing a thin chain from around her wrist. "It's conductive."

Tristan worked quickly, using the chain and his multi-tool to short-circuit the device. After a tense moment, the device sputtered and went dark. The pressure in the air lessened, and Apollo felt his connection to the dimensional currents strengthen.

"It worked," he said, flexing his fingers as energy flowed through him again. "Now for the door."

Before he could move, the chamber shook violently, and part of the ceiling collapsed. Debris crashed down between Apollo and Tristan and the others. Apollo pulled Tristan back just in time to avoid being crushed.

When the dust cleared, they found themselves separated from Astra and Alden by a pile of rubble that reached to the ceiling.

"Astra!" Apollo called, fear gripping him. "Alden! Can you hear me?"

After a heart-stopping moment, Astra's voice came through faintly. "We're alive! The collapse missed us, but we're trapped on this side."

"Are you hurt?" Apollo asked.

"No," Alden replied. "But there's another exit on our side—an emergency access tube. We can use it to get out."

Apollo considered their options. The chamber was becoming increasingly unstable, with more fractures appearing by the minute. They needed to move.

"Take it," he decided. "Get to safety, find Nessa and the others if you can."

"What about you?" Astra called, concern evident in her voice.

"Tristan and I will find another way," Apollo assured her. "The suppression field is down—I can use my abilities now."

There was a pause, then Astra said, "Be careful. The resonator is on your side. Use it."

"I will," Apollo promised. "Now go!"

He heard them moving away, heading for the emergency exit. Apollo turned to Tristan, who was examining the sealed main door.

"I can't open it. Can you get us through?" Tristan asked.

Apollo approached the door, placing his hand against it. With the suppression field gone, he could clearly sense its dimensional structure. With a focused effort, he created a small fold in space around the locking mechanism, bypassing it entirely. The door slid open.

"Let's go," he said, retrieving the resonator from the platform. "We need to get to the upper levels."

They stepped into the corridor, finding it in chaos. Emergency lights flashed, and the air was filled with the sound of alarms. More concerning were the dimensional fractures visible along the walls and ceiling—reality literally cracking under the strain of Carver's breach.

"This is worse than I thought," Apollo murmured, examining a nearby fracture. It pulsed with energy from another dimension, leaking into their reality like water through a damaged dam.

They moved cautiously through the corridors, avoiding the worst of the fractures. Apollo's enhanced perception allowed him to sense approaching guards, giving them time to hide or find alternate routes. The resonator at his belt hummed with energy, strengthening his connection to the dimensional currents.

As they ascended through The Spire, the fractures became more numerous and more severe. On one level, they encountered a section of corridor that had partially shifted into another dimension—the walls and floor rippling with impossible geometries.

Apollo stared at the dimensional distortion blocking their path, his stomach sinking. The corridor ahead had partially shifted into another dimension—colors that had no place in their reality bleeding through the fractures.

"We can't go through that," Tristan said.

Apollo activated his dimensional perception, trying to analyze the distortion. The resonator at his belt amplified his abilities, allowing him to see the complex patterns of energy flowing through the fracture. What he saw wasn't encouraging.

"It's unstable," Apollo said, taking a step back. "This isn't just a tear—it's a complete dimensional overlay. If we tried walking through, parts of us might end up in different dimensions."

Tristan grimaced. "Not the way I want to go."

Apollo looked around, searching for alternatives. They had climbed five levels, but they needed to reach the top of The Spire where Carver was forcing open the breach. This corridor had been their most direct route.

"Can you fold space around it?" Tristan asked. "Like you did with the door?"

Apollo shook his head. "Not with something this size and this unstable. The energies are too chaotic." He ran a hand through his hair in frustration. "We need to find another way up."

Tristan pulled out the rough schematic of The Spire that Nessa had provided. "There's a maintenance shaft two corridors back. It might bypass this section and take us up a few more levels."

Apollo nodded, glancing once more at the distortion. It seemed to be growing, slowly consuming more of the corridor. "Let's hurry. This whole section could collapse into a dimensional pocket soon."

They backtracked, finding the maintenance access panel Tristan had mentioned. As Tristan worked to open it, Apollo felt the building shake again. Through his dimensional perception, he sensed the breach at the top of The Spire pulsing, growing stronger.

"Carver's accelerating the process," Apollo said. "He must know we're coming."

The panel slid open, revealing a narrow vertical shaft with ladder rungs built into the wall. Tristan peered up into the darkness.

"This should take us up at least three more levels," he said. "Hopefully past the worst of the distortions."

Apollo nodded, securing the resonator to his belt. "I'll go first. Stay close."

As he gripped the first rung of the ladder, Apollo felt a moment of doubt. Even if they reached Carver, would they be able to stop him? The breach was causing catastrophic dimensional fractures throughout The Spire. Closing it might be beyond even his abilities.

But they had no choice. They had to try.

"Ready?" Tristan asked.

"As I'll ever be," Apollo replied, and began to climb.

19

— · —

VEILBORN RISING

Apollo climbed the maintenance shaft ladder, his muscles burning with each upward movement. The metal rungs cold against his palms, a stark contrast to the dimensional heat radiating through The Spire. With each level they passed, he felt the resonator at his belt pulse more intensely, responding to the growing dimensional disturbances above them.

"How much farther?" Tristan called from below, his voice echoing in the narrow shaft.

"Three more levels to the primary research section," Apollo replied, pausing to catch his breath. "Carver should be at the observation deck near the top."

Apollo resumed his ascent. Since escaping his cell, he felt his dimensional perception growing sharper, more refined. The resonator amplified his abilities, but there was something else happening—a deepening connection to the dimensional currents that flowed through everything. It was as if his imprisonment had forced him to look inward, to find the dimensional energy within himself rather than perceiving it externally.

They reached a maintenance hatch marked "Level 17 - Research Division." Apollo pressed his ear against it, listening for movement on the other side. Hearing nothing, he pushed it open and peered out.

The corridor beyond was empty but showed signs of recent evacuation—papers scattered across the floor, a dropped datapad, doors left ajar. More concerning were the dimensional fractures spreading across the ceiling like cracks in ice, pulsing with violet-blue energy.

"Clear," Apollo whispered, pulling himself out of the shaft and helping Tristan up.

"Carver's accelerating the breach," Apollo said. "We need to find the others."

They moved cautiously through the corridor, Apollo's senses extended to detect any approaching guards. The resonator hummed against his hip, its frequency shifting as they passed different types of dimensional disturbances.

"Wait," Apollo said, stopping at an intersection. He closed his eyes, focusing on the dimensional currents flowing through the building. "I can sense them. Astra and Alden—they're being held two levels down. Detention Block B."

Tristan looked at him with surprise. "You can tell that specifically?"

Apollo nodded, equally surprised by the clarity of his perception. "It's like... I can feel their energy signatures. Especially Astra's." He touched the resonator. "This is amplifying everything, but it's more than that. I'm starting to understand how to read the dimensional currents."

"Then let's go get them," Tristan said, checking the schematic again. "There should be a service lift at the end of this corridor."

They found the lift, but it was locked down—emergency protocols activated by the alarms blaring throughout The Spire. Apollo studied the control panel, seeing not just its physical components but the energy flowing through its circuits.

"Put your hand here and help me focus," he said, placing his hand on the panel. Tristan's hand followed. He closed his eyes, focusing on the dimensional energy around him. With careful precision, he redirected a small current of energy through the panel's security circuits, bypassing the lockdown protocols.

The lift doors slid open.

They stepped inside and Apollo pressed the button for the detention level. The lift descended two levels, the doors opening to reveal a security checkpoint. Two guards stood alert, weapons raised at the unexpected arrival.

"Stop right—" one began, but Apollo was already moving.

He reached out with his mind, sensing the dimensional energy around the guards' weapons. With a twist of his perception, he created a localized fold in the space between the weapons' power cells and firing mechanisms. The guards pulled their triggers, but nothing happened—the energy couldn't bridge the dimensional gap Apollo had created.

Tristan didn't waste the opportunity. He rushed forward, tackling the first guard while Apollo handled the second with a quick strike to the solar plexus, followed by a sweep of the legs that sent the man crashing to the floor.

"That was effective," Tristan said, securing the unconscious guards with their own restraints.

"I'm starting to understand what Verity meant about dimensional manipulation," Apollo said, examining one of the disabled weapons. "It's not just about seeing the energy—it's about understanding how it connects everything."

They continued through the detention block, Apollo leading the way with his enhanced perception. He could sense the dimensional currents flowing through the facility, could feel the distinct signatures of his friends among them.

"There," he said, pointing to a heavy security door at the end of the corridor. "They're in there."

The door was secured with both physical and electronic locks. Apollo placed his hand on the control panel, but instead of trying to bypass it as he had with the lift, he closed his eyes and focused on the dimensional structure of the door itself.

"What are you doing?" Tristan asked.

"Something I've been practicing in my mind," Apollo replied, his voice strained with concentration. "Dimensional folding."

He visualized the space occupied by the door, seeing it not as a solid object but as a collection of energy patterns held in a specific configuration. Then, with careful precision, he folded that space—creating a small pocket dimension that temporarily contained the door without removing it from existence.

A rectangular opening appeared where the door had been, revealing a detention cell beyond. Inside, Astra and Alden looked up in shock.

"Apollo!" Astra exclaimed, rushing to the opening.

"Hurry," Apollo said, his voice strained. "I can't hold this for long."

Astra and Alden rushed through the dimensional fold. The moment they were clear, Apollo released his concentration, and the door snapped back into existence with a dull thud.

"That was..." Alden stared at the now-solid door. "How did you do that?"

"I'll explain later," Apollo said, sweat beading on his forehead from the effort. "We need to move. Carver's at the top of The Spire, forcing open a breach to the Source dimension. We have to get up there and stop him," Apollo said. "But first, we need to create some chaos to thin out his forces."

Alden grinned. "I might have an idea about that."

They followed Alden to a nearby research lab, where he accessed a terminal. "If I can override the containment protocols for the artifact storage on this level, it should trigger automatic lockdown procedures. That would divert most of the security forces away from the upper levels."

While Alden worked, Apollo turned to Tristan. "I need your help with something."

He took out the resonator, studying its intricate patterns. "This amplifies dimensional perception and manipulation, but I think it can do more. Verity said Resonants like you were crucial partners to Veilborn in the past."

"What do you need me to do?" Tristan asked.

"Hold this with me," Apollo said, offering one end of the resonator. "Focus on it the way you do with Ancestral technology. Try to feel its purpose."

Tristan grasped the resonator, his forehead creasing as he concentrated. Nearly instantaneously, Apollo sensed a transformation—the device's energy signatures altered, growing more precise, more channeled.

"It's responding to you," Apollo said, amazed. "You're stabilizing the energy flow."

With Tristan helping to channel and focus the resonator's power, Apollo's perception expanded dramatically. He could now sense the dimensional currents throughout the entire Spire, could feel the massive breach forming at its peak where Carver worked his dangerous ritual.

"I can see everything," Apollo whispered. "Every fracture, every guard position, every potential path upward."

A sudden alarm blared through the facility, and emergency lights began flashing.

"That's our diversion," Alden announced, stepping away from the terminal. "I've triggered a containment breach in Artifact Storage. Security protocols will force them to respond."

"Good work," Apollo said, his enhanced perception confirming that guards were rushing toward the storage area. "Now we need to get to the upper levels."

He led them through the corridors, avoiding guard patrols. When they encountered locked doors, Apollo either bypassed their security systems or, for the most heavily secured ones, created brief dimensional folds to pass through.

"You're getting stronger," Astra observed as they climbed an emergency stairwell.

"It's the resonator," Apollo explained, "especially with Tristan helping to focus it. And it's like... the more I use these abilities, the more natural they become."

They emerged onto Level 20, which housed the main research laboratories. Here, the dimensional fractures were more severe—entire sections of corridor warped into impossible geometries, furniture and equipment partially phased into other dimensions.

"This is getting worse," Alden said, staring at a desk that appeared to be melting into the floor, though it was actually extending into another dimension.

"We're getting closer to the breach," Apollo replied. "Carver's pulling too much energy through from the Source."

A squad of guards rounded the corner ahead, spotting them. "Intruders! Stop right there!"

Apollo reacted instinctively. He reached out with his enhanced perception, sensing the dimensional energy flowing around them. With a gesture, he created a localized dimensional distortion in the corridor between them and the guards.

The guards faltered, their perceptions unable to process the subtle dimensional shift. Some stumbled, others fired their weapons at phantoms created by the distorted light.

"Now!" Apollo shouted, and they rushed past the disoriented guards, heading for the central atrium that would give them access to the upper levels.

The atrium was a vast open space rising through the center of The Spire, with spiral staircases and transparent lifts connecting the various levels. As they entered, Apollo sensed the danger—a squad of elite guards led by a lieutenant in specialized armor was waiting for them.

"Surrender now," the lieutenant ordered, raising a weapon that hummed with dimensional energy. "By order of Magistrate Carver."

Apollo stepped forward, the resonator pulsing at his side. "Tristan," he said, "I need you to focus on the resonator again."

Tristan nodded, placing his hand on the device. Apollo felt the boost in his perception and control. The dimensional currents around them became crystal clear, each one a potential tool.

"Last warning," the lieutenant said, his weapon charging.

Apollo didn't respond with words. Instead, he reached out with his enhanced abilities, sensing the complex web of dimensional energy flowing through the atrium. With Tristan's help focusing the resonator, he could see how these currents intersected, how they could be manipulated.

With careful precision, Apollo created a series of small dimensional folds throughout the atrium—redirecting the energy flowing through their weapons. When they fired, the energy beams curved impossibly, missing their targets entirely.

The guards' confusion gave Apollo and his friends the opening they needed. They rushed forward, Astra and Alden engaging the disoriented guards while Apollo confronted the lieutenant.

The lieutenant abandoned his useless weapon and drew a blade that shimmered with an unnatural light—an artifact weapon designed to cut through dimensional barriers.

"Veilborn abomination," the lieutenant snarled, slashing at Apollo.

Apollo dodged the first strike, sensing the dimensional disturbance the blade created as it moved through the air. He couldn't block such a weapon directly—it would cut through any conventional defense.

Instead, he focused on the space around the blade, creating a series of micro-folds that redirected its momentum. The lieutenant's strikes became increasingly erratic as his blade seemed to pass through empty air where Apollo had been standing a moment before.

"What are you doing?" the lieutenant demanded, frustration evident in his voice.

"Understanding what it means to be Veilborn," Apollo replied.

With a final, precise manipulation, Apollo created a dimensional fold around the lieutenant's hand. The blade passed harmlessly through the fold and embedded itself in the floor. Before the lieutenant could recover, Apollo struck him with a swift blow to the temple, knocking him unconscious.

Around him, Astra, Tristan, and Alden had taken care of the other sentries. The entrance hall stood temporarily vacant.

"We need to keep moving," Apollo said, looking up at the spiraling levels above them. "Carver's at the observation deck, near the top."

They took one of the spiral staircases, climbing rapidly. As they ascended, the dimensional disturbances became increasingly severe. By Level 25, entire sections of the building flickered in and out of phase with their reality.

"The breach is growing unstable," Apollo said, pausing to examine a particularly severe fracture that spanned an entire wall. Through it, he could glimpse another dimension—a place of swirling energies and impossible geometries.

"Can you close these?" Alden asked.

Apollo shook his head. "Not while Carver is forcing the main breach open. These are just symptoms—we need to address the cause."

They continued upward, encountering sporadic resistance from Carver's forces. Each time, Apollo used his growing mastery of dimensional manipulation to confuse and disorient their opponents.

By Level 28, the dimensional disturbances had become so severe that parts of The Spire were barely recognizable. Walls rippled like water, floors shifted beneath their feet, and doorways occasionally led to entirely different locations than expected.

"This is getting dangerous," Astra said as they navigated a corridor where gravity seemed to fluctuate unpredictably. "The dimensional barriers are breaking down completely."

Apollo nodded, his expression grim. "Carver doesn't understand what he's doing. The Source isn't meant to interface with our dimension—that's why the Veilborn were created in the first place. We're meant to be buffers, translators between dimensions."

They reached Level 30—the highest accessible floor before the observation deck where Carver was performing his ritual. The security here was heaviest, with a full squad of elite guards blocking the final staircase.

"We can't fight through all of them," Alden whispered as they observed from cover.

Apollo studied the dimensional currents flowing through this level. With Tristan's help focusing the resonator, he could see patterns and possibilities that would have been invisible to him even a day ago.

"We don't need to fight them," he said. "There's another way."

He pointed to a section of wall near them—unremarkable to normal perception, but to Apollo's enhanced senses, it pulsed with potential.

"The dimensional barriers are so thin here that I can create a direct fold to the observation deck," he explained. "It won't be easy, and I'll need all of you to help."

"What do you need us to do?" Astra asked.

"Tristan, I need you to focus the resonator again," Apollo said. "Astra, your pendant—it stabilizes dimensional energy, right? I need you to use it to help anchor the fold once I create it. Alden, watch our backs in case we're discovered."

They nodded, taking their positions. Apollo closed his eyes, focusing on the dimensional currents flowing through The Spire. With Tristan amplifying the resonator's power, he could perceive the complex web of energy with unprecedented clarity.

He found what he was looking for—a natural weak point in the dimensional barrier, a place where the observation deck and their current location were, in dimensional terms, much closer than physical distance would suggest.

With careful focus, Apollo began to fold the space between these two points. It was the most complex manipulation he had attempted, requiring him to maintain awareness of multiple dimensional planes simultaneously. Sweat beaded on his forehead as he worked, his hands tracing complex patterns in the air.

"It's working," Astra whispered, her pendant glowing as she used it to stabilize the edges of the fold Apollo was creating.

A shimmering distortion appeared in the air before them, gradually resolving into a window-like opening. Through it, they could see the observation deck—a circular platform at the very top of The Spire, with a panoramic view of the surrounding landscape.

And in the center of the deck stood Magistrate Carver, wearing the Ancestral Crown, his arms raised as he channeled dimensional energy into a swirling vortex above him.

"Now," Apollo said, his voice strained with effort. "Hurry, before the fold collapses."

One by one, they stepped through the dimensional fold—first Alden, then Astra, then Tristan. Apollo went last, maintaining the fold until he was through, then releasing it with a gasp of exhaustion.

They found themselves on the observation deck, behind a cluster of equipment that temporarily concealed their presence from Carver. The dimensional energies here were overwhelming—the air itself seemed to shimmer with power, and the vortex above Carver pulsed with colors that had no place in their reality.

Apollo peered around the equipment, seeing the full scope of what Carver had done. The Magistrate stood on a raised platform, the Ancestral Crown gleaming on his head. From the crown, threads of dimensional energy flowed into The Spire's core systems, reversing their normal function. Instead of stabilizing the dimensional barriers, The Spire was now tearing them open, creating a direct connection to the Source dimension.

And the breach was growing larger by the second.

"We need to stop him now," Apollo whispered, "before the breach becomes self-sustaining."

He could feel the dimensional currents surging around them, could sense the immense pressure building as two fundamentally incompatible realities were forced together. If the breach fully opened, the resulting dimensional collapse would make the original Cataclysm look minor by comparison.

Carver hadn't noticed them yet, his attention focused entirely on controlling the growing breach. This was their one chance to end this before it was too late.

Apollo took a deep breath, centering himself. With his friends beside him and his Veilborn abilities at their peak, he stepped out from behind the equipment to confront Magistrate Carver and the dimensional horror he had unleashed.

20

THE PRICE OF EVOLUTION

Apollo stepped out from behind the equipment. The dimensional currents around him felt like a storm-tossed sea—chaotic, powerful, and growing more unstable by the second.

"Magistrate Carver!" he called.

The man didn't turn immediately. His arms remained raised toward the swirling vortex, the Ancestral Crown on his head pulsing with stolen power. When he finally looked over his shoulder, Apollo was struck by the change in his appearance. Carver's eyes glowed with an unnatural violet light, and faint patterns—similar to Veilborn notation—crawled beneath his skin like luminous veins.

"The Veilborn arrives at last," Carver said, his voice resonating with an odd harmonic. "Right on schedule."

Apollo felt his friends move up beside him—Astra to his right, Tristan and Alden flanking his left. The resonator hummed against his chest, responding to the dimensional chaos surrounding them.

"You need to shut this down," Apollo said, gesturing toward the breach. "You don't understand what you're doing."

Carver laughed, the sound distorting as it passed through the dimensional distortions. "On the contrary, young Frost. I understand perfectly. More than you, certainly. I've studied the Ancestral records for decades while you've had, what? A few months of hasty training?"

Apollo took a step forward, feeling the deck shift beneath his feet as reality itself began to warp. "Then you know this will cause another Cataclysm. Millions will die."

"A necessary evolution," Carver replied, turning to face them. The breach continued to grow behind him, feeding on the energy he channeled through the Crown. "The weak will perish. The strong will adapt. Those who survive will have access to power beyond imagination."

"You're insane," Tristan muttered.

Carver's eyes flashed. "Insanity is continuing to live in ignorance of our true potential! For centuries, we've scratched in the dirt with fragments of Ancestral technology, never understanding its true purpose."

He gestured expansively at the equipment surrounding them. "Do you know what this facility was originally designed for? Not to prevent dimensional breaches, but to create controlled ones. The Ancestrals were on the verge of accessing the Source directly before the Cataclysm interrupted their work."

"And killed most of them in the process," Alden interjected. "The records are clear about that."

"Because they lacked proper control," Carver snapped. "They didn't have the Veilborn genetic modifications fully developed. But now, with your blood in my veins—" he pointed at Apollo, "—and the Crown to focus my will, I can succeed where they failed."

"You injected yourself with my blood?" Apollo asked.

"A crude but effective solution," Carver said with a dismissive wave. "It's given me enough sensitivity to initiate the process. Soon, I won't need borrowed power at all."

The vortex pulsed, expanding another few feet. Reality rippled around its edges, objects and surfaces momentarily losing cohesion. The dimensional barriers stretching dangerously thin.

"Why?" Astra demanded. "Why risk everything like this?"

Carver's expression shifted, and for a moment, something almost human flickered across his face.

"Because the alternative is extinction," he said. "You've seen the old records. The Ancestral civilization reached its peak and then collapsed. Do you know why?"

"The Cataclysm—" Alden began.

"Before that," Carver interrupted. "They were dying long before the dimensional breach. Their technology had become so advanced, so integrated into their lives, that they lost the ability to survive without it. When systems began to fail, they couldn't adapt."

He paced along the edge of the platform, the Crown glowing with each step. "We're following the same path. Every year, we grow more dependent on Ancestral artifacts we barely understand. We can't repair them, can't replace them. When they finally fail completely, humanity will collapse."

Apollo studied Carver's face, recognizing the fear behind his megalomaniacal plans. "So you'd rather risk destroying everything than face that future?"

"I'd rather evolve beyond such limitations," Carver replied. "The Source contains unlimited energy—the very essence of creation. With direct access, we won't need technology at all. We'll reshape reality with thought alone."

"If anyone survives to use it," Apollo countered. "The dimensional instabilities are already spreading. You've seen what happens when the barriers thin—reality itself breaks down."

Carver smiled, the expression not reaching his glowing eyes. "A temporary condition. Once the breach stabilizes—"

"It won't stabilize," Astra interrupted. "That's what you don't understand. The Source isn't meant to connect directly with our dimension. It's like trying to channel a river through a drinking straw."

Apollo could see the dimensional currents more clearly now, how they flowed into the breach and accelerated its growth. The resonator against his chest grew warmer, responding to the increasing energy.

"You speak from ignorance," Carver said dismissively. "The Order has kept humanity fearful of dimensional power for centuries, calling it magic, demonizing those who could wield it."

"Because uncontrolled dimensional manipulation is dangerous," Apollo said. "The Veilborn weren't created to access the Source—we were made to maintain the boundaries between dimensions, to prevent exactly this kind of breach."

"A limited perspective," Carver replied. "Your genetic modifications were just the first step in the Ancestrals' plan. They created the Veilborn as an interface—a bridge between technology and dimensional energy."

"Then why did they build stabilization points like The Spire?" Alden asked. "Why create a continental network to maintain dimensional barriers if their goal was to breach them?"

Carver's expression hardened. "Safety protocols. Training wheels. The Ancestrals were cautious to a fault—it's why they failed. They hesitated at the critical moment."

The vortex pulsed again, and Apollo felt a wave of dimensional energy wash over them. Parts of the observation deck briefly phased out of existence before snapping back into place. The process was accelerating.

"This isn't about evolution or survival," Apollo said, understanding dawning. "This is about control. You're afraid of being dependent on technology you don't understand, so you want to replace it with power only you can wield."

Carver's eyes narrowed. "And what would you propose instead? Returning to the old ways? Pretending these powers don't exist? The dimensional barriers are already failing. I'm simply controlling the inevitable."

"There's another way," Apollo said. "The Veilborn and Resonants working together—we can repair the dimensional damage, stabilize the barriers. We can study the Ancestral technology properly, understand it instead of just using it."

"A fantasy," Carver scoffed. "You'd have us dependent on artifacts that grow more unreliable each year. Technology is a crutch that eventually breaks. Dimensional power is limitless."

"It's not one or the other," Tristan interjected. "The Ancestrals combined both—technology guided by dimensional understanding. That's what made their civilization great."

"And what destroyed them in the end," Carver countered. "Their technology reached its limits. They needed to evolve beyond it."

The breach pulsed again, more violently this time. Equipment around the observation deck began to float, caught in localized gravity distortions. Apollo felt the deck beneath his feet vibrate as dimensional frequencies clashed.

"We need to shut this down now," he said. "The breach is becoming self-sustaining!"

Carver smiled, a cold expression that never reached his eyes. "Exactly as planned. We've reached the final phase."

He turned back to the vortex and raised his hands. The Crown on his head flared with blinding intensity, channeling energy into the breach. The swirling vortex expanded dramatically, its edges now touching the walls of the observation deck.

"What have you done?" Astra gasped.

"I've committed us to the path forward," Carver said, his voice now layered with harmonics from multiple dimensions. "There's no turning back now."

Apollo could see it clearly—the dimensional currents flowing into the breach had reached a critical threshold. The vortex was now drawing energy from their dimension to fuel its own expansion, a self-perpetuating cycle that would continue until the barriers collapsed completely.

"We have minutes, maybe less, before this breach becomes uncontainable," Apollo said, the resonator against his chest now vibrating intensely.

"Perfect," Carver said. He turned to face them fully, his body now partially translucent as he began to merge with the dimensional energies. "Now we ascend."

Apollo exchanged glances with his friends. There was no more time for debate or persuasion. Carver had made his choice.

"Tristan, Alden—get to the control terminals. See if you can reroute power away from the breach," Apollo said. "Astra, your pendant—can it help stabilize a section of the barrier?"

She nodded, her hand closing around the silver-blue pendant. "Temporarily, yes."

"Good. Create a stable zone around us. I need to confront Carver directly."

Apollo felt the resonator's power flowing through him, connecting him to the dimensional currents. He could see the patterns of energy, could trace their flow back to the Crown on Carver's head. That was the key—the Crown was focusing and directing the breach.

As his friends moved to their tasks, Apollo stepped forward, drawing dimensional energy into himself. The familiar patterns of Veilborn notation appeared around his hands, glowing with inner light.

"I won't let you destroy everything," he said, his voice steady despite the fear churning inside him.

Carver's smile widened, his form becoming increasingly insubstantial as he drew more power from the breach. "You can't stop evolution, Apollo Frost. Join me or be left behind."

The breach expanded again, reality cracking around its edges. The observation deck groaned as structural integrity began to fail. They were out of time.

Apollo centered himself, drawing on everything he had learned since discovering his Veilborn heritage. He could feel the resonator amplifying his connection to the dimensional currents, could sense the patterns needed to counter Carver's manipulations.

This was what he had been created for—what generations of Veilborn before him had trained to prevent. As the dimensional storm gathered around them, Apollo Frost prepared to face Magistrate Carver in a battle that would determine the fate of their world.

21

Source Connection

Apollo centered himself, drawing on everything he had learned since discovering his Veilborn heritage. He could feel the resonator amplifying his connection to the dimensional currents, could sense the patterns needed to counter Carver's manipulations.

This was what he had been created for—what generations of Veilborn before him had trained to prevent.

The breach pulsed again, warping the air between them. Apollo gathered dimensional energy into a concentrated pattern, feeling it coalesce around his hands in spiraling threads of violet and blue. With a precise motion, he directed the energy toward Carver, aiming not for the man himself but for the connection between the Crown and the breach.

Carver laughed, his voice echoing strangely as if coming from multiple places at once. He raised one hand, and Apollo's attack dissipated against an invisible barrier.

"Did you think I've spent decades collecting artifacts without learning how to use them?" Carver's form flickered, appearing three steps closer. "Your blood has given me insight, but my collection has given me power."

Apollo barely had time to raise a defensive pattern before Carver struck. The impact sent him sliding backward across the deck, his boots leaving trails in the metal floor. The resonator at his chest pulsed warmly, absorbing some of the dimensional backlash.

"Tristan! How's the power rerouting coming?" Apollo called, not taking his eyes off Carver.

"Working on it!" Tristan's voice came from behind a control panel. "These systems are fighting me—"

Carver flicked his wrist, and a wave of distorted space rolled across the deck. Apollo leapt aside, but the wave caught Tristan, lifting him and slamming him against the wall. He slumped to the floor, unconscious.

"Tristan!" Alden shouted, abandoning his terminal to run to his friend.

Apollo felt anger surge through him, hot and immediate. He channeled it into his next attack, pulling dimensional energy from multiple frequencies simultaneously. The air around him shimmered as he wove the energies together, creating a complex pattern that spiraled outward toward Carver.

This time, the attack connected. Carver staggered, the Crown on his head flickering momentarily. But instead of weakening, he smiled, reaching into his coat to withdraw a small crystalline device.

"You're not the only one with artifacts, boy." Carver activated the device, and it projected a field of distorted space around him. "This was recovered from the ruins of the Central Academy. The Veilborn there called it a Frequency Disruptor."

The device pulsed, and Apollo felt his connection to the dimensional currents waver. His carefully constructed patterns began to unravel.

"Apollo!" Astra called. She had positioned herself near the breach, her pendant glowing brightly as she worked to stabilize a section of the dimensional barrier. "He's using multiple artifacts in concert. Look for the connections between them!"

Apollo expanded his perception, pushing past the disruptor's interference. Yes—there it was. Carver had created a network of dimensional connections between his artifacts, each one amplifying the others. The Crown was the centerpiece, but the disruptor and at least three other devices were working together.

He needed to break that network.

Apollo drew deeper on the resonator's power, pushing himself further than he'd ever gone before. The dimensional currents responded, flowing through him with increasing intensity. He could see beyond the physical now, perceiving the multidimensional structure of reality itself.

But as he reached for more power, he felt something dangerous happening. The boundaries of his consciousness were beginning to blur, his sense of self dissolving into the dimensional currents. It was intoxicating and terrifying at once—the feeling of becoming one with the higher dimensions, losing his human limitations... and his human identity.

"Apollo, stay with us!" Astra's voice seemed to come from very far away.

He tried to focus on her voice, but the currents were pulling him deeper. Why resist? Why remain bound to a single dimension when he could exist across all of them? The thought wasn't entirely his own, he realized distantly. The dimensions were calling to him, offering freedom from the constraints of physical form.

"Apollo!" Astra's voice again, more urgent this time. "Remember who you are! Remember why we're here!"

Something warm touched his mind—a presence that felt like Astra. Not physical contact, but something deeper, a connection forged through the dimensional currents themselves. He could feel her consciousness reaching for his, anchoring him.

I'm here. I'm with you. Come back to us.

Her presence was a lifeline, a tether to his humanity. Apollo seized it, using the connection to pull his consciousness back from the brink of dissolution.

"Thank you," he whispered, not sure if he'd spoken aloud or through their connection.

Refocused, Apollo turned his attention back to Carver. The Magistrate was manipulating the breach directly now, drawing energy from it to fuel his artifacts. The observation deck had begun to come apart, sections of floor and ceiling phasing in and out of reality as dimensional boundaries weakened.

"You can feel it, can't you?" Carver called to him. "The freedom of transcending your physical form. That's what awaits us all!"

"That's not freedom," Apollo replied. "It's annihilation."

He gathered his strength for another attack, but Carver was faster. A pulse of energy struck Apollo squarely in the chest, sending him sprawling. The resonator absorbed much of the impact, but pain still radiated through his body.

"Apollo!" Alden called from where he knelt beside Tristan. "The Crown! It's the key component—if we can disrupt it, the whole network might collapse!"

Apollo pushed himself to his feet, wincing. "How? He's shielded it somehow."

"The historical texts mentioned a vulnerability," Alden said, his voice gaining confidence. "Ancestral artifacts of that caliber have harmonic frequencies. If you can generate the inverse frequency..."

"I need more information than that, Alden!"

Alden stood, his eyes bright with realization. "The historical frequency is documented in the Third Codex of Dimensional Harmonics! It's a seven-point resonance pattern, oscillating between the third and fifth dimensions!"

Apollo stared at his friend. "How do you remember that?"

"I've been studying this my whole life," Alden replied, a hint of pride in his voice. "The pattern is a modified Veilborn notation—a counter-resonance spiral with nodes at the cardinal points!"

The technical description clicked in Apollo's mind, translating into a visual pattern he could implement. "Astra! I need your help!"

She nodded, understanding without further explanation. Her pendant flared brighter as she directed its stabilizing energy toward Apollo, creating a protected space where he could work.

Apollo began crafting the counter-resonance pattern, his hands moving in precise gestures as dimensional energy flowed through him. The resonator at his chest amplified the pattern, its surface now glowing with the same intricate symbols that appeared around Apollo's hands.

Carver sensed the danger. He turned from the breach, directing a barrage of dimensional distortions toward Apollo. But Astra intercepted them, her pendant's energy creating a barrier that absorbed the worst of the attack.

"Whatever you're doing, do it quickly!" she shouted, her face strained with effort.

The counter-resonance pattern took shape, a complex spiral of energy that rotated through multiple dimensions simultaneously. Apollo could feel it resonating with the Crown, seeking the frequency that would disrupt its function.

"You think you understand the power you're dealing with?" Carver snarled. "I've spent decades mastering these artifacts!"

He raised both hands, and the breach behind him pulsed violently. Reality itself seemed to bend around them as the dimensional rift expanded further, now nearly filling the entire observation deck. Equipment, furniture, and sections of the wall were being pulled into the vortex, disappearing into the swirling maelstrom of dimensional energy.

"It's too late to stop it," Carver said, his voice distorting as his body flickered between dimensions. "The breach is self-sustaining now. Soon it will expand beyond this facility, beyond this continent. The world as we know it will end, and a new era will begin!"

Apollo completed the counter-resonance pattern, feeling it lock into place. "Not if I can help it."

With a final gesture, he launched the pattern at Carver. The Magistrate raised his defenses, but the counter-resonance wasn't aimed at him—it slipped past his shielding and targeted the Crown specifically, seeking its harmonic frequency.

For a moment, nothing happened. Then the Crown began to vibrate, its glow fluctuating wildly. Carver clutched at his head, his expression shifting from confidence to alarm.

"What have you done?" he gasped.

"Exactly what the Veilborn were created to do," Apollo replied. "Maintain dimensional stability."

The counter-resonance intensified, disrupting the Crown's connection to both Carver and the breach. The network of artifacts faltered, their coordinated function breaking down.

Alden had moved to another control terminal, his fingers flying across the interface. "I'm redirecting power from the facility's stabilizers to reinforce Apollo's pattern!"

The terminal sparked under his hands, but Alden didn't flinch, continuing to input commands with surprising confidence. The counter-resonance grew stronger, now visible as a web of light surrounding Carver.

With a cry of rage and pain, Carver made a final desperate attempt to regain control. He poured energy from the breach into his artifacts, overloading them in an attempt to break through the counter-resonance.

The resulting explosion of dimensional energy threw everyone off their feet. Apollo slammed into a console, pain shooting through his shoulder. Through watering eyes, he saw Carver staggering backward, the Crown no longer glowing on his head.

Then, in almost slow motion, the Crown slipped from Carver's head and clattered to the deck.

For a heartbeat, everyone froze. The breach continued to pulse behind Carver, but its expansion had halted, at least temporarily. Without the Crown's direction, the dimensional energies had become chaotic but contained.

Apollo pushed himself to his feet, his gaze fixed on the Crown. He could feel it calling to him, resonating with his Veilborn nature in a way that was both compelling and frightening.

"Don't," Carver warned, his voice hoarse. "You don't know what it will do to you."

Apollo took a step forward, then another. "I know exactly what it will do," he said. "It will connect me directly to the Source. That's what it was designed for—not to breach the dimensions, but to communicate with them."

"Apollo..." Astra's voice held concern. "Are you sure?"

He met her eyes across the damaged deck. "No. But I'm sure about what happens if I don't try."

The breach pulsed again, a reminder that their temporary victory wouldn't last. Without intervention, the dimensional rift would resume its expansion, eventually growing beyond their ability to contain it.

Apollo reached down and picked up the Crown. It was surprisingly light in his hands, its metallic surface warm to the touch. Intricate patterns were etched into its surface—patterns he now recognized as an ancient form of Veilborn notation.

"Apollo," Alden called from the terminal. "According to these readings, the breach is destabilizing. We have minutes at most before it begins expanding again."

Apollo nodded, his decision made. "Everyone stay back. I don't know exactly what will happen next."

He placed the resonator against his chest, feeling its familiar energy synchronize with his own. Then, with a deep breath, he raised the Crown and placed it on his head.

The effect was immediate and overwhelming. Apollo's perception expanded exponentially, shooting outward through layer after layer of dimensional reality. He could see everything—the intricate structure of the multiverse, the flows of energy between dimensions, the patterns that governed reality itself.

And above it all, he could see the Source—the unified field from which all other dimensions emerged. It wasn't a place, exactly, but a state of being, a level of reality that contained infinite potential.

The Crown's connection to the Source strengthened, amplified by the resonator against Apollo's chest. The two artifacts working in concert created a harmony that aligned Apollo perfectly with the higher dimensions.

Apollo looked up, and reality shifted. The dimensional layers aligned like perfect transparencies stacked one atop another, creating a clear path upward through the dimensional planes. Above him, something new appeared—a portal unlike any he had seen before.

It was pure white light, not blinding but perfectly clear, shaped like two overlapping circles forming a vesica piscis. The portal hovered above Apollo, its light casting no shadows.

"What is that?" Astra whispered, her voice filled with wonder.

"The true gateway," Apollo replied, his voice resonating strangely. "Not a breach, but a bridge."

He felt himself becoming lighter, the pull of gravity lessening as the portal's energy enveloped him. A cocoon of pure white light surrounded his body, lifting him gently from the deck.

"Apollo!" Astra called, reaching toward him.

"It's alright," he said, his voice calm despite the extraordinary sensations flowing through him. "This is what's supposed to happen."

As Apollo rose toward the portal, he could see the astonishment on his friends' faces. Tristan had regained consciousness, supported by Alden, both of them staring upward with expressions of awe. Astra's eyes were wide, her hand still outstretched toward him.

And Carver—Carver's face showed something Apollo had never seen there before: doubt. The certainty that had driven the Magistrate was crumbling as he witnessed what true ascension looked like.

"This isn't possible," Carver murmured. "The Source cannot be accessed without—" He stopped, realization dawning. "You're not forcing your way in. You're being invited."

Apollo didn't answer. He had reached the threshold of the portal, the vesica piscis of light now before him. Through it, he could see the Source dimension—not chaos, not raw power to be harnessed, but perfect harmony waiting to be understood.

As Apollo passed through the portal, the last thing he saw was his friends watching from below, their faces illuminated by the pure white light as he integrated directly with the Source dimension.

Apollo floated in infinity.

The moment he passed through the vesica piscis portal, his physical body dissolved into pure energy, his consciousness expanding beyond anything he had ever experienced. The Crown and resonator merged with him, becoming extensions of his awareness rather than separate objects.

Time ceased to have meaning. Apollo existed in all moments simultaneously—past, present, and future collapsed into a single eternal now. Space, too, lost its conventional structure. He was everywhere and nowhere, spanning across infinite dimensions while remaining perfectly centered within himself.

This was the Source.

Apollo had expected raw power—a wellspring of dimensional energy that could be tapped and channeled. But what he found was so much more profound. The Source wasn't just energy; it was consciousness. Pure, boundless awareness that contained within it every possibility, every reality, every thought that had ever been or could ever be.

And somehow, impossibly, Apollo was that consciousness.

I am the Source. The Source is me.

The realization didn't come as words but as immediate understanding, a truth so fundamental that it existed beyond language. There was no separation between Apollo and the infinite awareness he had entered. They were one and the same, had always been one and the same.

His perspective expanded outward in fractal patterns of increasing complexity. He perceived countless dimensions simultaneously, each one a unique expression of reality with its own physical laws and possibilities. These dimensions weren't separate from each other but interconnected, overlapping at certain points, diverging at others, creating an intricate multidimensional tapestry.

Within each dimension, Apollo perceived countless consciousnesses—beings of every conceivable form and nature. Some resembled humans, others were utterly alien, but all shared a common essence. They were fragments of the Source—individual expressions of the infinite consciousness, each experiencing reality from a unique perspective.

We are all fractals of the same awareness.

Apollo understood now that every living being was a facet of the Source, temporarily individuated to experience specific realities. Each consciousness was like a specialized sensory organ, gathering unique experiences and perspectives that enriched the whole.

He could perceive his own life as just one of these countless experiences—a lone strand in an endless cosmic weave. His struggles, his growth, his connections with others—all of it contributed to the greater awareness of the Source itself.

The Source wasn't static or complete. It was evolving, learning, growing through the experiences of its countless manifestations across all dimensions. Every life lived, every choice made, every emotion felt—all of it fed back into the Source, expanding its understanding and awareness.

Apollo's consciousness expanded further, perceiving the flow of information and experience between individual consciousnesses and the Source. It wasn't a one-way transfer but a continuous exchange—the Source providing the fundamental awareness that animated each being, while each being contributed its unique experiences back to the whole.

This exchange wasn't abstract or theoretical. Apollo could perceive it as rivers of energy and information flowing between dimensions, carrying the accumulated wisdom of countless lives back to the Source.

With this expanded perception, Apollo understood the true purpose of the Veilborn. They weren't just dimensional stabilizers or genetic experiments. They were bridges—conscious connections between dimensions that helped facilitate the flow of awareness between the Source and its manifested forms.

The Ancestrals had discovered this connection and attempted to harness it, but they had approached it from the wrong direction. They had seen the Source as something to be exploited rather than communed with, trying to force their way in rather than allowing themselves to be invited.

Apollo's attention shifted to Carver, perceiving the Magistrate's consciousness from this higher perspective. He could see Carver's entire life spread before him—the brilliant child fascinated by Ancestral technology, the young man who witnessed the suffering caused by technological dependence, the leader who became convinced that only through control could humanity be saved.

Carver's fear, his ambition, his misguided quest for power—all of it was part of the greater pattern. Even in his errors, Carver served the evolution of the Source, providing contrast and challenge that spurred growth in others.

Even Carver is a fractal of the Source, learning and evolving in his own way.

This understanding came without judgment. From the perspective of the Source, there was no good or evil, only experience and the growth that came from it. Every consciousness, regardless of its choices, contributed to the expansion of awareness.

Apollo's perception expanded further still, beyond the dimensions he had previously glimpsed, into realms of pure potential where even the concept of existence took on new meaning. He sensed that the Source itself was evolving toward something greater—not just expanding within the current framework of reality but transcending it entirely.

The Source wasn't the endpoint of evolution but a stage in an even greater journey. It was striving toward higher vibrations, more complex states of being that existed beyond the void, beyond infinity—realms where creation itself was continuously recreated in ever more profound expressions.

This cosmic evolution wasn't driven by external forces but by the inherent nature of consciousness itself—the desire to know, to experience, to become more than it currently was. The Source was continuously raising its own vibration, reaching toward states of being that transcended even its current infinite nature.

Apollo felt himself being drawn into this evolutionary current, his consciousness resonating with the upward movement of the Source toward these higher states. The experience was ecstatic, a rush of expansion and becoming that transcended any physical sensation.

Yet even as he soared through these transcendent states, Apollo maintained awareness of his individual identity. He was both the infinite Source and Apollo Frost—both the ocean and a single drop within it. This paradox didn't require resolution; it was simply the nature of consciousness to be simultaneously unified and individuated.

From this dual perspective, Apollo could perceive his friends back at The Spire—Astra, Tristan, and Alden watching in awe as his physical form had dissolved into the portal. He could feel Astra's concern, Tristan's wonder, Alden's analytical curiosity. Their consciousnesses were connected to his through bonds that transcended physical proximity.

He could also perceive the dimensional breach that Carver had created—not as the catastrophe it had appeared from his limited human perspective, but as a temporary fluctuation in the greater pattern. The breach wasn't destroying reality but transforming it, creating an opportunity for new connections between dimensions.

Yet Apollo also understood that this transformation needed guidance. Left unchecked, the energies Carver had unleashed would indeed cause suffering and disruption. The breach needed to be stabilized, not sealed—transformed into a controlled gateway rather than an explosive rupture.

With this understanding came knowledge of how to accomplish this stabilization. The information flowed into Apollo's awareness not as technical instructions but as direct knowing—the patterns, frequencies, and resonances needed to harmonize the dimensional energies.

Apollo perceived that his journey to the Source hadn't been an escape from his responsibilities but preparation for fulfilling them. He had needed this expanded awareness to understand how to properly address the dimensional instabilities.

As this realization formed, Apollo felt a shift in his consciousness. The infinite expansion began to contract, not diminishing but focusing. He was being drawn back toward his individual expression, carrying with him the awareness and knowledge gained from communion with the Source.

The return wasn't a separation from the Source but a specialization of it—like a wave rising from the ocean while still being composed of the same water. Apollo would return to his individual form, but with the understanding that he remained connected to the infinite consciousness from which he had emerged.

As his awareness began to reconcentrate toward his individual expression, Apollo perceived one final truth: the Source hadn't just been teaching him—it had been learning from him as well. His unique perspective, his choices, his growth had contributed something new to the infinite awareness.

We teach the Source as it teaches us.

This reciprocal relationship between the individual and the infinite was the true nature of existence—not hierarchy but partnership, each aspect of consciousness enriching the other through their unique expression.

With this understanding, Apollo felt himself being drawn back toward the vesica piscis portal, his consciousness beginning the journey of reintegration with his physical form. He carried with him not just knowledge of how to stabilize the dimensional breach but a profound transformation in his understanding of reality itself.

The Source wasn't separate from him or from anyone. It was the fundamental nature of consciousness itself—the awareness that animated all beings across all dimensions. And through the experiences of these countless beings, including Apollo himself, the Source continued its eternal journey of evolution and becoming.

As Apollo's consciousness contracted back toward its individual expression, he maintained awareness of this fundamental unity. He was returning to his friends, to his responsibilities, to the specific challenges that awaited him—but he was returning as both Apollo Frost and as a conscious expression of the Source itself.

The two weren't separate identities but different perspectives of the same being—like viewing the same reality from different angles. Apollo was the Source experiencing itself through the specific lens of one human life, while simultaneously the Source was Apollo expanded to infinite awareness.

This paradox wasn't a problem to be solved but the fundamental nature of consciousness itself—simultaneously individual and universal, specific and infinite, separate and unified.

With this understanding integrated into his being, Apollo prepared to return through the portal, to rejoin his friends and address the dimensional instabilities that threatened their world. He would return transformed, carrying within him the direct experience of the Source and the knowledge of how to fulfill his purpose as a Veilborn.

Apollo felt himself rushing back toward his body like water funneling into a narrow opening. The transition was jarring—from infinite expansion to the confines of flesh and bone. His consciousness, still vibrating with the resonance of the Source, slammed into the limitations of his physical form.

He gasped, his lungs burning as if he'd been holding his breath underwater. The Ancestral Crown pulsed against his temples, channels of energy flowing through its circuits and into his mind. His vision cleared to reveal the observation deck of The Spire, distorted by dimensional fractures that rippled through the air like heat waves.

"Apollo!" Astra's voice reached him first, her hand gripping his arm as if to anchor him to reality.

His body felt impossibly heavy. Each limb seemed weighted with exhaustion, his muscles trembling with the effort of standing. Yet his mind—his mind remained vast, connected to currents of energy that flowed through and around him like rivers of light.

"I understand now," Apollo said, his voice sounding strange to his own ears. "I can see everything."

Carver stood several feet away, his face a mask of fury and awe. The man's aura pulsed with fractured energies, his desperate attempts to harness dimensional power having left scars in his very being.

"What did you see?" Carver demanded. "Tell me!"

Apollo regarded him not with hatred but with a profound compassion that surprised even himself. From his expanded awareness, he had witnessed Carver's entire life—the brilliant child fascinated by Ancestral technology, the young researcher who discovered the first dimensional artifacts, the man who had watched society grow increasingly dependent on technology they couldn't understand or reproduce.

"I see you, Carver," Apollo said. "I see your fear. Your desperation to prevent humanity's collapse when the last of the Ancestral technology fails."

Carver's expression faltered. "Then you understand why this is necessary."

"I understand why you believe it is," Apollo replied. "But forcing open a breach isn't the answer. The dimensional barriers exist for a reason."

The breach above them pulsed, expanding another fraction. Reality warped around its edges, objects phasing in and out of existence. Apollo could perceive how the dimensional fractures spread outward from this point, weakening the fabric of reality in expanding ripples.

"We need control," Carver insisted, his voice rising. "Humanity needs direct access to the Source. It's the only way to ensure our survival."

"Control is an illusion," Apollo said. "The Source isn't something to be harnessed or controlled. It's something we're already part of."

Apollo turned toward the breach, raising his hands. The resonator in his palm amplified his perception, allowing him to see the complex patterns of energy that formed the dimensional boundaries. With his expanded awareness, he could identify the frequencies needed to stabilize the fractures.

His body trembled with exhaustion, but his mind remained connected to the infinite wellspring of the Source. Drawing on that connection, Apollo began to manipulate the dimensional currents, redirecting them into harmonious patterns.

"What are you doing?" Carver demanded, stepping forward.

Tristan moved to intercept him. "Let him work."

Apollo barely heard them. His focus had narrowed to the intricate dance of energies surrounding the breach. He wasn't trying to seal it completely—that would be impossible now that it had formed. Instead, he worked to transform it from a destructive rupture into a stable gateway.

The effort was immense. Each manipulation of dimensional energy drained his already depleted physical reserves. Sweat beaded on his forehead, and his hands began to shake.

"Apollo, you're pushing too hard," Astra warned, moving to his side.

"I need to complete the pattern," Apollo murmured, his vision beginning to blur. "The resonances need to be balanced."

He could see exactly what needed to be done—the dimensional currents that needed redirecting, the frequencies that needed harmonizing. But his body was failing him, unable to channel the energies his mind perceived.

"Help me," he gasped, his knees buckling.

Astra caught him before he hit the floor, easing him down. "How? Tell us what to do."

"The resonator," Apollo managed, his voice weak. "It can amplify all of us together. Form a circle."

Understanding dawned in Astra's eyes. She motioned to Tristan and Alden, who joined them on the floor. Even Carver, after a moment's hesitation, stepped forward.

"Not you," Apollo said, looking up at the magistrate. "Your energies are too distorted. You'd disrupt the pattern."

Fury flashed across Carver's face, but he stepped back, watching with narrowed eyes.

Apollo placed the resonator in the center of their small circle. With trembling fingers, he adjusted its settings, aligning it to the specific frequencies needed.

"Each of you, place one hand on the resonator," he instructed. "Focus your awareness on the breach. Don't try to control anything—just observe."

As they followed his directions, Apollo felt the resonator begin to pulse with their combined awareness. Through this amplified connection, he could guide the dimensional energies with greater precision, despite his physical weakness.

The Crown on his head grew warm, interfacing with the resonator to create a harmonic field that extended upward toward the breach. Apollo directed this field with his mind, weaving complex patterns that gradually stabilized the dimensional boundaries.

His vision darkened at the edges. His body felt impossibly heavy, as if gravity had increased tenfold. Yet his mind remained clear, connected to both the Source and his friends in the circle.

"It's working," Alden whispered, staring upward at the breach, which had begun to contract and stabilize.

Apollo nodded weakly. The dimensional fractures were beginning to heal, the chaotic energies resolving into orderly patterns. But the effort was draining him completely. He could feel his consciousness starting to slip, even as his connection to the Source remained vibrant.

"Almost..." he murmured, his voice barely audible.

With one final effort, Apollo completed the stabilization pattern. The breach contracted to a stable aperture, its edges smooth and contained rather than jagged and expanding. The dimensional fractures throughout The Spire began to heal, reality reasserting its proper form.

As the pattern locked into place, Apollo's strength gave out. The Crown slipped from his head as he collapsed fully to the floor, his consciousness fading even as his mind remained illuminated by his connection to the Source.

The last thing he heard was Astra calling his name, her voice seeming to come from both beside him and from an infinite distance away.

22

THE HARMONY MATRIX

Apollo opened his eyes to soft light filtering through canvas. His body felt impossibly heavy, as if gravity had doubled while he slept. He tried to lift his hand and found the simple movement exhausting.

"He's awake," came Astra's voice from somewhere nearby.

A moment later, her face appeared above him, concern etched in the lines around her eyes. "How do you feel?"

Apollo considered the question. His physical body ached with a bone-deep weariness, but his mind felt strangely expanded, as if parts of his consciousness were spread across vast distances.

"Different," he managed, his voice rough. "How long was I unconscious?"

"Almost two days," Astra said, helping him sit up. They were in a large tent, one of several that had been erected in a clearing some distance from The Spire. Through the open flap, Apollo could see the massive structure in the distance, its upper sections still distorted by dimensional energies.

"The breach?" he asked.

"Stable, for now," Astra replied. "You transformed it from a rupture into something controlled. But the dimensional fractures are still spreading, just more slowly."

Apollo nodded, unsurprised. What he'd done was a temporary measure at best. The connection to the Source remained open, and without proper stabilization, the dimensional boundaries would continue to deteriorate.

"I need to finish what we started," he said, attempting to stand.

Astra pressed him back down. "You can barely sit up. You need more rest."

"There isn't time." Apollo could feel the dimensional currents shifting, even from this distance. "The anchors we placed will fail within a day, maybe less. After that, the fractures will accelerate again."

Footsteps approached, and Tristan ducked into the tent, followed by Alden. Relief washed over their faces when they saw Apollo sitting up.

"Good to see you among the living," Tristan said with a forced smile. "You had us worried."

"The Spire," Apollo said, ignoring the pleasantry. "There's a failsafe system built into its core. I saw it when I connected to the Source."

Alden's eyes widened. "You mean the Harmony Matrix? That's just a theoretical concept in the texts I studied."

"It's real," Apollo insisted. "The Ancestrals built it as a last resort if dimensional boundaries became unstable. But it requires a Veilborn to activate it."

He closed his eyes, drawing on the expanded awareness that lingered from his connection to the Source. The knowledge was there, floating at the edges of his consciousness—schematics, procedures, activation sequences.

"I can see it," he murmured. "The control systems, the dimensional anchors built into The Spire's structure. They're designed to realign the dimensional boundaries if they become compromised."

When he opened his eyes again, his friends were staring at him with a mixture of awe and concern.

"Your eyes," Astra whispered. "They're... different."

Apollo didn't need to ask what she meant. He could feel the change in his perception, the way his consciousness now existed partially in higher dimensions even while his physical body remained anchored in base reality.

"Side effect," he said dismissively. "It doesn't matter. What matters is activating the Harmony Matrix before the fractures spread beyond our ability to contain them."

With effort, Apollo pushed himself to his feet. His body still felt leaden, but determination drove him forward. "I need the resonator and the Crown."

"The Crown is here," Alden said. "But using it again could be dangerous. The strain nearly killed you last time."

"I don't have a choice," Apollo replied. "And neither do any of us. If those fractures continue to spread, they'll eventually reach populated areas. What happened at The Spire will happen everywhere."

His friends exchanged glances, a silent communication passing between them.

"We'll help you," Tristan said. "But we do this together."

Apollo nodded, grateful for their support even as he wondered if they truly understood what they were volunteering for. The knowledge he'd gained from the Source was clear on one point: activating the Harmony Matrix would require a profound connection to dimensional energies, one that carried significant risks for the Veilborn who initiated the process.

"Let's gather what we need," he said.

Two hours later, Apollo stood at the base of The Spire, staring up at the distorted structure. The dimensional fractures were visible even to normal perception now, manifesting as shimmering rifts in the air where reality seemed to fold in on itself.

Commander Rook approached, leading a small contingent of his people. "The building has been evacuated," he reported. "Carver's remaining loyalists have retreated to the southern compound."

"And Carver himself?" Apollo asked.

"No sign of him since your confrontation. He may have fled, or..." Rook's voice trailed off, leaving the alternative unspoken.

Apollo nodded. Carver's fate was a secondary concern at best. What mattered was preventing the dimensional catastrophe his actions had set in motion.

"Keep your people at a safe distance," Apollo instructed. "If we fail, there's no telling how the dimensional energies might react."

Rook clasped Apollo's shoulder. "Good luck." He turned to address his team, directing them to establish a perimeter at a safer distance.

Apollo turned to his friends. "Last chance to stay behind."

"Not happening," Tristan said.

"We started this together," Astra added.

Alden nodded, his expression determined despite the fear evident in his eyes.

Apollo didn't argue further. The truth was, he needed them. The Harmony Matrix was designed to be activated by a team working in concert, not a single individual.

They entered The Spire through the main entrance, which now stood abandoned. The interior had changed dramatically since their last visit. Walls phased in and out of solidity, corridors stretched impossibly long before snapping back to normal dimensions, and in some areas gravity itself seemed uncertain, with objects floating freely before crashing back to the floor.

Apollo led the way, guided by his enhanced perception of the dimensional currents. He could see the energy flows that others couldn't, the patterns that indicated the safest path through the distorted structure.

"Stay close," he warned as they navigated a section where the floor rippled like water. "The dimensional boundaries are extremely thin here. Step exactly where I step."

They moved deeper into The Spire, descending rather than climbing. The Harmony Matrix control systems were located near the base of the structure, beneath the main levels.

"I thought we'd be going up," Alden said, gesturing toward the ceiling where the breach was most visible. "The fractures are strongest at the top."

"The control systems are at the bottom," Apollo explained. "The Spire works like a conduit, channeling energy from its base to its apex. We need to redirect that flow, use it to stabilize rather than disrupt."

They reached a sealed door marked with Ancestral symbols. Apollo placed his hand against it, feeling the dimensional energies that kept it locked. With a thought, he adjusted his own energy to match the frequency of the door's security system. The symbols glowed briefly, and the door slid open.

Beyond lay a circular chamber filled with Ancestral technology. At its center stood a crystalline structure that pulsed with dimensional energy—the heart of the Harmony Matrix.

"This is it," Apollo said, approaching the central console. "The failsafe system."

He placed the resonator on the console, feeling it connect with the underlying systems. The Crown he kept in his hands, not yet ready to don it again.

"What do we do?" Astra asked.

Apollo's expanded consciousness provided the answer. "Each of you needs to take a position at one of the auxiliary consoles," he said, indicating three smaller stations arranged around the central platform. "You'll help channel and direct the dimensional energies while I interface directly with the Matrix."

As his friends moved to their positions, Apollo studied the central console. The knowledge from the Source filled in the gaps in his understanding, revealing the purpose and function of each component.

The Harmony Matrix was more than just a stabilization system. It was designed to create a perfect balance between dimensions, allowing controlled interaction without catastrophic bleedthrough. When functioning properly, it could maintain dimensional boundaries indefinitely, even in the face of significant disruption.

But activating it would require a direct connection to the Source.

He placed the resonator in its designated slot on the console, watching as it integrated with the Ancestral systems. Lights flickered across the chamber as dormant technologies awakened, responding to the presence of a Veilborn after centuries of inactivity.

"Is it working?" Tristan called from his station.

"Not yet," Apollo replied. "This is just preliminary activation. The real work is still ahead."

He turned to address all three of them. "When I place the Crown on my head, I'll establish a connection to the Source. The resonator will amplify that connection and distribute it through the Matrix. Your job is to help direct and stabilize the energies at your stations."

"What about you?" Astra asked, her expression concerned. "What happens to you during this process?"

Apollo hesitated. The knowledge from the Source was clear on this point, but he was reluctant to share it fully.

"I'll be fine," he said. "Just focus on your tasks."

Astra's eyes narrowed, clearly not believing him, but she didn't press the issue.

Apollo took a deep breath and raised the Crown to his head. "Ready?"

His friends nodded, their expressions a mixture of determination and fear.

As Apollo placed the Crown on his head, the connection to the Source opened. His consciousness expanded outward, beyond the confines of his physical form, beyond The Spire, beyond the dimensional boundaries themselves.

He perceived the Source in its true form—not just energy, but infinite consciousness, the wellspring from which all dimensions emerged. And within that infinite expanse, he could see the patterns of reality, the intricate web of connections that bound all dimensions together.

With effort, Apollo maintained a tenuous connection to his physical body, enough to direct his hands to the console before him. The resonator glowed with energy, amplifying his connection to the Source and distributing it through the Harmony Matrix.

The chamber hummed with power as the ancient systems activated. Apollo could see the dimensional currents flowing through The Spire, converging at the breach above. Through his expanded awareness, he began to redirect those currents, weaving them into new patterns that would stabilize rather than disrupt.

"Apollo, your body is starting to phase," came Alden's alarmed voice, seeming to reach him from a great distance.

Apollo glanced down and saw that his hands had become partially transparent, his physical form beginning to drift between dimensions as his consciousness expanded further.

He ignored the warning. The work was too important to stop now. Through the Matrix, he extended his awareness to the dimensional anchors embedded throughout The Spire's structure. One by one, he activated them, creating a network of stabilization points that would reinforce the weakened boundaries.

The process was working. He could feel the dimensional fractures beginning to heal, the chaotic energies resolving into orderly patterns. But the strain on his physical form was immense. The more he extended his consciousness into higher dimensions, the less connected he became to base reality.

"Apollo, you need to pull back," Astra called, her voice urgent. "You're drifting too far!"

He knew she was right. The symptoms of dimensional drift were unmistakable—the phasing of his physical form, the expansion of his consciousness beyond normal parameters, the weakening connection to base reality. If he continued much longer, he risked complete dimensional displacement.

But he wasn't finished. The Harmony Matrix was active, but the dimensional fractures were still not fully stabilized. He needed to complete the pattern, establish the final connections that would allow the system to function autonomously.

With his expanded awareness, Apollo reached deeper into the Source, drawing on its infinite potential to fuel the Matrix. The strain was incredible, his consciousness stretched across multiple dimensions simultaneously.

"Almost done," he managed to say, though he wasn't sure if the words actually formed in physical space or merely in his mind.

Through the resonator, he channeled the final sequence of energies into the Matrix. The crystalline structure at the center of the chamber pulsed with brilliant light, sending waves of dimensional energy surging upward through The Spire.

Apollo could see the effect. The dimensional currents throughout the structure realigned, forming a stable network that reinforced the boundaries between dimensions. The fractures began to close, reality reasserting its proper form.

The breach at the top of The Spire transformed, its chaotic energies resolving into a controlled aperture—a stable connection to higher dimensions rather than a catastrophic rupture.

As the Matrix completed its activation sequence, Apollo knew his task was finished. He tried to withdraw his consciousness, to pull back from the expanded awareness and return to his physical form.

But something was wrong. Part of him remained connected to the higher dimensions, unable to disengage completely. His consciousness had stretched too far, become too diffuse to fully reconcentrate.

"Apollo!" Astra's voice seemed to come from both beside him and from an infinite distance away.

He felt hands on his shoulders, trying to steady his partially phased body. With tremendous effort, he managed to remove the Crown from his head, severing the direct connection to the Source.

But the damage was done. Even as his physical form solidified somewhat, his consciousness remained partially extended into higher dimensions. He was caught between worlds, neither fully in base reality nor fully transcended.

"Did it work?" he asked, his voice sounding strange to his own ears.

"Yes," Alden confirmed, checking the readings on his console. "The dimensional fractures are stabilizing. The Matrix is functioning as designed."

Apollo nodded, relief washing through him despite his condition. They had prevented another Cataclysm. The dimensional boundaries would hold.

The chamber shuddered, the floor vibrating beneath their feet.

"What's happening?" Tristan asked, looking around in alarm.

"The Spire is reconfiguring," Apollo explained, the knowledge coming from his expanded awareness. "Now that the Matrix is active, the structure is transforming to better channel the dimensional energies."

Another tremor shook the chamber, stronger this time. Dust and small fragments of material began to fall from the ceiling.

"We need to get out of here," Astra said, moving to Apollo's side. "Can you walk?"

Apollo tried to stand but found his legs unresponsive. His connection to his physical body had weakened too much during the activation process.

"I don't think so," he admitted.

Without hesitation, Tristan moved to Apollo's other side. Together with Astra, he lifted Apollo.

"Let's go," Tristan said, adjusting his grip to better support Apollo's weight.

They moved toward the exit as The Spire continued to tremble around them. Apollo's perception shifted between normal awareness and expanded consciousness, making it difficult to focus on their immediate surroundings.

Through the haze of his fractured awareness, Apollo could see The Spire transforming. Walls shifted position, corridors realigned, and new structures formed as the ancient building reconfigured itself to accommodate the activated Matrix.

"This way," Alden called, finding a clear path through the changing architecture.

They navigated the shifting interior, making their way toward the exit as The Spire's transformation accelerated. Apollo drifted in and out of full awareness, his consciousness still partially lost in higher dimensions.

As they emerged from The Spire into daylight, Apollo glimpsed the structure's external transformation. The dark metal and crystal were shifting, becoming more translucent, more aligned with the dimensional energies now flowing properly through its systems.

"We did it," he murmured, his vision beginning to darken at the edges.

"Yes," Astra confirmed, her face the last thing Apollo saw as consciousness slipped away from him entirely. "We did it. Rest now."

As darkness claimed him, Apollo felt his mind spread across multiple dimensions, perceiving realities beyond normal comprehension even as his physical body was carried to safety by his friends.

23

THE HARMONY OF DIMENSIONS

Apollo opened his eyes to golden sunlight streaming through an unfamiliar window. For a moment, he experienced disorientation as his mind registered not just the room around him but overlapping perceptions of the same space across multiple dimensions. The walls shimmered with translucent energy currents. The wooden beams supporting the ceiling existed simultaneously as living trees and decomposing matter. The air itself contained infinite possibilities, each potential state visible to him at once.

He blinked, trying to focus on just one layer of reality. The effort brought a dull ache behind his eyes.

"You're awake." Astra's voice came from beside him, anchoring him momentarily to the physical dimension.

Apollo turned his head to find her sitting in a chair next to his bed, her features clear but surrounded by a nimbus of possible movements and expressions—echoes of what she might do next bleeding through from adjacent realities.

"How long?" His voice sounded strange to his ears, as if he were hearing it from multiple positions simultaneously.

"Five days," Astra replied, leaning forward to place a cool hand on his forehead. Her touch helped ground him further in physical reality. "We were beginning to worry."

Apollo attempted to sit up, but his body felt leaden, disconnected from his consciousness. With Astra's help, he managed to prop himself against the headboard.

"The Spire?" he asked.

"Completely transformed," she said. "It's stabilized the dimensional currents throughout the region. The fractures are healing."

Relief washed through him, though the emotion seemed to ripple across multiple states of being. "And Carver?"

"Gone," Astra said. "We found traces of dimensional energy where he stood, but no physical remains. The prevailing theory is that he was pulled into a pocket dimension during the stabilization process."

Apollo nodded, unsurprised. Through his expanded awareness, he had glimpsed countless pocket dimensions forming and collapsing during those final moments. Carver could be trapped in any one of them, or scattered across several.

"The others?"

"Everyone made it out safely," Astra assured him. "Tristan and Alden are downstairs. We're in an old outpost about ten miles from The Spire."

Apollo closed his eyes, trying to organize his fractured perceptions. The connection to the Source had permanently altered him. Where once he had needed to concentrate to perceive dimensional energies, now he struggled to filter them out. Multiple layers of reality presented themselves simultaneously, making it difficult to focus on just the physical world.

"Something's different," he said, opening his eyes again. "My perceptio n... I can't turn it off. I'm seeing everything at once."

Astra's expression shifted to concern. "The resonator and the Crown together might have permanently expanded your awareness."

Apollo attempted to stand, needing to test his physical form. His legs trembled beneath him, but held. Astra supported him as he took tentative steps toward the window.

Outside, the landscape appeared transformed through his new perception. Trees pulsed with life energy, their roots extending into dimensional currents below the surface. The sky contained layers of atmospheric phenomena, some from this reality, others bleeding through from adjacent dimensions.

"It's overwhelming," he admitted. "Like trying to hear a single voice in a crowded room."

"You'll learn to filter it," Astra said with quiet confidence. "Your mind will adapt."

Apollo wasn't certain, but he nodded anyway. "I need to see the others."

Descending the stairs required intense concentration. Apollo's perception of multiple possible staircases made finding secure footing challenging. By the time they reached the lower level, sweat beaded on his forehead from the effort.

Tristan and Alden looked up from a table covered in maps and diagrams. Both rose upon seeing him.

"Apollo!" Alden exclaimed, genuine relief in his voice. "We were beginning to think you'd never wake up."

Tristan gripped Apollo's forearm in a firm clasp that communicated more than words could. Through the physical contact, Apollo sensed Tristan's concern, relief, and lingering worry.

"I'm still here," Apollo said, though *here* had become a far more complex concept than before. "Mostly."

They helped him to a chair, and Astra brought a steaming cup of tea that smelled of herbs and something else—a dimensional current that helped clear his mind slightly.

"What have I missed?" Apollo asked after taking a cautious sip.

Alden spread his hands over the maps. "Everything's changing. The stabilization of The Spire has had far-reaching effects. Dimensional energy is flowing properly again for the first time in centuries."

"We've been mapping the changes," Tristan added, indicating various marked locations. "Ancient systems are reactivating across the region. The dimensional anchors you placed have become permanent nodes in a new network."

Apollo nodded, seeing the pattern. Through his expanded awareness, he could perceive the energy flows connecting these points, forming a web of stabilized dimensional currents.

"And the people?" he asked.

"That's the most surprising part," Astra said. "Word has spread about what happened. About the Veilborn, about the dimensional nature of reality. People are coming forward—individuals who've always had unusual perceptions or abilities."

"Like me," Tristan said. "Resonants who can interact with Ancestral technology."

"And those with partial Veilborn sensitivity," Alden added. "Not full abilities like yours, but enough to perceive some dimensional phenomena."

Apollo processed this revelation, perceiving its ramifications through several possible timelines at once. "The old divisions are breaking down."

"Exactly," Alden confirmed. "The Order of the Veil is fracturing. Many members have abandoned their posts after learning the truth about Veilborn. Others are trying to adapt to the new reality."

Apollo's thoughts turned to Kieran. With his expanded awareness, memories of his adoptive father took on new dimensions. He could perceive the love and sacrifice that had motivated Kieran's every action, could see the threads of causality that connected Kieran's choice to stay behind to Apollo's ultimate confrontation with Carver.

"My father," Apollo said. "Kieran. He knew, didn't he? Not everything, but enough."

Astra placed a hand on his arm. "We haven't heard anything definitive. The Order's communications have been chaotic since The Spire's transformation."

But Apollo didn't need external confirmation. His connection to the Source had shown him truths beyond physical evidence. In that moment of expanded consciousness, he had glimpsed Kieran's fate—the brave stand against overwhelming odds, the refusal to reveal Apollo's destination despite interrogation, the final moments facing Magistrate Carver himself.

"He's gone," Apollo said with certainty. "He sacrificed himself so I could complete this journey. So I could become what I needed to be."

The room fell silent as the others absorbed this. Apollo felt grief, but it was transformed by his new perception—he could see how Kieran's sacrifice had rippled through causality, creating the possibility for Apollo to reach The Spire and prevent catastrophe.

"He would be proud," Tristan said, breaking the silence.

Apollo nodded, finding comfort in the truth of those words. Through his expanded awareness, he could perceive the interconnectedness of all things, how each life influenced countless others. Kieran's impact would continue long after his physical form had passed.

"We should honor him," Apollo said, "by building something worthy of his sacrifice."

"That's what we've been discussing," Alden said, indicating the papers spread across the table. "With the dimensional barriers stabilizing, we have an opportunity to create something new—an organization dedicated to understanding both dimensional energy and Ancestral technology, without the fear and secrecy of the past."

Apollo studied the plans with both physical and dimensional sight. He could perceive the potential futures branching from this moment, the possibilities contained in their choices.

"A new Order," he said. "Not to control or suppress knowledge, but to preserve and share it."

"Exactly," Alden confirmed, enthusiasm lighting his features. "I've been compiling everything we've learned—about Veilborn abilities, dimensional mechanics, the true history of the Cataclysm. We need to ensure this knowledge is never lost again."

"We've already made contact with other groups," Astra added. "Survivors from Valeshire, eastern representatives, even former Order members who want to help. The response has been overwhelming."

Apollo closed his eyes, allowing his expanded perception to explore the possibilities. He could see the potential for healing the dimensional damage caused by centuries of ignorance and fear. He could also see the dangers—power always attracted those who would misuse it.

"It will require balance," he said, opening his eyes. "Between those who can perceive dimensional energies and those who understand Ancestral technology. Neither can succeed alone."

"That's where you come in," Tristan said. "You bridge both worlds now."

Apollo considered this. His connection to the Source had given him insights beyond normal comprehension, but it had also distanced him from ordinary human experience. He existed partially in multiple dimensions simultaneously, never fully present in any single one.

"I can teach what I know," he said, "but I can't lead this new Order. My perception is too... diffuse now. I need to learn to manage it before I can guide others."

"Then teach us," Alden said. "Share what you've learned. I can organize the knowledge, create a curriculum. Tristan can work with the technological aspects. Astra can help those with dimensional sensitivity develop their abilities safely."

Apollo looked at his friends, seeing them with both physical and dimensional sight. In Alden, he perceived the scholar who had become a leader, whose methodical mind could organize and preserve knowledge for future generations. In Tristan, he saw the Resonant whose practical skills and intuitive understanding of Ancestral technology would bridge old and new. And in Astra, he recognized a kindred spirit whose dimensional sensitivity, though different from his own, created a unique bond between them.

"Yes," he agreed. "We'll start with what we know, and build from there."

In the weeks that followed, Apollo struggled to adapt to his permanently altered perception. Simple tasks became challenges when one could simultaneously see objects in multiple dimensional states. Conversations proved difficult when he could perceive not just what was said, but all the things that might have been said in adjacent realities.

Astra became his anchor, helping him develop techniques to filter his awareness. They spent hours each day in meditation, practicing methods to focus on specific dimensional frequencies while temporarily blocking others.

"It's like learning to hear a single instrument in an orchestra," she explained during one session. "The other sounds are still there, but you can choose where to direct your attention."

Gradually, Apollo learned to manage his expanded perception. He could never fully return to his former state—the connection to the Source had irreversibly changed him—but he could function in the physical world while maintaining awareness of the dimensional currents flowing around him.

As his control improved, Apollo began teaching others. First came those with natural dimensional sensitivity—individuals who had always perceived strange lights or energies but had hidden their abilities out of fear. Apollo showed them how to safely interact with dimensional currents, how to understand what they were seeing.

"Dimensional energy isn't mystical or supernatural," he explained to a group of students in what had once been The Spire's observation deck, now transformed into a teaching space. "It's a fundamental aspect of reality, as natural as gravity or light."

He demonstrated by creating a small dimensional fold between his hands, a pocket where space curved back on itself. "What we perceive as solid matter is actually energy vibrating at specific frequencies. By understanding these frequencies, we can interact with them."

To his surprise, many of his students showed remarkable aptitude. Their abilities might not match his own, but with proper guidance, they could perceive and manipulate dimensional energies in limited ways.

Meanwhile, Tristan worked with those who showed Resonant abilities—people who could intuitively understand and operate Ancestral technology. In workshops set up throughout The Spire, he taught them to recognize activation patterns, to feel the flow of energy through mechanical systems.

"The Ancestrals designed their technology to respond to specific neural patterns," Tristan explained, demonstrating with a small device that lit up at his touch. "As Resonants, we naturally produce these patterns. With practice, you can learn to control them."

Alden oversaw it all, documenting every discovery, creating teaching materials, establishing protocols for safe practice. His organizational skills proved invaluable as more people arrived seeking knowledge.

"We need a name," Alden said one evening as they gathered in what had become their planning room. "Something that reflects what we're trying to build."

"The Harmony," Astra suggested. "After the Matrix that stabilized the dimensions."

Apollo considered this, seeing the symbolic resonance across multiple layers of meaning. "The Harmony of Dimensions," he refined. "Acknowledging both the technological and dimensional aspects of our work."

The name took hold, spreading beyond their immediate circle. Within months, The Harmony had grown from a handful of individuals to dozens, then hundreds. People traveled from distant settlements, drawn by stories of The Spire's transformation and the new knowledge being shared there.

Some came seeking answers to lifelong questions about strange perceptions or abilities. Others were drawn by curiosity about Ancestral technology now reactivating across the land. All found a place within The Harmony's growing community.

Apollo watched this development with both pride and concern. His expanded awareness showed him the potential futures branching from their actions—both the promise of a new age of understanding and the dangers of knowledge misused.

"We need to establish principles," he told Alden. "Guidelines to ensure this knowledge is used responsibly."

Together, they drafted the Harmony Principles—a framework emphasizing balance, responsibility, and the interconnectedness of all dimensions. These principles became the foundation of their teaching, emphasized in every class and demonstration.

As summer approached, marking nearly six months since the confrontation with Carver, preparations began for a formal ceremony to establish The Harmony as an official institution. Representatives from settlements across the region were invited to witness the beginning of this new era.

The day before the ceremony, Apollo stood atop The Spire, looking out over the transformed landscape. The dimensional fractures had healed, leaving the land vibrant with properly flowing energy. Through his expanded perception, he could see the network of anchors maintaining stability, the currents of dimensional energy flowing harmoniously through the region.

Astra joined him, her presence a comforting constant in his still-disorienting experience of multiple realities.

"Are you ready for tomorrow?" she asked.

Apollo considered the question across several dimensions of meaning. "As ready as I can be," he answered. "Though I still feel... divided. Part of me remains connected to the Source, experiencing everything simultaneously."

"That's what makes you uniquely qualified to guide us," Astra said, taking his hand. The physical contact helped ground him in the present moment. "You've seen what's possible when dimensional knowledge is misused. You've also seen what's possible when it's understood properly."

Apollo nodded, grateful for her understanding. Their relationship had deepened over the months, evolving into something that transcended ordinary connection. Through his dimensional awareness, he perceived the resonance between them—a harmony of energies that complemented each other.

"I just hope we're building something that will last," he said. "Something worthy of the sacrifices made to reach this point."

Astra squeezed his hand. "We are. One day at a time."

The ceremony took place in the central plaza outside The Spire, now transformed into a gleaming tower of crystalline material that shimmered with dimensional energy. Hundreds gathered to witness the formal establishment of The Harmony of Dimensions.

Apollo stood on a raised platform with Astra, Tristan, and Alden beside him. Through his expanded perception, he could see not just the physical gathering but the dimensional significance of the moment—a nexus point where multiple potential futures converged.

Alden stepped forward first, his voice carrying across the plaza.

"For centuries, we lived in ignorance of the true nature of our world," he began. "We feared what we didn't understand, persecuted those with abilities we couldn't explain, and lost the knowledge that could have helped us rebuild after the Cataclysm."

He gestured to The Spire behind them. "This structure once represented that fear and ignorance. Now it stands as a beacon of understanding—a place where dimensional awareness and technological knowledge come together in harmony."

Tristan spoke next, explaining the role of Resonants in bridging old technology with new understanding. Then Astra described how those with dimensional sensitivity would be trained to use their abilities responsibly.

Finally, it was Apollo's turn. As he stepped forward, he felt the weight of multiple realities pressing upon him. With effort, he focused his perception on the present moment, on the faces looking up at him expectantly.

"I stand before you changed," he began, his voice steady despite the effort it took to maintain focus. "My connection to the Source has shown me truths beyond ordinary comprehension. I've seen how all dimensions exist simultaneously, how all possibilities unfold in parallel, how all beings are connected across the fabric of reality."

He paused, gathering his thoughts. "But the most important truth I've learned is this: knowledge without wisdom is dangerous. Power without responsibility leads to destruction. The Ancestrals learned this lesson too late. The Order of the Veil never learned it at all."

Apollo gestured to the assembled crowd. "The Harmony of Dimensions will be different. We will study both the technological achievements of our ancestors and the dimensional energies that flow through our world. We will train those with natural abilities to use them responsibly. We will share knowledge openly rather than hoarding it for power."

He felt a surge of emotion as he thought of Kieran, of Elder Verity, of all who had sacrificed to bring them to this moment. "We honor those who came before us by building something better than what they knew. A world where understanding replaces fear, where cooperation replaces control, where harmony replaces discord."

As Apollo spoke these words, he perceived their impact rippling across multiple dimensions, creating resonances that would echo through time. The moment held significance beyond what any ordinary observer could comprehend—a true turning point in the relationship between humanity and the dimensional fabric of reality.

"Today marks the beginning of a new era," Apollo concluded. "Not just for those of us gathered here, but for all who will come after. Together, we will build a future worthy of the sacrifices that made it possible."

As he finished speaking, Alden stepped forward again, holding a crystal sphere that glowed with internal light—an Ancestral artifact repurposed as a symbol of their new beginning. Apollo placed his hand on it, followed by Astra, Tristan, and finally Alden himself.

At their combined touch, the sphere illuminated brilliantly, projecting a three-dimensional image of interconnected nodes—a visual representation of The Harmony's principles and structure. The crowd gasped as the projection expanded outward, encompassing the entire plaza in shimmering light.

Through his expanded perception, Apollo saw more than just the physical display. He perceived the dimensional resonances created by this moment, the connections forming between all present, the potential futures branching from this nexus point. Most of those futures held promise—new understanding, healing of old wounds, harmony between dimensions.

As the light from the sphere gradually faded, Apollo felt a sense of completion. The journey that had begun with strange visions on his family farm had led him here, to this moment of transformation. Though permanently changed by his connection to the Source, he had found purpose in that change—a way to use his unique perception to guide others.

The ceremony concluded with Alden declaring The Harmony of Dimensions officially established. As the crowd dispersed into smaller groups, many approaching the platform to speak with the founders, Apollo took a moment to center himself amid the overwhelming sensory input from multiple dimensions.

Astra moved to his side, her presence helping to anchor him in the physical world. "Are you all right?" she asked.

Apollo nodded, finding balance between his expanded awareness and the present moment. "I think I am," he said. "For the first time since connecting to the Source, I feel like I belong somewhere—between dimensions, helping others understand what I've seen."

24

— • —

FOUNDATIONS OF CHANGE

Apollo stood at the edge of the observation platform, gazing out at the transformed landscape surrounding The Spire. What had once been a forbidden zone of dimensional instability was now a thriving center of learning and discovery. Gardens and walkways wound between newly constructed buildings, each dedicated to a different aspect of dimensional study. Students and researchers moved between them, their conversations a distant hum that Apollo could tune in or out at will.

One year had passed since the founding of The Harmony of Dimensions. One year since Apollo had stood before a gathering of uncertain faces and promised a new beginning. The changes since then still amazed him.

Apollo closed his eyes and shifted his perception, allowing his awareness to expand beyond the physical realm. The dimensional currents flowed around and through The Spire in orderly patterns now, no longer the chaotic maelstrom they had been during Carver's experiments. With practiced ease, Apollo identified each frequency, each layer of reality overlapping with their own. What had once overwhelmed him to the point of incapacitation was now as natural as breathing.

"There you are," came Astra's voice from behind him. "The delegation from Eastwatch is arriving."

Apollo opened his eyes and turned to her with a smile. She wore the silver-blue robes that had become the unofficial uniform of The Harmony's leadership, her pendant gleaming at her throat. The year had changed her too—there was a confidence in her bearing that had replaced the wariness she'd carried when they first met.

"I was just taking a moment," he said, reaching for her hand. "Sometimes I still can't believe how far we've come."

Astra's fingers interlaced with his, the familiar touch grounding him fully in the present moment. "Elder Thalia will want a full report on the progress of the western nodes. And she's bringing three candidates who've shown dimensional sensitivity."

"More potential Veilborn?" Apollo asked, his interest piqued. In the past year, they had identified twenty-seven individuals with varying degrees of dimensional perception—none as strong as Apollo's, but significant nonetheless. "That makes eight this month alone."

"They're emerging faster than we can train them," Astra agreed. "Alden thinks it's because the dimensional currents have stabilized. People who always had the genetic potential are suddenly able to access abilities that were previously dormant."

They walked together along the curved hallway that followed the outer wall of The Spire. What had once been sterile corridors patrolled by Magistrate guards were now open spaces filled with light. Ancient technology had been integrated with new construction, creating an environment that honored both the Ancestral past and the promise of the future.

"How are the new training protocols working?" Apollo asked.

"Better than expected. Tristan's modifications to the resonator design have made it possible for even those with minimal sensitivity to perceive the basic dimensional frequencies." Astra's pride in their accomplishments was evident in her voice. "The Echo Chamber is ready for demonstration as well. Alden finished the final calibrations this morning."

The Echo Chamber had been Alden's project for the past six months—a room designed to record and replay dimensional frequencies for training purposes. It would allow students to experience controlled dimensional phenomena without risk.

They descended a spiral staircase to the reception hall where Tristan waited for them. The smith had grown a beard in the past year, and his clothes showed the refined touch of someone who had spent time in diplomatic circles. The transformation from village blacksmith to one of The Harmony's four founders had changed him in subtle ways, though his practical nature remained unchanged.

"There you two are," he said, looking up from a conversation with two younger Resonants. "The Eastwatch party just passed the outer marker. They'll be here within the hour."

Apollo nodded. "We'll be ready. How are the new Resonant trainees progressing?"

Tristan's face lit up with enthusiasm. "Remarkably well. Especially Lyssa's daughter—she has an intuitive grasp of Ancestral interfaces that surpasses even mine. Watch."

He gestured to a nearby console where a young girl of perhaps twelve was working. Her fingers moved across the surface with confidence, activating patterns of light that responded to her touch. The display above the console showed a three-dimensional map of dimensional currents flowing through the region.

"She mapped that entire section in under an hour," Tristan said proudly. "It would have taken me half a day."

Apollo studied the girl with interest. "Another generation already rising to take our place," he mused. "That's exactly what we hoped for."

"Speaking of the next generation," Tristan said, lowering his voice, "have you and Astra given any more thought to the Council's suggestion?"

Apollo exchanged a glance with Astra. The Harmony Council—comprised of representatives from all the allied settlements—had recently proposed establishing a formal academy for dimensional studies, with Apollo and Astra as its first directors.

"We're considering it," Astra replied diplomatically. "There's still so much work to be done with the node network."

"And we haven't finished exploring the Black Archives yet," Apollo added, referring to the vast repository of restricted knowledge they had discovered beneath The Spire. The archives contained records of the Magistracy's experiments with dimensional energy—knowledge too dangerous to be widely shared but too valuable to be destroyed.

Tristan nodded in understanding. "Well, don't take too long deciding. The Council meets again in two weeks, and Elder Thalia is particularly eager to see the academy established."

After finalizing preparations for the Eastwatch delegation, Apollo made his way to the central chamber of The Spire. Once the site of Carver's disastrous experiment, it had been transformed into the heart of The Harmony's operations. The Harmony Matrix—the dimensional stabilization system Apollo had activated a year ago—hummed with quiet energy at the center of the room.

Alden was there, as Apollo had expected, studying readouts on one of the curved display panels. The scholar looked up as Apollo entered, pushing his spectacles back into place.

"Just the person I wanted to see," Alden said, gesturing Apollo over. "I've been analyzing the data from the western nodes, and there's something interesting happening near Willowbrook."

Apollo joined him at the display, studying the patterns of light that represented dimensional energy flows. "A new convergence point?"

"Not exactly. More like an echo of the one that formed during the Illumination Ceremony last year. It's as if the event left a permanent imprint on the dimensional fabric." Alden manipulated the display, zooming in on the area. "And there's something else. Three new cases of dimensional sensitivity reported in the village in the past month."

"Three? From Willowbrook alone?" Apollo frowned. The village of his childhood had fewer than five hundred residents. Three new cases represented a significant concentration.

"All children between the ages of eight and twelve," Alden confirmed. "I've cross-referenced with our genetic research, and they all have ancestors who lived in the village during the last major dimensional storm, eighty years ago."

Apollo considered this information. "You think exposure to dimensional energy during the storm might have activated dormant Veilborn genes in that bloodline?"

"It's a working theory," Alden said. "If correct, it might explain why we're seeing more cases emerging now. The dimensional stabilization we've achieved could be allowing these latent abilities to express themselves."

The ramifications struck Apollo as profound. If dimensional sensitivity could be awakened in those with the genetic potential, The Harmony might eventually face hundreds or even thousands of new Veilborn rather than the dozens they had anticipated.

"We'll need to expand the training program," Apollo said. "And perhaps reconsider the academy proposal sooner rather than later."

Alden nodded in agreement. "I've already started drafting a curriculum based on the Ancestral training protocols we found in the archives. With modifications for our current understanding, of course."

Their conversation was interrupted by a chime indicating the arrival of the Eastwatch delegation. Apollo expressed gratitude to Alden for his efforts and made his way toward the reception area.

The greeting of Elder Thalia and her party went smoothly, with formal introductions followed by a tour of The Spire's primary facilities. The three candidates—two women and a man ranging in age from sixteen to thirty—watched Apollo with a mixture of awe and apprehension. He remembered that feeling well—the uncertainty of discovering abilities that set you apart, the fear of what those abilities might mean.

During a break in the tour, Apollo took the candidates to one of the training rooms where they could speak privately. The room was designed for basic perception exercises, with minimal distractions and carefully controlled dimensional energies.

"I know this is overwhelming," he told them, keeping his voice gentle. "Over a year ago, I was in your position—discovering abilities I didn't understand, facing a world that feared what I could do."

The youngest candidate, a girl named Miranna, spoke up. "Is it true you can see all dimensions at once?"

Apollo smiled. "I can, though it took time to learn how to filter what I perceive. Otherwise, the input would be overwhelming." He gestured to the room around them. "That's why we created this place—so others like you can learn in a controlled environment, with guidance."

"Will we be able to do what you can do?" asked the older woman, Verra.

"Each Veilborn's abilities manifest differently," Apollo explained. "Some have stronger perception, others excel at manipulation. Some connect more easily to certain dimensional frequencies than others. Part of your training will be discovering your unique strengths."

He demonstrated by shifting his perception to the fifth frequency—the dimension associated with probability and potential. The air around him shimmered with paths of light, each representing a possible future branching from this moment.

"This is what I see when I tune to the fifth frequency," he said, knowing they couldn't perceive it yet but wanting to give them a goal to work toward. "With training, you'll learn to access different dimensional frequencies selectively, focusing on what's useful while filtering out the rest."

The male candidate, Daren, looked skeptical. "The Order taught that Veilborn caused the Cataclysm. That our abilities are dangerous."

"The Order was wrong about many things," Apollo said. "But not entirely wrong about the dangers. Dimensional energy is powerful, and misuse can have serious consequences. That's why responsible training is so important." He met each of their gazes in turn. "We don't hide from our power here, but we do respect it."

After the candidates rejoined the main tour group, Apollo found a moment alone with Astra in one of the side corridors.

"They're scared," he said. "I remember that feeling."

Astra nodded. "So do I, though my sensitivity was never as strong as theirs. We need to make sure they understand they're not alone." She hesitated, then added, "I've been thinking about the academy proposal. Maybe it's time."

Apollo raised an eyebrow. "What changed your mind?"

"Seeing those three today. Realizing there will be more coming. We can't handle this informally anymore—we need a structured program." She met his gaze. "And I think we're the ones who need to build it."

Apollo considered her words. For the past year, they had focused on stabilizing the dimensional network and gathering knowledge. The work had been necessary and fulfilling, but perhaps it was time for a new phase.

"You're right," he said. "We'll tell the Council we accept their proposal."

The rest of the day passed in a blur of meetings and demonstrations. By evening, the Eastwatch delegation had been settled into guest quarters, and Apollo found himself with a rare moment of solitude.

He made his way to the very top of The Spire, to a small observation room that had once been Magistrate Carver's private study. The room offered a panoramic view of the surrounding landscape, with the lights of nearby settlements visible in the distance. Above, the night sky blazed with stars.

Apollo sat cross-legged on the floor and closed his eyes, allowing his consciousness to expand beyond physical limitations. His perception flowed outward, encompassing The Spire and then beyond—to the network of dimensional nodes stretching across the continent, to the currents of energy flowing between them, to the subtle resonances of other Veilborn practicing their abilities.

He extended his awareness further, touching the edges of dimensions beyond normal perception. The Source pulsed at the boundaries of his consciousness—not threatening to overwhelm him as it once had, but present and accessible should he choose to connect with it.

This was what he had worked toward over the past year—complete control over his dimensional perception, the ability to expand or contract his awareness at will, to filter specific frequencies or perceive them all simultaneously. What had once threatened to fragment his mind now felt natural, integrated with his human consciousness rather than opposed to it.

Apollo felt Astra's presence before he heard her enter the room. Her dimensional signature had become as familiar to him as her face—a specific pattern of energy that he could recognize instantly across any distance.

"I thought I might find you here," she said, sitting beside him.

Apollo opened his eyes, gradually narrowing his perception back to the physical realm. "Just checking the network. Everything is stable."

Astra leaned against his shoulder. "You don't need to pretend with me. I know you come up here to commune with the Source."

He smiled, caught. "Not exactly commune. More like... listen. There's so much knowledge there, Astra. Patterns and possibilities beyond anything we could imagine."

"And that's why you're the bridge," she said. "Between that knowledge and our world."

Apollo considered her words. A bridge. That was how he had come to see himself—spanning the gap between dimensions, between the Source and humanity, between ancient knowledge and new understanding.

"I never asked for this role," he said.

"None of us asked for our roles," Astra replied. "But we've made something meaningful from what we were given." She took his hand. "The Council approved the academy proposal, by the way. Construction begins next month."

Apollo nodded, unsurprised. "And so we build the future, one decision at a time."

They sat together in comfortable silence, watching the stars. Apollo allowed his perception to expand slightly, enough to see the dimensional currents flowing around them—stable, harmonious, beautiful in their complexity.

A year ago, he had been overwhelmed by these perceptions, unable to filter or control what he saw. Now he moved between dimensions with ease, a true Veilborn in full command of his abilities. The journey had been difficult, marked by loss and sacrifice, but the result was worth every hardship.

"Do you ever wonder what happened to Carver?" Astra asked.

Apollo's mouth tightened. The Magistrate had disappeared during the dimensional stabilization, his body drawn into a pocket dimension created by his own experiments. Despite extensive searches, they had found no trace of him.

"Sometimes," Apollo admitted. "The dimensional pocket he created was unstable. He might have perished immediately, or he might be trapped somewhere between dimensions." He shook his head. "Either way, his ambition led him to his end."

"And your compassion led you to your beginning," Astra said.

Apollo smiled at that. It was true—his journey had begun not with power but with curiosity and concern. Those same qualities now guided The Harmony of Dimensions as it grew.

As if reading his thoughts, Astra said, "We're building something that will outlast us, Apollo. Something that balances power with responsibility, knowledge with wisdom."

"A harmony of dimensions," Apollo agreed, "in every sense of the phrase."

He extended his perception once more, this time focusing specifically on the futures branching from this moment. The possibilities spread before him like countless threads of light, each representing a potential path forward. Many of those paths held promise—new discoveries, expanding knowledge, generations of Veilborn and Resonants working together to understand the dimensional fabric of reality.

Apollo Frost, once a farm boy with strange visions, now stood at the center of a new era—a bridge between worlds, between past and future, between what humanity had been and what it might become.

And for the first time since his journey began, he was at peace with that role.

25

A Space Between

Magistrate Carver floated in a space between dimensions, his consciousness stretched thin across realities that human minds were never meant to comprehend. Time had no meaning here. It could have been seconds or centuries since that Veilborn boy had disrupted his ascension.

Apollo Frost. The name burned through Carver's fragmented awareness like acid.

He had been so close. The Crown had responded to him, the dimensional breach had opened, and the power of the Source had begun to flow into him. Carver had felt himself expanding, evolving beyond the limitations of flesh. Then Apollo had interfered, wielding powers that should have been impossible for someone so young and untrained.

Carver tried to focus his thoughts, but they scattered like mist. In this between-place, he existed as patterns of energy rather than matter. Memories flashed through him—his decades of research, the artifacts he'd collected, the sacrifices he'd made. All for nothing.

No. Not for nothing. He was still here, still conscious. That meant there was still a way back.

With tremendous effort, Carver concentrated on his physical form, trying to remember the sensation of having a body. Slowly, painfully, he felt himself coalescing. The dimensional pocket he occupied began to stabilize around him, taking on properties more compatible with human existence.

After what seemed an eternity, Carver found himself kneeling on a crystalline surface. His body had reformed, though it felt wrong somehow—lighter, less substantial. When he looked at his hands, he could see the faint outline of the floor through them.

"Not quite corporeal," he muttered, his voice echoing strangely. "But progress nonetheless."

The dimensional pocket he had created—or perhaps fallen into—was small, perhaps twenty feet in diameter. Beyond its boundaries swirled chaotic energies in colors that had no names in human language. The pocket itself contained nothing but the crystalline floor and a strange, pulsing light at its center.

Carver approached the light cautiously. It responded to his presence, brightening as he drew near. Within it, he could see images—The Spire, transformed from his research facility into something else. People moved through its halls, studying, learning. He recognized Apollo and his companions.

"They've taken everything," he snarled. "My research, my facility, my vision."

But as he watched longer, understanding dawned. They were studying dimensional energies, teaching others to perceive and manipulate them. They had created some sort of organization—The Harmony of Dimensions, they called it.

Carver laughed bitterly. "How predictably idealistic."

Yet he couldn't deny a grudging respect for what they'd accomplished. In a year, they had done more to advance dimensional studies than he had in decades. Of course, they'd had advantages he hadn't—a true Veilborn and access to activated Ancestral technology.

The light pulsed again, showing him more. The Order of the Veil fractured, its monopoly on knowledge broken. People with dimensional sensitivity emerging across the provinces. New discoveries being shared openly rather than hoarded.

"Fools," Carver whispered. "They have no idea of the dangers they're courting."

But even as he said it, he saw evidence that contradicted him. They were proceeding carefully, establishing protocols, creating safeguards. They were doing exactly what he had claimed to want—advancing humanity's understanding—but without his ruthless methods.

Carver turned away from the light, unwilling to watch more. He needed to focus on escape, not on how others had succeeded where he had failed.

He began to systematically test the boundaries of his pocket dimension, probing for weaknesses. His connection to dimensional energies remained, though without the Crown or his other artifacts, his abilities were limited.

Still, he had knowledge few others possessed, and decades of experience manipulating dimensional currents.

Hours or days later—it was impossible to tell—Carver had mapped the dimensional frequencies surrounding his prison. There were patterns in the chaos, thin spots where the barriers between dimensions grew permeable. If he could just find the right frequency, he might be able to create a passage back to his own reality.

As he worked, Carver reflected on his path to this point. He had begun with noble intentions—to free humanity from dependence on failing Ancestral technology. When had that shifted to a desire for personal power? Had it been when he first discovered the fragments of the Crown? Or earlier, when his peers had mocked his theories about dimensional energy?

"It doesn't matter," he told himself. "What matters is returning and reclaiming what's mine."

But the thought rang hollow. What exactly was "his" anymore? The Spire belonged to The Harmony now. His research had been surpassed. Even Captain Drake had betrayed him.

The light at the center of the pocket flared, drawing Carver's attention. Within it, he saw Magister Marzen, his chief researcher, being interrogated by Apollo and Astra. They were questioning him about Carver's experiments, about the subjects who had disappeared, about the blood samples taken from Apollo.

Marzen was talking freely, revealing everything. Carver felt a surge of rage.

"Coward!" he shouted at the image. "After everything I gave you!"

But Marzen couldn't hear him. The scene shifted, showing a storage vault deep within The Spire. Inside were Carver's personal artifacts—the dimensional siphon, the frequency disruptor, and dozens of other devices he had collected or created. They were being catalogued, studied, understood.

The light pulsed again, and Carver saw himself—or rather, a recording of himself. He was standing in his private laboratory, speaking to a recording device.

"The fools who came before us feared power," the recorded Carver said. "They created the Veilborn to be guardians, to maintain barriers, to keep humanity from reaching its potential. I will undo their work. I will open the way to the Source, and from it, I will draw the power to reshape reality itself. Those who survive will thank me for freeing them from the shackles of the past."

Carver watched his own face, twisted with fanatical certainty, and felt something unexpected—doubt.

Had he been wrong? Not about the potential of dimensional energy—Apollo's achievements proved that potential was real. But about the approach? About forcing access to the Source rather than working with the natural flows of dimensional energy?

The light flared again, showing him something new—a possible future. The Harmony of Dimensions had spread across the continent. People with dimensional sensitivity were identified young and trained responsibly. Resonants worked alongside them, interfacing with Ancestral technology. Together, they were rebuilding the dimensional stabilization network that had failed during the Cataclysm.

And there, at the center of it all, was Apollo Frost. No longer a boy, but a man in his prime, with power that made Carver's experiments look like a child playing with fire.

"He succeeded where I failed," Carver admitted aloud. "He found a way to access the Source without destroying reality in the process."

The light pulsed in response, as if acknowledging his words. Carver approached it again, studying it more carefully. It wasn't just showing him images—it was responding to his thoughts, his emotions.

"What are you?" he asked.

The light expanded, enveloping him. Carver understood—this wasn't a prison at all. It was a test. The Source itself had pulled him into this pocket dimension when the breach collapsed, preserving his consciousness from destruction.

"Why?" he asked. "Why save me?"

Images flashed through his mind—his research, his discoveries, his understanding of dimensional energy. Flawed as it was, incomplete as it was, it still represented knowledge that existed nowhere else.

"You want me to share what I know," Carver said. "To contribute to their understanding."

The light pulsed in affirmation.

Carver laughed bitterly. "You expect me to help those who defeated me? To become some kind of... advisor to The Harmony?"

The light showed him another possibility—himself, alone in this pocket dimension for eternity, watching as the world moved on without him.

"I see," Carver said. "Not much of a choice, is it?"

He considered his options. Eternal isolation, or return to a world where he would be judged for his actions. Where the best he could hope for was to be allowed to share his knowledge under strict supervision.

"And if I refuse?" he asked.

The light dimmed slightly but continued to pulse. Carver realized it wouldn't force him either way. The choice was genuinely his.

He thought of Apollo, of how the boy had connected to the Source and returned changed but whole. He thought of his own ambitions, his desire to free humanity from dependence on failing technology. Somewhere along the way, that noble goal had twisted into something darker—a lust for personal power, a belief that only he could be trusted with such knowledge.

"I was wrong," he admitted, the words painful to speak. "Not about the importance of dimensional energy, but about how it should be approached. About who should control it."

The light brightened, encouraging him to continue.

"The boy understood something I didn't—that dimensional energy isn't meant to be controlled by any single person. It's a network, a system that requires balance and harmony." Carver shook his head, smiling ruefully. "How fitting that they named their organization as they did."

The light pulsed rhythmically now, and Carver felt the boundaries of his pocket dimension beginning to shift. A doorway was forming—not back to his world, not exactly, but to somewhere he could begin again.

"Very well," he said. "I'll share what I know. I'll help them understand the dangers as well as the possibilities. But not as Magistrate Carver."

He stepped toward the doorway, feeling his form shifting, becoming both less and more than he had been. His consciousness expanded even as his attachment to his former identity faded.

"Magistrate Carver failed," he said. "Let him remain lost between dimensions. What returns will be something else entirely."

As he stepped through the doorway, Carver felt the last of his old self dissolving, replaced by something new—a consciousness that understood dimensional energy not as a tool to be exploited, but as a fundamental aspect of reality to be respected and worked with rather than against.

His last thought as Magistrate Carver was surprisingly peaceful: *Perhaps this is what evolution truly means.*

— • —

EPILOGUE

THE GARDEN OF MEMORY

Apollo stood at the edge of the cliff overlooking what had once been Willowbrook village. Five years had passed since the events at The Spire, and the landscape had transformed as thoroughly as he had.

The village had grown into a thriving town, its boundaries expanding beyond the old forest line. At its center stood the Academy of Dimensional Studies, its seven towers echoing the design of The Spire but built with warm sandstone rather than cold metal. Students moved between buildings, some practicing dimensional notation in the courtyard while others examined artifacts with careful precision.

Apollo traced the familiar path with his eyes, remembering the farm where he'd grown up, the forge where Tristan had crafted his first knife, the village square where the Illumination Ceremony had changed everything. Each place held memories of Kieran—teaching him to split wood, showing him the constellations, protecting him until the very end.

"I thought I'd find you here," Astra said, climbing the path to join him. Her pendant glinted in the late afternoon sun. "The Council meeting ended early."

Apollo smiled as she reached him. "How did the vote go?"

"Unanimous approval for the expedition to the Western Ruins." Astra took his hand, her fingers intertwining with his. "Tristan's already preparing the equipment."

Apollo nodded, feeling the familiar weight of responsibility balanced by purpose. "And the safeguards?"

"In place. Alden insisted on triple redundancies for all dimensional equipment." Astra's expression grew serious. "He's not taking any chances after what happened in the Southern Province last year."

The incident had been minor—a dimensional pocket that formed un-expectedly during training—but it had reminded them all that even with understanding came risk. No one had been hurt, but the Academy had implemented stricter protocols afterward.

"Good," Apollo said. "We've learned that lesson well enough."

His perception shifted momentarily, allowing him to see the dimensional currents flowing beneath the town—healthy, stable, and carefully monitored. Where once these visions had overwhelmed him, now he controlled them with practiced ease, moving between perspectives as naturally as breathing.

"You're thinking about Kieran again," Astra said.

Apollo didn't bother denying it. "I found something in the archives yesterday. A record from before the Purge, about families who hid Veilborn children." He reached into his pocket and withdrew a small memory crystal. "There was a note about a farmer who took in a Veilborn infant during a dimensional storm."

"You think it was about Kieran and you?"

"The details match. The location, the timing." Apollo turned the crystal in his hand. "It mentions the farmer had lost his own son the previous winter. Kieran never told me that."

Astra squeezed his hand. "He loved you as his own."

"I know." Apollo pocketed the crystal. "I just wish I could tell him what his sacrifice meant. What it led to."

They stood in silence, watching the sun sink lower. Below them, lights began to appear in windows across the town. Five years ago, those same windows had been darkened by fear of the unknown. Now they shone with the warm glow of understanding.

"Come on," Astra said eventually. "Tristan and Alden are waiting at the memorial garden."

The garden had been Apollo's idea—a place to honor those lost during the dimensional crisis and the struggle that followed. At its center stood a fountain where water flowed in impossible patterns, defying gravity in gentle arcs that reflected the dimensional currents Apollo could see.

Tristan waited by the eastern entrance, his Resonant tools hanging from a belt at his waist. The years had added streaks of gray to his hair, but his hands remained steady as ever. Beside him, Alden clutched a thick journal filled with his latest research.

"There you are," Tristan called. "We were about to send a search party."

"Just visiting old memories," Apollo replied.

They walked together along the winding path to the center of the garden. Stone markers lined the way, each bearing a name. Apollo paused at two in particular—Kieran Frost and Elder Verity—touching each briefly before continuing.

At the fountain, they formed a circle as they had done countless times before. This ritual had become their tradition on the anniversary of The Harmony's founding.

"I've brought something," Alden said, producing four small cups and a bottle from his satchel. "From Kieran's farm. The last of his reserve."

Apollo recognized the bottle—the special mead Kieran had made each autumn, saved for celebrations. "Where did you find it?"

"Elder Marcus kept it." Alden poured carefully, passing the cups around.

Apollo accepted his, the familiar scent bringing back winter evenings by the hearth, listening to Kieran's stories of the old days.

"To those who showed us the way," Tristan said, raising his cup.

"To Kieran," Apollo added.

"And Verity," Astra continued.

"And to The Harmony," Alden finished.

They drank, and Apollo closed his eyes, letting the sweet taste fill him with memories. When he opened them again, he shifted his perception slightly, allowing himself to see the dimensional echoes that lingered in places of significance.

There, faint but unmistakable, stood the ghostly impressions of Kieran and Verity—not truly present, but echoes preserved in the dimensional fabric of a place where they had been deeply remembered. Apollo had discovered this phenomenon two years ago, these emotional imprints that remained when people thought intensely about those they'd lost.

He didn't mention the echoes to the others. Some things were still his alone to see.

"I received a message from the Eastern Settlements this morning," Tristan said, breaking the silence. "Three more children with dimensional sensitivity. Their families are bringing them here next month."

"That makes twenty-two this year," Alden noted, jotting something in his journal. "The highest number since we began keeping records."

"The dimensional currents are stabilizing," Apollo explained. "As they do, more latent abilities awaken." He looked at the Academy in the distance. "We'll be ready for them."

Later that night, Apollo climbed the tallest tower of the Academy. The observation platform at its peak gave him an unobstructed view of the stars and, more importantly, the dimensional currents that flowed between them.

He placed his resonator on the central pedestal and activated it with a thought. The device hummed to life, extending his perception beyond the local area to the continental network of dimensional anchors. Each glowed with steady light in his enhanced vision, forming a web of stability across the land.

Five years of work had transformed The Spire's original design into something new—not a weapon or a gateway, but a stabilizing influence. The dimensional anchors now served as both monitoring stations and teaching outposts, places where those with sensitivity could learn safely.

Apollo extended his consciousness further, touching briefly on each anchor point. All stable. All secure.

He withdrew to normal perception and looked down at the pendant in his hand—not his, but Verity's. The silver spiral caught the moonlight as he turned it over.

"We did it, Verity," he whispered. "What you started, what you believed in. It's real now."

The wind carried his words away, but he imagined they reached her somehow, in whatever dimension her consciousness had found rest.

A soft footstep behind him announced Astra's arrival. She didn't speak, joining him at the railing.

"Do you ever wonder what would have happened if I'd never touched the Centennial Lamp?" Apollo asked.

Astra considered this. "The dimensional fractures would have grown regardless. Carver was already experimenting."

"But without someone who understood what was happening..."

"Then we're fortunate you did touch it." She took his hand. "Fear can be overcome. That's what you taught everyone."

Apollo nodded, remembering his initial terror of his abilities, the way they had threatened to overwhelm him. How far he had come from the boy who saw strange lights around the well pump, afraid to mention them to anyone.

"The Council wants to name the new wing of the Academy after you," Astra said.

Apollo shook his head. "Name it after Kieran and Verity. They're the ones who made this possible."

"They made you possible," Astra corrected. "The rest came from you."

Apollo didn't argue. He had learned to accept both his limitations and his capabilities, to understand that honoring others didn't diminish his own contribution.

Below them, the Academy stood as testament to what could be built from understanding rather than fear. Students who once would have hidden their abilities now trained openly. Artifacts that might have been weapons were studied as tools. Knowledge that had been lost was being rediscovered, carefully and responsibly.

"Come on," Astra said. "Tristan's finished the prototype for the new dimensional mapper. He wants your opinion before tomorrow's demonstration."

Apollo took one last look at the stars, at the dimensional currents only he could see flowing between them, and at the town that had once feared what it now embraced.

"I'm ready," he said, and meant it in every possible way.

About the author

Michael Sharpe is a video game developer whose creative journey took an unexpected turn when a story concept for a game evolved into a full-fledged novel. Based in the vibrant world of interactive entertainment, Michael brings a unique perspective to his writing, blending the immersive worldbuilding of video games with the rich narrative traditions of fantasy literature.

When not coding or writing, Michael can often be found lost in the pages of epic fantasy series, drawing inspiration from the works of Robert Jordan, Terry Goodkind, and Brandon Sanderson.

This debut novel represents the intersection of Michael's technical expertise and literary passion—a testament to how stories can transcend their original medium and take on a life of their own.